Totally Bound Publishing books by Liia Ann White

Masters of Haven
Somewhere in Between

I0526290

Masters of Haven

SOMEWHERE IN BETWEEN

LIIA ANN WHITE

Somewhere in Between
ISBN # 978-1-80250-993-9
©Copyright Liia Ann White 2022
Cover Art by Kelly Martin ©Copyright November 2022
Interior text design by Claire Siemaszkiewicz
Totally Bound Publishing

SOMEWHERE IN BETWEEN

Dedication

This one's for Mum, my constant inspiration and
biggest cheerleader.
You would have loved this book.

Chapter One

Amara entered the club and fought the sudden urge to flee. It had been eighteen months since she'd stepped foot inside Haven, Perth's most exclusive BDSM club, and so much had changed in that time. This used to be her safe haven, the one place she never had to hide her true self. Where she could let go of her control issues and let her submissive side come out to play. Now, it was a strange place. It was somehow more daunting. She didn't belong here anymore.

With her best friend by her side, she signed in as a guest and handed over her completed waiver and membership forms. The dim lighting from chandeliers and wall sconces cast red and gold glows around the main room. The only well-lit section was around the bar. Everything spoke of darkness, pleasure and sex — the wooden flooring, darkly painted walls, exposed beams that held an assortment of chandeliers.

There was no artwork on the walls anymore. Instead, they were decorated with an array of toys free for anyone to use. Even the position of the bar had changed. Now set against the far-left wall, the oblong wooden bar top sat as a feature of the room. Chains hung from the top beams and deeply set metal links were inserted into the wooden top. *Perfect for naughty little submissives*, she thought.

A dance floor took up a small portion of the converted warehouse, and the rest of it was taken up by an array of black and brown lounges, armchairs and small tables. But there was plenty of empty space for play, for submissives to be splayed out as tables, as one man currently was. A Domme sat on a black leather lounge and had her boot-covered feet resting on his back. The look on the man's face, that smile of pleasure and desire as he looked straight ahead while his Domme spoke to him... Amara knew that feeling well and missed it deeply. It filled her with envy.

The familiar scents of leather mixed with sweat and sex invaded her nose as she inhaled deeply. The sounds of leather slapping flesh, bare hands smacking arses and cries of pain and pleasure were comforting. It had been far too long since she'd been involved in any of this. Despite her good reasons, she mentally kicked herself for taking such a long break. The atmosphere of the club called to her. She'd missed this, needed this. When she'd frequented it previously, it had still been a public club. Now, under new ownership, it was private and exclusive. She'd been lucky to get access to a temporary membership. If she hadn't been helping with a demonstration, she wouldn't be here at all.

A hand touched her back and guided her towards the bar. Her friend Larissa gestured for her to take a seat on a red leather-covered stool and took a seat beside her.

"Haven looks so different now," Amara said as she looked around.

"Yeah, the new owner did a complete renovation before he opened it up. He's always changing things around, though," Larissa said.

"You'll have to introduce me so I can thank him for allowing me in."

"I can't believe he gave you a month-long pass. Good thing we vouched for you, isn't it?"

Amara regarded her friend with a small smile, despite the sadness and anxiety that filled her. "Too bad I won't be using it other than tonight."

No matter how badly she wanted to, she wouldn't be returning. She simply didn't have the time. She was a twenty-eight-year-old woman with almost no social life. And wasn't that just a little depressing?

"You will be coming back next week. You promised me." Larissa's stern expression told her there would be no give on her promise.

"Fine, I'll come back next week. But after that, you know I can't."

"I know why you *say* you can't. I'm sure you could work something out."

Amara accepted her drink from the bartender, thankful for the interruption. She didn't want to talk. Not tonight. Tonight was about her dipping her toes back into the old lifestyle she'd loved so much to see if there was still a spark there. Not that she expected to play with anyone tonight. Now that she looked around to see all the other women nearby, she realised it definitely wouldn't be happening. They all held such confidence, self-assurance. Two things she was now severely lacking.

What had happened to her? She used to saunter around confidently, knowing how to turn on her sexual appeal like a switch. Once upon a time she would have shown up in a latex skirt and a tight corset, sexy as hell.

Now, she wore a multicoloured pleated skirt that was too short for her comfort and a tight black top that showcased her large breasts and veered attention away from everything else. She'd gained weight and had more fat rolls than she used to, bigger curves than she was comfortable with. In some spots, she was just plain round. She used to love her curves, the roundness of her belly, the mounds of her breasts, the softness of her thighs, but now… Now it was all too much.

"Stop fidgeting," Larissa scolded her, slapping her hand gently. "You look great."

Amara hadn't realised she was pulling at the hem of her skirt, trying to cover her thunder thighs that peeked out below the pleated fabric. Taking a sip of her soda, she clasped the glass in both hands and held it in her lap.

"I can't believe I let your husband talk me into this," she mumbled.

"You're doing him a big favour. The other sub pulled out and he needed someone with big boobs to model for him. You have amazing breasts," she told Amara in a matter-of-fact tone. "You're really helping him out."

Larissa's husband, Agin, was one of the Masters of Haven. A select few Dominants were voted in as Masters and Mistresses by the members. As a result, they were called upon to conduct demonstrations and help out with mentoring newer Dominants, as well as helping submissives by negotiating scenes for them.

Back when Amara had frequented Haven, there had been none of that. It was a public club with professional bouncers as well as experienced Dominants doing dungeon monitor duty. Now it was all done in-house. Even the bartenders and attendants were club members who got discounted rates on their memberships in return for their work. Perhaps that was how Amara could become a full member. Larissa had suggested it to her on the drive over. She could wait tables and serve drinks. It would be a great way to get to know people, too.

Shaking her head, she wiped her mind of that thought. She wouldn't be joining. Other than the fact that she could never afford the dues, she wouldn't be able to commit to it. A wave of anxiety washed over her, cooling her skin as her palms began to sweat. Tonight, she was going to be a model for Agin for his rope demonstration. A very talented rigger, he'd called on her before for practice when he needed a body type different from his petite wife's.

Tonight, she would be half naked in front of a room full of strangers, on display, wrapped up in rope. Previously, she'd been a total rope bunny but had never managed to find a rigger of her own. She could do without it, though, and leave it as a special treat to indulge in once in a while. What she really desired— needed—was submission and masochism. Those two parts of her she would never be able to ignore. In not playing for so long, she felt like she'd lost a part of herself.

Oh God, I can't do this.

She gulped her drink nervously and began to fidget again.

"Don't even think about backing out," Larissa warned. "Agin needs you tonight. He chose you because your body is perfect. He chose a specific design just for you."

"I'm just so nervous." So nervous she wanted to burst into tears.

Fuck, what had happened to her? When had she become so beaten down, so pathetic?

"You have nothing to be nervous about. The demonstration isn't until later. For now, we'll just sit here and relax. After the demo, if you want to play, you can play. If you want to leave, you can leave. No pressure."

"I shouldn't have come so early. All it's doing is making me more anxious."

"It's good for you to get out of the house for the night. Belle will be here soon, and it'll be just like old times."

Amara forced a smile. The trio of them had always hung out here. Just three little submissives looking to get into trouble.

"You'll have to look upstairs while you're here. They're private rooms now and they're all themed. Grayson does an amazing job. He's always changing things around, so it never gets stale."

"I assume that's the owner."

"Yeah, you'll meet him later. He attends all the demonstrations. He's very hands-on."

"It has a different vibe, too. Or maybe it's just me," she admitted sadly.

"Hey, none of that." Her friend rested a hand on her bare knee. "Tonight, you are just like the old Amara. Confident, vibrant, sexy as hell and open to anything. Once the Dominants see you all roped up, you're going to stand out like a beacon and be fending off their offers."

Amara let out a laugh that was far too bitter. She definitely didn't hold her friend's confidence. Larissa scanned the room, clearly looking for her husband. Larissa and Agin had the sort of relationship Amara had always dreamt of. The Dom and sub had met in this very club a couple of years earlier and had been inseparable ever since. Amara remembered the night they had met. The look on Larissa's face when he asked her to scene with him. The happiness and contentment that had glowed from her afterwards. She knew, right then, that her friend was a goner.

On cue, Agin approached, tall, broad-shouldered and intimidating as hell in all black. He enclosed her nape with one hand and the other woman shivered in response, a big smile spreading across her face as she looked up to him. Bending, he kissed her long and hard. Amara averted her gaze and tried to ignore the pang of envy that shot through her chest.

"There's my girl," Agin said, a hint of an accent still evident even though he'd been living in Australia for twenty years. "Amara, you look divine."

Amara couldn't help but blush. Agin always complimented her. And he never lied. He really did see her as an attractive woman, even if she didn't believe it herself. The fact that the man was a Dom just made her happier. Maybe someone else tonight would see her as attractive. Maybe she would get lucky.

"Thanks. It's been so long since I wore nice clothes, I wasn't sure what would still fit me."

"Well, you definitely chose well. It's nice to see you wearing something other than a T-shirt and jeans," he teased.

"Hey, some men like the casual look." Not that she'd experienced it herself.

His eyes darkened as he regarded her. "But all men appreciate when a woman shows off her body, especially one like yours."

Anywhere else, she would have called him a perv and hit him. But not here, not in Haven. She was very aware that he was a Dominant, a well-respected one at that. Here, she showed him the same respect she would show any other Dominant.

"The showcase isn't until eleven and I'm on dungeon monitor duty until then."

That explained why he was wearing a silver-trimmed leather vest along with his silver wristband that showed he was a Master.

"Amara, if you need anything before then, you come and find me. If a Dominant wants to scene with you, I will help you negotiate. You are here under my protection tonight. You are not to play without my knowing."

"Okay."

"You, wife." He looked down at Larissa with nothing but desire and ownership. "You are to stay in the submissive area until I retrieve you."

At Amara's confused expression, Larissa pointed to an area on the opposite side of the large room where a cluster of men and women were gathered, some cuffed, like Larissa, or collared—the taken submissives—and others bare of such garments—the available submissives.

"Now, get your arses over there before I spank them," Agin said with a smile and patted his wife on the butt.

"I love you, Sir," Larissa said as she stood.

Her husband shot her a wicked smile. "Don't tempt me to shirk my responsibilities, woman."

He gave her one more kiss before leaving to patrol the room. When inside the club, Agin was very much the powerful Dom. Although friendly with everyone, he had an aura about him that wasn't approachable, not to a submissive at least. It had taken Amara months to become comfortable speaking freely with him in a lifestyle situation. It still amused her because outside of the BDSM environment, he was incredibly approachable. The two sides of his personality were like chalk and cheese.

Amara grabbed a Pepsi Max and met Larissa in the submissive area, the two of them sitting on a two-seater red leather lounge. She suddenly felt like a tiny mouse cornered by a starving alley cat. A couple of Doms walked by, assessed the two of them, gave them both pleased smiles and moved on. Amara had forgotten how difficult this part of the night could be. Sitting alone, waiting for a man or woman to approach her, never knowing if she would be propositioned or overlooked. It was damn nerve-wracking. Right now, she hated it. Putting up her barriers, she steeled herself and set her attention on her friend, not on the strangers walking by.

A little while later, their friend Belle approached, walking by a couple of men who all but leered at her as she strode by. The woman was a freaking Amazon — with light-brown skin and dark eyes, she was tall, curvy in all the right places, while remaining muscular and toned yet somehow still soft. Her black hair was placed in a series of elaborate braids before culminating in a high ponytail. She was always dressed to impress and tonight was no exception. She wore a black latex skirt, a black corset and sky-high fuck-me heels. The woman was a true picture of beauty. But it was her smile that always caught Amara's attention. Before they were friends, Amara had been attracted to her. But she had quickly friend-zoned Belle and they had been inseparable ever since.

"Hey, ladies." She greeted them each with a kiss before sitting on a chair beside them. "When did you get here?"

"About half an hour ago," Amara said. "I thought you'd be off playing with your new friend."

"Ayden's not here yet. Just wait till you see him, Amara. The guy is built, *everywhere*."

"And I'm sure he'd appreciate us knowing all about it," Larissa added with a laugh.

Belle stuck to strictly physical relationships with men. In the five years Amara had known her, she'd only had one relationship. She had strictly D/s relationships and even they didn't last long.

"He likes his public play. You might see it all later," Belle added with a wink.

Amara laughed. Belle had come a long way from the little newbie who was terrified to embrace her submissive side. Now, she was one of the most confident women around.

"What time does Agin need us?"

"Not until eleven."

"You're a free agent until then," Belle told Amara with a knowing smile. "How about we go do a lap?"

"I'm not sure I can play tonight."

"Come on. Last week you were all excited about the prospect. What changed?"

"I showed up and was reminded just how much I've changed since I was here last."

Just how much her body had changed. God, even her attitude sucked now. She should have been here just having fun with her friends, enjoying a night out. Instead, all she could think about were the negatives. When the fuck had she become such a pessimist? She'd always been such a positive person.

"The longer I'm here, the worse I feel about myself. Look at these women. They're all so beautiful. And I'm just a fat, frumpy mess."

"You're being ridiculous." Belle grabbed her hand and stood, not giving her a chance to say no. "Come on, let's go."

Amara followed her friend through the club, Belle catching stares from just about every unattached Dominant in the place. A few men approached her, completely ignoring Amara's presence. That made Amara feel even shittier than she already did. The lump building in her throat threatened to cut off her air. Tears burned her eyes as she forcefully blinked them away. Belle rejected one more Dom as they made their way towards the back of the club.

"I thought you and Ayden weren't exclusive," Amara said, after pointing out she had rejected all the other Doms.

"We're not, but I don't feel like meeting anyone new tonight. Not when I've planned a scene with him."

"So, it's okay for you to reject the idea of a scene, but not me. You hypocrite."

"*I* haven't been out of the game for a year and a half. You have." Belle nudged her as they turned to head back towards the submissive area. "You need to get back on the horse, so to speak."

"You know I don't have the time to see anyone."

She barely had any time to herself at all. She definitely didn't have the time to date or sleep with anyone on a regular basis. Belle gave her a sad smile and wrapped her arm around her shoulder briefly in a comforting manner.

"I know you don't, sweetie. But I see life passing you by and I absolutely hate it. A couple of years ago you would have been all over this place. You would have put yourself out there. Now, you won't even look anyone in the eye."

Amara had no comeback because it was true. She was different now. Life had changed her. And not for the better.

"Well, looks like you've caught someone's attention."

Following Belle's eyeline, Amara saw Eddie, a man who had topped her for a few months before everything went to hell. As handsome as ever, he flashed her a grin and headed towards her. His muscular legs powered his long strides and his broad shoulders were encased by a black silk shirt. Amara remembered exactly how his body looked beneath all that clothing, how his flesh felt against hers, his body overpowering her as he gave her the best orgasms of her life. They hadn't seen each other for long before she broke it off, but the man held promise to be a permanent Dom, maybe more. He had always made her feel so utterly feminine and that wasn't something she experienced on a daily basis.

"Well, if it isn't little Amara." His voice was as smooth as ever. Bending, he kissed her cheek, his dark hair brushing her temple. "I didn't expect to see you here tonight."

"How have you been?"

"Well." He looked her up and down, his gaze pure sex. "You look amazing."

Amara frowned at his lie. She looked far from amazing. But the look in his eyes told her that was exactly how he saw her. He'd never been one to mince his words.

"Thank you." She forced a smile.

Belle had scooted off to the side to converse with a Domme, watching Amara from the corner of her eye. She'd never been a subtle person but her hand gesture made Amara laugh.

"What have you been up to?"

"Not much. I've been really busy with work."

Good, Amara, that's not technically a lie.

"How have you been?"

"Great. I actually met someone not long after we split." He looked over her shoulder. "Here she is now."

A short, curvy brunette approached, a collar around her throat, the look of a thoroughly loved submissive spread across her features. She tucked herself under his open arm and gave Amara an assessing gaze.

"Amara, this is Cynthia. Pet, this is my old friend, Amara."

The woman offered her a smile and nodded slightly, obviously not having permission to speak. Amara smiled at the other woman, then Eddie.

"Well, it was good seeing you again."

"Yeah. You too." His gaze ran over her one last time. "If you're interested in playing tonight, come and find me. I've missed that hot little body of yours."

Amara opened her mouth to speak but nothing came out. She certainly hadn't expected that from him. Not when he had a sub of his own. Then again, Eddie had always been partial to threesomes with two women. Fond memories of the two of them playing with another female submissive ran through her mind for a moment. Yeah, they'd definitely had a lot of fun together. With a cocky chuckle, he ran a finger down her cheek before leaving with his submissive. God damn, the man was still as sexy as ever. And he'd just made her feel better about herself than she had in a very long time.

Belle stepped back to her side, a grin on her face.

"What are you waiting for? Go scene with him."

As hot and dominant as Eddie was, he hadn't incited that tingle in her. Not like he used to. His touch had done nothing for her, his words nothing more than mere flattery. There was nothing inside her but a cold emptiness. Maybe she was broken.

* * * *

Amara sat in the submissive section and caught up with her friends. It was the first time she'd seen them in weeks. And, for a moment, it was just like old times. A certain sense of security came over her, along with contentment. But the second the topic turned to her, Amara's mood plummeted. There was only ever one thing going on in her life now and it was as depressing as it was heart-breaking.

"How's your mum doing?" Larissa asked as she sipped at her soda.

"She's fine," Amara replied with a sad smile. "Each day is much the same now. But her moods are slowly getting worse."

"She's not getting more abusive, is she? I know that was a concern."

Amara shook her head. "No, she's more depressed. She has a doctor's appointment next week. I'm going to discuss putting her on antidepressants. He's been offering them for months, but I think it's time to bite the bullet."

"I'm sorry, sweetie," Belle said, resting a gentle hand on her knee.

"Are you still having this week off?" Amara nodded to Larissa. "Good. Each time I see you, you're getting more and more worn down."

"I feel it too. Like a part of my soul is being chipped away each day."

Amara's once full life had been narrowed down to one thing—caring for her disabled mother. After her mother had suffered a catastrophic stroke eighteen months earlier, Amara had been forced to care for her. She no longer worked, barely socialised and had no time for herself. But this next week she had rented out a house in a quiet, semi-rural area, where she could do nothing but relax and spend time with herself. And she couldn't wait.

"Have you given any more thought to getting further help? More than just once a week."

Amara shook her head. "Because she's so young, she doesn't qualify for government assistance. Any further help, Dad would have to pay for. And he thinks I should be able to handle it all by myself. He has no idea."

It had all but broken her spirit at this point. For the first few months, she'd had help organised by the hospital. She'd gone into survival mode and had been able to look after Mum with minimal help. But soon after, she crashed. Now, every day was a struggle to get through without breaking down. She spent most nights when she was finally alone crying her eyes out.

"Maybe after this week he'll change his tune," Larissa offered. "After all, he's never looked after her by himself for more than a few hours, has he?"

"He's never dealt with her on a bad day, either. A part of me feels guilty for thinking this, but I hope this week is really hard on him, so he'll finally realise what it's like for me. I'm sure he thinks we just sit around gossiping all day."

If only that were the case. Instead, Amara spent her days watching her mum like a hawk, making sure she didn't do anything to hurt herself. Like grabbing a knife by the blade, which she'd done a couple of months ago. The stroke had fundamentally changed her. Her personality was very different and her brain didn't process. She had a shorter temper, got tired easily, forgot a lot. Some days, she was a giant toddler, having tantrums, throwing things, calling Amara names... Amara shook her head to dismiss the negative thoughts

21

and tried to focus on the here and now, on being with her friends.

"We should probably go get changed," Amara said, looking at the large clock above the bar. "Agin will be ready for us soon."

Larissa and Belle exchanged worried glances but didn't say anything further. Amara was grateful for that. She didn't want to discuss her depressing life any further.

Agin showed up shortly after and ushered them to the locker room to get changed. After undressing and putting her clothing in a locker, Amara looked at herself in the mirror, her friends on either side. They really did all have different bodies. While Belle was the muscular and curvy Amazon, Larissa was built like a dancer, all long, slender limbs, narrow hips and small breasts. Petite was the right word for her. Then there was Amara. Hourglass-shaped with plenty of padding. On a good day, she liked her new body. On a bad day, all she could focus on was how fat she was now. All because she didn't have the time to look after herself like she used to.

"Come on, pets." Agin's booming voice came from the locker room door. "It's time."

The three of them filed out, Larissa completely naked, Belle wearing a thong, Amara wearing a pair of lace panties. Amara had never been shy about being naked in front of others but right now she wanted to cover herself up. Agin handed her a blanket and she gratefully wrapped it around herself while they walked through the club. Anxiety tore through her as they reached the back room, past the dungeon where more serious play was going on.

A small crowd had already gathered with more people filing in to watch while Agin set up his ropes.

Agin stopped midway through and gave his wife a very pleased, assessing gaze while ignoring the other women in the room. Amara smiled. Even surrounded by naked women, he only ever had eyes for his wife. It was a sweet thing to witness. Not only was he a good Dom, he was also a good man.

He began the demonstration with Larissa, wrapping black rope around her torso, concentrating on the intricate design. He ended up adding a crotch knot, something he only did when he planned on torturing her, usually when Larissa had mouthed off to him. Belle's design was on the torso only, the light blue rope a beautiful contrast to her light-brown skin.

When it finally came to her turn, Amara managed to drop the blanket that covered her and move into the centre of the room where Agin motioned for her to stand. As she stood with her hands clasped on top of her head, her heart was beating so hard in her chest it began to hurt. Her breath caught in her throat several times as she forced herself into a submissive headspace. Staring at the ground, she focussed on nothing other than Agin working the dark blue rope around her pale skin. The second it touched her skin, she sank deeper. As it wound around her torso, it began to feel like a nice warm hug on her bare skin.

"Remember, I'm going to touch you tonight, pet," he whispered in her ear. "Let me know if you are uncomfortable with it."

"It's fine," she replied without looking at him.

After all, she hadn't been touched in so long, even the touch of her best friend's husband would be welcome.

As she looked down at the floor, Amara felt herself slipping into that all too unfamiliar headspace where she enjoyed being wrapped up in soft rope. Her breath became slow and deep as he worked the rope around her breasts, cupping them gently while he worked, testing the circulation. Catching a hint of her nervousness, he leant down to whisper reassurances in her ear. She managed to focus on only him, not on the other eyes watching her, assessing her body. But it was hard.

Agin continued to speak throughout the demonstration, his words blurring in her mind as she slipped further into that happy place. By the time he was finished, she was content and floaty. Being wrapped up in the firm rope work felt right. More right than anything had in too long. It was like coming home. She'd missed the feeling so much. When she thought he was finished, she dared a peek, looking down to see Agin's handiwork. She received a stinging slap to her butt.

"No peeking, little miss," he told her with a smirk.

"Sorry," she mumbled but scowled at him. Then she remembered where she was and who he was. "Sorry."

He gave her a stern look, but his lips tilted up at the edges. Amara had forgotten what it was like to deal with Dominants in their element. And Agin was definitely more on the strict side. She focussed on giving in to that submissive side she'd ignored for eighteen months. In her everyday life, she was dominant through and through, an alpha female. Yet in the bedroom or an environment like Haven, she was wholeheartedly submissive. By the time he'd finished, she had slipped nicely into a submissive headspace and let him do with her as he wished.

Agin let her hands drop to her sides, pointing out how the rope supported her large breasts. He pulled her hair out from its clip on the top of her head. Her hair cascading across her shoulders sent a shiver down her spine, awakening her sensitive skin. She let out a small sigh, enjoying the feeling of being wrapped up like a present. Her breasts were held up and out, open for anyone to play with. Daring a peek at the crowd, she noticed all the eyes on her, and her lower belly suddenly tingled with anxiety. The Dominants and riggers were watching her, looking down at her body, at Agin's artwork, yet avoiding her eyes. All except for one.

The man's piercing gaze landed right on hers. Hidden at the back of the crowd, the man was the epitome of tall, dark and handsome. With hair that fell over his forehead and full pink lips pressed into a firm line, he was drop-dead gorgeous, the kind of man Amara had always been attracted to. There was a flutter in her belly, a tingle in the small of her back as he held her gaze. His eyes pinned her, leaving her unable to look away from him. He made her feel nervous.

Managing to tear her gaze from him, she quickly looked to her friends who were still off to the side. They looked at her with kind eyes and reassuring smiles. She could handle those looks. The look that the clearly Dominant man was giving her? Not so much. It did things to her insides that she wasn't ready to feel tonight.

Chapter Two

Sullivan stood at the back of the crowd and watched the shibari demonstration coming to a close. Agin was a fellow Master of Haven—not one he knew particularly well—but he couldn't deny the man did beautiful work. The Dom was working on a curvy little sub with the most amazing breasts he'd ever seen. Encased in the deep blue rope, her milky skin all but glowed in the lighting. Her rosy pink nipples stood erect as Agin brushed his knuckles against them. Her dark brown hair fell down her back and her big light-brown eyes stared at the ground as the man finished up his work.

The pretty sub was unfamiliar. He hadn't seen her at the club before. And she was definitely intriguing. At the beginning of the demonstration, she had appeared sad, almost defeated, a heaviness weighing her shoulders down, yet when the rope work began, she had lightened, her eyes glistening as she reached what he recognised as a submissive headspace. At one point, Agin had whispered something in her ear and a smile spread across her full pink lips. Her entire demeanour changed. Her eyes danced with amusement for a moment before she composed herself.

When he'd finished, Agin gave the sub a kiss on the cheek and ran a hand down her back. She shuddered beneath his touch and looked up at him adoringly. Not as a submissive would look at her Dom, but how a woman would look at a treasured friend.

The three rope-clad subs lined up as Agin went through the different designs for each body type one last time. Sullivan looked around at the riggers and Dominants who hung on his every word. The man had quite a reputation amongst the BDSM community and Sullivan understood why. He was very knowledgeable and clearly loved working with rope. He took pride in his work and went into great detail throughout the demonstration.

Grayson came to stand beside Sullivan, watching over his domain. "He's good, isn't he?"

"He's definitely captivated everyone," Sullivan replied to his best mate. "Who's the little sub on the end? I haven't seen her here before."

"She's a friend of his. Hasn't been here in quite a while but used to frequent it before I took over."

When Grayson had bought Haven, he had turned it into a private club to avoid some of the messes the previous owner had dealt with. He had also made a point of getting to know each and every member.

"Do you know if she's available?"

"Free and single according to Agin." His friend shot him a knowing look. "Going to play, are we?"

Sullivan smiled, looking the pretty little sub up and down once more. "Most definitely. I mean, look at her."

At first, he'd thought she was cute but not particularly beautiful, until she had smiled. Her smile lit up the entire room and did things to him that he hadn't experienced in quite some time.

"Yeah, look at her. All wrapped up like a gift just waiting to be opened." Grayson clapped him on the shoulder. "You'd better make your move before somebody else snaps her up, mate."

A number of men and women headed for the little sub like hungry sharks descending on an injured fish. She turned into a shrinking violet before his eyes. The confidence she'd displayed during the demonstration was gone. Agin remained by her side the entire time, backing her up each time a new Dominant approached, nodding each time she rejected their offer to play.

Sullivan watched as, one by one, the Dominants were politely turned down. He was surprised when one particularly popular Domme approached the woman only to be rejected as well, although the woman brought a definite flush to the little sub's cheeks and chest. The woman returned to speaking with her friends, periodically turning to look around while Agin packed up his gear. The sub constantly ran her hands over the rope. Her face brightened when Larissa pointed to one particular area between her breasts and Sullivan saw the mystery girl's face flush, her pupils dilating. It was obvious she loved being roped up but wasn't interested in playing. Why enter the club then?

Sullivan saw his friend Ayden approach the Amazon, greeting her with a hard kiss before he cuffed her. With a few words, he left her with her friends and approached him.

"She's your new submissive?"

"That's Belle." The other man nodded. "She's something, isn't she?"

"She certainly is." Sullivan saw the definite appeal of the incredibly gorgeous woman. Though he preferred his women small and round and curvy. Soft. Small enough for him to throw around, with enough padding that he could never truly hurt her. Exactly like the little brunette who was turning down every Dominant who approached her.

"What do you know about her friend?"

"Only that she came tonight as a favour to Agin. He needed an extra model at the last minute. Belle said she wasn't sure about playing tonight or not."

"That would explain why she's rejecting everyone."

Ayden frowned. "I'm not sure. She comes across as a little icy, too. Closed off."

Sullivan frowned at his friend. "I wouldn't ever call her icy."

"Maybe icy isn't the right word. But look at her body language."

He did. He saw a very nervous submissive who wasn't comfortable in her own skin being paraded around in front of others. The way she continuously covered her breasts by crossing her arms, how she looked at the ground or off to the side when approached by a Dominant. No, he wouldn't call her icy.

"Anyway, I've got a sub to torture."

"Have fun."

He watched as Ayden led Belle out of the room, noting the slight hunching of the little brunette's shoulders as she was left with only two friends. Agin wrapped an arm over her shoulder in a show of protection. She melted into him and gave him a grateful smile as she peered up at him before he let her go. Damned if she wasn't the cutest thing he'd ever seen. It brought out all his protective instincts at once.

He wanted to wrap her up, place her in his lap and stroke her hair while she told him all her worries. He'd take them away. Make her smile. Hell, he wanted to tie her up himself and spank her until she forgot all about her troubles and cried out his name.

Amara felt completely out of place. Larissa and Agin were socialising for the moment while Belle was off playing with her Dom, like she should have been. All the Dominants who approached her in the demo room had been nice enough, some even gorgeous, like the one towering blonde Domme, yet none incited that feeling of arousal inside her. Maybe she'd been right earlier. Maybe she was broken. Maybe her tastes had changed. After all, she'd changed a lot over the last year and a half. Maybe what she wanted out of sex had, too.

Sitting at the bar alone, she cradled her bottle of water, tightened the blanket around her shoulders and began to feel sorry for herself. *Fuck. Stop being pathetic.* She scolded herself and stood. Mustering all the courage she could find, she held her head up high and decided to do a lap of the club. Still feeling the mild high of being roped up, Amara wandered past a couple of scenes that piqued her interest.

One of them was Belle, strapped to a spanking bench, a vibrator inside her, nipples clamped, crying as Ayden walloped her with his bare hand. The loud smack rang throughout the room, sending a shiver down Amara's spine. She'd never particularly enjoyed being spanked, but right now she would give about anything to be in Belle's position. Just not in public. The next scene was between a Dom and his female sub. Cuffed to a St Andrew's cross, the woman wore rope and a pair of clamps tethered to a chain as the Dom ran a flogger up and down her inner thighs. He ran the instrument up her pussy, giving it a light slap and the woman's head dropped to the side, a blissful smile on her face, eyes glazed over, well and truly in subspace.

A pang of envy tightened Amara's chest. She'd never experienced true subspace. It was the one part of the submissive experience she'd always missed out on. All thanks to her control issues, she had never trusted anyone enough to let them take her there. Plenty of Doms had tried, but none had succeeded. Even Eddie, who had been an amazing Dom with a great reputation, hadn't been able to get her there. She couldn't imagine being that blissed out on endorphins and brain chemicals that she left her body and went elsewhere. *It must feel amazing.*

With a small sigh, she turned to leave and walked smack bang into a wall of muscle.

"Sorry," she muttered as she looked up.

Mister tall, dark and handsome who had been watching her at the demo was now smiling down at her. Dark brown eyes watched her with an assessing gaze while his cheek dimpled ever so slightly as he gave her a crooked smile.

"Leaving so soon, little sub?"

She opened her mouth to speak but nothing came out. That feeling she'd hoped to experience all night came roaring to the forefront. A fluttering in her chest, a rush of blood headed to the juncture of her thighs, but most importantly of all, the small of her back tingled with arousal. He ran one finger down her cheek, leaving a hot trail in its wake, the simple touch setting her nerve endings alight.

The woman behind her climaxed loudly, her scream sending a shiver through Amara's body. It didn't go unnoticed by the stranger standing before her. His long, lean body crowded her as she spun around to watch the scene again. Amara turned to see the Dom lean in and kiss his sub tenderly, running his hand over her bare skin while she rode out the remainder of her orgasm. The sexy stranger leant down so his lips grazed her ear, the action sending a shudder throughout her body.

"I've noticed you turning everyone down tonight. Is there a particular reason for that?"

"I... I haven't been interested in any of them," she admitted.

But she was interested in this one. Good God, she was wet just from feeling his body pressed against her back, his breath warm on her neck.

"Would you be interested in doing a scene with me?"

Her mouth went dry as she turned to look up at him. This sexy stranger could have any woman in the club. Yet he'd asked her to play. Was he for real?

Yes. Oh, please, yes.

She gave him a small nod then shook her head. "I couldn't..."

Looking around the room, she felt her self-consciousness come back. Being half naked while participating in a demonstration had been bad enough. Being touched, coming in front of other people? No, she definitely couldn't do that. She couldn't have people see her body like that.

"Public play is not your thing, is it?"

Looking up at him, she licked her dry lips. "Sorry, but no. Not now..."

"How about a private scene then?"

She hesitated, despite feeling herself become wetter by the second.

Go for it, her inner voice spoke up. *What have you got to lose?*

The voice was right. She probably wouldn't make it back to the club for months. This was her one chance to play. And she'd missed it. God, she'd missed it. Not just sex but being close to another person. Being touched, worshipped, desired.

"I'd like that. But I need to find my friend, Agin, to tell him."

"You're under his protection tonight."

She nodded.

"All right then, let's go find him." He took her hand in his and led her towards the back of the main room. "I'm Sullivan, by the way."

"Amara."

The stranger smiled down at her as he walked by her side and damned if it didn't light up her entire world. "Nice to meet you, Amara."

* * * *

True to his word, Agin helped with the initial negotiation, acting as a mediator between Amara and Sullivan. She felt like a complete newbie, even though she'd negotiated by herself dozens of times. They went over hard limits, her expectations as well as his. When Agin was comfortable enough with the two of them to continue, he let her go, as long as she promised to find him as soon as she was done playing.

When the two of them came to an agreement, Sullivan led her upstairs to one of the private rooms, the honeymoon suite. Set up as a sexy cliché of a suite, complete with a canopied bed covered in red silk and bedding, the room also contained a deep red loveseat, a large armoire off to one side and a small door that led to a bathroom. An assortment of toys hung from hooks and shelves on the far wall by the bathroom, but

Sullivan had, of course, brought his own toy bag. Setting it on the large armoire, he turned to face her and watched her for a moment.

She felt completely naked beneath his gaze, then she remembered she almost was. The shibari had made her feel as though she was fully clothed. Thankfully she'd worn cute underwear tonight. She couldn't imagine having someone like him see the regular plain cotton undies she usually wore. Unfortunately, expensive undergarments and clothing weren't something she could afford to treat herself with any longer. There was a damn lot she couldn't afford anymore.

"What was that thought?" he asked in a gentle tone.

She hadn't realised she was frowning until he spoke. With an effort, she forced a smile and brought her gaze back to his. "It's nothing."

He narrowed his gaze. "This won't work if you lie to me, Amara."

She slumped her shoulders. He was right. "It was nothing that concerns you, then. I'm fine, really." Her smile was genuine this time. She was looking forward to playing with him. Being touched by him. Being fucked by him.

He offered her a small smile and closed the distance between them, moving one finger beneath her chin to tilt her head up. Remaining still, he continued to watch her with those dark, dark eyes. The flutter in her gut reminded her how excited she was to scene with him. During their negotiations, her mouth had gone dry, her heart hammering against her ribcage. As he continued to watch her, the feeling got worse. The tingle in the small of her back began to take over as her mind went blank and all she focussed on was the man before her.

Seemingly pleased, he leant down and pressed his lips against hers. He sipped and teased her lips at first until she tilted her head and brought her hands up to rest on his chest. Then he deepened the kiss and oh, what a kiss. He slanted his mouth over hers, his tongue sweeping past her lips to glide against hers. He tasted of a hint of mint and man. He fisted a hand in her hair, tilting her head back further, holding her right where he wanted her. With a light moan, she gave herself over to him, submitting almost completely. She'd always loved being manhandled, having someone's fist gripping her hair tightly to control her movements.

God, it was good to give over control again. She was so tired of always being in control of everything. This was exactly what she needed. He continued to ravage her mouth before the kiss became sweet and slow. Arousal tore through her, wetness pooling between her thighs as she pressed them together to try to soothe the ache as her clit came to life. Amara pressed her chest against his, her sensitive nipples bunching as they rubbed against the smooth fabric of his shirt. His other hand came to rest on her bare waist as another low moan emitted from her throat, an involuntary sound as she lost herself in the kiss.

"Well," he said when he pulled away from her, his dark eyes on fire with reciprocated desire. "There's definitely something there."

Yes, there definitely was. Something she hadn't experienced in a very long time. She continued to watch him as his fingers danced along her waist, beneath the rope around her ribs, toying with it.

"This really is beautiful work," he commented, looking down at the ropework. "Your safe word is 'ice', correct?"

"Right."

"The club safe word is 'red'. Use either and everything stops." He moved around her, his fingers

35

leaving a burning trail on her skin as he looked her up and down while she followed him with her eyes. "I understand it's been a while since you've been with anyone. If it becomes too much for you and you wish to slow down, take a break, use 'yellow'. Understood?"

"Understood." She nodded.

"If at any time I ask you for a colour and you're happy to continue, tell me you're 'green'."

Amara smiled. She was more than familiar with the traffic light system. She'd been involved in the BDSM lifestyle since she was eighteen and had plenty of experience in it. Yet Sullivan appeared to be a careful man. She got the impression he was like this with everyone he played with, not just those who were out of practice.

He continued to run his fingers along her skin as he stood before her, then placed an open palm between her breasts, his eyes on her face, even as her chest moved up when she sucked in a breath. The shibari made everything more sensitive. Her skin was on fire, breasts swollen to an almost painful point. Her nipples pebbled when he moved to palm her breasts. Unable to hold in her gasp, she avoided his gaze, embarrassed by her eager response.

"Look at me, Amara." His tone was gentle but there was no doubting it was an order. "When we play, I want your beautiful eyes on me at all times, unless I instruct otherwise."

She immediately moved her gaze to his, finding herself captivated by him.

"You've given me permission to use you tonight." He spoke into her lips before he kissed her softly. "Have no doubt that I will well and truly use your body for my own devices. I intend to fuck you, sweetheart. Just like you asked."

His words of promise sent a shiver down her spine, her breaths increasing as she continued to stare up at him.

"But first, I intend to pleasure you."

He pressed one open palm to her chest and pushed, gesturing for her to move back. She did, until the backs of her thighs hit the high bed.

"On your back in the centre of the bed, little sub."

Little sub. The reminder of their titles sent her further into the submissive headspace she desired to get lost in. Following his instructions, she moved, propping herself up on her elbows while looking at him. He undid the buttons of his shirt and slipped it off his shoulders. Holy shit, his body was something else entirely. All long and lean, toned and muscular, he was absolutely mouth-watering. A smattering of dark hair covered his toned pecs, and a thin line of hair led down his abdomen to disappear into his pants, to the spot she really wanted to see. He moved — no, prowled — over her, straddling her, his knees on either side of her hips. Grabbing both of her hands, he forced her to lie flat on her back and reached up above her.

Wrapping soft Velcro cuffs to both of her wrists, he ran a finger beneath them to check the tightness, then tugged on them before moving down her body. Her heart pounded, blood rushing through her ears, and it was all she could do not to retreat from his heated gaze. The man exuded power and dominance. Sex. His dark eyes watched her, gauging her every response to him. No doubt he'd noticed her breathing increased as soon as he closed the cuffs around her wrists. The feeling of helplessness as she tugged at the restraints had her wet and ready for him. All she wanted was for him to tear off her panties and fuck her into oblivion.

Anxiety joined the desire when he sat back and just looked at her, not moving a muscle. Of course she was anxious. She was strapped to a bed, pinned beneath a complete stranger. Even though Agin had sworn he had a good reputation in the club—after all, he was a Master—he was still unknown to her. Movement in the glass panel of the door caught her eye. One of the dungeon monitors peered in the door, watching them for a moment, checking on them and their situation. She'd forgotten about the monitors.

She was safe. She would be fine. She could do this. She *would* do this.

Now, all she had to do was lie back and enjoy the ride this sexy stranger was going to take her on.

Dipping his head, Sullivan kissed her, nothing more than a simple peck. She had told him she enjoyed kissing, that a good kiss could turn her on more than some people touching her pussy. Apparently, he was testing out that theory. He lowered his body onto hers, the heat of his body enveloping her as he took her mouth. The kiss began sweet then soon turned to one of pure dominance. He claimed her, plundered her mouth, taking what he wanted in the way that only a Dom could.

Fuck, she'd missed this feeling, being completely and thoroughly owned by someone. She'd forgotten how much she loved having a big male body blanketing her own, the sense of comfort and security it gave her. She moaned into his mouth as she pulled against the restraints, wanting to touch him.

One hand made its way down her waist, across her hip, then disappeared beneath the fabric of her lace panties. *Holy fuck*. He cupped her mound, one finger dipping between her folds, slipping in a little too easily.

"You're wet, sweetheart," he murmured into her lips. "You really do enjoy kissing."

The sound that came from her was a cross between a whimper and a moan. He applied pressure with his fingertips, moving his hand out to rub around her clit. Her hips arched into his touch as he kissed her again, taking her breath away. She was too sensitive. One finger dipped inside again, teasing her entrance as his tongue mimicked the movement. He breached her in one agonisingly slow movement, his finger curling inside of her before he removed it.

Another whine came from her when he pulled his mouth from hers, a wicked grin spreading across his face. The bastard was enjoying tormenting her. And she loved every second of it. A second finger joined the first as he thrust them roughly in and out of her cunt.

"Holy shit," she said at the intrusion.

Even she could feel how tight she was as she clamped down on his fingers. He moved his fingers, stretching her, preparing her for what was to come. A very smug smile spread across his full lips as he moved, bringing his legs between her thighs spreading hers. He lowered himself down her body and pulled one nipple into his mouth. Hot and wet, his tongue swirled around the taut peak until it became painfully hard. His jeans scraped against the sensitive skin of her inner thighs as he moved his thumb in circles around her swollen clit. It was all too much for her to process and she felt herself slipping further and further down into that place in her mind she hadn't visited in far too long.

He sucked on her nipple, biting down gently, sending waves of pleasure straight to her clit as she arched her back. A moan came from her, long and low. He sucked hard, closing his sharp teeth around the swollen peak. She cried out, opening her eyes to look down at him. He moved, his teeth grazing the sensitive underside of her breast before he returned to her nipple and bit down, hard.

"Fuck!"

Her fingers clenched, itching to touch him as a wave of helplessness washed over her, combining with incessant arousal. She'd always enjoyed pain with her pleasure, sometimes more than she thought she should have. But then again, she was a masochist. It was in her to enjoy pain. And this man knew all about the right kind of pain.

"You have beautiful breasts," he murmured against her burning skin before moving down her body.

His fingers continued to pump in and out of her, curling inside of her while he moved to her neglected breast. Amara dared to look down and found one of the most erotic sights she'd ever seen—this drop-dead gorgeous man licking, teasing and sucking her breast while his arm moved, pumping up and down while he finger-fucked her.

Fuck. She wasn't going to last much longer.

His movements ceased. He trailed his lips and tongue down her stomach while he curled his fingers beneath the fabric of her panties. She closed her eyes again and lost herself in the feeling of his soft lips on her skin, his fingers pulling off her panties. They slipped off her legs and he made his way back up, pressing a series of open-mouthed kisses to her inner thighs. A soft kiss, a sharp stinging bite, a lick to soothe it. Fuck, she loved being bitten. He sank his teeth into her tender inner thigh, right below her pussy, and she cried out at the feeling. Doing the same to the other side, he bit a little harder and she arched her hips, craving more. He gave a low chuckle and removed his mouth from her. She opened her eyes to find him lowering his mouth towards her...

"You don't have to..." Her words were lost as he parted her folds and ran his tongue directly over the top of her clit.

Holy shit. She dropped back onto the bed and it shifted beneath her. She dropped as she lost herself in the sensation. Sparks of desire tore through her as he flattened his tongue over her clit, then ran the tip of it up one side, down the other, around and around. Her breaths came in short, sharp pants as her fingers curled into a fist, nails digging into her palms. He hooked his arms around her thighs, holding her completely still to stop her writhing. Being pinned down only turned her on more—being unable to move while he tormented her with his tongue had her orgasm building, burning through her veins.

His hot, wet tongue flattened as he licked directly over the top of her throbbing clit. She cried out as her orgasm roared through her bloodstream, awakening all the nerve endings in her body. Her hips tried to buck beneath his iron grip, but she was stuck, completely immobile.

Two fingers suddenly thrust inside of her, and she lost the ability to think. She came, lost in a wave of pure bliss. Her legs shook around his shoulders, body writhing, pussy grinding against his face as she rode out what might have been the single most intense orgasm of her entire life.

Chapter Three

Sullivan lifted his head and watched the most beautiful sight he'd ever seen as Amara rode out the aftershocks of her climax. Skin flushed, breasts swollen, nipples softening, she was quite a sight. She'd cried out loudly, shaking with her entire body, giving herself over to it completely. There was no hiding for her. He'd never seen anyone like her. She'd fought so hard to hold on to control right up until the moment she came. And she came so wholeheartedly. It had been months since he'd been with a sub so sweet and responsive. She arched into his touch and whimpered as he licked over her clit one last time.

"You come beautifully, sweetheart," he told her as he sat up on his heels.

She opened her glassy eyes to look at him, nothing but surrender in them as she watched him. Fuck, she was gorgeous. His erection strained painfully against the zipper of his jeans. He wanted to torment her some more, to see her writhe beneath him. But she'd asked him for a hard fuck and that was what she would receive. He stood to undo and remove his jeans then sheathed his cock in a condom before returning to his previous position between her thighs.

He moved back to her amazing breasts, sucking one soft nipple into his mouth while he pinched the other between his thumb and finger, enjoying the sweet moans and cries he got from her. She sucked in a harsh breath when he bit down gently that spurred him on further. He continued his ministrations, alternating breasts until her nipples were hard peaks beneath his touch.

Positioning his cock at her entrance, he hesitated, reining in his control. As much as he wanted to thrust right into her, she'd warned him it had been a while since she'd had sex. He needed to take it slow. He pushed in, just the tip, and found her so fucking tight he had to pause. It was like entering a virgin.

"Fuck, Amara," he muttered as he inserted his cock an inch further. "You're going to test my patience."

"Patience is overrated," she said with a laugh.

Fuck, he loved her laugh. With clenched teeth, he inched his way inside her so agonisingly slowly it took all his self-control. Sweat beaded across his forehead as he focussed all his energy on not ramming into her sweet little cunt. When he was finally buried to the hilt, he remained completely still, noting the mild look of discomfort on her face. Her inner muscles clamped down on him, a tight wet fist clenching around his cock.

Jesus fucking Christ. When was the last time he had felt this way with a woman?

"You're so fucking tight."

"I tried to warn you it had been a while." Her voice was husky as she teased him. "Just don't go too easy on me. I told you, I like it rough."

He pulled out a few inches, then thrust back in. She threw her head back and moaned loudly, saying his name in a harsh whisper. Repeating the movements, he stayed in control, in and out, until she moaned in pure pleasure. Then he began to really move.

Within a few minutes, her cunt spasmed around him, a flush spreading across her cheeks and down her chest as another orgasm began to take over. Losing himself in her, Sullivan moved up onto his knees and angled himself so his cock brushed against her G-spot. He knew he'd found the right location when she threw her head back and pulled against the restraints. He bit down on the inside of his cheek as she erupted around him. She closed her thighs around his hips, her cunt clenching over and over, muscles rippling down the length of his rock-hard cock. Her entire body shook and shuddered beautifully as she slowly came down, eyes opening to nail him with her piercing gaze.

He pushed her thighs up, moving her legs until her ankles rested on his shoulders. He loved this position. It enabled him to drive long and deep. Her eyes still glassy from her orgasm, she looked up at him and bit down on her bottom lip. Fuck, that look drove him wild. He focussed, fucking her hard and fast, enjoying the way her tits shook with each thrust. His movements became harder, more erratic as his own orgasm built from the base of his spine, his balls tingling.

Moving a hand down between her thighs, he found her very swollen, hard clit and pressed against it in a way he knew bordered between pleasure and pain. She came with a cry, her body trembling beneath his, ankles clamped on either side of his neck. His own orgasm took over, heat rushing from his balls straight up his shaft as he continued to thrust into her. He erupted inside of her hot cunt, her channel clenching around him as she milked him dry. Every part of him tingled, from the top of his head to the tips of his toes. Each muscle trembled as he stayed still for a few moments, holding her legs to his chest.

Eventually, he moved, slipping out of her tight, still throbbing pussy. Removing and discarding the condom, he undid her restraints and massaged her shoulders, enjoying the small moan she gave him. His face and lips continued to tingle as he tried his hardest to regain his composure. He couldn't remember the last time he'd come so hard. Lying down on the bed, he propped himself up on an elbow and looked down at her, relishing the look she gave him.

Lips swollen from his kisses, cheeks flushed from coming, she watched him with those light-brown eyes and reached a hand up to cup his cheek. Taking the hint, he dipped his head so she could kiss him. It was a light, sweet kiss that he smiled into.

"Thank you," she said quietly.

Before she got comfortable, he needed to remove the ropes from her body. Reaching beneath her, he undid the knot from behind her neck, thankful Agin hadn't done it up too tight.

"Let's get this off you, then get you settled."

She made a small sound but sat up, her eyes hooded. She let out a sigh as he unwound the rope from her soft skin. It was a shame to undo such beautiful work, but it had been on long enough. And he selfishly wanted to hold her skin to skin without a barrier in place. Dropping the ropes to the ground, he reached for a soft blanket from the bedside table and wrapped it around her back. Lying by her side, he pulled her into him, careful to keep her bare chest pressed against his.

Holding her felt right, like she belonged nuzzled against him. How the hell did a stranger burrow herself under his skin after one single fuck? If he wasn't careful, he could get himself into trouble with her.

Sullivan remained lying on the bed while Amara peeled herself from him and made a move to sit up. She tried to shuffle off the bed, but he reached out and clamped his hand on her bare thigh, his fingers digging in.

"Where do you think you're going?" He made sure he kept his tone deep and dominant.

She looked down at him, eyes all wide and innocent. "We're done. I thought…"

"You thought wrong, little sub. I'm not done with you yet."

Biting the inside of her bottom lip, the beauty hesitated for a second before moving to prop herself up on one hand. He reached up and ran his knuckles along the outside of her left breast, smiling when her nipple pebbled in response. The blanket fell off her shoulders, revealing her smooth, pale skin. Skin he wanted so desperately to bite into and taste.

"Your breasts really are beautiful."

Her cheeks flamed in response as she tried to cover herself up. He sat, grasped her wrists and held her hands on the bed. Her pupils dilated as she melted into his hold.

"This body is still mine. Don't you dare try to hide it from me."

He saw her submission before she shuddered. She parted her lips as she kept her eyes on his. Her muscles relaxed as he let go of her wrists and moved slightly so he could cup both breasts in his hands. Large, heavy and round, they were still perky. And somehow both soft and firm. He'd always been a breast man, but Amara's were in a class all on their own.

Leaning forward, he took the opportunity to lick the left nipple, then the right, blowing cold air on them until they puckered. He could just imagine them clamped until they were ruby red, with jewels and weights hanging off them. Yeah, that would be quite the sight. Pinching one nipple between his thumb and finger, he grinned at the little squeak she gave him. He pinched the other, then both at the same time. She all but melted into him as she moaned in response. She had sensitive breasts. He'd always loved that in a woman.

He moved to run his tongue along her throat, kissing the spot over her pulse gently.

"As sexy as you are," he said against her throat. "I'm afraid I'm going to need a few more minutes."

A wicked smile spread across her lips, her eyes dancing as she looked at him. "You'd better make it worth my while. I've had a lot of offers tonight, after all."

Well, where had this bratty little vixen been?

"Are you asking for a punishment?"

Her eyes widened as she realised that she'd just sassed a Dom. "No, I just..." She sighed. "Fuck. I'm sorry."

She averted her gaze and bit her lip.

He gave her a soft kiss. "You're forgiven, this time. Next time, I'll spank you for that."

It was evident she hadn't been with a Dom in quite some time. He could tell as much from the way she had fought her submissive side during negotiations. She felt a need to be in control at all times. Agin had said as much too, also warning him of her stubborn streak which might get her into a little trouble. Yet as soon as they'd been alone, she'd yielded to him, her sub side shining through.

Lucky for her, he was an easy-going Dom and let his subs get away with far more than any other Master in the club would. That was why he would let her get away with teasing him tonight. Next time, and there would be a next time, he wouldn't be quite so lenient.

"Did you enjoy yourself?"

Her cheeks flushed. "I did. Very much."

He pushed her onto her back and busied himself with her breasts. With one knee bent up, her dark hair spread out across the deep red bedding, she was truly a picture of beauty. Insatiable. Submissive. And all his.

Pulling away from her breasts, he ran his hands along her silky-smooth skin, enjoying the way her muscles twitched beneath his touch. Those pink lips were parted, her eyes piercing as she looked directly into his.

"So, what do you do for a living?"

Her entire body froze, tensing as though he'd just told her he liked to shoot kittens for fun. He'd asked a simple enough question, though, hadn't he? He wanted to get to know her, rather than sitting in silence while they both recovered enough for him to take her again.

"Amara?"

Her eyes wide, she propped herself up on both elbows and made an effort to cover herself once more. "I'd rather not…"

"It was a simple question. But if you'd prefer, I can busy myself in other ways."

He made a move for her, running his hand up her inner thigh. Letting out a small breath, she opened herself up to him, happy for the distraction of his touch.

"Lie down and let me enjoy this luscious body of yours."

Those whisky eyes widened again as she looked at him with an expression of mild shock and disbelief.

"My body has never been referred to as luscious before."

He frowned down at her. Had she really never been told how beautiful her body was? Because it was definitely luscious. Beautiful, soft, curvy, mouth-watering. Fucking hot. A man could get lost in those nooks and crannies. He could spend hours licking, kissing and biting his way along her pale flesh, never getting his fill of her.

"Luscious is the only word to do it justice."

She frowned at him, her lips pursed into a thin line. This time, she nudged his hands out of the way and moved to cover up her breasts. Yeah, someone had definitely made her feel bad about her body. He would spend the next couple of hours showing her just what he thought of it. He would make her feel as beautiful as he saw her.

He'd called her luscious. That was the first time she'd ever been described that way. Before, men had called her curvy, voluptuous, even beautiful. But never luscious. That certainly wasn't how she saw herself. Fat, overweight, flabby. That was how she saw herself. Especially now that she was lying curled up in the arms of an amazing specimen of a man. He was strong, lean, muscular and oh so gorgeous.

As her mood darkened and her thoughts turned on her, she realised what was happening. Fucking sub drop. Why was she experiencing sub drop? She'd only ever experienced it when the scene was particularly intense, or she was going through a hard time in her life. Of course, the last eighteen months had been a rough time. Maybe it was now all culminating and causing her to crash. The scene with Sullivan had been amazing. She'd felt better than she had in years. And now it was over.

She quickly moved to stand, slipping off the bed to wrap her arms around herself.

"Hey." He followed her, blocking her view of the bathroom door where she wanted to escape to.

Her bottom lip trembled. Tears began to fill her eyes.

"It's like that, is it?" he said gently. "Come here," he said, even as he wrapped his arms around her.

Not waiting for a response, he scooped her up in his arms and tucked her into his chest, holding her tight. God, it was good to just be held. How long had it been? Months. Probably years. Her brave resolve crumbled in his hold.

"Come on." He led her to the love seat and sat down, pulling her on top of him.

"You don't… I'm…"

Too heavy. Too fat. Too goddamned needy. The words were lost as a sob escaped her throat and she collapsed into a heap on the stranger's lap. Fuck, she was a mess. How utterly embarrassing. She'd never experienced true sub drop before, but this was far worse than any other time she'd ever crashed.

Sullivan didn't say a word, but simply kept his arms wrapped around her, his cheek resting on the top of her head as he rocked her gently. He pressed a kiss to her head, her forehead, her cheeks. She felt wanted. Cared for. Treasured.

No. She couldn't get attached to a Dom after one night. She was smarter than that. Uncurling her legs, she set her feet on the floor and grounded herself. She'd gotten what she needed from him, and then some. Time to move on. He didn't need to deal with her drop. She could do that herself.

"I'm sorry about that." Amara swiped at her cheeks and composed herself in a well-practised move. She was a master of masking her emotions now. "I need to go."

"Don't apologise," he said sternly, running his knuckles down her cheek. His touch was warm and soothing. "If you really need to go, I will take you to Agin. You are not to be alone right now."

She stuck out her jaw stubbornly and shook her head. "I'm fine."

"You are not," he snapped. "You're crashing and I will not leave you alone to deal with it. If you won't let me tend to you, you will let him do it."

Damn Dom. She'd forgotten how perceptive they could be. Hugging her arms around herself, she scooted off his lap and looked for her clothing. He quickly dressed himself and helped her with her underwear when her fingers didn't work. Wrapping the blanket around her, he wrapped one strong arm over her shoulders and led her downstairs. At least her legs worked well enough for her to walk.

"Have Lenny grab my bag, will you?" Sullivan said to the dungeon monitor they walked by. "I'll be downstairs."

Amara found Agin with Larissa curled up in his lap, clearly deep in subspace, needing him to care for her. That damn pang of envy returned. What Amara wouldn't give to be in that position, having a Dom of her own to care for her. To look at her the way her friend looked at his wife. But it wouldn't happen. Not any time soon anyway.

"May I go get dressed?" she asked in a quiet voice, looking up at Sullivan.

"You may. But come right back here, sweetheart." His tone wasn't forceful. If anything, it was soft and sweet. Yet he continued to radiate dominance that she couldn't ignore.

She scurried off to the locker room and dressed in a hurry, her fingers fumbling with her clothing. God dammit, why couldn't she even dress without trouble? Expecting to feel better once dressed and moving around, she found herself sorely mistaken. That hollow feeling in her chest just got bigger. Emptier. All she wanted to do was go home and cry herself to sleep.

Making her way back to her friends, she found that Belle had joined them, fully dressed and ready to go. No sign of sub drop for her. Sullivan sat in the lounge opposite Agin, saw her approach and moved to wrap his arm around her waist. She sighed into his warmth and allowed herself to touch his shoulder lightly and lean into him. He pulled her to stand between his legs and sat her down on his knee.

Back straight, her entire body tensed again as she realised what she'd done. She'd just willingly sat in the stranger's lap because she sought comfort. Brushing her hair over her shoulder, Sullivan pressed a kiss to her cheek and regarded her with his dark gaze.

"Agin has his hands full, so you're stuck with me until he's ready to leave."

"I'm fine. Really." She stood again.

"Amara. *Sit.*"

Stunned by the order, she obeyed and plonked herself down on his thigh. He wrapped his arms around her once more and scooped her legs up so she sat in his lap properly. Pulling her against his chest, he leant back and curled her body into him, positioning her just how he wanted her.

"I hear you have a bit of a stubborn streak when it comes to aftercare," he murmured for only her ears.

"So, you are to stay right here in my lap and relax until I give you permission to move. Is that clear?"

Dammit. She nodded and settled into him.

"Just let me take care of you, my sweet."

So she did. She curled up in his lap, hugging the blanket around herself, allowing him to comfort her. Eventually she closed her eyes and focussed on the fact that she was being held and comforted. And she loved every single second of it.

Chapter Four

Sometimes Amara felt like she was drowning, barely able to keep her head above water. Her soul and spirit were withering away bit by bit, sinking into the abyss. Today was one of those days. It had been two days since she'd met Sullivan, the sexiest, most caring Dom she'd ever been with. And she hadn't been able to get him off her mind since. He'd asked to see her again, asked for her number, but she'd refused. Eventually she'd given in and agreed to see him at the club on Friday. After all, he would have forgotten about her by then.

Shaking her head, she focussed on the task at hand. She didn't have time to think about the sexy stranger who'd fucked her so hard he'd caused her to drop. He had completely blown her mind. What she wouldn't give to go back there with him.

Handing her mum a bowl of oats and fruit, she moved to the kitchen to get the morning medications ready. Her dad sat on the couch, focussed completely on the television, not paying any attention to his wife.

Inwardly, Amara sighed, wishing she could afford to be that way. To tune out, remain completely ignorant to what was going on around her.

As soon as that thought crossed her mind, Amara saw Mum put her spoon down and make a move to scoop the scalding hot oats with her bare hand.

"Mum," she called out, her tone harsh. "Use your spoon."

For a moment, the older woman regarded her with confusion before her brain kicked into gear. She picked up the spoon and continued to eat. That was why Amara could never zone out. She had to pay attention at all times out of fear her mother would hurt herself again.

"When are you leaving?"

"As soon as I get showered, I'll be out of your hair."

"Good," Mum responded with a slight frown.

Amara couldn't help but be hurt by her response. It couldn't have been easy for her parents to have her around twenty-four-seven. But she didn't exactly enjoy it either. She missed her old life to the point where it was painful to think about. Eighteen months ago, she'd had a life she loved. A career she excelled at, a house of her own, a social life, a love life. Now? She was twenty-eight, living with her parents and caring for her mother full-time. It wasn't the life she'd envisioned for herself. It wasn't fair. But life wasn't fair.

Her entire life now revolved around Mum. Watching her, helping her with mundane tasks, taking her to appointments, stopping her from wandering during the night. Amara was never alone. Never had time for herself. She'd alienated all her friends other than Larissa and Belle, who wouldn't let her cut them off. She barely left her parents' house anymore. That was why visiting Haven on Friday night had been such a big deal for her. But this week she was finally taking a break, staying at a rental house by herself for the entire week where she had nothing to do but focus on herself. And she couldn't wait for it.

After leading Mum to the bathroom, Amara turned off the water, got her under it, put some shower gel on the loofah and made sure Mum washed herself properly before leaving her to rinse off alone. That was one of the hardest parts of caring for her, making sure she completed simple tasks such as washing herself and brushing her teeth.

The stroke that changed her had been catastrophic. One day, she was a vibrant, happy, fun-loving fifty-six-year-old woman, the next she was a shell of her former self. After a two-week coma, she'd been left unable to move the right side of her body and unable to speak.

Amara had witnessed the entire thing. She and Mum had just gotten back from the movies when her words began to slur. After getting her settled on the lounge, Amara slipped away to call for an ambulance, knowing that her mum was either having or was about to have a stroke. All the signs were evident. When she returned to the room, she found her seizing on the chair. It was the single most terrifying experience of Amara's life. To this day, the memory triggered extreme panic and anxiety in her.

That began Amara's journey to full-time caregiver. She didn't have a choice. With her older brother living in Sydney and her dad running his own busy company, it quickly became evident that it was up to Amara to quit her life and care for Mum. At times it made her bitter, angry, downright hostile. But who wouldn't be that way when they had zero time for themselves? Still,

Amara hated how jaded she'd become. She'd always been such a positive person. Now, she'd lost herself in becoming a carer and couldn't find a way out.

What Amara really missed was getting a full night's sleep. With her mum wandering throughout the night, she never slept deeply or for more than a couple of hours. The last time they'd tried Mum on sleeping pills, they had caused her to sleepwalk. Amara had woken one night to find her standing at the end of the driveway with no explanation as to why she was outside and no memory of getting out there.

Dad was standing in the kitchen when she returned, going over the comprehensive notes Amara had left for him. She knew she'd probably gone overboard but she needed to make sure everything was covered. There was a lot her dad didn't know about caring for Mum. He'd never done it for more than a few hours. Amara had taken on that responsibility, and he was okay with that. This week would definitely be a wake-up call for him.

"Her next lot of meds aren't due until dinner, but make sure she takes them while eating. The anti-seizure meds upset her stomach."

Dad looked up, a smirk on his face. "I can give her medication, Amara. It's not that difficult."

The man really was in for a rude awakening.

"If my job was just about giving meds and feeding her, I wouldn't always be so tired and grumpy, would I?" she snapped.

He gave a *humph* in reply. Amara sighed, closing her eyes. One thing she'd become recently was short-tempered. Sometimes she was flat-out nasty. She'd even begun to see a psychologist for her mood issues. While she didn't have depression, she did have post-traumatic stress disorder mixed with control issues and a buttload of grief she'd never gotten to deal with. Why? Because there was no downtime. No time for her to grieve, other than that half an hour each night between her mum going to bed and her collapsing into her own bed. That was when she let go and cried. But she didn't really deal with her emotions, just let them out before pushing them back down.

Her dad had no idea what she went through every day, no matter how hard she tried to explain it to him. He just didn't listen.

"I washed her hair yesterday, so it won't need doing until Tuesday. But you'll need to help her. She gets confused between the shampoo and conditioner and soap. She's got enough meds to last and I bought some more puzzle books. Tony will give you a break on Wednesday and I suggest you use that time to rest."

Tony, the professional caregiver, had been a lifesaver for Amara. After six months of doing it alone, she'd managed to discover she was entitled to one day of professional help each week. He came in to look after Mum while Amara went about doing all the things she couldn't do with Mum in tow. It usually involved grocery shopping, deep cleaning, her own appointments and sometimes even sitting out in the garden to relax and recollect her thoughts.

"Just please make sure you listen for her during the night. You don't realise how much she wanders because you get to sleep through it."

Since the stroke, her parents had been sleeping in separate bedrooms, at opposite ends of the house, so Dad could get a good night's sleep because he worked long hours.

"I'll be sleeping with her. It'll be fine." He gave her a reassuring smile before placing the instructions back on the fridge. "I've got this."

Oh, how she wished she could believe him. All Amara could do was hope he had a rough week and would finally give in and organise the professional help that she desperately needed. Maybe she would also grow wings and be able to fly away from all the stress in her life.

"I'm only half an hour away if anything happens."

Like hospital trips. Mum was now taken to the emergency room every few weeks. From little things like small falls where she would twist her ankle, to the time she burned herself because she didn't use any cold water in the shower and her brain didn't process pain properly on some days. All of those things had happened when Amara wasn't being hypervigilant. It was what made her such a panic merchant now.

"She'll be fine," he told her confidently. "She's not an invalid."

No, she wasn't. Luckily, Mum was still able to do some things for herself. She just needed a little help. She was still able to socialise with her friends every couple of weeks. She was able to occupy herself for small spans of time. But on a bad day she could be awful. She argued, fought, threw things, hurled insults at Amara that cut her to the core. And all of those things ate away at Amara's soul.

* * * *

Amara lay back in the bathtub of the rental house that had been her home for the week. An audiobook played in the background, rose-and-lavender-scented bubbles danced along the water line and her muscles began to relax. The past few days had been wonderful. She'd done nothing but pamper herself. Sitting out in the beautiful garden, catching up on reading and TV shows she'd missed out on over the past few months. She'd even meditated at one point. And tonight, she was going to Haven to hopefully treat herself again. Last Friday had been so much fun, she hoped she'd get the chance to repeat it.

After dressing, Amara assessed herself. Tonight, she'd chosen a fitted royal-blue top with a low neckline and three-quarter sleeves that covered her flabby upper arms, a tight black skirt that hugged her thunder thighs a little too closely and a pair of ankle boots that hid the one part of her body that wasn't overweight. Her clothing was all a little tighter than she would have liked, showing off the lumps and bumps she had, but since she had no money to buy new clothing, she had to make do with what she had. And hopefully the top was low enough that nobody would look past her impressive cleavage. The one part of her body she'd always appreciated was her boobs. Despite the back and neck pain they caused, they did always look great.

After Amara parked at the back of the club, a wave of anxiety about knocked her down and she began to lose her nerve. Neither of her friends had arrived yet and she couldn't bring herself to enter the club alone. Not where she would feel like a lamb being led to slaughter. God, she was pathetic. She missed her confidence. She used to have it in droves, too much probably. Once upon a time, she would have marched inside Haven with her head held high, looking around for someone who piqued her interest. She'd been mistaken for a Domme many times because of the way she carried herself. That wouldn't happen now.

She smiled a sad smile just as Larissa knocked on her window.

"Why aren't you waiting inside?"

"I got anxious and couldn't go in alone," Amara admitted as she got out of the car.

"Come on." Larissa linked their arms. "Let's get you a glass of liquid courage and go find that hottie from last week."

Sucking in a deep breath, Amara stood by the bar and sipped at her bourbon and cola. As much as she hated to drink before a scene, she definitely needed the drink to calm her nerves. Larissa sat on the stool beside her and chattered on about her week at work. The two of them used to work together as property managers for a successful real estate firm. It was how they'd met. Amara missed the work. She'd been toying with the idea of returning to work part-time but couldn't figure out how to bring it up with her parents. Since her dad would have to pay for a carer to take over her responsibilities, she couldn't commit to anything without his approval.

"There he is." Larissa's voice pierced the fog in her brain.

Following her friend's eye line, she found Sullivan approaching, that gorgeous, sexy-as-sin smile on his face. He strode toward her. The man exuded confidence, power and sex. All the submissives he walked by followed him with their eyes. Yet he'd chosen to approach her. Why? Amara hadn't been able to figure that out.

"Good evening, sweetheart." He greeted her with a quick kiss on the cheek before welcoming Larissa.

"I wasn't sure you'd be here tonight," Amara admitted.

"I would never miss an opportunity to see you." His voice was deep and smooth as a well-aged whisky. It did things to her insides. "I'll be waiting over there." He gestured to a table in the far back corner where a man she vaguely recognised sat at a table in a roped-off area. "When you're finished here, come to me."

Amara gave a quick nod and a barely audible "Okay" as her mouth went dry. Her heart leapt into her throat.

Sullivan strode away to join his friend, then kept his eyes on her as she finished her drink.

"Oh God, how does he affect me like this?"

"You mean turn you into a timid little submissive eager to please him?" Larissa laughed. "Sweetie, the man has a gift. I've seen him play quite a bit and he can definitely turn it on when he needs to."

"I forgot what it felt like to submit to a man." Amara took a long sip of her drink and rested the empty glass on the bar. "I've spent so long being in charge all the time."

"And wasn't it fun to let go last week? To submit to him?"

Her insides quivered as a smile spread across her face. "I felt complete for the first time in years."

"And tonight, he can push you even further. Just imagine what next week will bring."

"Riss, I'm not coming back next week."

"Amara…"

"I can't. Hell, Dad was pissed off enough at me last week because he had to stay up late with Mum."

"Too bad," Larissa snapped. "You need to do something for yourself. If you take one night a week, what's going to happen? Nothing. He will have to step up and help you."

Amara was too tired for this argument. Larissa didn't have to deal with her dad's bad mood, his silent treatment when she'd done something he deemed wrong or selfish. And he had called her selfish last week because she'd been out until three a.m. and needed a sleep in the next day. She knew Larissa was looking for her best interests, but tonight was not the night for it.

"The only reason I came tonight is because I can spend all day tomorrow sleeping to recover. I won't have that luxury normally."

"Amara..."

"I know you're looking out for me, and I appreciate it. But I just can't, okay?"

Larissa gave her one more look, her chin set stubbornly, but she let it go.

Chapter Five

Sullivan watched the sweet little sub approach as he continued to speak to his friend. She stopped beside him, hands clasped behind her back, eyes down as she waited for him to turn his attention to her. Without looking, he held an arm out, pleased when she stepped into it silently, allowing him to wrap his arm around her waist. She was so warm and soft and sweet against his side. He inhaled her scent, the faintest hint of cherries and pure female. There were no harsh perfumes or heavily scented soaps for this woman. He loved that.

"Are you ready?" he asked her.

"When you are," she replied quietly. "I'm happy to wait."

He'd noted last week that not once had she called him 'Sir', not like most submissives did automatically. It was part of her charm, her refusal to give him that. Pointing to the floor at his feet, he waited while she knelt without a word. Running his hand over her hair, he continued his conversation. Amara had been well trained by someone—her posture was perfect, back straight, hands palms up on her parted thighs. He noted her skirt was too tight for a perfect slave position but near enough for him.

"Sweetheart, I don't believe you've met Grayson."

She shook her head. "I haven't," she said with a smile as she looked towards the man sitting on the armchair opposite him.

"Grayson, this is Amara. My little sub from last week."

"It's a pleasure to meet you, pet." He greeted her with his usual charming smile that made most subs swoon at his feet.

"Thank you for allowing me into your club. I'm sorry I didn't get a chance to introduce myself last week. I appreciate your generosity."

Grayson gave her a genuine smile and leant forward in his seat. "Thank you for helping Agin last week. It was a fun demonstration to watch."

Her cheeks flamed with a deep blush as she avoided his gaze.

"I hope you enjoy yourself tonight as much as you did last week." He winked at her.

"Oh, she'll enjoy herself all right," Sullivan said, gripping the nape of her neck. "All right, little sub. Up with you."

She moved to her feet without pause and stood with her hands clasped behind her back once more, not saying another word.

"Don't let me keep you from your entertainment," Grayson said to Sullivan, raising one dark blond brow.

Smiling at the insinuation, Sullivan stood, towering over the submissive. Right now, she looked like prey, ready for him to pounce on. His cock hardened further, pushing against the zipper of his pants uncomfortably.

"If you'll excuse us," he said to his friend. "I'll see you tomorrow."

He grasped Amara's upper arm in a firm grip and turned her, pushing her ahead of him towards the stairs that led to the private rooms. He'd reserved one for the entire night, in the hopes that he would be entertaining himself with Amara for hours to come. One of the perks of being a Master of the club was that he could reserve equipment and rooms for the night, which definitely made the responsibility worthwhile.

Stepping into the *Arabian Nights*-themed room, Sullivan dropped his toy bag on the armoire by the door and pointed towards the floor. Amara knelt again in slave position, her skirt hiked up enough for her to assume the beautiful stance.

"Take your top off. Hands behind your back."

She moved without hesitation, clasping her hands at the base of her spine, pushing her breasts up and out, begging for his hands. He smiled as she looked up at him. He bent down to press a gentle kiss to her lips.

"When we're in a scene, if I ask you to kneel, this is how I want you to present yourself. Breasts out for me."

With her plump lips parted, cheeks slightly flushed with arousal, chest moving as she breathed a little harder, there was no doubt she was aroused. He straightened and wandered around her in a circle, assessing her.

"Whoever trained you did a good job."

She didn't respond.

"You have permission to speak, my sweet."

"Thank you."

"How long have you been involved in the lifestyle?"

"Since I was eighteen," she told him in a confident tone. "But I've been interested in it since I was much younger."

He raised a brow and regarded her with a smirk as he leant his butt against the chest of drawers behind him. "How much younger?"

"When I was twelve, I read an erotic novel and it intrigued me. Thanks to the wonder of the internet, I did my research and decided to test it out when I was an adult."

"Go on."

"I lost my virginity at eighteen in a very vanilla fashion, and it did nothing for me." She licked her lips and avoided his gaze for a moment. "After that I joined an online community, found like-minded people and the rest is history."

"Interesting."

He moved to wander around her once more. He'd had a similar experience—lost his virginity at seventeen, didn't enjoy it as much as he thought he would, then, thanks to Grayson, had discovered BDSM. Running a finger down her spine, he enjoyed the shiver that came from her. His fingers danced along her bare shoulders, along her collarbone and down the front of her top. She sucked in a little gasp as he palmed her breast beneath her bra, flicking her peaking nipple with his thumb.

"Was your training done by one Dom?"

She shook her head. "I took a few classes with a fellow submissive. But mostly I learned from the Dominants I played with. Nobody in particular took me under their wing, so to speak. I focussed on learning as much as I could by playing with different men and women when I used to visit Haven before…"

She trailed off and he removed his hand from her, standing once more.

"You've scened with both men and women?"

A small nod. "I'm bisexual."

Good to know. "Have you ever had two Dominants at once?"

"No," she answered immediately. "I've had threesomes with another submissive but would never play with two Dominants at once. I prefer to focus all my energy on one at a time."

He smiled at her. Right answer. Because while he had shared in the past, he didn't particularly enjoy it. And he would not enjoy sharing Amara.

"From now until we finish, you are not permitted to speak." He kept his tone even. "If you feel the need to ask a question, you may begin with 'excuse me, Sir' and I may give you permission. Do you understand?"

She hesitated, avoided his gaze.

"What is it, sweetheart?"

"Do I have to call you 'Sir'? I have… I have a bit of an issue with that."

"With calling a Dom 'Sir'?" That was certainly different.

She nodded and damned if her embarrassed expression wasn't the cutest thing he'd ever seen. "It doesn't feel right calling anyone other than my permanent Dom 'Sir'."

He couldn't help but smile down at her. "While it is something I enjoy, you do not need to refer to me as 'Sir' if it makes you uncomfortable. If you need to ask a question, simply use my name. Do you remember my name?"

She frowned up at him, a little scowl on her beautiful face. "Of course."

"Say it."

He saw her internal struggle. Last week, Agin had warned him she was a very stubborn, headstrong individual in her everyday life, often refusing to give in to the demands of others. And he was seeing evidence of that right now.

"Sullivan."

He loved hearing his name on her sweet lips. Smiling down at her, he bent, cupped her face and kissed her again. "Just say that if you have any question about what we're doing. Other than that, or your safe word, you will say nothing at all." He gripped her chin firmly. "Although cries and moans of pleasure and pain are definitely encouraged."

A visible shudder spread through her. He'd barely touched her and she was responding to him. That pleased him immensely.

"Now, stand and strip please."

Obeying without hesitation, she stood, stripped off her clothing and folded it, placing it on the floor beside the armless lounge behind her. She stood with her hands clasped behind her back, legs slightly parted.

"Eyes on me, sweetheart." Those big, whisky-coloured eyes caught his, all but hypnotising him. "I want your eyes on me all night."

He dipped his head to catch a kiss. When he drew back, she had shut her eyes, so he watched as she opened her eyes slowly and looked directly into his when he pulled away. "Good girl."

Her smile told him she enjoyed his praise. She really was a sweet little thing.

"Part your legs a little more for me."

She did so and he ran a finger along her pussy, feeling incredibly smug when he found her already wet for him. Bringing his finger to his mouth, he tasted her. There was nothing like the flavour of an aroused woman. The action elicited a small sigh from her, and he looked down to find her pupils dilated, cheeks flushed a little more.

"You taste delicious, my sweet Amara."

He could see her fight not to avert her gaze in embarrassment. Why did hearing how they tasted embarrass so many women? He would never understand it.

Moving to his toy bag, he pulled out a pair of nipple clamps. Last week, she'd told him she was a masochist as well as submissive, but didn't require pain to get off like some did. So, tonight, he would test out her pain threshold. Capturing one nipple between his lips, he pinched the other, teasing them until they became erect points. He bit down gently and was rewarded with a sharp intake of breath. He bit a little harder and heard a sigh of happiness come from her parted lips, followed by a small moan. Oh yes, she definitely liked pain. Biting a little harder, he pinched the other nipple and twisted. She moaned, the sound hardening his cock to a painful point.

He applied one clamp, tightening it until the nipple began to turn a beautiful deep red. Amara's breath quickened, her breasts straining with each breath while she sucked in a hiss that told him she was at her limit. He adjusted the other to the same point and took a step back to admire his handiwork. His pretty little sub would definitely look great with jewels and chains hanging off her. Next time he would try them out. Tonight, he had other things in mind.

"Up against the bedpost, facing me, arms above your head."

The woman moved, positioning herself as instructed, the position forcing her breasts up and forward. She winced as the clamps pinched her nipples a little further and her swollen breasts were forced upward. He ran his tongue along each peak, enjoying the small whine and shiver he received when he touched her. Running his knuckles along the underside of each breast, he noted the shudder that spread through her, goosebumps erupting on her skin, her nipples hardening even further.

Dropping to his knees, he ran his hands down her body, unable to resist touching her any longer. He dug his fingers in along her ribs, along the roundness of her belly, the curve of her hips, down her soft thighs as he parted them then moved back up. She had such soft, supple skin. He couldn't wait to mark it. To sink his teeth into her flesh. To have those thick thighs wrapped around his waist as he ploughed into her.

"Amara," he said sternly. She'd closed her eyes on impulse and snapped them open at his tone. "Good girl."

Reaching above her, he pulled out one of the many silk ties that were attached to each post of the bed and brought it down to restrain her wrists.

"Your safe word is 'ice', correct?"

A firm nod, a little smile on her lips.

"Remember 'red' works, too."

Tugging gently at the tie, she smiled up at him when she noticed him watching her intently. The woman definitely liked bondage. Unable to resist, he dipped his head for a gentle kiss and reached behind her for another restraint. This one went around her torso, pinning her back against the wide post of the bed.

Mouth still on hers, he reached down and inserted a finger into her tight little pussy.

Breaking the kiss, she gasped and threw her head back at the intrusion. Her muscles clenched around his finger, clamping down on him as he withdrew. When he spread her wetness to her clit, it hardened and throbbed beneath his touch before he plunged two fingers inside of her sweet, sweet cunt, enjoying the small cry she gave him.

"I'm going to take you tonight, Amara," he murmured into her ear, his cheek resting on hers. "But there will be nothing fast about it this time."

Her thighs tried to close but he shoved a foot between hers, knocking her legs outward again.

"Stay nice and wide open for me, sweetheart."

He continued to thrust his fingers in and out of her. She was well and truly aroused in no time and her eyes never left his.

Oh yes, tonight was going to be fun.

* * * *

Amara watched as Sullivan took a few steps back and looked at her, his gaze assessing. She'd just come from his fingers alone, her chest heaving, body still tingling as her head continued to spin. She licked her dry lips as he removed his black shirt and moved to his toy bag. His back was just as sexy as his front. All taut lines and lean muscle. She wanted to trace them all with her tongue. She itched to reach out and touch him, her fingers tingling.

He turned to face her with a flogger in his hand and a smile on his face. Her entire body quivered and his smile turned into a grin as he approached her. When was the last time she'd been flogged? She didn't even remember. But she'd always loved a good flogging. Sullivan gripped her chin, tilting her head up towards his.

"Enjoy it, do you?"

Removing the restraint from around her waist, he undid her wrists and moved her towards the centre of the bed. He turned her so she was facing away from him and dropped the flogger onto the bed. Gripping her wrist, he pulled a cuff from the top post of the bed and placed it around her wrist.

Were there restraints all over the damn bed?

He attached a cuff to her other wrist so her arms were in a V position. Her nipples pulsed with each rapid heartbeat as the clamps pulled on them, shocks of pain shooting straight to her clit.

Anticipation was abundant as he pushed her hair over her shoulder and pressed his bare chest against her back. Oh God, the feeling of his body against her was such a fucking turn-on. She'd always had a sensitive back. She'd told him that last week. Apparently, he had remembered. He pressed a gentle kiss to her spine, between her shoulder blades, his tongue flicking out to taste her. She let her head drop to the side as her eyes drew closed, enjoying the feeling of his soft yet firm lips on her bare skin.

Both of his hands were on her, smoothing over her skin, touching and caressing her. She tried to focus on the feeling of his hands and lips on her, rather than the pit in her stomach that appeared as she thought of what her body must look like right now. He pressed his lips to her shoulder, then across her back to the other. He nuzzled her neck as his hands made their way down her waist to grip her ass firmly.

"You have an amazing ass, sweetheart." His voice was a low, arousing rumble in her ear.

But she didn't. It was too wide, covered in cellulite dimples, not nice and round and perky as she would have liked.

A sharp sting hit her left cheek as he smacked her.

"No thinking, little sub. Especially not negative thoughts about this hot little body."

She gave a low moan as he cupped the sting, his fingers a bruising grip as he pressed his very large, very hard erection against her butt. How did he make her feel so damn alive?

"That's my girl."

He fisted her hair, turned her head and stole a kiss. Then he disappeared, leaving her feeling cold and empty and alone.

The strands of the flogger began to run up and down her back, awakening her warm skin. The threads of leather soon hit her upper back in a smooth and slow rhythm, running up and down her back, avoiding her spine and kidneys. Her head fell forward as the blows became harder, bordering on medium pain. Soon, she lost herself in the sensation, her nerve endings alight with pleasure.

He ceased the movements just as she felt herself slipping away, reaching forward to cup her pussy, slipping a finger around her clit. Pushing a finger inside of her, he thrust in a steady rhythm, gliding past her swollen tissues as he built her up to the edge of orgasm before he pulled out and resumed flogging, harder this time.

The pain woke a part of her that she hadn't felt in a very long time. A part that fulfilled her need to let go. The stinging on her skin sent shivers down her spine, and the shocks of pain had need spiralling through her. He stopped for a moment, then she felt sharp teeth biting down on that sensitive spot where her neck met her shoulder. Crying out in ecstasy, she nearly came right then, her clit throbbing with such need it began to hurt. His teeth sunk into her skin, and she forced herself to breathe through it, enjoying the sharp ache. It burned, causing tears to spring to her eyes. Licking over the spot, he left her and resumed flogging, leaving her lost in a fog of sensation.

Whacks against her back and thighs gave way to fingers inside of her, hands caressing her breasts, lips on her neck, teeth biting the sensitive skin of her throat. Then more flogging, then a hard body against her burning back. Fingers brought her to the edge once more. This time she was so close she could taste her orgasm on the tip of her tongue. Then white lights filled her vision as she exploded around his fingers. Everything inside of her tensed and released, her entire body quivering with release, desire a rush through her bloodstream as her body gave way completely and her mind blurred.

* * * *

Amara very slowly returned to her body, becoming aware that she was being held. Something warm and soft was wrapped around her. Arms banded tightly around her body as Sullivan's scent enveloped her. A voice murmured, vaguely audible through the ringing in her ears. A hard erection pressed against her ass and she tried to move her head but found it too heavy to stir.

"You back with me?" The deep male voice pierced the fog in her brain.

"Mmmmm." She managed a murmur and that was it.

A low chuckle sounded as the arms tightened around her. Sullivan. She was in Sullivan's lap after he'd just brought her to the most mind-blowing orgasm she'd experienced in a long time. How the hell had he moved her? She'd been restrained against the bed, standing until she came. He must have somehow undone her arms and carried her with him. Strong, strong man. She was no lightweight.

"Drink this," he said gently.

A bottle of water appeared when she opened her eyes and he wrapped her fingers around it. She didn't think, just tipped the bottle and drank as instructed. Her mind slowly returned to normal, her thoughts making sense once more. She managed to sit up straight and found herself looking into those beautiful dark chocolate eyes. He smiled down at her, his eyes soft.

"Did you enjoy yourself, little sub?"

"That was insane." Her voice was husky, her throat raw. Had she screamed? Oh God, she had. She'd screamed when she came. That hadn't happened in…ever.

"I'd say you definitely enjoyed the flogging."

"Mmmhmm." Her back and thighs were still warm and welted, deliciously sore.

He pressed a kiss to her lips that was so sweet she wanted to cry. Brushing her hair behind her ear, he continued to watch her with careful eyes. Then it clicked. Subspace. She'd hit subspace. Finally.

"That's never… I've never…"

Goddammit, why couldn't she finish a sentence? Because it was an embarrassing thing to admit.

"You've never reached subspace before?"

She shook her head and bit the inside of her bottom lip.

Those strong, warm arms tightened around her and his soft lips pressed against her temple.

"I find that surprising." At her look, he explained, "You're incredibly responsive. You slipped away easily. It was a beautiful thing to watch."

Resting her head back on his shoulder, she snuggled further into him. She became very aware of his thick erection beneath her and squirmed into a seated position, looking at him.

"Don't worry, sweetheart. We're nowhere near done yet. You just needed a little break."

"Good," she said on a sigh. He rewarded her with a quiet laugh and a kiss that took her breath away.

* * * *

Amara slowly became aware of her surroundings again, her brain caught up in the same fog as earlier. After a very intense round of lovemaking where she'd come so often she'd lost count, she had slipped into subspace again and lost complete control of her body. At one point, she'd cried because her body was so overly sensitive, and he refused to stop tormenting her. He'd flogged her again, thrown her onto the bed, tied her up spread-eagled and fucked her. Then he'd shoved her legs up so her ankles were around her ears, fucked her again, rolled her over, fucked her until she cried then had gone down on her until she was a boneless pile of flesh beneath him. Then he fucked her until they both came so hard their bodies shook.

Opening her eyes, she found herself in Sullivan's lap once again, curled up with her head resting on his shoulder. He tightened his arms around her while he conversed with another man. She had been well and truly and thoroughly fucked. But right now, she felt so cared for it hit her deep inside, in that place she kept locked away where nobody could reach it.

Never had a Dom looked after her the way Sullivan did. He was so attentive and sweet yet remained strict and authoritative. At one point she'd spoken without permission and he'd pinned her pelvis down and finger-fucked her so mercilessly she thought she might pass out. And he'd done it with a wicked grin on his gorgeous face.

As she became more aware of her body, she realised it was aching in the most delicious way. Her pussy was swollen and tender, her breasts still sensitive from being manhandled and flogged. Her nipples were raw. Even her ass hurt from where he had gripped her so hard she was sure she would have bruises for days to come.

She was satiated in a way she'd never experienced before. Even when she thought she'd had a great scene, she now realised she'd never truly let go. She'd never trusted someone enough to let her mind slip away. Or maybe she just hadn't been ready before. No. It was Sullivan. There was something different about him. He was unlike any Dom she'd met.

"I must say, she never reacted that way with me," a voice across from her said with slight amusement. "She's something else, though, isn't she?"

"She sure is." Sullivan's chest rumbled beneath her ear as he spoke.

"Make sure you take care of her."

"That sounds like a warning." He sounded almost amused.

"Just a reminder that she's special," the other, familiar-sounding man said. "I'll leave you to it."

Amara heard the other man leave and lifted her head to find them sitting in a quiet corner of the main room. The recovery corner, Larissa had called it last week. Running her hands over her eyes, she moved to sit up properly and found herself feeling incredibly weak. Sullivan locked his piercing eyes with hers.

"There she is," he said with a smile. "Here."

He handed her a bottle of red sports drink. She definitely needed it. After drinking the entire thing, she propped herself up on his lap and tried to regain some composure. She was completely naked beneath the blanket and tightened it around her, incredibly self-conscious.

"Uh-uh. None of that." He inserted a hand beneath the blanket and pushed it aside, running his hand along her breast. "I want you open for me to touch."

A blush heated her cheeks, but she didn't try to close the blanket again.

"So, my sweet." He ran his fingers through her hair, down her cheek and along her throat. She'd noticed that he was always touching her in some way. "When can I see you again?"

She froze. The spell was broken. *Time to turn back into a pumpkin, princess.*

"You can't... I mean... I can't..." She swallowed past the lump forming in her throat. "I won't be coming back here..."

Why did she keep losing the ability to speak in front of this man?

"Then you'd better give me your number."

She could do that, couldn't she? No. Right? No. She didn't have time to date. But she also really liked him. And not just because he had a magical cock. And fingers. And tongue. God, she was already burning the candle at both ends. Adding in seeing someone to the equation of her life would just make her feel worse. But... Having a stress relief in her life might work in her favour. She felt beyond amazing right now.

"I'm not asking for a relationship, sweetheart." He ran a hand up and down her back. "But you have to admit there is something between us. I feel we both owe it to ourselves to explore that a little further."

The man did have a point. Biting the inside of her lip, she thought it through. What harm could it do? She could see him maybe once a week, have some great sex, feel refreshed and recharged like she had last week. And dammit, she deserved to do something for herself.

Feeling brave, she nodded and held her hand out. "Give me your phone."

Amara programmed her number into his phone and handed it back to him with a kiss as butterflies of excitement fluttered around her stomach.

"I can only do weekends. Probably only once a week. I have... I don't have much free time."

"We'll sort something out." He kissed her softly, sweetly. "Now, relax back into me. You're not going anywhere for a while."

She did, leaning into his warmth, resting her head on his shoulder once more as she watched the world go by around her. In that moment, she had no worries, no cares. She just focussed on the feeling of a heated male body beneath her, wrapped around her, calming her.

Chapter Six

Amara felt happy and light on Sunday as she headed home after her week away. Seven nights away from home had been just what she needed to rest and recuperate. She almost felt like her old self again. But not quite. Because that old, carefree, fun-loving Amara was gone. The weight of responsibility now pushed her down.

She stepped inside her parents' house and heard her mum's angry tone. So much for a breezy homecoming. Making her way inside, she greeted both parents, Mum barely registering her presence, a permanent scowl etched on her face. She continued to stare at the television and knitted, giving Amara a small grunt of recognition. Dad sat at the dining table going over paperwork, a weary expression on his face. That alone told Amara he'd had a tough week looking after Mum. It wasn't often her father appeared tired.

A wave of unwelcome guilt washed over Amara. Guilt for taking the week off to be selfish. Guilt at forcing someone else to do her job. And that carer's guilt that she never got rid of, no matter how hard she tried. It was always right there, hovering in the back of her mind. Except for when she was with Sullivan. With him, it had disappeared. She gave a sigh as she thought of her night with him. She hadn't heard from him since then, but that wasn't a surprise.

Dinner time rolled around quickly, and she prepared a plate of food for Mum, handing it to her while Dad got his own, shooting her a look of thanks when she took over for him. She prepared the medications and stood beside Mum, who still hadn't spoken to her. Nothing like an awkward homecoming to bring her crashing back down to reality.

"Pill time," Amara said in the singsong voice she always used when announcing it.

Scowling at her, Mum put more food in her mouth and turned her attention back to the television.

"Mum, you need to take your meds."

"No, I don't." She stuck her chin out stubbornly and Amara knew she was in for a fight.

"Yes, you do," she said in a firm voice, the one she reserved for days like this where Mum was difficult and fought everything. "Take them and I'll leave you alone for the rest of the night."

"Why don't you leave me alone, period? You abandoned me all week. You don't care about me."

"Mari," Dad warned her.

"No, Drew. If I don't want to take them, I don't have to. Neither of you can force me to."

"Do you want to have another seizure?" Amara snapped. "Because that's what will happen if you don't take your medication."

"Good," she snarled. "Maybe this time it will kill me."

Amara recoiled as if she'd been slapped. Flashbacks of her mum seizing filled her mind, and she did her best to fight it.

"Mum, please," she said in a quieter voice.

"I'm not fucking taking them," she responded like an angry, foul-mouthed child.

Something inside Amara snapped. All week, she'd been happy. Relaxed. Carefree. Four hours back home and she was already exhausted. All the work from the week had come undone. Being sworn at by her own mother just topped off her bad mood.

"Fine," Amara snapped and left the room.

In the kitchen, she crushed the pills into a cup of tea and set it on the table beside the couch, in the hopes her mum would drink it. Once she'd eaten herself, Amara did the dishes, Dad joining her after a minute, a solemn expression on his face.

"She's been like that since she woke."

"Did she not sleep well?"

Lack of sleep usually caused Mum's bad moods.

"Barely got three hours in. She was up and down all night. At one point I found her in the middle of the backyard, flat on her back. I have no idea if she'd fallen or laid herself down, but it was a fight to get her up and inside."

Amara nodded, knowing exactly what he'd experienced. "That's usually how it goes."

"You've been saying that, but I didn't realise how bad it was until this week."

Amara's soul lifted. Now that he'd spent a week in her shoes, did he finally understand how difficult the last year and a half had been for her? She concentrated on the dishes, swallowing past the lump in her throat as she focussed her attention on the task at hand. Dad left and returned to his living room. The one good thing about him not being an emotional person was he didn't push Amara when she was upset. Her tears always made him uncomfortable. The bad thing was that it left her feeling incredibly alone all the time. She no longer had anyone to emotionally support her.

* * * *

Later that night, Amara found herself lying awake in bed, unable to sleep. Mum had never drunk her tea and refused to take her medication again before bed. And now Amara was absolutely terrified that she was going to have a seizure. Fear rippled through her at the thought. She felt herself becoming more irritable by the second, which only impeded her further attempts to sleep. Her psychologist described her insomnia as trauma induced, which was dead on.

At half past midnight, Amara heard Mum grunting as she got out of bed. Listening with a keen ear, she heard her use the toilet then wander into the living room. Rolling out of bed, Amara followed the light to the kitchen where she found Mum standing in front of the open fridge half awake, staring into space.

"Mum," she whispered. "What are you doing?"

"I'm hungry."

"You can't be hungry. It's midnight. You need to go back to sleep," she said gently.

Mum paused for a moment then looked at her in confusion. "It's midnight?"

Amara nodded and stifled a yawn. "You've only been in bed for two hours."

Relief filled her when Mum closed the fridge and she realised she wasn't going to fight Amara. She ushered her back to bed without an issue, tucked her in and gave her a goodnight kiss — something Mum insisted on every night since her stroke.

Mum stayed in bed until four a.m., then woke and wandered through the house again. The sound of the back door had Amara jumping out of bed.

"What are you doing?"

"Going to water the garden," she replied innocently, her hand resting on the sliding door.

"Leave it until later. Let's go back to bed."

"What time is it?"

"Four a.m."

She looked at her in confusion. She was always confused during the nights while half asleep.

"Let's go back to bed."

Though the specifics changed, each night was the same in essence. Mum woke to perform some mundane task, queried the time then let Amara usher her back to bed. Sometimes she fought her. Sometimes it was easier for Amara to help her complete the task then get her back to bed. Some nights, she woke and flat-out refused to go back to bed. Those nights were the worst for Amara.

* * * *

When Amara woke at six a.m., she found her mum in a far more cheerful mood than when she'd gone to bed. Taking her morning pills without incident, she ate her breakfast, then hopped in the shower happily. Dad sat at the dining table where Amara was going over the calendar for the week and watched her with careful eyes.

"How often was she up last night?"

"Twelve-thirty, four and five."

"Amara, you need help."

"I do," she agreed without hesitation.

For months, she'd been asking him for professional help and her pleas had fallen on deaf ears. Was he finally going to listen to her now? She wasn't cut out to be a full-time carer. She never had been. She'd done it because nobody else would. And because her mum — her pre-stroke mum — would have done the same thing for her.

"I'm sorry I didn't see it before." He ran a hand over his cropped hair and rested his elbows on the table. "I don't know how you've been doing it. This week absolutely exhausted me."

"Now you know why I'm always in such a foul mood," Amara stated.

It was no secret that her moods had gotten worse in recent months. She'd gotten sick more often, was always tired and it had taken its toll on her. Until the last week away, she'd been finding herself with less and less energy each day. And those were very bad traits for a caregiver to have.

"I want to discuss your future with you. It's evident you can't keep doing this full-time. I can see it wearing you down. So, I'm going to cut back my hours at work to help look after your mother."

Amara dropped her pen and looked up at her dad in shock.

"Tony will work Wednesday through Friday each week, beginning this week and, when you're ready, you can look into returning to work."

Sitting in stunned silence, Amara was completely unsure of what to say. She couldn't believe what she was hearing. It all sounded too easy. Her dad was finally on her side.

"What you've done is admirable, Amara. We are both so proud of you for stepping up. But she's not going to improve any further and you should be allowed to have a life again." He gave a quiet sigh and looked directly at her. "I'm sorry I haven't been giving you enough help. I'll be stepping up in the evenings to give you a hand and I'll take over on the weekends."

Amara bit the inside of her lip to stop herself from crying.

"I realise now that I haven't given you much support. But I intend to make amends. Whenever you want some time off to go out with your friends, let me know and I'll look after your mother."

"But then you'll just end up in the same situation as me."

"I'm her husband. It's my job to look after her. One that I've let slide for far too long."

Where was all this coming from? "Dad —"

"Amara. Let me do this."

Tears blurred her vision as she forced herself to look away from her dad. Tears of relief. Grief. Guilt. God knew what other emotions she had been hiding for so long.

"Can you even afford to work part-time?"

While he ran a very successful electrical business — one he'd built from the ground up — she knew that came with a lot of overheads.

"I definitely can," he told her. "And that is not something you need to worry about."

But she would. It was a part of her now to worry. She wanted her parents to live their golden years in comfort, not scraping by. They had both worked so hard for so long specifically for that reason.

When she eyed him sceptically, he added, "I've been thinking about going part-time for a while now and have discussed it with all relevant parties. Anything management can't handle, I can deal with from home. And money is not an issue."

She'd always known her parents had money to spare, but finances were a thing they'd never discussed in her family.

She hastily wiped her tears while he sipped his coffee.

"I've discussed it with Tony and he's beginning this week to give you some time off so your mum can get used to the new routine before you look for work."

Mum required a routine now. It was apparently common in people with damage to the part of her brain that had been affected by her stroke.

"And Mum's okay with this?"

"We discussed it at length this week. It was her idea to have Tony step up ASAP. Luckily, he's available to help. She knows you want your own life again and brought it up with me a few weeks ago."

"What about nights, though? I could honestly handle caring for her during the day if I got a proper night's sleep again."

"I'll come with you to her doctor's appointment on Friday. Whether we try new sleeping tablets or get a night-time carer, something's got to give. He can advise us either way."

Amara remained silent for a couple of minutes while she went over everything in her head. She could get her life back. Go back to work, maybe even move into her own house again. She could be a daughter instead of a carer. She wouldn't have to harp on her mum all day, every day. That was something she hated doing with a fiery passion. She hated treating her mother like a patient.

"Starting today, you will look after her Mondays and Tuesdays, Tony will be here Wednesday through Friday and I'll take over on weekends. We can be flexible between us, obviously, but that's how I want it to work from now on. You've done a great job over the last eighteen months. It's time you're rewarded for it."

"Thanks, Daddy," she said as her throat closed up. How many years had it been since she'd called him that? "You have no idea what it means to me."

"I really am sorry it took me so long to realise you were suffering."

"I appreciate that," she replied with a small smile. And she really did.

She was going to get her life back.

* * * *

Amara met Larissa at a small café near her office, waiting until she arrived almost fifteen minutes late. The previous couple of days had been much easier on Amara. Her dad really had stepped up. He'd taken over last night, leaving her to have some time alone while he watched over Mum as she watered the garden. He'd fed her and given her the medications. All Amara had to do was get her into bed. Amara was feeling much better about herself. She was more positive than she'd been in a long time.

Her friend appeared flustered, hair slightly messed, cheeks pink, as she dropped her bag on the floor and flopped into her chair.

"Well, don't you look a sight," Amara teased.

"God, it's a nightmare right now." She ran her hand over her weary face. "Roger just acquired a new rent roll and it's an absolute nightmare. I haven't seen something so mismanaged since we took over that rent roll from the South Perth office. Remember how much fun that was to deal with?"

Amara did remember and it wasn't. They'd copped so much abuse from tenants who were used to getting away with everything. Some of them were months behind in their rent and the owners were fed up with poor management. The first couple of months after taking over had been filled with court dates to evict tenants, make-up inspections of neglected houses, owner inspections and so many breach notices they'd had to work overtime to keep up. But it was all part of the challenge of being a property manager and, for whatever reason, Amara had thrived on the stress. She'd enjoyed the job so much and missed it.

The two of them ordered lunch and eased into conversation, Amara filling her in on the changes that were happening at home. She was excited about the fact that she was going to be looking for part-time work soon.

"Since you're going back to work soon, can I offer you a job?"

Amara choked on her water and stared at her best friend. "I'm sorry, what?"

"We're going to hire another PM anyway. It might as well be you. Besides, I'm the senior PM now. I have hiring and firing power. I've already run it by Roger and he's willing to make you a competitive offer. You can begin part-time. We can be flexible with your hours if something happens with your mum *and* you get to be part of our fun office again."

"Well, I can't say I hadn't hoped I would work with you again."

"Have you got time to stop by after lunch? Roger is in the office for the rest of the day."

Amara eyed her friend suspiciously. "Why do I feel like this lunch was one big set-up?"

"It's actually a happy coincidence." Larissa laughed. "Roger was told the rent roll was self-sufficient with no big issues. We thought it would be fine splitting it amongst the three of us, but that's clearly not going to work."

"Okay, I'll go meet with him when we're done here."

"Great," Larissa replied gleefully. "Now, on to the juicy stuff. Please tell me you've made plans to see Sullivan again."

Amara's nerves about returning to work turned into nerves of rejection. "I haven't heard from him yet."

Her friend frowned and pouted. "Well, that sucks. I'd hoped to get some gossip from you."

"No gossip here." Amara shrugged as her phone vibrated in her pocket. "Well, speak of the devil."

"Ooohhh, what did he say?" Larissa leant over the table with her hands clasped in front of her.

"He wants to go out on Saturday."

"And you're going to say yes because you just told me your dad is happy to take over on the weekends, so you have no excuse."

Damn, she was right. "Why am I so nervous?"

Massive butterflies thudded around Amara's gut. Her heart thumped in her chest, cheeks flaming.

"Because you haven't had a date in over eighteen months. But you know he's a nice guy. You've already slept with him. And he has a great reputation at the club."

"I bet he does." Amara bit her lip at the memories from Friday night. "The man knows how to treat a woman."

"He has all the single submissives falling at his feet."

"I know why. But that makes me even more nervous. I'm so out of practice. I don't even remember what it's like to date."

"Please, girl, it's like riding a bike."

"But what about all the awkward getting to know you stuff? I'm not ready for all that. I just want some amazing sex from him. For now, anyway."

"Then ask to catch up at the club or his house. Then there's no pressure for a real date. If you end up not liking him, you can get laid and leave."

It sounded so crass. "I just don't think I'm up for seeing anyone regularly yet. I need to sort my life out first before I bring someone else into it."

"That's completely understandable. And from what I've heard, he's not after anything serious anyway."

"What makes you say that?"

"He plays once or twice with a woman, then moves on. He never sees them for more than a weekend."

Amara paused, her text from Sullivan open on her phone as she read it again. He'd definitely asked her on a date. And he'd already played with her twice. So, what exactly did a date mean to him?

"Don't think about it so hard," Larissa told her. "Past Amara would have jumped all over this. Gone in guns blazing, ready to fuck the guy's brains out regardless of whether or not he was after a commitment."

Amara sighed. She was right.

I'm free on Saturday.

She waited on bated breath for his response.
He texted her his address.

Be at mine at five and we can go out for dinner before we get down to business.

Amara hesitated. As tempting as it would be to have a proper date with Sullivan — and it was — it was safer if they stuck to sex only, for now at least.

How about we skip dinner and just spend the night in your bed?

He didn't respond immediately. Those three dots of reply taunted her.

We can do that.

I'll be there at six.

She added a smiley-face emoji.

I can't wait.

With a smile on her face, she put her phone down and looked up at her friend. "It's done. I'm seeing him on Saturday night for some no-strings D/s play."

"Thatta girl. And I expect a phone call on Sunday to give me all the juicy details."

* * * *

The meeting with Roger went well and he offered Amara a job on the spot, three days a week with a very competitive salary. He even agreed to give her a month before she started, which Amara hadn't expected. The entire drive home, she couldn't wait to tell Mum all about it, and her date. But she wouldn't tell her about the date just yet. Mum would ask for details and, since she had no boundaries now, she would keep asking for them no matter what Amara said.

After a quick stop at the grocery store, Amara got home and found her mum sitting at the dining table working on a large puzzle with Tony.

"How was your day?" Amara greeted her with a big smile.

"Great. Tony took me for a walk that tired me out. Then we started working on this puzzle. Oh, and Bridget called."

She relayed almost the entire conversation she'd had with Bridget, her oldest and best friend. Bridget was one of the few people who didn't treat Mum as disabled. She and her husband Dave had been her parents' friends for decades, since before they got married, and they remained close.

After Tony left at five, Amara took Mum outside for their usual routine of a bit of relaxing before Dad arrived home. The two of them sat on the large outdoor lounge that overlooked the once pristine, now severely neglected garden Mum had worked so hard on before her stroke. Amara had inherited her love of gardening, finding it relaxing and even meditative. Maybe she could start fixing the garden up now that she would have weekends free to do so.

"So, tell me about your day. Why you've got that big smile on your face."

"I told you about the job," Amara said, pulling her leg beneath her. "I'm excited about the prospect of working again."

Mum tilted her head and gave her that knowing look she'd always had — the look that said she knew Amara was hiding something from her. Even with brain damage, she knew Amara better than anyone.

"Okay, fine, I wasn't going to tell you, but I've got a date on Saturday night."

"A date?" Mum's face brightened, eyes dancing as she smiled. "That's wonderful, peanut."

The use of her childhood nickname always made Amara's heart swell.

"I met him when I went to the club to help Agin a couple of weeks ago."

"The BDSM club?"

"That's the one. I saw him again on Friday and we're catching up on Saturday."

"Oh, Amara, it makes me so happy you've met a boy."

Time to pump the brakes. "Don't get too excited. It's just sex."

She waved a dismissive hand at her. "Why don't you want a real relationship?"

"You know why, Mum."

But her gaze said she had no idea.

Amara sighed. "Right now, I don't have the time. I need to get used to our new routine before I invite someone else into my life. Besides, I've been burned too many times. I put so much effort into a relationship and it always ends badly."

Amara had only ever been in three serious relationships. One when she was nineteen that had ruined her life, completely destroyed her confidence and forced her to start her life all over again. Another was a rebound with a girl who had started out sweet and ended up being a controlling asshole and the last was with a guy who couldn't handle her being so independent. She discovered he was after a full-time Dominant/submissive relationship and had tried to manipulate her into one. All had ended bitterly.

"For now, sex only is all I'm after. It's easier that way."

"You say that, but your smile says otherwise." Mum poked her cheek and grinned. "I haven't seen that smile in a long time. You really like this boy."

Amara rolled her eyes.

"I may have had a stroke that broke my brain, but I'm still your mother," she said, her voice suddenly stern. "I know you better than anyone else. You want a partner and a family. That's never going to happen if you don't go looking for it. Sex only won't lead to a happily ever after."

In that moment, she wasn't a stroke survivor with brain damage. She wasn't ill. She was just a mum giving her daughter life advice. And Amara had missed that so much.

"I'm happy things are happening for you again. You were stuck in a rut for a long time. I didn't think you'd ever get out of it. I want to see you live your life. Go out, have fun, be young. But remember, you also need to settle down and give me lots of grandchildren to spoil. Do you understand me?"

"Yes, ma'am." She gave her a mock salute. "Don't worry, I'll eventually give you a couple of grandkids to spoil."

Eventually.

Chapter Seven

Sullivan waited for Amara to arrive at his house, feeling like a nervous young teen waiting to go out on his first date. He'd spent the day cleaning, organising his still quite vacant home. He had the bare necessities but there was no real personality about it. No artwork hung on the walls, no photographs, even though he'd lived there for three months already. The house was just lacking. Would she notice or even care? The lack of garden would prove he hadn't lived here for that long. But he couldn't explain why he hadn't decorated the house at all.

Shaking his head, he took a sip of his Pepsi Max and leant against the kitchen island bench top, unable to sit down. Amara had been so hesitant to give him her number last week. What if she backed out at the last minute? She seemed a little flighty when it came to seeing him outside of the club. He wasn't used to that. Most of the women he'd played with at the club couldn't wait to get back to his house, almost all of them asking to see him outside of the club. But he didn't do that. Not anymore. He kept his home a safe place just for him. So, what on earth had gotten him to invite Amara over? Right—she was different, special. She made him feel things he hadn't felt in years.

He hadn't been able to get her off his mind since that first night. The way she felt pressed against him. How she'd writhed beneath him in the sweet agony of her beautiful orgasms. The way she looked when pinned below his body, restrained and unable to move, completely helpless and utterly tempting. The way she smiled, her laugh. The gorgeous grin and little giggle she gave after coming.

He'd never had a scene partner as responsive as her before. So eager to please, so giving. He hadn't once had to push her to submit. She gave herself over willingly. Gave everything to him without hesitation. He'd never known a sub like her.

A car pulled in his long driveway and nerves knotted in his gut. He pushed off the bench top, running his hands over his pants, checking himself over one last time as he made his way to the door. *Good God, man, get a hold of yourself.*

His heart leapt to his throat when she knocked on his door. Damn, when was the last time he had been nervous to see a woman? He took a moment to compose himself and reached for the doorknob. Amara stood on his step, her shoulders squared, chin up in a way that had her exuding confidence and dominance. He completely understood why she'd been mistaken for a Domme before. She held herself in a very guarded way. Some people wore their submission on their sleeve with their emotions. But not his Amara. *His.* Yes, she definitely was his now.

Her face softened when she saw him, a smile spreading across her full lips as she looked up at him. He looked her up and down. She wore tight jeans that showcased her thighs and wide hips. A plain black top hugged her curves and dipped down to show off those amazing breasts. Damn, he wanted to wrap himself around her right now. He couldn't wait to have that little body at his mercy tonight. In his bed. He would make her beg and plead for release. He'd make her cry out her ecstasy. And he would love every single second of it.

"Hi." He greeted her with a smile. "You look great."

"Thanks." A beautiful blush crept across her pale cheeks.

Taking her small hand in his, he led her through the entry towards his open-plan living area. The large kitchen, dining and living area somehow felt warmer with her presence in it. He'd purposely built the home with his future family in mind. This was his long-term home. His dream home. One that he'd worked his ass off to be able to afford.

Her eyes came to rest on the television and a broad grin spread across her face as she rested her hands on the back of the large U-shaped lounge.

"Oh, I love *American Dad!*" she commented.

"I knew I liked you," he responded, bringing his hands up to rest on her soft shoulders. "Can I get you a drink?"

Those light-brown eyes pierced his as she turned to look up at him. "A water would be great. Thanks."

"Make yourself comfortable." He gestured to the lounge, watching as she settled on the edge of it, her trepidation evident.

He came to sit beside her with two glasses of water, placing both on the coffee table. Resting against the couch, he stretched one arm out on the back of it, his fingers moving on their own accord to play with her hair. She leant into his touch, and he smiled to himself. He noted the small shudder that spread throughout her body.

"This is a really nice place."

"Thank you. I've only been here a few months, but it's home."

"I couldn't help but notice you're on a lot of land."

"It's ten acres." He smiled when her eyes widened.

"Ten acres is a lot for one man to have to himself."

"I saved my entire adult life to have a big house on a big property. I want my future children to have space to run around and play on."

Idiot. One way to scare off a woman was to mention his desire for a family too early. Especially a woman who was clearly not eager for a relationship.

"That is the dream. I grew up on five acres and loved it. We even had our own go-kart track at one point."

The more she spoke, the more he liked her.

"Now that would have been fun."

His fingertips lightly grazed her cheek, sending heat across his skin as he brought them down to brush her collarbone.

"So, tell me about yourself, Amara."

She gave a small frown. "Doesn't that defeat the purpose of this being just about sex?"

"You know as well as I do that a D/s relationship needs to involve emotion. I need to know about you if I am to read you properly." He let his hand drop, brushing his knuckles over her breast lightly before resting them on her warm thigh. "If I'm going to be your Dom, I need to know you."

She raised one dark, elegant brow and put her glass back on the coffee table. "And who said you're going to be my Dom? Maybe I just want one more night with you."

"Call it wishful thinking," he teased.

"Or being presumptuous," she said. "Although you do have a point. We should at least know the basics about each other."

"What do you do for work?"

She froze, her entire body tensing just as it had at the club.

"I'm about to start working as a property manager again. But for the last eighteen months I've been a full-time carer for my mum."

Now it was his turn to freeze. No wonder she looked like she had the weight of the world on her shoulders. He knew from first-hand experience how hard being a caregiver was.

"She had a stroke. So… Yeah. That's why I don't get much time to myself." She bit the inside of her bottom lip, something he had noticed she did when avoiding a conversation topic or when she was nervous. "That's why I didn't want to make plans to see you again."

She waited for him to respond.

"That must be hard." He continued to run his hand over her thigh. "I cared for my own mum for two years, a long time ago. I know how difficult it can be."

She regarded him for a minute with those whisky-coloured eyes of hers. A number of emotions ran through them before she settled and regained her composure.

"What about you? What do you do?"

"I'm a physiotherapist and own a gym."

Smiling, she ran her gaze over his body, undressing him with her eyes. "Well, that makes sense, given your physique." A blush took over her cheeks. "I mean, it's evident you look after yourself."

"Relax, sweetheart," he said as he bit down a laugh. "You can objectify me all you want."

She offered him a small smile as she did just that. He grew hard at the hunger in her eyes.

"I imagine you don't get much time for yourself, running two businesses."

Most women who heard what he did for a living either assumed he was rich because he owned his own businesses or that he was a workaholic. Truth be told, he was neither. He'd worked his ass off to get into the comfortable position he was in now. But now he'd gotten himself into a place where he could work regular hours and still afford his mortgage while taking the time off when he needed. The gym basically ran itself and was more enjoyable than his physio clinics, yet he was a great physiotherapist.

"I have a healthy balance now. Working for yourself definitely has its perks as well as its drawbacks. I bet you don't get much spare time being a caregiver."

"I have help now. I'm trying to get out more and live my own life again." She shifted uncomfortably, pulling the neckline of her top up.

She wasn't as at ease with him as he'd hoped she would be. Running his fingertip along the curve of her top, he pushed it down further and gave her a sultry smile.

"Don't cover yourself up around me, my sweet. You seem to forget I've already seen you naked. And will again tonight. In fact…" He shifted in his seat. "Take off your top."

Her eyes widened. "Excuse me?"

"You heard me." He used his Dom tone. "Don't make me repeat myself."

She didn't. To his surprise, she sat up straight, pulled off her top and sat back, huddling her arms around her waist, looking down at her body. She definitely had some body image issues. All he saw was wonderful, pale flesh that he couldn't wait to get his hands on.

"So, you haven't had help before now?"

She gave a sad shake of her head but forced a smile that didn't reach her eyes. He remembered all too well how painful and lonely it was to be a sole carer. It hadn't ended well for him.

"Let's talk about you."

"Why are you so uncomfortable with yourself?"

A small shrug. "I'm not, I just don't have that interesting a life. I'm a carer, that's all I do. It's not something I like to talk about."

He was beginning to see that. "Fine. For now, you can ask anything you want about me."

"You mentioned you work for yourself. Do you just work in one clinic?"

"I work in one and hire a couple of staff for the other. The gym runs itself. Most of my job is staff management and paperwork. That's why I still work as a physio, so I get my people fix in."

"You must be very smart and savvy to run three businesses on your own."

Taken aback by the compliment, he smiled in response. Most people asked him for free advice or asked where his offices were so they could get a cheap appointment to see him. None ever commented on his brain.

"You must be very strong and patient and compassionate to be a carer," he complimented her right back, enjoying the blush it coaxed from her.

"Patient, no. But I've always been compassionate. I inherited that from my mum."

A few moments of silence followed before Amara turned to face him, careful to keep her stomach covered up. He would work with her on that, force her to see the beautiful woman he saw over the flaws that she chose to focus on.

"So, are we done with the getting to know you portion of the evening? Can we move on to the fun stuff?"

Sullivan choked on a laugh. "Well, aren't you a forward little submissive?"

"There is one thing you need to know about me, Sullivan."

Bloody hell, he loved the way his name rolled off her tongue.

"I'm a sexual submissive, but that's it. In every other aspect of life, I'm dominant. I am in charge of my own life. I don't take shit from others, and I won't stand for being pushed around. If we're going to continue to see each other, you need to accept that."

He raised his brows, cocked his head and regarded her. His initial assessment of her was correct. She was a dominant woman. But there was absolutely no doubt in his mind that with the right Dom she would become submissive in more ways than just in the bedroom. He just needed to earn her trust to take her to that point.

"I appreciate your honesty. While I'm not a fan of full-time D/s relationships, I do like having a naked submissive on my lap while I watch television at night. I can slip into Dom mode at times other than when I'm in the club. And I believe you would slip into a submissive state in private as well."

Scoffing, she straightened her shoulders and stuck her chin out. "And what makes you say that?"

"Did you not take your shirt off because I asked you to just now?"

She bit her plump bottom lip and avoided his gaze. "I guess I did do that, didn't I?"

"You did."

Reaching over, he cupped her breast through her bra and ran his thumb along the smooth skin. Her mouth opened slightly on a small gasp as he dipped his thumb beneath the lace of her bra to find her nipple, already erect.

"Times like these when we are not technically in a scene, I will take over. Not always, but sometimes I need to dominate. Is that going to be okay with you?"

Her lashes fluttered as she looked up at him. "As long as you understand that sometimes I am not going to be in the mood for it."

"We can negotiate as time goes by," he agreed. "As long as you understand that I won't tolerate topping from the bottom. Ever. So don't even try it."

A smirk spread across her lips, her breath catching in her throat as he ran his thumbnail along her nipple. "Wouldn't dream of it."

"Brat."

He leant forward and took her mouth in a deep kiss. She submitted immediately, all but melting into him as his hands caressed her breasts, tongue plunging into her mouth. Breaking the kiss, he rested his forehead against hers in an intimate touch, enjoying her rapid breathing.

"This soft little body is mine when we're together. Tonight, I will do what I want, when I want and you will give it to me, willingly."

She gave a small nod as her pupils dilated further.

"I remember your safe word. I also use the traffic light system. Since we're playing in private tonight, you may become overwhelmed." He moved a hand to cup the nape of her neck in a firm grip. "If anything becomes overwhelming, use 'yellow' and we will slow down and talk it through."

"Do you remember my hard limits?"

"I do."

He definitely remembered her unusual hard limit of no anal play whatsoever. Most women were reluctant to try it at first, but Amara had made it a hard limit and would never negotiate on it. Not that it bothered him. There were plenty of other ways he could amuse himself with her body and mind.

"Then I won't need to use 'yellow'."

"Brave little sub." He smiled and stood, bringing her with him.

"I also made a safe call. You've got until midnight."

A safe call. Clever girl.

"Follow me."

He grabbed her hand and pulled her with him to the bedroom where he intended to well and truly use and abuse her body in the best way possible.

Amara followed Sullivan past the front door, by a closed door, to his bedroom, a very large master suite with a king-sized black steel canopied bed right in the centre of the room. It had clearly been custom made with bondage in mind. There were extra railings on it, including two thick beams that reached across the centre of the bed, clearly available for suspension play. She was sure there were restraints all over the edges and ends of the frame.

Dark blue carpet matched the deep blue and grey bedding. A large black armchair sat in one corner of the room, dark chests of drawers finishing off the room, all set off against light grey walls and black timber blinds. The entire room screamed of masculinity and Amara loved it.

Sullivan all but tore off the rest of her clothing then stood and regarded her with his muscular arms folded over his chest. The man exuded dominance without even trying. Naked beneath his gaze, she'd never felt quite so vulnerable. At the club, she was always aware of dungeon monitors, and of the fact that if she screamed or safe worded, someone would come running to her rescue. Yet here, in this practical stranger's home, there would be no help if she got in over her head. And still, she found herself wanting to give herself over to him completely. What was it about him that made her feel safe? She'd never opened up to or trusted a Dom so quickly. Even when dating someone, it took her weeks to feel this comfortable with them.

Perhaps it was the fact that he was a Master of Haven that made her feel extra safe. He took a threatening step forward, not moving his arms from over his chest and dipped his head to kiss her. The slow, languid kiss was a promise of what was to come. Arousal tore through her veins, heartbeat increasing, breath coming in short sharp pants as he pulled away from her. She pressed her thighs together, trying to ignore the wetness that pooled there, trickling down the inside of her thighs.

Fuck, she was so turned on right now, she could dry hump him and get off. But she waited patiently. She wanted to please him. To serve him. So why were the tendrils of nerves clawing at her lungs? Because she was alone with him. It was just the two of them.

He pulled back and ran his hands up and down her bare arms in a soothing manner. "Easy, sweetheart. We'll take it slow."

She shook her head. Despite her nerves, she felt herself slipping deeper into the submissive headspace. That tingle in the small of her back began to take over the longer she looked into his eyes.

"No. I don't want to go slow."

He ran his knuckles over her cheek, and she sighed into his touch as it sent a shiver down her spine.

"From now on, I don't want you to speak." His tone was stern even as a smirk spread across his lips, his eyes dancing. "Although I expect to hear those beautiful sounds you make." He leant forward to brush his lips against her ear. "I'll allow you to beg as well."

She bit down on a smile. She'd never begged in her life. Yet if anyone could get her to do it, it would surely be this man.

He kissed her again, a gentle press of his lips to hers as he taunted her. Parting her lips with his tongue, he slowly devoured her. Cupping her breasts, he used his thumbs to tease her sensitive nipples as they hardened beneath his touch. His tongue ran along hers before his teeth scraped against her bottom lip. He bit down hard enough to pull a gasp from her. She reached up to grip at his forearms, digging her nails into his skin as heat pooled in her core. Tilting his head, he continued to kiss her, taking, plundering, absolutely dominating her. The man really knew how to kiss. It was all consuming.

Sullivan moved a hand to the centre of her chest, resting between her breasts as he pushed her back towards the bed. She settled in the centre of it, swallowed by the bedding. He followed her, his body blanketing hers. She let out a small moan as he pressed his clothed body against her naked one. The feeling of his jeans scraping on the soft skin of her inner thighs as he settled between her was one she relished. The fabric of his shirt brushed against her aching nipples, causing her to arch into him.

He ran his hands over her naked body, caressing and teasing her until they came to rest on her waist, pinning her beneath him, holding her still. He used his lips, tongue and teeth to explore her neck, finding the spot that was still tender from his bite last week. He paused, gave a low groan and bit down, so hard she cried out and had to breathe through it. Instinctively, she reached for his head, tangling her fingers in his thick, silky hair to hold him in place as he applied more pressure with his teeth.

"Fuck!" she cried out as she wrapped her legs around his waist.

How the hell could one bite send her into a frenzy? She'd forgotten how much she loved being bitten, but now that Sullivan had, it drove her wild. His tongue flicked out to soothe it before he sucked on the spot, his lips trailing further down her throat and up to her ear.

"Fuck, I love your responses, sweetheart."

Her response was to grind her pussy against his thick, hard erection through his jeans. If he didn't get some part of him inside of her soon, she was going to explode. He lifted his head up to look down at her, bringing his hands up to grip hers that now rested on his shoulder. Moving both above her head, he stretched her arms up and gave her his Dom look.

"No more touching and no moving," he ordered. "Keep your hands up there for me."

Her clit throbbed painfully with need. Her entire body heated as she nodded in reply. Mental restraint had always been a big turn-on for her, even more so than physical bondage. She would force herself to stay still, no matter how difficult it was. Sitting up, he stripped off his shirt and rested back on his heels. Good God, he was beautiful. Her fingers clenched as she fought the need to reach out and touch him.

"You seem to enjoy biting." He lowered himself onto her body, shuffling down to her torso. "So, I'm going to bite you again. And it's going to hurt. But you aren't going to move a muscle, are you, sweetheart?"

She looked down at him and shook her head, licking her suddenly dry lips.

"Now put your head down and breathe. This is going to hurt."

Closing her eyes, she tried to relax as she waited. His lips brushed the sensitive skin of her waist, right where it dipped below her ribs. There was no other warning. His teeth suddenly sank into her. Every single muscle in her body clenched and tightened against the pain. *Fuuuuuuck*. She wanted to cry out.

Tears burned her eyes before her body began to convert the pain. The bed sank beneath her as she gave herself over to the pain that now turned into pleasure, shooting straight to her clit. Her pussy clenched, feeling very empty. A whimper escaped her throat as he loosened his grip on her and pulled away, pressing a small kiss over the hurt.

"Good girl," he whispered as he kissed his way towards her breasts.

Those two words filled her with such pride. She'd pleased him, just as she'd hoped to. One hand suddenly appeared between her folds and he swore when he found her sopping wet.

"Fuck, Amara. You really did enjoy that."

Barely fighting the urge to buck her hips, she remained still while he plunged a finger inside of her then removed it just as quickly. Propping himself up on his forearms, he lowered his head and caught a nipple between his lips. He sucked, hard. Crying out, Amara arched her back, begging for more before forcing herself down. He caught her eye, narrowed his gaze for a moment then went back to tormenting her breast with his mouth. His tongue flicked over the taut peak, around and around in slow, torturous movements while he pulled the other between his fingers, pinching hard, running his fingernail across the centre of it.

When he bit down on her nipple, the pain sent shocks of pleasure straight to her throbbing clit. He swapped and repeated his moves on the other breast, licking, sucking and biting down while manipulating the other between his fingers, palming her breast, kneading it with a firm hand, leaving her a panting mess beneath him.

"Please…" She fucking begged. "Sullivan, please…"

"Please, what, little sub?" His voice was thick with lust.

"Please fuck me."

"Since you asked so nicely." The smile in his eyes told her that was exactly what he'd been after. He'd wanted her to beg.

Lithe and limber, he moved off the bed, pulling off his jeans and underwear in one movement, and sheathed himself with a condom. Her clit became impossibly hard and throbbed, begging him for attention. Her pussy clenched as she thought of being invaded by him.

Yes, fuck me. She wanted to cry out, but merely whimpered instead.

Spreading her thighs with strong, large hands, he settled himself between them and hovered over her. Capturing her mouth in a searing kiss, he pressed her further into the bed until she felt herself sinking into it. From the top of her head to the tips of her toes, she tingled with awareness and arousal. She'd never been so turned on in her life. She might burst if he didn't touch her.

His cock brushed against her folds, teasing her. She couldn't help herself and arched her hips, trying to seek the friction she so desperately needed, only to receive a sharp slap on her inner thigh. She squeaked in response and looked into his very serious dark eyes.

"Don't move."

Oh God, she loved that tone. There was no room for disobedience.

She whined loudly. "I'm sorry."

Flashing her a wicked grin, he dropped his head and enveloped her mouth in a kiss so ravenous she almost came. Teetering on the edge of self-control, she whimpered into his mouth when his hand danced along her waist, grasping the spot where he'd bitten her. It sent a jolt of sweet, delicious pain through her body. That hand moved to cup her mound, one finger tapping lightly on her clit. That was all she needed to let go. He swallowed her cry as she came hard. Her entire body bucked beneath him. Her thighs clenched around his waist.

She lost herself entirely. Her breaths came in sharp ragged movements as her entire body trembled and shook beneath his. *Holy shit, that was intense*. His finger continued to move around her throbbing clit, up and over, down one side then up the other, before the tip ran directly over the top of the hard nub. She sucked in a hiss between her teeth at the painful sensation as her far too sensitive clit was touched.

His response was a wicked chuckle before he rustled on the bed and it dipped beneath him. A cuff wrapped around her thigh, just above her knee. She moved her head with great effort and looked down to find him splaying her open as he adjusted the strap to hold her there. He repeated the move with her other thigh. The bastard did have restraints attached to the bed frame.

Splayed open for him, she was completely unable to move as she tried to fight against the cuffs.

"That's a pretty sight," he said as he looked up at her from his position hovering over her cunt. "Now you're nice and open for me."

A finger dipped inside her, her pussy clamping down on it straight away.

"Very nice."

He dipped his head, his tongue darting out to lick directly over the top of her clit. *Holy shit*. She nearly came again. Throwing her head back on the bed, she closed her eyes and lost herself in the sensation of his skilled touch. He inserted another finger, eliciting a gasp and moan from her. In and out, he rotated his fingers at a leisurely pace while his tongue lashed at her rapidly hardening nub. Daring to look down at him, she saw him close his lips over her clit as he sucked it into his mouth.

"Oh God," she moaned and dropped her head again.

She couldn't handle it. She was going to come again. How the hell did he manage to get her so close to the edge so damn quickly? His fingers curled inside her, hitting her G-spot as his tongue continued to lash at her. Her eyes slammed shut as white pulsed in her vision, her entire body burning with desire.

"Oh, pleeeease," she whined.

"Please, what?" he teased her. The bastard was toying with her, dragging it out, keeping her orgasm just out of reach.

"Please make me come," she said breathlessly, her words barely audible.

He shifted the position of his hand, his fingers curled against her G-spot as he began to move in a brutal fashion, thrusting up and down.

"Come for me, sweetheart."

At his words, she let go completely. Liquid desire shot through her veins, tears burning her eyes as she came harder than she ever had in her life. She cried out — screamed — as he continued to move and suck on her, wringing out every last drop of her orgasm.

Her body limp, she barely registered his touch as he kissed his way up her body, paying more attention to her breasts. She was done. She was dead. Could someone die from coming too hard? He curled two fingers inside of her once again, finding her G-spot with the ease of a well-practised Dom, and finger-fucked her in a brutal fashion. She'd never felt anything like it.

Another orgasm crashed over her without warning. Her fingers clenched painfully into the doona as she fought against the urge to touch him, to wrap her arms around his broad shoulders.

"Oh God," she moaned when he pressed his body against hers.

Every muscle in her body ached and burned. Somehow there was still arousal left in her, the need to come building more and more as he pressed his cock against her entrance, holding it there, refusing to enter her.

"I love watching you come," he said against her lips, the erotic words sending a shiver throughout her entire body.

He inserted himself inch by gruelling inch, slowly spearing her body in the most primal way. With a low moan, she tried to wrap her legs around him only to find she was still restrained. Opening her eyes, she looked into his dark gaze while he seated himself and remained unmoving.

"You disobeyed again," he said as he reached behind his back.

She hadn't realised she'd moved her hands to touch him. Biting on her lip, she widened her eyes as she quickly moved them back above her head.

"Lucky for you, I enjoy feeling your hands on me." He pressed a kiss to her lips. "You may touch me now."

Further desire unfurled in her belly as she dared to return her hands to his shoulders. At his smile of approval, she ran them along his biceps, digging her fingers into his flesh as he began to move inside of her. He thrust in and out of her, slow and steady at first, switching to a hard, fast, ferocious rhythm. Burying himself deeper inside of her with each thrust, he ground his pelvis so it pressed against her swollen clit with each movement.

She completely lost herself in the wave of sensations that took over. Her skin on fire with need, her entire body trembled. Wave after wave of pleasure flowed through her veins, heart pounding in her chest as she struggled to breathe. Shifting onto his knees, Sullivan moved so the head of his cock brushed against that sensitive spot deep inside of her.

The room flashed white and everything exploded. She tightened her arms around his shoulders, nails digging into his back as she held on for dear life. A wailing rang in her ears. Was that her? Oh God, she'd never heard that sound come from her before. He buried his face in her neck and followed her into bliss, groaning as he thrust his cock impossibly deeper inside of her, burying himself in her cunt. It twitched and jerked as he came inside of her.

Amara's throat burned as she tried to control her breathing. She tightened her arms around his shoulders and pulled his body towards hers, welcoming his heavy weight as he relaxed against her. She revelled in the feeling of his body pressed against hers, her chest heaving, sensitive breasts grazing the crisp hairs on his chest, sending further arousal through her. Groaning when he slid out of her, she let him go, waiting for him to remove the restraints so she could press her thighs together.

Her body was so completely satisfied and oversensitive, every nerve ending was alive and pulsing. He settled beside her, wrapping his arms around her to pull her body against him. Resting her head against his chest, she brought one arm up to lay across his waist and lay like that until she gathered the strength to move.

* * * *

Several hours later, Amara lay sprawled across Sullivan's chest, her leg draped over his thigh comfortably, chest heaving as she fought to catch her breath. She was completely and utterly undone. She hadn't been so well fucked in…ever. Her entire body was still throbbing. Her mind blurred with happiness and an endorphin rush as she fought to clear her head. Fought and failed.

"Did you enjoy yourself, little sub?" he murmured into her hair, that arrogant lilt to his voice.

He bloody well knew she'd enjoyed herself. His distant neighbours probably knew too. At one point she'd screamed so loudly she'd lost her voice.

"I don't want to move," she all but whined.

"You don't have to."

"Good," she murmured into his chest. "I don't even think I can."

Too many men she'd been with had gotten their rocks off and felt the need to leave immediately. No aftercare at all. But Sullivan was a different type of man. He was a different type of Dom. He'd left her a quivering mess, sent her into the oblivion of pure bliss then wrapped a blanket around her and pulled her into him, pressing her against his chest. He'd scooped her up into his lap and held her, given her water to guzzle down, even fed her chocolate at one point. He'd held her patiently, giving her time to recover before he tried speaking with her. He had asked how she felt, how she'd enjoyed their scene, but most importantly—he had actually listened.

Yeah, the man did aftercare beautifully.

He moved beneath her, lifted his head and pressed a quick kiss to her lips before shuffling out from beneath her.

"I'll be right back."

He slipped on his underwear and disappeared, leaving her alone.

She felt bare. Empty. Alone. *Oh no.* She didn't want another sub drop. Not after such a perfect night. *Please, no.*

He reappeared with a glass of water and a red sports drink, which he handed to her. Shifting into a half-seated position, she smiled as she took the bottle from him and pulled the blanket around her shoulders.

"Drink. You definitely need rehydrating after that last round."

He flashed her that wicked grin of his and pressed his soft lips against her forehead.

"Thanks." She smiled before she began to guzzle the drink greedily. "I don't think I've ever come so many times in one night."

"There's something a man likes to hear."

He scooped her into his arms and pressed a kiss to the top of her head. The hole inside of her began to fill, thankfully. She wasn't alone. He would never leave her alone. He wasn't that kind of man.

Turning on the television for background noise, he lifted her with little effort and pulled her into his lap. God, it felt good to be held by him. He was such a comforting presence.

"How are you doing? Are you crashing at all?"

She shook her head against him. "I thought I was, but it's gone now."

"Make sure you tell me if you ever begin to feel it. What we did was pretty intense at some points, especially with the pain. I would be surprised if you didn't feel yourself dropping."

"I'm fine." She looked up at him. "Really."

He tightened his arm around her and let out a low sigh she probably wasn't meant to hear. "Is it too early to ask when we can do that again?"

His voice was a rich tenor that rolled over her skin, making her shudder lightly. She smiled and curled further into him.

"I was thinking the same thing."

Throughout the night they'd discussed her situation, how she barely had time to herself but was working on it again. He'd been very understanding and promised not to push her.

"I think I need to stick to weekends for now."

"I'm happy to work around you."

He continued to run a soothing hand up and down her arm, while the other remained a steel band around her back.

"Answer something for me. You're clearly a confident, self-assured woman. Why were you so against playing in public at the club?"

She frowned and bit the inside of her lip, avoiding his gaze as she shuffled back slightly. She really didn't want to talk about that right now, not while she was still riding the high of the night.

"Amara."

"Can we not talk about this now?"

"You're going to have to talk about it with me eventually. I'd like to know why you appear so ashamed of your beautiful body."

Giving him a huff, Amara dropped the bottle on the bed behind her. "Fine. I've gained a lot of weight since becoming a carer. I don't have time to exercise like I used to. I'm not comfortable with my body as it is now. Not like I used to be anyway."

He frowned down at her. "Has anybody made you feel bad about how you look?"

"No. This is all internal. I used to love my body." She sighed, remembering the body she used to have. Bigger and curvy yet toned. There was no flab, not like there was now. "I used to have more tone. Now I'm just flabby."

"Well, allow me to show you how much I appreciate the body you have now."

Shuffling her off his lap, he moved to place a kiss on each of her breasts.

"This lush, voluptuous…"

A kiss to her rounded stomach.

"Soft, supple little body."

She shuddered as he continued to place open-mouthed kisses on her stomach, along her waist. Down her hips…

"I love having it wrapped around me." Another gentle kiss. "Pressed against me." A nip on her inner thigh. "Pinned beneath me…" He kissed her mound. "I love having it writhing beneath me, begging for release."

His words, his actions, made her feel desirable. Wanted. Sexy.

"I absolutely love your body, Amara."

She could see herself easily falling for this man who enjoyed her so openly. He knew just what to say… *No.* There would be no falling for him. This was just sex. Amazing, mind-blowing, life-changing, absolutely incredible sex.

Settling next to her, he looked at her with hard eyes. "What was that thought?"

"Nothing," she responded in a knee-jerk reaction. She really wasn't used to men being so open with her, asking about her thoughts and feelings.

"Amara, you don't have to tell me everything, but don't lie to me."

"I just don't want to talk about it."

He ran his knuckles down her cheek in a gentle touch before pressing his lips to hers.

"When I was caring for my mum, I was often told 'you can't care for someone else unless you care for yourself first'."

"Something my psychologist tells me constantly."

Crap. Why the fuck did I say that? A great way to scare him off, making him think I'm a headcase.

"My psychologist often tells me I don't take care enough care of myself. That's what I intend to do for you from now on, my sweet Amara. I intend to spoil myself by spending time with you."

"You see a psych?" She couldn't hide the surprise from her voice.

"I have depression. It would be stupid not to."

"Oh." His honesty shocked her. "That's definitely the smart thing to do."

Her alarm went off, piercing the comfortable silence between them. It was time for her to make her safe call and go home.

"I have to go," she said reluctantly.

"Amara, I'm sorry if…"

"Oh no, it's nothing you said," she assured him as she slipped on her underwear. "I need to make my safe call and get home. I have to get up at six for my mum's routine and need to at least try to get some sleep."

After dressing, she moved to straddle Sullivan on the bed, her hands on either side of his face as she kissed him softly and deeply.

"Thank you for tonight. It was fucking amazing." She grinned. "Pun intended."

He kissed her again, so deeply that it made her toes curl.

"We'll work out a time to do it again as soon as possible."

Flashing her that killer smile, he replied, "I look forward to it."

Walking her to the front door, he opened it and escorted her to her car in nothing but his underwear. He wrapped an arm around her to kiss her one more time.

"I'll text you."

"I can't wait," she replied honestly before getting into her car.

She smiled the entire way home. Sullivan had made her feel more alive than she had in years. Not only because of the sex but their easy conversation. They got along so well. She felt a small twinge inside her chest. If she wasn't careful, she really would easily fall for him. And that was something she couldn't afford right now. At least, not until she sorted herself out.

Chapter Eight

On Monday morning, Amara came down hard from her night with Sullivan. After getting only two hours of sleep, she woke feeling exhausted, depressed and honestly devastated. She was all alone in the world, with no one on her side. Nobody in her corner to back her up. After lying in bed for a few minutes, she fought back tears of loneliness and exhaustion and rubbed her eyes before rolling out of the bed.

She'd never had a come-down hit her so hard, especially two days after the fact. But she'd also never had a night like the one she'd had with him. She had ridden the endorphin rush yesterday, feeling happy and cared for all day. She'd called Larissa and told her all about the night, unable to wipe the goofy smile off her face. Then Belle had called asking for details and her reaction had been much the same. But sometime during the night, she'd crashed hard and begun crying, sobbing quietly into her pillow as existential loneliness washed over her soul.

Jumping in the shower, she lingered for a few minutes longer than usual, hoping the scalding water on her skin would help perk up her mood. It didn't. After brushing her teeth, she left the bathroom to find her mum in the kitchen, making her own breakfast unsupervised. Hovering in the doorway, Amara watched as she managed to heat up the oats and cut the banana with no issues. This was good. Amara needed to let go a little. But it was difficult. She felt the need to hover closely, to take over and help. But that wasn't what Mum needed now. Even Tony didn't help her as much as Amara did.

After asking the professional carer for advice last Friday, Amara made the conscious effort to let go a little more each day. She watched as Mum hesitated when the microwave turned off. Opening the door, she reached in for the scalding bowl but backed off when she saw Amara approach. Handing her a tea towel, she gestured for Mum to use it. The other woman's brain kicked into gear. Amara continued to watch as she moved the bowl to the bench, scooped her banana and berries into the oats and took a mouthful.

Good job.

"Sit down and I'll bring it to you," Amara said when her mum got lost in her own thoughts and began to stare into space.

Amara got her own breakfast and sat on the lounge beside her. The fracture inside of her remained, no matter how hard she tried to put on a brave face for her mother.

"You look tired," Mum said with a frown. "You didn't sleep well, did you?"

"Not really."

"Did I sleepwalk?"

"Yeah." Amara rubbed her eyes. "I think these new tablets are worse than the old ones."

Tears brimmed in Mum's hazel eyes as she avoided her gaze. "I'm sorry."

"Hey, it's okay." Amara reached for her hand, holding it gently. "At least when you sleepwalk, you're amusing. Last night you told me you were taking the cat for a walk and couldn't find the leash."

Amara smiled slightly at the memory of her mum wandering around the kitchen, rummaging through the drawers looking for a leash that didn't exist. They'd never even owned a cat.

"Did I do anything else?"

"You tried to brush your teeth with Vegemite. Almost had it in your mouth by the time I realised what you were doing."

She'd covered her toothbrush in the thick black spread and was lifting it to her mouth when Amara caught her and shouted for her to stop. Luckily, she kept a spare toothbrush for Mum because she'd also previously tried brushing her teeth with soap, dishwashing liquid and moisturiser.

Amara laughed along with her mum despite her fatigue and bad mood. She'd always loved seeing her mum laugh. It didn't happen enough anymore.

"I think we'll try the different pills tonight and see if they work better. You need to get more sleep."

"So do you."

"I'm okay," she lied. She was far from okay.

Tears pricked her eyes as she suddenly realised that she hadn't heard from Sullivan yesterday. Even after they'd spent an amazing night together and he'd assured her he couldn't wait to see her again.

Oh my God, stop this shit, she scolded herself.

Even knowing her thoughts weren't rational, that they were a product of the sub drop, didn't help. It never did.

Amara blinked rapidly, forcing the tears away. She tried not to get emotional in front of Mum anymore. She couldn't handle seeing her daughter in tears. It sent her spiralling into a depression every time.

Stay strong. Be brave. You've got this.

"When are you starting work?"

"In a few weeks. They want me to start this week but it's a little soon for me."

"You need a break between jobs," Mum said thoughtfully.

"Exactly. A nice little holiday. And I want to make sure you get used to Dad looking after you instead of me."

"Tony will still be helping, too."

Amara nodded. "He will."

"That's good. He's a nice boy."

Amara forced a smile. Mum had always liked Tony and usually behaved well for him. She hadn't on Friday. While Amara and Dad were at the doctor's, she'd had a full-blown breakdown and thrown a tantrum. She only calmed down once Amara got home and Mum realised she hadn't abandoned her. Because Amara had been the sole carer for so long, Mum had become reliant on her, expecting her to always be there for her. Unfortunately, that wasn't always going to be possible, especially now that she was going back to work. Yet on Friday she'd been sure Amara had done just that, left her forever. Her reactions weren't rational anymore. It was all a product of the brain damage.

While Tony was fully capable of handling her, Amara worried because sometimes Mum would only calm down for her, much like how a child would only behave well for their mother. There was something about seeing Amara that made her relax more often than not.

"You'll get used to the new routine. Then I'll be working, and you and Dad can have some more alone time. I plan on going out more on weekends for that reason too."

"Good," was her mum's only response.

"So, now that we're alone..." Mum leant forward, an eager expression on her face. "Tell me about your date."

Amara felt crushed. Previously, she would have told her mum all about it, giving her all the basic details. But she couldn't do that now. Not only because Mum's brain didn't work properly, but because she felt awkward about it. But her mum had always been her go to woman, the one person she could run to for advice, tell her deepest, darkest secrets to. And she simply couldn't do that anymore. That only fuelled the loneliness that lived inside Amara today.

"It was fun. We had a great night."

Mum grabbed her arm and squeezed it a little too tightly. "I want details."

"Let's just say he's a great Dom."

"Oooohhhh." She rubbed her hands together. "Tell me more."

Amara laughed. "I won't give you details, Mum. But he's a great guy. We have the same taste in movies, music, TV shows. He even likes to hike. He's really sweet and just seems like a really good guy. I'm hoping to see him this weekend."

"You like him," Mum interjected.

Amara paused and considered lying. But she really did like him. A lot.

* * * *

Sullivan hadn't been able to get Amara off his mind. It was only Tuesday and he'd considered texting or calling her every day since Saturday. He'd been riding a high since he saw her. Their night together was, simply put, amazing. He'd never felt such an immediate connection with someone. He'd gotten so lost in their scene that he'd almost ended up topping out. He couldn't forget the way she felt pressed up against him. The way she fit perfectly curled up in his lap. The way she teased him playfully. Her smile lit up his world and her laugh filled him with joy. She was an incredible woman.

He'd hit Domspace hard and kept waiting for the crash, but it didn't come. Instead, he continued to ride high, unable to wipe the stupid smile from his face all week. Of course, it was the first thing Grayson noticed when he entered the treatment room at Sullivan's office.

"How'd your date with the little subbie go?"

"It was great," he told him simply. "She's something special."

"And?"

"And that's all I'm going to say."

He began to work on his best mate's injured knee, hoping he would drop it. But, of course, he didn't. The man could be damn invasive when he wanted to be. It was a part of what made him such a good Dom.

"The smile you've got plastered on your face says you experienced something more than just great sex."

"I can't lie, I'm hoping I can convince her to pursue something more. There is definitely a connection between us."

"Is that why you felt the need to invite her into your home?" He raised his brows and gave him a smirk. "You haven't taken anyone home in years."

"Honestly, I can't tell you what compelled me to do it. Maybe I hoped she'd be more comfortable at my house. She has some body image issues and isn't comfortable playing in public."

"And we all know how much you enjoy a public scene."

It was true. He really did love a public scene. There was nothing like showing off his beautiful submissive, knowing others were watching her as she got off by his hands. Previously he'd indulged in allowing other Doms to touch his subs, but that would definitely not be happening with Amara. He was already feeling very possessive of her.

"Whatever your reason, I'm glad you gave in. It's about time you found a nice girl to settle down with. You've been alone for far too long."

His friend was right. He'd been alone for over two years, never taking a woman on more than twice. One weekend was his limit. But deep down he wanted the happy ending. He wanted a wife, someone to be the mother of his children. He'd built his home to fill with love and laughter and that was never going to happen if he didn't begin dating, or at the very least using a submissive for more than a couple of days to see if there was a deeper connection between them.

His ex, Katerina, had done a number on him. She'd burned him, left him untrusting of women for too long. She'd started off as a sweet submissive, one who wanted nothing more than to please him. Then, somewhere along the line, she'd turned greedy and had become vindictive when they'd split up. He couldn't believe he'd read her so wrong. It had made him doubt how good a judge of character he was.

"Have you sorted things out with Jessie?"

Grayson flinched at the mention of his full-time submissive that he'd been having doubts about recently. "I uncollared her last night."

"Damn. I'm sorry."

They'd been together for three months, which was quite a while for Grayson. Last month, he'd confided in Sullivan that he didn't gain as much satisfaction from full-time domination as he used to. As he'd gotten older, he'd come to realise he wanted something part-time or just in the bedroom. Almost all of Grayson's previous relationships had been full-time D/s and Sullivan had never understood how he handled it. Sullivan just wasn't built that way and would never take on that amount of responsibility for a woman.

"I just couldn't do it anymore. It's too much responsibility for me now. I found it exhausting rather than thrilling." Grayson winced as Sullivan touched on a sore spot in his thigh. "I've promised to help find her a new master. If you have any ideas of who might be suitable for her, let me know."

"I'm sure we can introduce her to some Doms on Friday. Justin's recently single and a full-time master. Perhaps he'd be interested in her."

"I had thought of him. He might have too heavy a hand for her though. She barely coped with me at the beginning."

Sullivan continued to work on his friend's injured leg.

"Shall I inform the Masters and Mistresses you're no longer available to touch the submissives?"

He smiled as he began to pack up his gear for the day. "While I'm with Amara, I won't be playing with anyone else, no."

"You'll be disappointing a lot of sweet women. Though I am glad to hear it."

"If I can convince Amara to join me on Friday, it will be evident to most of them that I'm off the market."

Grayson frowned. "Your tone says she might not join you."

"Perceptive as always." He snorted. "She has a complicated family situation and doesn't get much time to herself. I feel like I'm pushing it by asking her to see me this Saturday."

"Complicated how?"

"She's a carer for her mother. She doesn't get much time to herself. I get the feeling that her family hasn't been particularly supportive, and she's been fighting to get help. I'm sure it's why she wants to keep our relationship casual."

"Hell." He ran a hand over his hair. "She's found the right man to understand her situation, hasn't she?"

Grayson had been with Sullivan every step of the way while he'd cared for his ill mother. They had been friends since childhood, and Grayson was the one person who hadn't abandoned him when life got difficult. If it weren't for Grayson, Sullivan would have completely lost himself while caring for his mum. He'd been there for him when he crashed. He gave him more leeway than other friends when his depression acted up. The man really was the best friend Sullivan could have asked for.

"I'd better get locked up. I have to go visit Mum now," Sullivan said, the words tightening his throat.

"You sure you don't want company?" Grayson offered but Sullivan shook his head.

The last thing he wanted anyone else to see was how his mum reacted to his presence now. Gone was the loving, caring mother he'd known for the first half of his life. She'd been replaced by a virtual husk of her former self.

"No, but thanks. I'll see you on Friday."

Sucking in a deep breath, he drove towards the care facility his mum now lived in. Guilt and anxiety were a weight in his gut as he turned in the driveway. She'd been living here for over ten years but visiting her never got any easier. Carer's guilt was real and each time he stepped inside the home, it reared its ugly head and threatened to shatter him. It was a constant reminder that he'd failed as a caregiver. As a son. On some days he believed he was a complete failure. Luckily, today wasn't one of those days.

Sullivan made his way to the locked wing of the home where his mum lived and signed himself in on the visitor's registry. Bea, one of the few nurses his mother would interact with, spotted him and waved. She was sitting at a table with Mum, actually having a conversation with her. He couldn't remember the last time he'd had a civil conversation with his mum.

When she'd first moved into the facility, he'd visited her every day, trying to claim back the relationship they used to have. Then the visits happened every other day. Now, he was down to seeing her once or twice a week at most. It was easier on both of them that way. She never reacted well to his presence. Almost every time she became belligerent, even violent. It made the nurses' jobs harder in the days that followed and often sent him spiralling into a depressive state.

When Mum turned her head to look at him, he felt his heart skip a beat. Maybe tonight would be a good night. The closer he got to her, he realised that wouldn't be the case. There was no recognition in her eyes. She only had fleeting moments of clarity and spent most of her days staring into space, not interacting with another living soul.

Now she sat before him, a shell. Gone was the vibrant, caring, sweet mother he knew. The last time he'd spoken with her doctor, he'd noted she was becoming more withdrawn as the dementia got worse.

"Violet, you've got a very handsome young visitor," Bea said, patting his mother's arm as he sat beside her.

Mum continued to watch him, her blue eyes vacant. Her dark hair was showing more grey each time he saw her. It was no longer thick and wavy. Now it was straight and stringy, lifeless just like her eyes.

"Hey, Mum."

She frowned as she tried to place him.

"It's Sullivan," Bea reminded her before she left them alone.

"Sullivan," his mum said with a small smile as he leant forward to kiss her cheek.

She was far calmer than she had been last week when he'd visited. She'd spent most of the visit yelling at him to leave her alone, calling him awful names. She had even hit him at one point. Every hostile interaction chipped away at his soul. Some days he wondered why he even bothered to visit her when she so clearly hated him.

Because she's still Mum.

"Where have you been?" she asked him in a quiet voice.

"I've been working. Sorry, it's been a few days."

She shook her head. "You know better than to get home after dark."

Sullivan sighed lightly. His mum often lived in the past now. Apparently today she saw him as the teenager he'd been before she'd decided alcohol was more important than he was.

Don't be bitter, he had to remind himself.

"Sorry, I got held up."

"Did you lock the door behind you? You need to keep the door locked."

"I did."

"The man came again last night," she told him, her eyes suddenly filled with distress. "He stole my purse. You need to call the police."

And just like that, she was gone. Off to the other world she lived in.

"It's okay. I caught him on my way in. I've put your purse in your room. He won't be coming back. The police have him."

She blanked for a few moments, that glazed expression coming over her eyes, the one that absolutely broke him. Though they might have had a complicated relationship in the years that followed the accident, she was his mum and he still loved her dearly. Seeing her like this was an awful thing to witness. But it was all her fault.

"Joseph," she said quietly. "Where's Joseph?"

The mention of his dad was always hard for Sullivan. It had been almost twenty years since the accident took him and Brady away from them and it hadn't gotten any easier to deal with. There was a large permanent hole in his soul that could never be mended.

"Dad's gone, Mum."

"Gone..." She trailed off, then her eyes snapped up to his. "So is Brady."

"Yeah..."

They sat in silence for a few minutes, while he held his mother's frail hand and others went about their lives around them. Mum continued to stare blankly out the window, not a single iota of recognition in her eyes.

At least she's not angry.

Those days were the worst—the days where she cursed him for still being alive, wishing his brother were here instead. Some days, Sullivan wished for that too.

Bea approached and asked for a minute of his time, ushering him off to the office to speak with him in private.

"She's getting like that more often. I'm so sorry, Sullivan."

He gave a small shrug. "It's better than the alternative."

"She had another outburst this morning, took it out on her room. Smashed almost everything inside it."

Great. He ran a hand over his now weary face. "I'll replace everything."

One of the reasons he had to stop looking after Mum by himself was her tendency to smash everything breakable around her. His mum—his old mum— would be absolutely appalled by her behaviour now. She had always been so gentle, so sweet and caring. She had been a mother to everyone when he was growing up. Hardly ever raising her voice, she'd only ever smacked them a handful of times. She was the best mum two boys could have asked for. Then the accident happened and everything about her changed.

"The doctor is hoping the new antidepressants will begin to work within the next week or so and will help stop the outbursts."

"I hope it does for your sakes. I'm sorry you have to deal with her outbursts so often."

The nurse didn't respond. She didn't need to. Sullivan had done enough research into alcohol-related dementia to know what his mum's future held. She would eventually lose touch with reality completely. She'd withdraw into herself, lose the ability to do anything for herself at all. Hell, she was already almost there. She already needed assistance in dressing, bathing and eating.

When he'd been caring for her, she would go for days without bathing or changing into clean clothes, insisting she'd just done it. That was when he knew she wasn't going to get any better. She'd continued to go downhill from there.

Once Bea dismissed him, leaving him with a bill for the destroyed items from his mum's room, he returned to Mum and did what he usually did. He had a one-sided conversation and told her about his day, his life. He mentioned Grayson in the hopes she would respond, but she didn't.

He became more depressed the longer he stayed. She didn't get any other visitors. When she'd begun drinking heavily, she'd alienated herself from all of her friends. They had no family left. It was just the two of them.

Now it was just him.

What he wouldn't give to know what was going on in her head now. Did she recognise him? Did she understand what he was saying to her? Did she even care? Bitterly, he realised he knew the answer to all three questions was probably no. Even when he'd given up his own apartment to look after her, she hadn't cared. Instead, she'd hurled abuse at him, thrown things at him, hit him. But he'd continued to look after her because it was the right thing to do. For fifteen years, she had been the most amazing mum to him. He did it for that woman.

After the accident, she'd become inattentive at first. The grief of losing her husband and oldest son had broken her and she'd forgotten about the son she had left. Sullivan had been forced to grieve alone. Without the help of Grayson and his parents, he wouldn't have gotten through the next few years sane. It still hurt him to think about, more than he had ever cared to admit.

Then Mum had hit the bottle—hard. It eroded her personality. She was a mean, angry drunk, often leaving him to fend for himself for days. He'd begged and pleaded with her to go to rehab so many times, but his pleas fell on deaf ears. So often, he had tried to cut her off, to stay away from her, but she'd grown very manipulative. He was constantly giving her money for food, even though he knew she spent it on booze. Eventually she moved on to painkillers. She'd sold his and Brady's collectibles to pay for her habit. When she'd tried to sell one of Dad's most prized possessions, he'd put his foot down and removed all the valuables from the home while she was out on a bender one weekend.

By the time he realised he needed to move in to take care of her, her hatred had well and truly set in. He was at university at the time and had to shift to part-time over the next two years while he cared for her. He found it incredibly hard to cope but he held on, in the hopes that she would come through and revert back to his old mum. But she didn't.

Sullivan would never forget the day it became obvious she needed to be locked in a home with full-time nurses to care for her. He'd woken at two a.m. to find her bedroom empty, the front door wide open. She was wandering the streets in the middle of winter, barefoot and wearing nothing but a thin nightgown. Yelling and swearing at invisible people, she'd swung her arms out, throwing punches at hallucinations.

He'd barely managed to restrain her, copping a beating himself before the police showed up. One of the neighbours had thought they were two drunks having an argument and had called the cops. Not that Sullivan blamed them. He probably would have done the same thing. He'd managed to convince the police not to take her and made up his mind that she needed to go into a home.

He'd felt so guilty for entertaining the idea of putting her into a facility that it took him another two weeks to make enquiries. The decision had hit him hard. He'd failed as a carer. Failed as a son. Now, he knew he wasn't being fair on himself. He hadn't been equipped to do the job by himself. He never should have taken it on in the first place.

"I miss you, Mum," he said as he watched her vacant blue eyes staring out the window.

His heart ached constantly for what he had lost. For the loving mother he had lost. While the surrogate family he'd made for himself filled his life with love, it wasn't the same as his real family. It would never be the same.

"I should get going."

She squeezed his hand, a spark of recognition coming to her eyes. "My baby boy."

His heart lifted. "Yeah, Mum. It's me."

Tears burned his eyes as the blank gaze returned. That was all he got out of her. She let go of his hand and continued to stare out the dark window. He pressed a kiss to the top of her head as he stood.

"I'll see you soon."

And he left, feeling as empty and depressed as ever.

* * * *

Incredibly drained, Sullivan spent an hour or so stretched out on his lounge, staring at the television. He was completely exhausted. Then Amara came to the forefront of his mind. What incredibly random timing.

Although, there was something about Amara that lifted his spirits. The first night he saw her, he had been depressed for days and seeing her pulled him right out of it, made everything right in his world.

Well, wasn't that an unhealthy way to think of a woman?

He should send her a message to let him know he was thinking of her. Women liked it when a man showed interest, didn't they?

I know you said weekends only, but I would love to see you sooner. I haven't been able to get you out of my head.

Pressing send before he chickened out, he instantly regretted it and threw his phone on the couch. *Talk about clingy.* He ran a hand over his face and through his hair, inwardly cursing himself. Then his phone made a sound.

How about I text you tomorrow and let you know? I'd like to see you again too.

She replied with a winking smiley-face emoji.

He smiled, a big stupid grin that he couldn't stifle. For Christ's sake, he wasn't supposed to get all giddy over a woman. He was a grown-ass man. He was a Dom. He should have been more composed than that.

Sounds good to me. How was your day today?

A few minutes later, she replied.

Fine. The usual. I'm just trying to relax a bit now before the nightly routine begins. How was yours?

He hesitated, and found himself wanting to tell her how awful his night had been. Fuck, what was wrong with him? He didn't share his emotions like that. He really was exhausted tonight.

The usual. I'll let you get back to relaxing.

I'll text you tomorrow.

She responded with a kissy-face emoji. He responded in kind and dropped his phone. Had he just come across as a stage-five clinger? Probably. What a fool.

Chapter Nine

Amara woke after a peaceful sleep, feeling well rested and ready to tackle the day. She'd managed to get six full hours of sleep, with her mum's new sleeping tablets keeping her fast asleep for eight hours. Unfortunately, that meant she hadn't woken during the night to use the toilet and had wet the bed. That set the tone for the rest of the day.

Two more accidents followed throughout the day, plus a total breakdown where she cried for no reason other than the fact that she had brain damage and her emotions didn't process correctly anymore. After comforting her for an hour, Amara managed to get her settled enough that she could continue the puzzle she'd been working on with Tony. Amara handed the reins over to him and took a few moments to try to centre herself as her own emotions brimmed at the surface, threatening to take over.

Seated on the outdoor lounge, she closed her eyes and enjoyed the warm summer sun beating down on her exposed skin. A smile spread over her face as her thoughts drifted to Sullivan. As drained as she was today, she couldn't wait to see him tonight. After a small argument with Dad, he finally agreed to look after Mum and put her to bed so Amara could go out. It was part of their new agreement, but he was taking some time to get used to it. On the whole, his attitude had changed since her week away, but sometimes he fell into old habits, expecting Amara to do everything. Still, she felt more appreciated in the last couple of weeks than she had in the previous eighteen months.

Pulling out her phone, she texted Sullivan.

You still free tonight?

He responded immediately.

You bet. What time can I expect you?

Is seven okay?

Perfect.

* * * *

By the time evening rolled around, Amara was well and truly ready to get out of the house and get a physical stress release. Mum hadn't paid any attention to Tony throughout the afternoon, instead insisting Amara do everything for her. The carer might as well have not been there. Spending the entire afternoon paying close attention to her mum exhausted Amara. Depression and sadness took over her emotions and by the time she was ready to leave, she felt the need to cancel on Sullivan. But no, she wouldn't. She had made plans and she would stick to them.

After dinner, she asked Dad again if he was okay to look after Mum for the night.

He shot her a disapproving glance. "One of these days, I'm going to be insulted by your lack of faith in me."

Amara flinched. "That's not the issue. I know you're fully capable of doing it —"

"Amara," he said softly. "I'm teasing."

She found a smile on his face. *Great.* She was in such a bad mood she couldn't even recognise her own father's teasing.

"Sorry, it's been a long day."

"So you said."

On the verge of tears, she tried her best to suck it up as she changed into a singlet top and jeans and grabbed her bag of toys. Sullivan had specifically reminded her to bring any toys she had this afternoon so that he could see what she enjoyed using on herself. Nervous butterflies thudded around her stomach as she drove the twenty minutes to his house. She'd managed to give herself a little pep talk, putting her mind in a better mood. Now she had that mild anxiety that filled her whenever she was seeing a Dom mixed with excitement.

Appearing fresh out of the shower, Sullivan opened the door for her and greeted her with a long, deep kiss. He smelled good enough to eat. She loved that he didn't use strong colognes. He smelled of his soap and a purely masculine scent that was all him.

He took the bag off her and raised his brows as he gauged the weight of it.

"Whoa, how much stuff do you have in here?"

"A girl has to have her own stash. It's unsanitary to only use a Dom's toys."

"And this has nothing to do with you being a control freak, does it?"

She laughed loudly. He knew her well already. That was the exact reason she had so many toys of her own. She liked to buy what she liked, not trust a Dom to get the right toy for her. Unless she was dating them seriously, she'd never allowed a Dominant to buy her anything. Now that she thought about it, that was quite an unhealthy way of thinking.

"Some of them are brand new." She'd bought them to use with Eddie but never got the chance to use them.

"How was your day?" he asked as he led her to his bedroom.

"In a word, shithouse. But I'm here to forget all about it."

He turned to face her as he dropped the bag on the bed. Wrapping his strong arms around her waist, he took a moment to just look at her. It made her feel oddly naked and uneasy. She began to shift in his grasp.

"I'm sorry you had a rough day." He bent to press a kiss to her lips. "But I will definitely make you forget all about it."

He kissed her again. This time it was warm and inviting. Dragging his lips across her cheek, down her jawline, he nipped the sensitive skin before moving down to her throat. She cupped the back of his head as he licked and sucked his way down her neck then back up before he captured her mouth again in a hot, searing kiss that had her curling her toes into the thick carpet.

Sullivan emptied Amara's bag on his bed, a slew of vibrators, dildos, cuffs, clamps, ties and blindfolds spread out on the bed. She really did have a lot of toys. Far too many for a submissive.

"I have a cane too," she told him. "But that's a little too conspicuous to sneak out of the house with."

"I suppose you don't want your parents knowing what you're up to while you're here."

"Oh, no, they know. I told them exactly what I was headed here for."

He stopped his movements, mild shock on his face. "You're serious?"

"I've always had a very open relationship with my family. They know I'm in the lifestyle. My brother is a Dom, so they've overheard us discussing it from time to time and have asked questions."

"Wow."

She laughed. "You think that's bad. I told my mum when I had my first orgasm during sex."

"We definitely have very different relationships with our families."

"We were taught never to be ashamed of sex or our bodies. But we were also taught to be safe, that sex was something special, not to go around fucking anyone with genitals."

He smiled. "That's a good way to raise kids."

"I'm sure they regret it sometimes. When I lost my virginity, I came home and told them and their best friends. Just blurted it out all proud that I'd lost my V card."

Choking on a laugh, he ran his knuckles over her cheek. "You are definitely a unique woman, Amara."

God, she loved how he said her name. He made it sound like the most beautiful word in the English language.

"I am nothing if not unique."

Dipping his head, he pressed his lips to hers in a tentative, shallow kiss. She brought her hands up to cup either side of his face and tilted her head to deepen the kiss. Desire unfurled deep in her belly as he fisted one hand in her hair and took over. His tongue swept across hers, tasting her. All Amara's worries for the day disappeared into the kiss. She moved her arms to wrap around his broad shoulders and pressed her body against his. Nothing else mattered in that moment, just the feeling of him taking over her body.

Sullivan slipped his hands beneath the hem of her top, his hands leaving a scalding trail across her bare skin. He reached down and gripped her ass, his fingers digging into the flesh through the denim. It sent a shockwave of desire straight to her core, where liquid heat pooled between her thighs. She moaned into his mouth as he continued to ravage her, hands roaming over her body, his fingers applying the slightest amount of pressure on her sensitive points.

Eventually, he pulled away and rested his forehead on hers in an intimate gesture she adored. He took a moment to just stand there, as though he was breathing her in. She let her hands roam over his body as he stood unmoving, his fingers digging into her hips as her hands made their way to his groin.

Everything about Sullivan made her nerve endings fire on all cylinders. His touch, God, his touch, did things to her that she hadn't experienced before. "Strip to your underwear. I'll pick out what we're going to play with tonight."

Making quick work of her clothing, Amara stood in her bra and panties while he put her toys back in her bag. She noted that he'd kept out her favourite pair of nipple clamps. Anticipation tore through her at the thought of being pinned beneath him while he attached them.

He stood in front of her, regarding her with his head tilted ever so slightly. His gaze was pure Dom. All delicious intimidation and raw sexuality. Fighting the urge to cover herself up, she clenched her fists at her side and awaited his instructions. With a light kiss to her shoulder, he moved to stand behind her. Running his fingers lightly across her shoulders and down her back, he spread one hand open on her upper chest and applied pressure to her trapezius. Closing her eyes, she focussed on his touch as it loosened the tension in her muscle. Then his thumb dug in even further and the pressure quickly turned painful.

Hissing in a breath, she let out a small sound before he let go and repeated the movement on the other side. He followed up the pain by pressing his lips to the hollow of her throat, his tongue flicking out to taste her skin. Undoing the clasps of her bra, he pushed the straps over her shoulders, his hands following their trail as he kissed her neck again. Dropping her head back, she invited him to kiss her neck, grateful when he licked and sucked his way up to the sensitive spot just below her ear. Hands never leaving her sensitive skin, he reached forward to hold the heavy weight of her breasts in each hand, moulding and kneading the flesh until her breath came in small pants. He teased and plucked her nipples, pinching them hard, eliciting a moan from her.

"Oh God…"

"I love how sensitive your breasts are," he murmured into her ear, sending a shiver down her spine. "I can't wait to clamp and torture them."

"Please…" She clenched her thighs at the promise.

He trailed his hands down her, to her underwear as he lowered himself and kissed his way down her spine. Closing her eyes, she focussed on nothing other than his touch, the press of his soft yet firm lips just above her pelvis, where her spine dipped. His tongue flicked out to tease the skin as he pushed her underwear down her legs. Pressing a kiss to either of her butt cheeks, he lingered there for a moment, biting into her flesh hard enough to send a jolt of pain directly to her clit. She pressed her thighs together and let out a low moan. He repeated the action then moved back up her body to stand behind her, his rock-hard erection pressed against her ass.

With a small sigh, she leant back into him, resting her head on his chest. Without warning, he bit down on her neck, hard. Almost too hard. Breathing through it, Amara exhaled a long low moan as she pressed her body back against his, reaching her hands behind until he captured them in his own. With their fingers entwined, he brought their hands up to her waist and rocked his cock against her ass, then bit down on her neck again, sucking hard enough this time to bring tears to her eyes.

Oh fuck, he was amazing. He knew just how much pressure to apply when hurting her, never going over that threshold to what was unbearable for her. How the hell did he know?

"On the bed," he murmured into her ear. "Assume the position."

Crawling onto the bed, she knelt in the centre of it and sat up just as he'd asked her to last week—hands clasped behind her back, her breasts thrust out, head up to watch him, her eyes never leaving his gaze.

"Very nice," he said as he came to kneel on the bed before her.

She loved receiving his praise. It completed that part of her that missed submitting to a Dominant. Spreading his knees until he was at the right angle, he began an assault on her breasts. Licking, sucking, biting and squeezing, he tortured her for several long minutes until her breasts ached and her nipples were so hard, they could cut glass. Each sensation sent jolts of pleasure straight to her clit which throbbed painfully with need.

One hand reached behind her to grasp her hair right at her scalp. She sucked in a breath as he tipped her head back forcefully.

"I'm going to push you tonight," he said against her lips. "If you feel uncomfortable with anything, you tell me. No being brave. Understood?"

She nodded as much as she could in his fierce grip. "Understood."

Giving her a smile, he held out his other hand which now had her favourite tweezer clamps. After sucking each nipple one more time, he blew on them to cool them to harder points and attached each clamp. He moved to the bedside table where he picked up a chain.

Oh shit.

Attaching the chain to each clamp, he tugged it gently. Amara cried out and closed her eyes against the beautiful pain. Pain radiated throughout her body, from her nipples straight to her soaking wet pussy.

"Evil Dom," she said as she frowned at him, unable to stop herself.

"Naughty sub." He pulled the chain, harder this time. "You're just asking for a spanking, aren't you?"

She froze. She really wasn't. She'd never enjoyed spanking much. Although with Sullivan, maybe it would be different.

"No more talking," he warned before taking her mouth in a commanding kiss. "On your back, arms up, legs spread into a V."

She obeyed him as he left the bed and dug around in the large wardrobe where he kept his toys. The room was so big she couldn't see him. He returned with several items in his hands, including a fucking Hitachi wand. God, she both loved and hated those things. Whoever had invented them was definitely a sadist.

Attaching lined cuffs to her wrists, he brought them together and attached them to something above her. She pulled. He'd restrained her to the bed. Unable to escape, she looked down at him, watching as he moved around the bed, the mattress shifting beneath his weight. A pair of cuffs were wrapped around her ankles, which he then attached to more restraints on the bed posts.

"I can see you've had a hard day, little sub," he said gently. "I want you to let go tonight. Do absolutely nothing other than focus on me."

Wait. "Does that mean I look like complete shit?"

Tears pricked her eyes. *No, dammit. Fuck off.* The last thing she wanted to do was to cry in front of him. The whole point of seeing Sullivan was to have fun and forget her negative emotions.

He ran his knuckles over her left cheek. A soft, tender touch.

"That's not what I mean. But I see sadness in your eyes. I want to take it away."

She closed her eyes against the unwelcome intrusion of emotion that his words elicited. But the image of her mum completely inconsolable on the floor today made its way to the forefront of her mind. One stray tear leaked from her eye before she swiped her face against her arm to get rid of it.

"Kiss me," she asked without looking at him. "Please, just kiss me."

"Because you asked so nicely."

He pressed his chest against hers, the sharp stab of pain in her nipples causing her to whimper into his mouth. He took her in a deep, wet kiss. When he ground his denim-clad cock against her pussy, she had the feeling she was in for the ride of her life.

* * * *

A couple of hours later, Amara lay almost completely boneless beneath Sullivan. Almost, but not quite. He'd lost count of how many orgasms he'd given her, finding himself lost in Domspace for most of the night. Each orgasm had forced her to let go a little more. He had worshipped her beautiful body, kissing, licking and biting his way across nearly every single inch of it. He'd fucked her in several different positions until her voice had gone hoarse from her cries. At one point, he'd thought she would slip into subspace, right where he wanted her, but she hovered on the precipice. She needed more pain.

Placing the clamps back on her overly sensitive nipples, sans chain, he smiled when he received that little hiss of pain when he tightened them, just enough to hold them in place this time, just enough to divert her brain. Her clit throbbed beneath his fingers as he slowly slid his cock through her slick, passion-swollen cunt. She cried out when he buried himself to the hilt, her eyes unfocussed as she continued to watch him. *Good girl.*

That was what he wanted to see.

Determined, he began to thrust in and out in a slow and steady rhythm. The groan that came from her sent vibrations through him, down his cock to settle in his balls that drew up against his body. *Fuck.* Clenching his jaw, he kept his orgasm at bay.

Amara whimpered that beautiful little sound when he shifted his position, pressing his chest against her soft breasts. He kissed his way down her throat, finding the spot he'd bitten hard earlier and closing his teeth over it. The sob she let out told him she was one step closer to slipping away completely. The way she clamped down on his cock told him she loved the sensation. Her eyes closed. She threw her head back as she cried when he let go. She was so fucking beautiful. And almost there.

"Get ready," he warned her.

When he released the left nipple clamp, ripples tore through her body as her pussy clamped down on his cock and began to spasm.

"Ow, ow, ow," she cried as he sucked the peak into his mouth to soothe the pain. "Oh fuck," she moaned as the pain clearly turned to pleasure and she writhed beneath him.

"Ready for the next one?"

"Noooooo," she whimpered in the most gorgeous, endearing way.

Muffling a cry, she bit down on her arm as he removed the remaining clamp. She spasmed around his cock again and he pressed a finger to her clit and rubbed mercilessly. She screamed, completely letting go of her inhibitions as she came apart beneath him, all around him.

What a beautiful sight.

Once her orgasm subsided, he gave in to his own, thrusting in and out while continuing to torture her softened clit.

"Sullivan." Fuck, he loved when she said his name like that, half crying, half panting. "I can't."

She fought against the restraints. "Please, I — "

"Amara," he scolded her.

Her eyes snapped open, glistening with fear and arousal as she looked up at him.

"You will come, one more time."

"I can't." She sobbed. "I can't handle another one."

"You can." He pinned her with his gaze. "For me."

Her cheeks flushed further, pupils dilating as she gave in to her need to please him. Shifting onto his knees, he fucked her hard. His orgasm rose from the small of his back to his balls which drew up against his body, rushing up his shaft. He pressed against her clit and her entire body seized up, inner muscles clenching and contracting around his cock. She fell apart, her body shaking violently as she came. He let go, allowing her to drag him down with her, her cunt milking his cock completely dry.

He tingled from head to toe, chest heaving with each laboured breath as he looked down at her. Fuck, she was amazing.

He collapsed onto his hands, careful to hold his weight off her. Her breath came in short, sharp pants while she tried — and failed — to regain her composure. He pulled out of her and she let out a loud whimper of a sigh. Then her tears began to fall.

Mission accomplished.

Moving swiftly, he got rid of the condom, removed her restraints and grabbed a soft blanket he'd kept on standby. Scooping her up, he moved to sit on the large armchair by the window and wrapped the blanket around her tightly as sobs shook her entire body.

It had pained him to see her when she first arrived, barely holding it together while she pushed her emotions down. She had put on that brave face, but he knew she needed to let go, to purge all the emotion she had been holding on to. One thing he'd quickly learned about Amara was that she shut herself off too quickly. She dealt with her emotions internally rather than sharing. But she needed to share, to feel, especially with her Dom. How else could he take care of her? And he felt a deep-seated need to take care of her. She called to all his protective instincts when she appeared hurt.

He wanted—needed—her to feel safe in his arms. Having her there felt right. She belonged there. With him. And he would hold her for as long as she needed. Resting a cheek on the top of her head, he whispered sweet nothings to her while she continued to cry it out.

When she finally came to, she wiped her cheeks and looked at him with the most gorgeous sheepish expression he'd ever seen. A blush painted her tear-stained cheeks, her whisky eyes searching his.

"Feeling better?" he asked softly as he caressed her cheek.

She nodded in response.

"Was it as intense as it looked?"

She cuddled further into him, filling him with pure joy. "Mmmmmm."

When she tilted her head seeking a kiss, he happily obliged, enjoying the feeling of her pillowy soft lips against his. He tasted the salt of her tears, mixed with the feminine taste that was pure Amara.

"I needed that." She let out a sigh. "How did you know?"

"It's a Dom's job to know these things."

"You're definitely the best Dom I've ever had."

Wasn't that something that just made his heart swell with pride?

"Thank you, sweetheart."

She stretched out her legs for a moment and let out a long low moan that had his cock hardening again.

"I don't want to move," she whined even as she snuggled further into him.

Why did she always feel the need to get up and move immediately after a scene? He enjoyed nothing more than having a sleepy sub in his arms. She'd obviously dealt with Dominants who didn't enjoy aftercare. The fools.

"You're not going anywhere," he murmured into her hair.

* * * *

Amara eventually left Sullivan's lap, leaving him feeling empty. He watched from his position in the chair as she dressed herself slowly, almost gingerly, as though her muscles weren't quite ready to move yet. She was quite a sight. Her hair was a mess of dark brown falling over her shoulders, eyes hooded in sleepy satisfaction, lips red and swollen from his kisses. He couldn't ignore the sense of pride and ownership that filled him when he noticed the marks and bruises that were scattered across her pale skin. He'd been careful to only leave marks where nobody would see them, other than one big bite mark on her neck. That was an accidental and blatant mark of ownership. He smirked. It was something he couldn't bring himself to regret.

They made plans to see each other on Saturday and an idea came across his mind. Moving to his wardrobe, he searched for the little box that sat on a shelf of brand-new, unused, toys and pulled it out.

"I have an idea for Saturday," he said as he stood beside her. "How about we go out for dinner, and we use this?"

He handed her the box and watched as she opened it and found the remote-controlled vibrator he'd never had the chance to use on a woman. Because it would have involved going on a real date outside of the club. And he didn't date his subs. Not until Amara.

"What do you say?"

Her body betrayed her expression. Her face flushed, a subtle shudder running down her spine as she smiled up at him, pupils dilating when she met his gaze. Yes, she clearly liked the idea.

"Okay. But only because I've never used something like this in public before."

"Neither have I," he admitted. "I hear they can be a lot of fun."

He'd previously seen Grayson use a similar device on a former submissive of his at a party. She had barely controlled herself and, at one point, came so hard while speaking with Sullivan that her legs gave out and he had to catch her. All because Grayson had complete control.

He took the box from her and tossed it on the bed, catching her lips in a kiss so hot it had him ready to go another round.

"I should go," she said reluctantly when he withdrew.

"I'll see you on Saturday."

Walking her to her car, with a hand resting on the small of her back—because he needed to be touching her at all times—he gave her one last kiss that left her breathless. Damned if he didn't miss her as soon as she drove away. He was definitely getting attached to her. And it scared the hell out of him.

Chapter Ten

Amara felt like a new person. All week she'd been sleeping a full six to seven hours each night. She'd been spending more time by herself, even getting her hands dirty in the garden earlier today. And she had an absolutely amazing new Dom. For the first time in a long time, she was happy.

On the drive to Sullivan's, she had to push down the guilt she felt for abandoning her parents by reminding herself they also needed time together to be a couple. She made her way to Sullivan's front door, now noticing the severe lack of garden in his front yard. She would have had so much fun working on Sullivan's bare yard, starting a new garden from scratch.

Belle would have a great time. The landscaper loved nothing more than starting with a blank canvas. She owned a very successful business and had landscaped Amara's old house from scratch, letting her help on weekends. Now that the house was rented out, her poor garden had been severely neglected. Belle had offered several times to fix it up for free, but Amara would never take advantage of her friend like that. Nor could she afford to pay her to do it.

Smoothing out the skirt of her blue-trimmed black dress, Amara noted her sweaty palms. She was nervous about going on a real date with Sullivan. Why was she so nervous? He'd seen her naked and writhing several times and had held her while she cried. There were no boundaries between them — only emotional ones. That was why she was nervous. She was going on a real date for the first time in years. Even when she'd been with Eddie, they hadn't gone out for dinner. They had spent all their time at one of their houses or at Haven. They hadn't really dated.

Sullivan opened the door and pulled her from her musings. Her nerves suddenly got far, far worse. She was definitely playing out of her league. No, they weren't even playing the same game. Sullivan had dressed in perfectly tailored black dress pants and a deep blue button down with the sleeves rolled up to reveal his muscular forearms. She couldn't help but ogle him. His hair was messed in its usual, sexy-as-hell style, his face freshly shaven and he smelt...mouth-watering was the only word that came to mind. The scent of his soap mixed with that musk of man that was all him. It was so endearing she wanted to sink her teeth into him.

"Wow," she said, unable to stop herself.

Wetness pooled between her thighs, her clit throbbing with each beat of her heart. He was definitely out of her league.

"Wow yourself." His hungry gaze ran up and down her body as he licked his lips. "You look amazing."

Tipping her head up, she gave him a quick kiss and deepened it when he wrapped his arms around her waist, pulling her body firmly against his.

A slow, sensual smile spread across those full lips and his eyes crinkled as he held up a small remote. "The toy is on the bed. Put it in and we'll head off."

Amara's cheeks flushed as she dashed past him to obey his request. She couldn't believe she was going to do this, actually play with someone in a public, vanilla space. When she met him in the entry, the vibrator came to life inside of her. Her knees all but gave out and she grasped onto his forearm to balance herself.

She gasped. "Holy shit, that's strong."

That evil Dom grin she'd come to love spread across his face. "Oh yeah, this is going to be fun."

On the drive to the restaurant, Sullivan turned the vibrator on and off several times just to torment her. Of course, he insisted it was so he could test the strength of it. Amara was so turned on by the time he parked the car, she wanted him to turn back so she could fuck him as soon as possible. Yet he wouldn't let her come. At one point he turned on the vibrations so high and at such an intense pulsing, she nearly came on the spot, crying out loudly, but he turned it down immediately, leaving her hovering right on the edge. She made a move to take things into her own hand — literally — but he scolded her and swore he would punish her later for it. She had yet to be punished by him but had no doubt it would be creative and harsh. And something she didn't want.

As they made their way inside the fancy restaurant, Amara's legs were slightly wobbly as she tried her best to hold it together. She looked around and realised they were at a very fancy restaurant that she would never dream of attending herself. Swanky was the word she'd use to describe it. Decorated in rich, dark colours, the tables were set out to accommodate privacy for the diners. The wait staff wore impeccable black and white suits fancier than Amara's outfit. She immediately felt self-conscious and pulled at the skirt of her dress, wishing it was longer, fancier and covered up more of her.

Sullivan caught her movement and wrapped a possessive arm around her waist as they were led to a very private table in the back of the restaurant. Holding a chair out for her, he made sure she was seated before seating himself, ever the gentleman. He sat on the opposite side of the table to her, his heated gaze running down her body as she shifted uncomfortably in her chair. Right then, she wished he was sitting next to her with an arm around her.

The waiter took their drink orders, frowning when they both refused to see the wine list. Amara wasn't much of a drinker, but she had always hated the taste of wine.

"You don't drink?" she asked him as she took a sip of her water.

"Mental illness and alcohol don't mix well," he said in a matter-of-fact tone.

"Oh, right. I'd forgotten about that." She really had forgotten he had depression. Either he hadn't had an episode when he'd been with her, or he was a master at hiding it.

"I don't mind if you drink, though."

She shook her head. "I'm not a big drinker. Besides, I need to keep my wits about me tonight, so I don't make a fool of myself in public."

His eyes danced with mischief as he leant back in his chair, a broad smile on his handsome face. His hand disappeared into his pocket, and she braced herself for the toy to come to life inside of her. It didn't. She blew out a long breath and relaxed a little. This was going to be a long night.

"Can I ask you a personal question?" She bit the inside of her bottom lip. "And feel free not to answer it."

"Shoot."

"How long have you had depression for?"

He didn't skip a beat. "I was diagnosed at seventeen."

"That's young."

He gave a casual shrug. "It is what it is."

Without warning, the vibe came to life, buzzing right against her G-spot. *Fuck.* The constant low hum of satisfaction burned through her veins. Sucking in a gasp, she adjusted her position as her legs went weak, before glaring at Sullivan, who smiled wickedly. He had a way about him that was not only playful, but also portrayed pure and utter dominance at the same time. She knew from experience with others that it was a fine line to walk, yet he seemed to do so effortlessly. Amara had to wonder how many years of experience he had at being a Dom.

"You could have warned me you were going to do that," she snapped despite the pleasure roiling through her body.

He leant forward and licked his lips in a way that had her wanting to kiss him. "You forget, sweetheart. For the rest of the night, your body is mine and mine alone. I will do with it what I please." He shifted back in his seat. "There will be no warning."

Oh God. Her insides melted at his words, his tone, his power. Every time his hand disappeared beneath the table from now on, she would have to prepare herself.

Amara had taken a few minutes to adjust to the constant state of arousal she was in. Sullivan didn't alter the speed or pulse of the vibrator until their food arrived. Quickening the pace, he set it to a rhythmic pulse that brought her so close to the edge he could smell her arousal. He could almost fucking taste it on his tongue. Her hands gripped at the table as she wiggled in the chair in the most delicious way. A warm pink flush spread across her cheeks. Her lips swelled as she repeatedly bit and licked them. Her eyes were hooded as she scowled up at him. Fuck, she was so cute.

"Can you at least turn it down so I can eat? Please?" she added hastily.

Only because she asked so politely, he ceased the vibrations altogether. He smiled when she exhaled a long sigh of relief. She'd told him she didn't want to come in public, but he could see the longing in her eyes. She might not have wanted to, but she needed to. And wasn't it a Dom's job to give his submissive what she needed?

Of course, he had selfish reasons for tonight's play. Seeing her all wound up and aroused in the restaurant had been such a turn-on for him, his erection pressed uncomfortably against the zipper of his pants. It would be good for her to let go in a public space. Maybe this way he could lower her inhibitions and one day get her to do a public scene with him in the club.

Amara moved a forkful of pasta towards her mouth and hesitated when he moved his hand to his pocket. Each time he moved, she stopped and prepared herself.

"Don't," she warned him even as a smile spread across her lips.

He couldn't have her telling him what to do now, could he? Waiting until she put the fork between her lips, he flicked the remote. Her knee hit the bottom of the table as she jumped. Shit, he hadn't expected that much of a reaction. He smothered a laugh and continued to watch her. Eyes hooded, lips parted, cheeks and chest flushed, she looked a treat.

"I regret letting you do this to me," she said between laboured breaths.

It was amazing how she appeared so in control while simultaneously letting go.

"No. You don't," he told her, enjoying her return smile.

While she might have complained, she was enjoying herself immensely. Anyone could see that. Lucky for her, her back was to the rest of the patrons and nobody else could see her responses. He turned it up a notch and watched in satisfaction as she dropped the fork onto her plate and tensed. Each muscle in her body began to tremble as she looked up at him helplessly. Getting off on her expression, the position he'd put her in, he gave her a small nod and smirked as she clamped one hand over her mouth and gave in. It was the most subtle orgasm he'd ever seen, but she came on a small squeak, her muscles shuddering, cheeks a beautiful deep red.

Fuck, she was gorgeous. Even when trying to hold it in, she came beautifully and wholeheartedly. Her entire body trembled, her eyes closing while she bit down on her lip as she rode out the aftermath. Letting out a low "fuck," she looked up at him, pure submission in her eyes.

"What do you say?"

She panted a breath before looking at him. "Thank you."

"Good girl."

She smiled at his praise.

Busying himself with his meal, he kept both hands on the table and she eventually followed suit, obviously feeling safe enough that he wouldn't torment her while she ate. He needed her to eat. She would require her energy for what was to come later.

They began to talk about life, his work, her past, but he wanted—needed—to know more about her. He couldn't help but note she had cleverly avoided his deep questions about her life, preferring to keep to surface topics. She didn't discuss her past relationships. Yet she had no problem talking about her childhood and family. She talked endlessly about her friends and how supportive of her they were. He wanted to learn everything there was to know about this wonderful woman he'd found.

Their conversation soon turned to him, and trepidation filled him. He wasn't ready to discuss his family situation with her, but the question was inevitable. After all, he knew all about hers and she knew nothing about his. Yet he didn't want to talk about it. Not yet. He couldn't bear to see 'that' look of pity come across her face, the same expression everybody gave him when they realised he was alone.

Then she asked the question. He froze mid-chew and tried to compose himself.

"I just realised you know all about my family and situation, but I know nothing of yours."

He took a deep breath and steadied himself. Having lost his appetite, he dropped his fork on his plate and looked at her.

Suck it up, man. She deserves to know.

"There's not much to tell. My dad and brother died in a car accident when I was fifteen and my mum is in a care home."

He waited for the look, that obligatory 'I'm sorry' that always came, but it didn't. Most people clammed up when he told them of his family, but not Amara.

"Is your mum sick?"

A bitter smile. "You could say that. She has alcohol-related dementia."

"That must be hard."

Only Amara would say something like that.

"It used to be. She was a very mean drunk. But since the dementia has taken over, she's more vacant than anything. She doesn't recognise me most times I visit."

Rubbing his chest to try to relieve the ache he felt, he avoided her gaze. He'd just told Amara more about his family than any other woman he'd been with in years. He had always felt the need to keep them at arm's length. So why the hell had he told Amara? Because she was different. He really liked her. He knew she wouldn't judge him.

And she hadn't given him that look of pity at all.

"Sullivan." Reaching over the table, she held his hand in hers and gave it a light squeeze. "I'm sorry, I shouldn't have asked."

"You weren't to know."

And he didn't blame her for asking. But as the black dog of depression tried to take over his mood, he regretted telling her. He forced himself to take a breath and squeezed her hand. Using Amara as an anchor to the present, he looked at her. The smile she offered wasn't one of pity. It was warm. Caring. Gentle. Sweet.

* * * *

For the rest of the night, Sullivan lulled Amara into a false sense of security, not touching the remote once more. After paying the bill, with a little fight from Amara who tried to insist she pay her half, he turned on the vibrator to stop her and force her to give in to him. It worked a treat, as she shut her mouth immediately to stop from crying out. Feeling smug, he excused himself to the bathroom and hovered in the doorway, adjusting the vibe. She leant forward, elbows on the table as she squeezed her thighs together, her face growing tight as she inched closer towards an orgasm.

With a sense of satisfaction, he went about his business and returned to find her speaking with Agin and Larissa. This was going to be interesting.

"Are you all right?" he heard her friend ask. "You look a little flustered."

Sullivan couldn't hide his smile as he approached.

"I'm here with Sullivan, so..." She didn't continue as he approached the table.

Turning the vibrator way down, he gave her a little relief, grinning when she shot him a look of thanks and recovered.

"Good to see you," Agin said, shaking his hand.

"And you."

"I have a feeling I know exactly what's going on beneath the table now," the other man said with a smile as he reached his arm around his wife's waist. "We're planning something similar tonight."

The two women shared a look and Amara visibly swallowed.

"He wouldn't even let me eat in peace," she said in a breathy tone that made his cock hard.

He rested a hand on the nape of her neck and squeezed gently. "That is the entire point of the exercise. To push your limits in public."

"Yeah, well, you definitely did that," she muttered.

"Now I'm scared," Larissa chimed in, her cheeks blushing as she looked at Agin with wide eyes. "Please let me eat without turning it on."

The other man laughed. "Now where would be the fun in that, pet?"

Larissa actually gulped and shifted her weight. "On that note, we'll leave you guys to it," she said in a tone that told him Agin had just turned on the toy.

"Have a fun night, you two," Agin added before ushering his quivering wife away.

Sullivan turned the vibrator back on, enjoying the little whimper Amara gave as she stood and it shifted inside of her. Switching it to a strong, steady rhythm, he steadied her as they made their way to the car. Once seated, she began to squirm and let out a little sound of impatience that made him rock-hard.

It took all his will not to move the seat back and fuck her right there in the car. No, he'd wait until he got home where he could take his time with her. But, for now, she needed another release.

Leaning over, he claimed her mouth, slipping his tongue between her teeth. It danced with hers as he gripped her chin and held her in place. She all but wilted beneath his touch, in the most delicious way.

When he moved his hand to thrust it into her hair, she let out a throaty moan and tried to press herself against him. He slipped his other hand up her thigh, beneath her dress and found her panties sopping wet.

Fuck! She was testing his control. He clenched his fist in her hair and gave a low growl, taking her mouth even harder.

When he massaged her clit over the thin, lacy material, it took mere seconds to get her entire body to quiver beneath his touch. She came with a cry. He pulled away, drinking her in, watching the beautiful sight. Eyes dark, she looked at him as she rode out her orgasm, squeezing his hand between her thighs.

"Don't you look a sight," he commented smugly. "Let's get you back to my place before I take you right here."

He pressed a kiss to her lips one more time before forcing himself to focus and drive.

Continuing to play with the vibrator on the drive home, he watched her slip further and further into that submissive headspace he wanted her in. They were five minutes from his house when he slipped his hand between her thighs, teasing her clit. She came so quickly he hadn't anticipated it. This time, she sagged against the car seat and her eyes glazed as she slipped away into subspace.

Shit. Fuck.

"Amara." He said her name softly.

She only murmured in response, completely zoned out as she linked her fingers with his. He hadn't meant for her to go that far.

Rookie fucking mistake, Sullivan.

Angry at himself, he sped home, scooped her out of the car and carried her inside when her legs wouldn't work. She cuddled into him, burying her face into the crook of his neck. She whispered something unintelligible and tried to lift her head but failed.

"Shh, just relax," he said soothingly as he settled on the couch with her. "You're okay."

He, however, was not. He was pissed. *What a fucking asshole.*

Coming to curled up in Sullivan's lap, Amara was completely unaware of how much time had gone by. Forcing herself to sit up straight, she looked into his dark-chocolate eyes and found him smiling down at her. But it didn't reach those beautiful eyes. The last thing she remembered was coming in the car, a harsh wave of arousal washing over her. Then everything had blurred.

"Welcome back," he said, his knuckles grazing her cheek in that tender way she loved so much.

"What happened?"

"I'm afraid I overwhelmed you a little."

That was putting it lightly. Her orgasm hadn't felt quite strong enough to send her into subspace, but she'd also never had quite such a long build-up to one before. Rubbing her hands over her eyes, she completely forgot she was wearing make-up tonight. Crap. She'd no doubt smudged mascara all over her face.

"Goddammit. Give me a second."

Standing on shaky legs, she made her way to the ensuite and checked her reflection. No panda eyes, luckily. But her eyes looked different, glassy, almost like she was drunk. She guessed she was drunk, on endorphins. Sullivan had removed the vibrator while she'd been out of it. He appeared in the mirror, resting a shoulder on the doorframe as he regarded her with another empty smile. Why did he suddenly seem so different?

"How are you feeling?"

"Great." She turned to face him with a sultry smile. "Ready to go another round."

She stepped up to him, resting her hands on his chest in the hopes that he would hold her. After a few moments he did, resting his warm hands on her upper arms before trailing them down to her waist. She took the opportunity to try to undo his shirt buttons, but her damn hands wouldn't work.

"Thank you for taking such good care of me." She pressed a soft kiss to the exposed skin of the top of his chest.

"It's my job to take care of my sub."

His sub. Those two words alone were a turn-on for Amara. Right now, she wanted him to claim her, to take her roughly. When he didn't make a move, she reached up to touch his face, daring to make the first move to kiss him. His mouth slanted over hers as she sucked his bottom lip into her mouth and bit down gently.

Hint, hint, she wanted to say.

His hands remained on her waist as he took over the kiss, digging his fingers into her flesh before moving them to her hips where he anchored her body against his. His erection pressed against her stomach, long and thick and hard as ever. He continued to kiss her, hard, and she gave herself over to him completely, letting out a small moan into his mouth.

Turning, he guided her towards the bed. He became hungrier, more forceful. His hands roamed her body, moving down to her ass where he pulled at her dress and slipped his hands beneath her underwear to grasp her bare ass. She gasped into his mouth as her clit throbbed, hardening at his ministrations.

Pulling away from her, he looked down at her, his gaze dark and hungry.

"Dress," was all he said while he worked on his shirt.

He quickly undid the buttons, throwing the clothing on the floor. Her mouth watered as she took in the glory of his body, all golden skin over taut, lean muscle. Dropping her dress on the floor, she fought the urge to cover her body, barely. Sullivan reached behind her, pressing his lips to hers softly as he undid the clasp of her bra and pushed it off her. Falling to his knees before her, he hooked his fingers beneath the lace of her panties and pressed a firm kiss to her mound.

Ever so slowly, he pushed the lace down her legs, the action sending shivers down her spine. She was so open to him when naked, so self-conscious. Yet he never made her feel anything but beautiful and desired. The look on his face right now while he stared at her pussy made her feel like he was going to eat her alive. And that was exactly what he did. Parting her folds, he licked over her too sensitive clit. Her knees gave way beneath her, threatening to buckle completely when he sucked the engorged nub into his mouth. She held on to his shoulders to keep her balance, looking down at the erotic sight before her. Standing, he ran his hands up her bare skin, letting them settle on her breasts where he caressed her nipples with his thumbs, kneading her mounds in his large hands.

Completely naked, she followed him as he led her to the bed, so she straddled his lap. There was definitely something different about him. There was a darkness to his expression as he watched her settle on top of him.

It worried her. He looked almost triggered. Reaching around her, he grabbed a condom from the bedside table and sheathed himself, his thumb grazing her clit purposely as he moved.

"I really hate those fucking things," she grumbled.

She'd always hated the feeling of condoms, preferring to go bareback wherever possible.

"Better safe than sorry."

He was right, of course. But she knew she was clean and trusted him when he told her he also was.

"I have an IUD. There's no chance of me getting pregnant."

"A conversation for another time," he mumbled against her lips, then he slid his cock inside of her.

"Oh my God." She moaned into his mouth, which stayed just out of reach when she tried to kiss him.

He began to move beneath her, holding her hips in place as he thrust in and out in short, sharp movements. There was no foreplay, nothing gentle about it. This was a fucking, plain and simple. And it felt incredible.

Amara gave herself over to him as he pounded into her from below. His hands stayed on her hips, controlling her movements, keeping her still when she tried to undulate with his movements. Taking the silent hint, she tensed and kept herself still above him. Holding on to his shoulders, she looked at him, taking in the almost haunted look in his eyes. Then she saw him finally give in. His breaths turned into laboured pants. She loved that she had that effect on him. Loved the small moans and groans that came from him as she squeezed his cock with her inner muscles. She did that. She turned him on. She had made him come. Fuck, it was a turn-on.

Without warning, he pulled out and switched their positions, pinning her body beneath his. Arousal tore through her as she clung to him like a lifeline, her arms tight around his shoulders. He reached under her thighs, grabbing her beneath the knees to push her thighs up and out. She was completely and utterly open to him now, unable to move, helpless to his ministrations. He thrust into her hard and long and deep, his pelvis grinding against her swollen and throbbing clit with each thrust. His movements became more frantic as his cock twitched inside of her. He came, driving deeper and deeper, not stopping until he was completely spent.

Chest heaving, she looked up at him, her fingers digging into his biceps, fingernails in his flesh. That was fucking intense. Sullivan watched her for a few moments, that inscrutable expression in his eyes, before he withdrew and moved down her body. She cried out as his mouth closed around her clit, his tongue flat and wide as it pressed against the swollen aching nub. Not a second later, she came, her thighs pressing against the sides of his face as she gripped the bedding. Heat tore through her as her hips bucked against his face, every nerve ending in her body pulsing with ecstasy.

Amara's body went limp and she found herself, once again, completely unable to move, save for her chest heaving as she tried to suck in as much oxygen as possible. How the hell did he do that to her every single time?

He hopped off the bed, discarded the condom then returned to pull her body on top of his. He moved her as if she weighed nothing, which was definitely far from true. Her body blanketed his, her head resting on his chest as she lay completely satisfied.

No words were spoken. The two of them lay skin to skin in total silence. He danced his hands up and down her back, causing chills to erupt over her body. As her satisfaction wore off, she became aware of his tense muscles beneath her. She couldn't quite shake the feeling that something was wrong with him. Now that she thought about it, he'd been different for the later part of the evening. He wasn't as present as he usually was. Wasn't quite in control.

* * * *

Sitting on the edge of the bed after dressing, Amara looked back at Sullivan, concern filling her. He'd pulled on a pair of sweats but hadn't moved other than that. His jaw remained tight, his eyes hard as he stared at the ceiling. She'd lost him somewhere along the line. Something was definitely going on in his head. She felt an overwhelming sense of protectiveness for him, but was it her place to bring it up? Would he even tell her what was wrong? Getting him to talk about himself tonight had been like pulling teeth.

Shuffling to face him, she reached out and grabbed his hand. "Hey, you okay?"

He gave another smile that didn't reach his eyes. "Fine. Just tired."

It was obvious he wasn't going to share with her what was on his mind.

There's my cue, she thought glumly. "I'll get out of your hair then."

When he didn't dispute that, her heart dropped, rejection settling in her gut. Without another word, she made her way to the living room to pick up her handbag and found him waiting for her in the entry.

His shoulders were slumped, the usual aura of confidence about him missing. But it was his eyes that made her heart ache for him. They looked haunted and sad and cold. So cold. The man she'd spent the night with had gone. Was he depressed? She didn't have much experience with it other than with her mum, but she couldn't shake the feeling that he was now depressed.

She wanted to push him. To force him into talking with her, to tell her what was wrong. But it wasn't her place. She wasn't his girlfriend. She was just a woman he was fucking. Still, she reached for him, wrapped her arms around him and held him. She didn't want to let go until she knew he was feeling better but when he held her with little commitment, she pulled away and took a step back.

"Thank you for tonight. I had a lot of fun, even with all the torture," she added with a grin.

"You're welcome. Drive safe."

He gave her a small, empty kiss before she left, feeling completely and utterly useless.

The feeling grew on her drive home and by the time she drove in her driveway, she felt worthless too. What good was a woman if she couldn't improve the mood of the man she was seeing? So often with her, the lines between D/s and partnership blurred. It was one of the downsides to having a full-time D/s relationship with someone. She got attached far too easily. She really had to do something to stop it before she got too attached to him.

Chapter Eleven

Feeling like absolute shit, Sullivan stayed in bed until ten the next morning. Why the fuck did his depression have to rear its ugly head while he was with Amara? He'd been having a great night with her and he'd ended up ruining it. The expression on her face as she left had him feeling like a total asshole. She'd looked worried and defeated.

First, the depression had tried to make itself known when they'd spoken of his family. He'd managed to keep it away, until he fucked up and she slipped into subspace all because he'd not been paying close enough attention and he lost control of himself. He'd let his focus lapse, had missed the warning signs, like a fucking newborn Dom. He had fifteen goddamn years of experience—he knew better than to get lost in himself like he had. He'd fucked up, all because he had been having too much fun tormenting Amara.

Now, as he lay in bed alone, his muscles felt like they were lined with lead. Letting out a groan of frustration, he rolled onto his side and stared at the clock on his bedside table. He really should get out of bed. But why? He didn't have anything to do today. He had no responsibilities. Nobody was waiting for him. He could stay in bed all day and nobody would know or care.

Fuck depression. He knew his worth, he really did. But right now, the black dog was winning. Maybe he should head to the gym to stave it off. Or go for a hike. It had been weeks since he'd been hiking. But, being a Sunday, the trails would be filled with couples and families out enjoying each other's company. It would just remind him of what he still didn't have. At thirty-five, he had really thought he would have a family of his own by now. He thought he would be happy. While he was happy to a certain extent, he wasn't complete like he wanted to be.

His phone vibrated on the table.

I wanted to check you were okay. You seemed a little off when I left and it worried me.

Sweet Amara. The perceptive little sub had noticed he was off last night. Of course she had. Despite her constant reminders that they were in a purely physical relationship, she couldn't help herself but be worried about him. She cared. And he couldn't pretend that he didn't absolutely love that.

I'm okay. I didn't mean for things to get so out of hand last night.

Why was it so much easier for him to tell her this via text?

Things didn't get out of hand. You should know I would tell you if they did. I'm not some meek little new submissive who can't handle herself. I had a lot of fun.

He did know that. She didn't pull her punches. If he'd truly fucked up, she would have told him, he didn't doubt that. She was nothing if not honest.

It was amazing. You were amazing. You are *amazing.*

I didn't mean for you to go into subspace in the car when I couldn't care for you properly. I'm sorry.

Did you hear me complaining? No. So stop beating yourself up about it or I'll come over and do it for you.

A genuine smile of amusement spread across his face. His little sub certainly was a fighter, that was for sure.

I'm sorry if I triggered you. I really did enjoy myself.

Clenching his phone in his hand, he tried to ignore the anger tearing through his veins at her apology. She'd done nothing wrong. She had no reason to apologise to him. Ever.

Against his better judgement, he called her.

"Hey," she greeted him.

"Don't ever apologise to me," he told her in that dominant tone that overtook when he was playing with her.

"Sorry," she replied. "I mean…" That beautiful laugh. "You know what I mean."

"Amara, I am sorry it got too intense in the car. It hadn't been my intention but I lost myself a little. My intention was to torture you then take you over the edge once I got you home."

"Well, you definitely did that." She laughed again. "I had a lot of fun. Even when Larissa and Agin showed up and I became more embarrassed than I'd ever been in my entire life."

He grinned at the memory of her face when she'd spoken to her friends. Playing in the club in front of them was one thing, but apparently doing it in a public space was different.

"Now I know to take it easier next time. And there will be a next time."

The thought of playing with her in public again made him hard as granite. What he really wanted was to do a public scene with her at the club, to show her off to the other members. But he needed to work on her body image issues before that would happen. He'd never understand how a woman could judge herself so harshly. Amara had a body to die for. All soft, mouth-watering curves that he loved sinking his teeth into. Each time he saw her naked, he felt like an overexcited virgin ready to blow his load prematurely. Her body was pure perfection.

She laughed in reply and he found himself wanting—needing—to see her again. "Have you got plans for today?"

"None at all. Mum and Dad have gone out for the day so I'm all alone."

"I was thinking of going for a hike," he lied. "Would you want to join me?"

She hesitated, her silence deafening. "Sure, I'd love to."

Sullivan found himself excited at the prospect of seeing her again. It wasn't even about sex. He just wanted to see her. Fuck, he wanted to date her. When was the last time he wanted to date a woman? Not since Katerina had threatened to take him to the cleaners and ruined his trust in women almost completely. But Amara was different from other women. She was unlike anyone he'd ever met.

* * * *

Amara met Sullivan at the base of a hiking trail she used to frequent before her mum got sick. When she met his gaze, it took her a few moments to realise he was depressed. That was what had been wrong with him last night. It wasn't anything either of them had done—he was just depressed. Greeting him with a long, slow kiss, she looked up at him.

"Hey, you look a little better today."

He gave her a smile and reached for her hand. "I'm much better now that I'm with you."

Flushing, she bit her bottom lip but held his gaze. "You do know how to make a girl feel good."

He kept her hand in his as they began to hike the easier portion of the trail. Halfway through, she needed to take a break, thoroughly embarrassed by her lack of fitness. Her face was on fire, her legs were crying out for her to stop moving and she could barely catch her breath. It was fucking humiliating.

Yet Sullivan didn't make her feel bad about it once. Whenever she needed to slow down or take a quick break, he would simply take the opportunity to kiss her, pull her into his body, touch her in some way. At one point, he'd begun openly groping her and turned her on so much her panties were still wet. God, she loved how much he touched her. She'd never felt so wanted.

They sat on a large boulder overlooking the city. She felt completely at ease with him. Despite the fact that she was out of breath and her face felt so red it was probably beginning to turn purple.

"I can't believe how much fitness I've lost," she commented as she put her water bottle in her small backpack.

"Well, you have had other priorities, haven't you?"

She offered him a smile. Even when he could have, quite easily, he didn't make her feel bad about herself. Other people she'd dated would have. One of her previous partners took every opportunity he had to make her feel bad about herself, always telling her she could be thinner or fitter. But Sullivan was different. He was better than that. He would never make her self-conscious of her body. She knew that for a fact.

"Before Mum got sick, I would have done this hike without breaking a sweat. Now look at me."

He lifted his sunglasses to look her up and down. The heat of his gaze made her shudder. How did he do that?

"Anyway, can I ask you something about last night?"

His shoulders tensed ever so slightly. "Go ahead."

"Did I trigger you when I asked about your family?"

His smile faltered. It gave her all the answer she needed. "Perceptive little sub."

She felt guilty. Her curiosity had gotten the better of her and she'd sent her Dom into depression. It hadn't even crossed her mind that there might be a reason he never discussed his family. Now that she knew, it filled her with guilt.

"I'm sorry. I just realised you know way too much about my family. If I'd known it was a sore spot, I wouldn't have mentioned it."

He reached out and ran a hand over her ponytail, tugging it gently. "What really got me was the fact that I was stupid enough to let you go into subspace while I couldn't care for you properly."

"That wasn't your fault."

He pursed his lips into a thin line that told her he felt otherwise. He dropped his sunglasses back over his eyes.

"We don't have to discuss them again. I don't want to bring you down."

She flinched when he didn't respond. The silence she received was deafening. *Talk about putting your foot in your mouth.*

"My brother was two years older than me." He startled her when he spoke. "I used to follow him and Grayson around, copying everything they did, getting under their feet. But they never once made me feel like an annoying little brother, even though I'm sure I irritated the shit out of them. Brady was a great big brother. He was my best friend." He smiled. "We did everything together."

She smiled at the soft tone of his voice when he spoke of his brother.

"My dad was my hero. That man could do no wrong in my eyes. He was a good man."

"And your mum?" she asked.

"She was the best mum two boys could have asked for. She was gentle, sweet, kind yet held her own amongst the three of us. She rarely raised her voice. She was an amazing woman. Held a strength that was necessary for dealing with the three of us."

Amara rested her hand on his bent knee and shuffled closer in an effort to comfort him. She could see the intense pain on his face as he continued to speak.

"After the accident, she hit the bottle hard. That fact that she lost her husband and son was too much for her to handle. I get that. But I lost her when I lost them too. I had to grow up very fast while trying to grieve."

Amara entwined her fingers with his, happy when he let her.

"It was hard for her, I get that. But it was hard on me, too. I moved out as soon as I graduated high school, intent on living my own life far away from her. But I kept getting sucked back in. She needed help taking care of herself so I moved back in to look after her. Once the dementia set in, she went downhill fast."

"How long has she been in the home?"

"Over ten years." He squeezed her fingers. "She gets quite abusive. Often hurls abuse at the nurses, throws things at them."

"Did she do that to you?"

"Yeah." His heartbreak was evident in his voice and it broke Amara. "She was very abusive when drunk. She even hit me."

Amara couldn't hold in her gasp. Drunk or not, a parent should never hit their child in rage.

"Sullivan," she said gently, "I'm so sorry you had to deal with that alone. That must have been incredibly difficult."

"I've gone through enough therapy now to realise the mum I grew up with is gone. She left the day of the accident."

186

This man. This beautiful, sweet, caring, unbelievably kind man had lost his entire family and somehow still managed to function. Amara couldn't imagine what he must have gone through. How he must have felt. But the fact that he had the strength to continue on alone proved what kind of person he was.

Feeling incredibly close to him, she rested her head on his shoulder and continued to hold his hand, while he sat in silence. Looking out over the city, she enjoyed the peace and quiet of the bushland around them.

* * * *

After finishing the hike, they headed towards the car park, Amara feeling so very close to Sullivan in that moment that she didn't want their time together to end. A perky little blonde crossed the car park and caught Sullivan's eye. A smile lit up his face as he held a hand up in a casual wave and Amara couldn't help but feel a pang of self-doubt hit her. Was this the sort of woman he usually dated?

Amara couldn't help but give her a once-over, noting her incredibly fit appearance. There was no doubt in her mind that he knew her from the gym. She had the sort of body Amara used to dream of having before she realised that her genetics would never allow it. Muscular, toned, fit yet still soft and feminine. She was hot.

"I didn't know you were coming for a hike today. You could have kept me company," the other woman said.

"It was a last-minute thing. And I managed to convince Amara to come with me, so it worked out."

He wrapped an arm around her shoulders and pulled her into his body.

The woman regarded her with a warm smile and raised her brows. "So, you're the famous Amara," she said in a sweet voice. "I'm Ellie."

"It's nice to meet you." Amara shook the hand she held out.

"Ellie's one of the trainers at my gym."

Well, that certainly made sense, given her appearance.

"We picked a nice day for it. Tomorrow is going to be forty degrees again," Ellie commented in disgust.

Amara couldn't help but groan. She'd always hated the heat of summer. The days where it was over forty degrees, she didn't leave the comfort of the house if she could help it. Unless it was to jump in a pool, of course.

"I take it you're not a fan of the heat either," Ellie said with a laugh.

"I may have been born here, but I am not built for Perth summers."

"I'm from Melbourne, so imagine how I feel."

She merely laughed in response, along with Sullivan.

"She always complains," he teased. "I keep telling her to move back to Melbourne, but she won't. I think she just likes to whinge."

The other woman hit him lightly. "Oh please. You would be lost without me and you know it."

Sullivan threw his head back and let out a loud, absolutely heart-warming laugh. It lit up Amara's world as she looked up at him.

"And on that note, I'll leave you guys to it. It was great to meet you, Amara."

"Yeah, you too, Ellie."

Ellie wandered past them and Sullivan squeezed his arm possessively around Amara's shoulders.

"She seems like a fun person."

"She is. She basically runs the gym for me and does a great job, despite her age."

She did look younger than Amara, perhaps in her mid-twenties. Yet Amara knew better than most that maturity and age didn't go hand in hand.

Sullivan led her down the gravel path towards their cars, keeping his hold on her. All day, he'd been touching her in some way. A gentle pat on the butt here, a light caress on the shoulder there. She loved how tactile he was. How his touch was firm yet gentle. Always leaving her wanting more. So much more.

After waiting for her to put her things in her car, he dipped his head and kissed her. And oh, what a kiss. Her toes curled inside her sneakers, heart beating hard against her ribcage, and it had nothing to do with the hike.

"Thank you for coming today." He smiled down at her. "It was exactly what I needed."

"I'm glad I could help." Although she wasn't sure she'd actually helped at all. If anything, she'd probably made him feel worse by forcing him to open up about his family. He was still visibly depressed. The lines that bracketed his mouth were tense, but he did appear a little more positive than when they first arrived.

"I'll see you on Wednesday?"

"You definitely will." She grinned and kissed him quickly one last time.

She couldn't wait to see him again.

* * * *

On Saturday, Amara was having a much-needed girl's day with Larissa and Belle. Usually, spending the day watching movies, gossiping and eating too much cheese was a perfect outing for her. But today, Amara was in a mood and hadn't been able to pull herself out of it.

Mum had had a rough week, filled with depressive episodes, tantrums and, this morning, she had thrown her puzzle book at Amara and told her she was an overbearing bitch. All because Amara had asked Dad if Mum had taken her medications. She should be used to it by now, but every time her mum took out her bad mood on her, it made Amara feel like absolute shit. And this morning, she had felt like an overbearing bitch. She was still finding it hard to turn off her carer mode. Even being surrounded by her supportive friends couldn't get her to switch her mind off or cheer up.

Trying to get past it, Amara plastered a smile on her face even though her mind was focussed on home. Was Dad coping with Mum? Had she gotten any better once Amara had left? Was she pushing the limits and doing things she shouldn't? Taking a sip of her drink, Amara tried her hardest to focus on the present, on spending time with her friends.

Her friends soon turned the conversation to Sullivan. As she was happy to talk about him, Amara's mood began to shift. She gave them all the gory details. She loved that her friends were also in the lifestyle, both submissives, so she could tell them everything without fear of being judged.

"So, you're really still insisting this is just about sex?" Belle shot her a sceptical look after she told them about their hike together. "You didn't even sleep with him on Sunday. That's not what fuck-buddies do. You know that. I wouldn't dream of doing something like that with Ayden. We catch up, we fuck, we part ways. That's how it works."

"That's all it is." Amara couldn't even convince herself when she said that anymore. Things had begun to slip into a grey area between the two of them. "He was having a rough day because of something I'd said the previous night. I felt responsible. I owed it to him to try to rectify it. That's all it was."

"All I'm going to say is that your face lights up whenever he's mentioned," Larissa interjected.

Amara blushed, knowing it was true. She lit up when he was mentioned. But she couldn't help it. He made her giddy. He brought out the best in her, forced her to talk about herself between scenes, made her share her emotions in a way that no one else did.

"He does make me feel special."

"And you deserve to feel special," Belle said as she crossed her long legs. "But the fact that he's texting you today when you're seeing him tonight does suggest that he's after more than just a physical relationship."

He'd been texting her on and off all day. It had started with a random story of him finding an injured bird at the gym this morning, continued with flirtatious jokes then ended with promises of what was to come tonight. Those promises left her far too aroused for comfort.

"I see where you're coming from." Larissa backed her up. "But no strings can only last for so long. Somebody always catches feelings."

Her words hit Amara right in the chest. She'd only known Sullivan for a month, but during the last couple of weeks, they'd spoken almost every day. She was beginning to really like him. After all, how could she not? He was everything she'd ever wanted in a partner. They had fun together and he made her smile more than she had in a very long time. He made her laugh. He understood her rude and sarcastic humour more than her friends did.

"If his reputation at the club is anything to go by, you're special to him too," Belle said as she popped a cracker with cheese into her mouth.

"And that means…" Larissa poked her.

"He hasn't taken a sub for longer than a weekend in over two years. And he *never* plays with them outside of the club. I overheard Ayden and Grayson speaking with him on Friday while I was recovering, and he even said he might attend a party Grayson is having in a few weeks. He apparently won't do that with just any submissive."

When Amara had first heard he didn't take submissives home, she'd been surprised, especially considering he had restraints attached to nearly every piece of furniture in his home, including the outdoor lounges, as she'd discovered this week. But it was something he refused to talk about. She knew his previous relationship had ended badly but that was it. He wouldn't discuss it any further with her and she hadn't pushed.

"See? You are special to him," Belle said.

"I don't want anything more than what we have now," she stated, hoping she could fool her friends.

In reality, she longed for a partner of her own. To start a life with someone, start a family, get the happily ever after she'd always dreamed of. But she wasn't in the right frame of mind for that now, not even close.

"You have to move on at some point, though. You might as well try it with the man who has kept that goofy smile plastered on your face since we began talking about him."

Amara tried to compose herself but couldn't wipe the smile from her face. She really did like Sullivan a lot. But she was the one who had put the sex only limitation on their relationship. And he'd very happily agreed to it.

"I'm not in the right place to do it now. Not until I get my life together a little more."

Nobody would want to get seriously involved with her right now. Not while her life was such a mess. That was what she would keep telling herself, anyway.

Amara's phone went off a while later, but it wasn't Sullivan. It was her dad.

Your mum had a little fall. She's fine but she hit her head so I'm taking her to the hospital now.

And just like that, her good mood was ruined. "Fuck."

Nausea and worry churned her gut as she read the message again.

"Mum had a fall. Dad's taking her to the hospital."

"Is she okay?"

"He said she's fine. He's taking her because she hit her head."

And when she hit her head, Mum was at a high risk of having another seizure. One that might very well end her life or leave her in a vegetative state. Nerves ran rampant throughout Amara's body, pumped along by adrenaline. Her leg bounced up and down as she fought the urge to stand and pace.

She immediately wanted to see Sullivan. He would make her feel better. He would hold her. Comfort her.

Make her forget her worries. *For fuck's sake.* Her friends were right—she'd caught feelings. What absolutely perfect timing.

"He's got it handled, Amara," Larissa said gently, resting her hand on Amara's.

She asked Dad if he wanted her to meet him at the hospital and he assured her they would be okay. It was just to get her quickly checked out.

"I'm sure she'll be fine," Belle offered. "Despite what your worries may tell you, your dad is fully capable of looking after her. She is his wife, after all."

Amara knew their comments were coming from a good place, that they were trying to reassure her. But they didn't understand. How could they?

What was she doing to fall?

She was putting a wine glass away and lost her balance.

Dad's response had her staring at her phone in disbelief. Why the hell was she trying to put a wine glass away on the top shelf of the kitchen cupboard? She wasn't meant to reach for high shelves at all because she had such poor balance now. Was Dad just not paying enough attention?

This was why Amara had so much trouble letting go. Dad didn't watch Mum like he should. Mum would always try to push the boundaries. She was like a toddler who'd been told not to push a button—she was going to do exactly that.

Sucking in a deep breath, Amara tried—and failed—to force away the irrational anger building inside of her. She hated it so much. Hated how familiar she had become with it. But now wasn't the time to scold her dad for not paying close enough attention.

"I know what you're thinking. But she can't be monitored twenty-four-seven. At the end of the day, she is still an adult. She's going to make mistakes and things like this are going to happen."

Larissa's words triggered Amara. She *should* be watched twenty-four-seven. That was what Amara had been doing for a year and a half. That was what she'd given up her entire life for. To make sure she was safe.

Each time she let go a little, something bad happened. And nobody else understood. Her friends had never come close to losing a parent. They didn't understand the panic it instilled in her.

"She *needs* to be watched constantly," Amara exclaimed angrily. "Any bump on the head could trigger a catastrophic seizure. One she might not recover from!"

Belle wisely sat silent while Larissa spoke up. "She is a very headstrong woman, just like you. She's going to do what she wants. Accidents are unavoidable. You know that."

"What I know is that I already lost her once. I'll be damned if I don't do everything within my power to make sure I don't lose her again. Not until she's old and grey and frail." Tears spilled over her cheeks. "You have no idea what it feels like. I've already lost my old mum. She's gone, she'll never be the same again. And I grieve for her every single day. I need to do what I can to make sure I don't lose the mum I have left."

Shoving to her feet, Amara stomped outside to get away from the other women. Nobody other than Jackson knew what they'd lost. Their mum might still be alive, but she wasn't the same, not even close. She was no longer the woman Amara could run to for life advice. They didn't sit like they used to, chatting for hours on end, discussing everything and nothing. Now she was less tolerant. Grumpy and depressed more often than not. Stubborn. Pushy. Inappropriate.

Amara stood on the open patio, her hands shaking as she barely held it together. Hot, angry, grief-filled tears splashed down her cheeks. She shouldn't have come today. She should have stayed at home and watched Mum. Then she wouldn't have fallen.

And now, Amara had just snapped at her friends, people who cared for her, and thoroughly embarrassed herself. Time to go home.

She headed inside, wiping her cheeks as she dared to look at her friends. They both sat on the edge of the couch, watching her with careful eyes. Yeah, they were mad at her.

"I'm sorry. I shouldn't have snapped at you."

"No, you shouldn't have," Larissa said sternly. "Now come here."

Begrudgingly, she sat between the two of them, sighing as her friends bracketed her and each wrapped an arm around her. Belle rested her head on top of Amara's and a sob broke free even as she tried to stifle it with her hands.

"I'm just so terrified she'll die. Every time I leave the house, I'm scared it will be the last time I see her alive."

"We don't know what you're going through, but we're trying to look out for you."

"The way you've been dealing with this is not healthy. You're burning out. Your mood swings are erratic. You're tired all the time. You're not even enjoying your time with us. You're always worried about what's going on at home. I know it's going to be hard, but you need to stop worrying about what's going on while you're not there. You can't control everything," Belle said, her gentle hand running up and down Amara's back. "You should also talk to us more about it. Let us help you."

They were right. She needed to lean on her loved ones more. Since she couldn't rely on her emotionally stunted dad and brother for support, she should lean on her friends.

"Maybe you need to speak to Sullivan about this."

Amara stared at Larissa in disbelief. "No, I…"

"You told me he'd been a carer for his own mother. He can help you more than we can. Ask him, just as a friend, for advice. I'm sure he'd be more than willing to help."

But he wouldn't. He didn't open up about his time as a caregiver. He'd never truly gone into detail about his experience, even when Amara had complained about her own difficulties. After last weekend, she couldn't push him into discussing it either. The last thing she wanted was for him to become depressed because of her again.

"This is only like the fifth time I've ever seen you cry," Belle commented. "That alone says you're not as open with your emotions as you should be."

Her friend had a point.

"I hate crying in front of others."

Amara had grown up believing that crying was a sign of weakness. Crying in front of others was never an option for her. That was why she saved her tears for the pillow, where they belonged, when she was completely alone and nobody would see her.

"Amara." Larissa ran a hand over her hair and looked down at her with kind eyes. "You've scened in front of us. You've come in front of us. There's not much more emotion and soul baring than that. So, why don't you ever cry in front of us?"

"Crying shows weakness. I hate being weak."

Now that she'd said the words out loud, she realised how completely wrong it sounded. She would never say anything like that to someone who cried in front of her. On the contrary. So why did she think of herself as weak for crying?

Her emotions really were all messed up.

"I'm sorry, but that may be the most backwards-ass thing I've ever heard come out of your mouth." Belle laughed. "You know you sound crazy when you say things like that, right?"

Amara choked on a laugh and smiled up at her. "I do, don't I?"

"What you're going through is emotional. You need to learn to rely on us for the support you don't get at home."

Why did her friends have to make so much sense all of a sudden?

"Now, how about we put on a triggering movie and get more tears out of you, so you'll feel better? Nothing cleanses me like a good cry."

"Time to play sadist and make the little subbie cry," Belle teased as she reached for a cracker and stacked on too much cheese. "Cheese and tears. There's nothing better for a woman."

Chapter Twelve

Sullivan waited impatiently for Amara to arrive. When she'd texted him earlier to say she might have to cancel because her mum had fallen and gone to the hospital, all he could do was sit back and wait in the hopes she wouldn't bail on him. She hadn't and would arrive any minute.

He stood in his bathroom and admired his handiwork. He'd never run a bath for someone else but had to admit he'd done a good job. Tealight candles lined the outer edge of the tub, the light dancing off the tiled walls, flickering against the lavender-and-rose-scented bubbles. Even he wanted to jump in and relax and he wasn't a bath kind of guy. Hopefully Amara would appreciate it, or at least appreciate the effort he went to for her.

She sounded as though she'd had a rough few days and he wanted to take care of her. That was what he planned on doing tonight. He'd run a bath, cooked for her, planned on spending the night pampering his little sub, even deciding to give her a massage to lull her into a sense of relaxation. And tonight would go as he'd hoped, even if he had to spend the entire night in Dom mode. He'd noticed that her independent streak made it difficult for her to switch off at times.

Tonight wasn't even about sex. And when was the last time he'd cared for a woman without the incentive of sex? Not for a very long time.

Amara knocked on the front door and his heart about leapt out of his chest. Fuck, he couldn't wait to see her again. He'd missed her and it had only been a few days. He opened the door to find her looking far more tired than he'd expected. This week had been rough on her indeed. Eyes rimmed with dark circles, she looked at him through her dark lashes. All he wanted to do was scoop her into his arms and hold her tight.

Greeting her with a long, languid kiss, he took her handbag from her and led her to the bathroom. Her eyes went wide when she saw the tub, grateful tears glistening in them as she looked up at him.

"You did this for me?"

He ran his hands up and down her soft, bare arms and dropped a kiss to her head. "I have a special night of pampering for you."

Her bottom lip trembled as she turned to wrap her arms around his waist and buried her head in his chest. His protective nature took over as he comforted her. He took a moment to enjoy the way her body fit against his, so perfectly. Yeah, she definitely belonged with him.

"Get in before it gets cold," he said gently and pressed a kiss to her forehead. "I'll be right back."

Checking on their dinner, he set the sauce to simmer and returned to the bathroom, just in time to hear a low moan as she settled herself into the tub. He had to remind his cock to stay down. Tonight was about her, not him. Of course, his body didn't listen and reacted to her little sounds as she seated herself.

Amara looked a real treat. Hair tied up on the top of her head, with loose tendrils curling around her face, she rested her head on the edge of the tub. Cheeks pink, eyes closed, a small smile spread across her lips. He watched her closely and something switched in him. This wasn't just about sex anymore. He was falling for her.

He enjoyed spending time with her, watching her little mannerisms. The way she would blink rapidly when deep in thought. The way she bit the inside of her bottom lip when trying to stifle a smile. How she looked at him when she thought he couldn't see her. How she looked at him right now with that beautiful lazy, sated smile spread across her gorgeous face.

"You know, the only thing that would make this better right now is if you were in here with me."

"That's not why I did this. Tonight is about pleasing you."

She sat up, giving him a peek at her pale breasts, her light pink nipples just out of sight. "And it would please me if you joined me."

He smirked. Who was he to say no to a beautiful woman?

Moving further forward in the tub, she waited as he stripped off his clothing and slipped in behind her.

"Now I'm very glad I splurged on the extra-large tub," he murmured as she leant back against him.

His cock became painfully erect as she pressed her back against his chest. Wrapping his arms around her waist, he stretched his legs on either side of her and inhaled her sweet cherry scent as she settled against him. Having this soft, beautiful woman wrapped in his arms did things to him. He found himself happy she couldn't see the pleased expression on his face right now.

"Thank you," she said as she turned her head to nuzzle his neck. "I really needed this."

"You're very welcome. But this is just the beginning, sweetheart. You won't know yourself by the end of the night."

He planned on spending the rest of the night with her relaxed against him, her supple body pressed against his. As long as he was touching her, he would be very happy tonight.

* * * *

Hours later, Amara lay sprawled across Sullivan's bed, unable to move. She had well and truly let go tonight. The long, sensual massage he'd planned had inevitably turned sexual to the point where she was begging for him to take her. Satisfaction swelled inside of his chest as he pushed a lock of sweat-dampened hair off her face. She'd insisted on a heavy scene and had asked him to flog her. While he wouldn't usually give in to her request on any other night, tonight was all about her. And he'd decided to please himself by spanking her for the first time after flogging her sweet ass until her skin welted. It had taken a while to get her there, but she had finally ended up sobbing in his arms. And damn, it was a beautiful sight.

She hissed in a breath as he rubbed a soothing salve on the welts on her luscious ass. He gently massaged it in, careful not to be too firm with his touch. Pressing a kiss to the small of her back, where her spine dipped in that delicious way, he smiled against the soft skin. He loved her body so much, he could happily spend hours kissing his way along it, using his fingers to trace every single line and dimple on her flesh.

"I'm afraid you're going to be sore for a couple of days," he murmured as he stretched out next to her.

"Worth it," she mumbled, a satisfied grin on her face.

She was definitely a masochist. He'd never considered himself a sadist, but watching her get off as he hurt her did things to him that he hadn't felt before. Next time he would use her cane and see what it did to both of them.

"How do you feel?"

"Amazing," she said on a yawn. "I don't want to move but I also want a cuddle."

He ran a finger down her cheek, traced her lips, pleased when she flicked her tongue out to lick his fingertip.

"If you want cuddles, then you need to move." He chuckled at her moan of response.

In the cutest way possible, she moved onto her hands and knees and crawled up on the bed so he could pull the covers back for her. Slipping beneath them, she stayed on her knees and fell into his waiting embrace. Head resting on his chest, she folded her hands in his lap as he wrapped his arms around her.

A few seconds later, she gingerly moved to sit down. She sucked in a breath when her ass touched the bed, her cheeks flushing with arousal at the pain. The woman was insatiable. Sitting down properly, she let out a low moan and rested her full body weight against him. He welcomed it and ran a hand up and down her back in the comforting way he knew she appreciated. The position of her hands on his inner thigh combined with her small whimper and moan had his cock hardening again.

Fucking hell.

Pressing a kiss to the top of her head, he relaxed back on the headboard and held her, enjoying the feeling of his little sub—his woman—in the security of his arms. She hummed her satisfaction as her eyes drifted closed and she relaxed into him.

As he let his mind wander, he wondered if she had any idea how hard he'd already fallen for her. And how easily she could hurt him.

* * * *

Amara lay curled up on the bed, in Sullivan's arms, barely paying attention to the television. Instead, she focussed on the contentment that swelled inside of her. Tonight, he'd cooked for and fed her. He'd given her the most relaxing and arousing massage of her life. Then he'd well and truly fucked her into total submission. Afterward, he'd made sure she'd stayed hydrated and fed her chocolate from the stash he kept in his bedside table just for her. He had made her feel so utterly special that she didn't know what to do with it.

He'd burrowed his way deep inside her, to that place she kept locked away after her last epic fail of a relationship. Despite her reservations, she'd let him in.

It was no longer just about sex with him. He was special to her.

Fingers splayed on his abdomen, she smiled when the muscles twitched beneath her touch. One day she would get permission to lick his entire body.

"Thank you for tonight," she said without moving. "You're an incredible man."

"You're an incredible woman." He pressed his lips to her hair. "And you need to take better care of yourself."

She sighed audibly. First her friends had lectured her, and now the man she was sleeping with was going to.

"Before my mum went into the care home, I was her full-time caregiver for two years. Towards the end, I had help twice a week while I was at uni, but that was it. I had no time to myself. I recognise the signs of someone burning out, Amara, because I did it myself."

She looked up at him. "I assumed you had professional help. You never said you did it alone."

He nodded. "I did my best. I thought of nothing but her, much like I suspect you've been doing with your mum."

He ran a hand along her upper arm to squeeze her shoulder before trailing it back down again.

"My mother ended up barely able to do anything for herself. I had to help feed her, clothe her, bathe her. It was hard, but I coped with it, until I didn't. I ran myself into the ground."

"Did your friends lecture you like mine did today?"

A sad smile. "I didn't have friends other than Grayson. And twenty-something guys don't exactly share their emotions."

That made her so sad for him.

"I kept getting sick. My moods were out of control…" He kissed her forehead when she moved to look up at him. "I know it's hard to let go, but you need to. For your own sake. You have help. The sort of help I would have killed for."

She immediately felt guilty. He was right. Her dad really had stepped up over the last month. He'd been doing the job on the weekends, but also helped her at night and gave her more freedom than she'd previously had. She was grateful for it but had been having trouble letting go. Perhaps she needed to discuss her control issues with her psychologist when she next saw her.

"You start work this week. You'll need some downtime. And I don't mean time with me. You need to do something specifically for yourself each day."

"But I feel so guilty each time I do something selfish." She licked her dry lips. "Even coming here tonight, as much as I wanted to…it was hard to leave her."

"I know." He offered her a reassuring smile. "But trust me when I tell you, you don't want to run yourself into the ground. It's very hard to get back out."

She sat up properly to look at him, keeping her hand on his stomach as she propped herself up with her other.

"Once my mum was settled in the care facility, I checked myself into the hospital for exhaustion. I ended up on the psych ward for two weeks. My depression spiralled out of control. It took me a long time to get my life together after that."

Amara saw the pain in his haunted eyes. Touching his cheek, she ran her fingertips over his stubbled jaw, along his soft lips, bringing them to rest on his chin. To think that he had gone through that all alone, without any family support… It broke her heart.

"I'm sorry you had to go through that. It must have been awful."

"It was. And I don't want to see it happen to you. You're too special. And I won't sit by and let it happen."

"Thank you for sharing that with me."

When he offered her a weak smile, she realised he was getting depressed again. She noticed the heaviness of his shoulders, that look in his eyes as they darkened. The lines around his mouth became tight, as did the laughter lines around his eyes. He might have been a professional at reading her, but she was getting better at reading him too.

Incredibly protective of him, she moved to straddle him and wrapped her arms around his shoulders to hold him tight. They might have been completely naked, his cock pressed against her pussy, but there was nothing sexual about her touch. It was a hug of pure comfort and support. He wrapped his arms around her waist and buried his face in her hair, letting out a low, quiet sigh. She smiled, because he was finally allowing her to comfort him properly. She wanted to know him, really know him. And she would make it her mission to discover everything about him.

* * * *

A few hours later, Amara sat forward on the bed, legs crossed, cradling her water bottle in her lap as the two of them watched a comedy on his large television. Her butt had protested her sitting in one spot for too long and she had to keep moving. Sullivan ran one hand up and down her back in the way she adored. Closing her eyes, she focussed on the sensations playing across her skin as he used his fingertips to gently caress her. Her entire body shuddered at one point and he chuckled lightly.

"That feels so nice."

"We need to have a conversation."

She tensed. They'd already had a pretty intense conversation tonight, now he wanted to have another? "What kind of conversation?"

"The exclusivity one."

Thinking back to what Belle had said earlier, Amara realised just how big a deal this was for him. Sullivan didn't do exclusive. He didn't see women on a dating level. Yet he'd done that with her.

"I'm not sleeping with anyone else," she told him. "Nor do I plan to."

"Good." She turned to find a smile that lit up his face. "Neither do I."

Hope surged inside of her. "Does that mean what I think it means?"

"I'm willing to get rid of the condoms if you are."

She answered by crawling into his lap, kissing him so deeply she ended up very aroused and very, very wet.

"I can get tested again this week," she offered. "My last one was while I was with Eddie, but I haven't been with anyone since."

"I trust you when you tell me you're clean. You're hardly the sort of person to lie about that."

"I can't ever imagine lying to you," she said as she cupped his face in her hands.

"Do you want me to get tested again?"

She shook her head. He'd shown her his test results from three months earlier. He was clean and always careful. "I trust you."

Kissing him again, she pressed her chest to his. He pulled her up onto her knees and devoured her mouth, sending arousal shooting through her. He grew harder beneath her, his erection pressing against her entrance as she forced herself not to sit down on him.

"Can we start now?"

"We can." He ran his thumb along her lower lip as he cradled her face in his large hands. "If you promise me something first."

"Anything," she replied without hesitation.

"Every day this week, I want you to do something for yourself. For an entire hour." His thumb moved to her chin, tilting her face so she had no other choice but to look directly into his eyes. "I'm asking you as your friend, but I could order you as your Dom."

My Dom. The thought sent a shiver down her spine. He was officially, exclusively hers.

"Okay." Her voice was barely audible. "I promise."

"Good girl," he said against her mouth.

She loved being called a good girl, but when Sullivan did it, it filled her with more than just pleasure. It filled her with acceptance. Joy. Completion.

Gripping at her hips, he pulled her down to spear her with his cock. He filled her so completely she cried out. His fierce hold stopped her when she tried to move her hips.

"Fuck, you feel amazing."

She let out a sigh as she focussed on nothing more than him filling her without a barrier between them. It felt so much more intimate. She clenched her inner muscles around his cock and moved her hands to grasp at his shoulders. The look he gave her was one of pure want and lust.

"Keep your hands there. Do not move."

He leant in to kiss her, all tongue and teeth and hunger. The kiss remained demanding as he moved, thrusting in and out of her, lifting her on and off his cock as he took complete control. She might have been on top, but she had zero control. She loved every second of it. They were skin to skin. His cock was velvet over steel as it brushed against her G-spot. He leant forward and pressed his body against hers, bending his knees up behind her, the position moving him even deeper inside her cunt. Holding on to him, she kept her eyes on his and enjoyed the ride.

Chapter Thirteen

Good luck today.

The three simple words warmed Amara's heart and almost eradicated the anxiety she'd been feeling since she woke. Today was her first day of work in almost two years and she was nervous, for so many reasons. Yet Sullivan's text made her feel at ease. She'd gone through her morning routine, got Mum ready before Tony arrived and prepared to leave. Leaving her was difficult but not as difficult as she'd thought it would be. She was in good hands with Tony, and Dad would be home in the afternoon to help. She was going to have a good day.

Once she arrived at work, Amara made sure her brain stayed switched on all day. She paid close attention to what Larissa and the other property managers told her about the new rent roll. It had indeed been left in a mess and remained that way. Her day was filled with introducing herself to owners who had present issues, discussing breach notices with tenants, organising inspections for the next month and showing a house on her way home. She had well and truly been thrown in the deep end. But she'd loved every second of it.

The following two days were much the same. She never had a chance to worry about how Mum was doing because she didn't have a spare second to herself. She looked forward to getting into a routine — she loved being back at work and being a productive member of society once again.

"You're still a natural," Larissa told her as they prepared to leave the office on Friday afternoon.

"It's been an interesting few days but I'm enjoying it. I can't thank you enough for getting me the job."

"Please." She waved a dismissive hand. "You got the job yourself. And you've already taken so much off my plate. You have no idea how much you've helped."

"And you're okay to take over Mondays and Tuesdays?"

"Anything urgent will be passed on to me. Otherwise, it's yours to work with. Eventually, you'll build it up and can work full-time. Until then, this arrangement is fine with me."

Amara hugged her friend before leaving, feeling light and happy. She arrived home to find that her dad had been called into work this afternoon and it was just Tony looking after Mum. Apparently, he'd had a hell of a day. Mum had been in fine form, yelling, crying, becoming so depressed she told him she didn't want to live anymore.

Welcome home.

"Where the fuck have you been?" Mum snapped when Amara entered the living room.

"I've been at work."

"Fucking bitch," she snarled under her breath as she glared at her. "You abandoned me. You don't care about me."

Her words cut Amara to the core. This was exactly what she'd been worried about, her mum feeling abandoned because she'd returned to work.

Mum's mood quickly shifted and she cried, sobbing into her hands as she curled up in the recliner. "I don't want to be here anymore."

Amara sat on the edge of the couch and tried to console her.

"I don't want to be a burden. I hate it."

Amara's heart broke into a thousand tiny pieces as she wrapped her arm around her mum. "You are not a burden. I love spending time with you." She pressed a kiss to her head. "I love you."

"Then why haven't you been here all week? Why did you leave me?"

"Because I need to work," Amara said as she ran her hand over her mum's hair like she would a child.

Mum didn't speak any further, just continued to sob until she cried herself into exhaustion. Amara hated seeing her so depressed. She felt completely useless, unable to console her. She'd been having more outbursts like this but Amara had no idea why.

Once Mum was asleep on the couch, Amara moved to lock the front door, poking her head back in the living room before intending to change her clothes. When her eyes came to rest on her mum, everything else ceased to exist.

Eyes wide open but not registering anything, Mum stared in her direction. Her entire body twitched and shook.

"Fuck." Amara didn't have time to react. She rushed over and rolled her onto her right side, holding her in place as she reached for her phone. She was having another seizure. A bad one.

"It's okay, Mum," she said as she dialled triple zero. "You're okay."

She sent Dad a text while she waited for the emergency operator to take down the pertinent details. Sucking in a deep breath, she tried to force herself to keep calm but felt panic rising, threatening to take over.

"Have you got her on her side?" the operator asked in a calm and soothing tone.

"Yes. She's drooling but her lips aren't blue." *Not like last time.*

With her eyes still glazed with that awful vacant stare, Mum's seizing began to slow, becoming more of a twitch rather than a shake. Mum voided her bladder and eventually began to moan as she came out of the seizure.

"You're okay, Mum, just stay still." Her voice somehow remained calm and steady. "You had another seizure. The ambulance is on the way. You're okay."

To the operator, she said, "She's coming out of it now."

"You're doing a great job, Amara. Just stay on the line with me. The ambulance isn't far." The operator paused, typing away in the background. "While she's not seizing, make sure the door is unlocked for them."

Amara rested a hand on her mum's cheek. "I'm just going to unlock the door, okay? I'll be right back."

Running out of the room, she moved faster than she ever had, unlocking and opening the front door before rushing back to the living room. The operator continued to speak to her, assuring her everything was okay, but panic began to fill her again when she laid her eyes on Mum.

She was seizing again, her muscles tense and shaking far more violently than before. Sheer terror coursed through Amara's veins as she approached her mum's side again.

"She's seizing again," she cried. "It's really bad this time."

The world began to blur around her, the operator's voice ringing in her ears over the sound of blood rushing by with each heartbeat. Sirens wailed in the distance, but she barely paid attention to them. Her sole focus was on Mum, whose lips were now turning blue. Amara was vaguely aware of the ambulance pulling into the driveway, the officers making their way through the house. One of them touched her arm gently, ushering her out of the way so they could work. She felt nothing. She was completely numb but brutally aware that this might be the last time she saw her mum alive.

Stepping to the side, she allowed the ambulance officers to work while trying not to completely lose her shit. They injected her with something, took her vitals, put her on the gurney once the seizing ceased and strapped her down. Then the seizing began again.

Why is this happening? was all she kept thinking.

"We're taking her to Midland, you can meet us there," one of the ambos said.

Snapping out of her daze, Amara nodded. She knew the drill. Drive to the hospital alone, then wait until Mum was stable enough to be seen. Alone. All fucking alone.

She tried calling Dad again, but it went straight to voicemail. Sending him another text, she updated him, knowing full well he wouldn't receive it. His phone was probably flat yet again. Amara sat alone in her car and waited for the ambulance to leave, more alone than she had ever been in her entire life.

Calling her brother, Jackson, Amara hoped speaking with him would stop her from freaking out again. She needed to stay alert enough to drive to the hospital.

"Hey, sis, what's up?" he answered cheerfully.

"Mum's had another seizure," she blurted out. "I'm driving to the hospital now, but I can't get hold of Dad and I'm starting to freak out."

Heart thumping against her chest, adrenaline and fear tearing through her veins, she'd lost the feeling in her hands as she gripped tightly on the steering wheel. Her face began to tingle as she panicked.

Jackson swore. "Wait for Dad to get home and drive together. I don't want you driving in this state."

She clearly wasn't holding it together as well as she'd thought. "I'm already on the road. I can't sit at home. I can't leave her there by herself."

"Then stay on the phone with me until you get there. I need you safe."

"I will," she sobbed. "I hate this." She began to cry hard, tears blurring her vision as she sped down the highway.

"So do I. I'm sorry I'm not there."

Hearing those words from her big brother made all the difference. Sometimes she felt like an only child because he was so disconnected from them. Him living on the other side of the country absolutely sucked. She hated it. She missed him. But having him on the phone with her right now made all the difference.

Amara stayed on the phone with Jackson until she parked. He'd managed to distract her and calm her down somewhat so she was no longer crying. Sitting in the far back corner of the emergency waiting room, she curled into herself and tried to shake the image of her mum seizing. She couldn't. The scene played over and over in her mind while she sat alone. Mum, flat on her back, drooling and moaning helplessly, eyes vacant, glazed, completely blank. Amara's chest ached at the awful memory, her heartbeat rapid and irregular. Her head began to spin as she panicked again, losing the feeling in her face and hands.

I'm not built for this.

How the hell could she ever leave her mum again? What if she hadn't been home this time to help? What if Dad had been looking after her and not paying close enough attention? She could have died. She might still...

Phone in hand, Amara stared at it and found herself wanting to call Sullivan. He would comfort her in the way only he could. She texted her friends instead to let them know what happened. Of course, her beautiful friends offered to sit with her while she waited but she told them to stay at home. There wasn't much they could do to help.

Right now, Amara wished she had a partner. Someone to rely on wholeheartedly. Someone in her corner to help. But she didn't. She was completely alone, sitting in a crowded waiting room, crying by herself.

Amara's face was still tingling and her breathing became erratic, short and sharp. Her head spun. Her chest hurt with a sharp, stabbing pain. *Shit*. She was having a panic attack. Cupping her hands over her mouth and nose, she tried to control her breathing. This wasn't her first panic attack—she'd had several while

Mum was in the coma, then when she first began caring for her. She could calm herself down. She had to.

Breathing into her hands, she scanned the room as she tried to focus on other things. The emergency room on a Friday night was not a great place to be. There was an obvious drug addict, strung out and screaming at the nurse trying to help him. A middle-aged man with a very deep gash on a clearly broken arm tried to keep his cool while he watched the spectacle. There were infants screaming, children crying, parents barely holding it together. Then there were the people who appeared as though there was absolutely nothing wrong with them, like they shouldn't be in a hospital, let alone a busy emergency room.

Amara's breathing became less harsh. Her chest pain eventually dulled to a light ache. She moved to hug herself and leant forward in her seat. Her phone vibrated, startling her. It was Sullivan asking how her day at work had gone. *Horrible. Absolutely shit. I need you.* She wanted to text him, but she didn't. Instead, she waited a few moments.

With shaking hands, she texted him back.

Mum had another seizure. I'm at the hospital. I'll text you later.

A few minutes went by, but he didn't reply. Of course he didn't. Why had she thought he would? He wasn't her boyfriend. Her life was a mess. He didn't need to deal with it. No normal man would want to be a part of it, so why would Sullivan?

"Amara." Dad's voice rang in her ears.

She looked up to find him walking towards her. She'd never been so relieved in her life. Worry etched on his face, he stopped before her. There was no hug, as much as she needed one. Her dad wasn't a hugger.

"My phone died after I read your text."

Goddammit, Dad! she wanted to scream at him.

"I haven't heard anything." Her voice was raspy. "They're really busy. I don't know if they'll even let us back there."

"I'll go check."

Dad, being her dad, lined up at the clerk's desk, a determined expression on his face. He didn't panic like Amara did. He always kept his emotions in check. She had no idea how he did it.

The heavy-looking double doors to the patient area opened and a slender man entered the room. "Mari Jones?"

They were both in front of him in a flash.

"You can come in and see her, but only one at a time."

Amara glanced at her dad, knowing he would be the one to see her first. "I'll wait here."

* * * *

Amara took her place in the far corner of the room and rested her elbows on her knees. After texting Jackson with an update, she barely contained her tears when she read his reply.

I'm flying over Sunday. I'll be there at five in the evening.

Relief flooded through her very soul. He was flying over to see them. He was finally coming home again. Much like their dad, he wasn't good with words or emotions, but his actions spoke louder than words.

Stay strong. She's in the best place possible.

He was right. She knew that. But until she laid eyes on her mum, her mind would keep going over the worse-case scenarios. The neurologist had warned them several times that another seizure could change her further, for worse. It all depended on the severity of it. And this had been a bad cluster fit.

Oh God. The feeling of helplessness and panic returned, and she curled up into a ball, wrapping her arms around her legs. Tears blurred her vision and she did her best to suck it up and stop them from falling. Two male dress shoes entered her line of sight before someone squatted before her. A hand came to rest on her elbow, long fingers gently wrapping around it.

"Amara."

She looked up and stared into Sullivan's dark eyes. She let go immediately. Without a word, she threw her arms around his shoulders and held on for dear life. Tears fell, relief crashing over her as she buried her face in his neck. He knelt and just held her while she cried. He was here. Sullivan was with her. She wasn't alone.

Sullivan moved to the chair next to Amara and pulled her into his lap, continuing to hold her as tightly as he could without hurting her. Seeing her so vulnerable broke him. If it had been a person who had put her in this state, they would be flat on their ass right now with an imprint of his fist in their face. Unfortunately, there wasn't anything he could do other than just be there for her. The second he had walked in the room, he had seen her huddled in the corner, barely holding it together, with tears in her big eyes as her bottom lip and chin began to tremble. All he wanted to do was scoop her up and take away her pain. So he did.

Eventually, she pulled back from him and rested her forehead against his. Her light-brown eyes looked directly into his, still shimmering with tears.

"You didn't have to come." Her voice was thick from grief and the obvious panic she felt.

"Of course I did." He pushed a lock of hair behind her ear. "You needed me."

The second that he'd read her text, he'd left his house without a second thought. His need to protect her, to be there to comfort her, outweighed everything else. She needed someone and he wanted to be that someone. It was as simple as that.

The heartbreak and vulnerability in her eyes just about broke his heart. "It's okay," he said gently as she moved to rest her head on his shoulder, her laboured breaths hot on his neck.

"Have you heard anything yet?"

"They just let my dad in to see her."

She scooted off his lap, no doubt feeling self-conscious as people around them began to stare.

"Can I get you anything?"

She offered him a sad smile and shook her head. He pressed a soft kiss to her forehead and pulled her back into him, pleased when she relaxed into his side. Her head rested on his shoulder and her breathing slowed as her muscles melted into his hold. He'd half expected her to turn him away when he arrived. His stubborn little sub always wanted to handle things alone. But he needed to be there for her as much as she needed him. To help her. To support her. Hell, he needed to be with her, period.

Yeah, he had well and truly fallen for this woman. And wasn't that just a kick in the nuts?

The one thing Sullivan hadn't thought of in coming to this hospital was the memories it would bring back of his own mum being admitted. He'd spent many nights alone in this very emergency room. He remembered how terrifying it had been sitting there by himself, not knowing what was happening. The last time he'd been here, he had heard his mother screaming through the doors, hurling abuse at the doctors and nurses trying to help her. Eventually, they'd given her a sedative. He had no good memories of being at this hospital, until now.

Holding Amara, being able to comfort her, would be a good memory. It made him feel wanted, needed even. And she did need him, even if she wouldn't admit it. The way she currently clung to him proved that.

A few minutes later, the doors to the patient area opened and a tall, broad-shouldered man around sixty exited with a visitor's wristband in his hand. Amara jumped up and made a beeline for him, relief evident in her expression.

It suddenly hit Sullivan that he was about to meet Amara's dad. *Shit.* He hadn't prepared himself for that possibility. He was definitely not ready for it.

"She's okay," the other man said. "She's awake and alert, just a bit loopy. You can go in for a few minutes."

Amara let out a deep, trembling breath and took the wristband from him. "Is she different?"

Her dad smiled and shook his head. "No, she's the same."

Amara let out a sob as her shoulders slumped in relief. Sullivan rested his hands on her shoulders to remind her he was there for her. She composed herself and straightened. "Sullivan, this is my dad, Drew. Dad, this is Sullivan."

"I gathered that," Drew said and held his hand out. "Nice to meet you, Sullivan."

He shook the other man's hand. "You too, sir. I'm sorry it's not under better circumstances."

"Will you be okay here for a few minutes?" Amara asked him.

"Of course." He gave her a smile even as a tidal wave of anxiety washed over him.

He was about to spend time stuck with the father of the woman he'd been sleeping with. Without being able to prepare himself. Fuck.

Amara gave him one last look before moving to the patient area and leaving him alone with her dad.

Chapter Fourteen

Standing by her mum's bedside, Amara's nerves ran rampant through her veins. Her gut flip-flopped, though the panic began to subside as she saw her mum. Catching Amara's eye, Mum gave her a lazy, doped-up smile. She was the same.

"Hey, peanut," she said, using Amara's childhood nickname.

"Hey, Mum." She bit back tears of relief as she leant forward to give her a kiss. "How are you feeling?"

"They gave me some really good drugs."

Relief flooded Amara at the sound of her voice. The tone was the same, even though her words were slurred. She appeared as alert as she could be, given they'd no doubt pumped her full of muscle relaxers and anti-seizure medications. She hadn't deteriorated like the doctors had warned she might. Like Amara had been fearing.

"You sure know how to scare the shit out of me." Amara tried to laugh and choked on a sob instead.

Mum reached for her hand. "I'm sorry I scared you."

"I'm so happy you're okay. I feel so much better now that I've seen you."

They sat in silence for a few minutes as Mum's eyes began to drift closed. The nurse stopped by and informed them she would be admitted for the night.

"You should get home. There's nothing you can do here."

Amara smirked. Mum had always been more worried about others than herself. It was a peek back to her old mum. She had always been caring for others.

"I'll see you in the morning, okay?"

"Okay, sweetie," she replied sleepily. "Tell your dad to go home as well. I'll be fine here."

Amara laughed as she stood. "Yeah, right. You know he'll be staying with you."

Mum rolled her eyes and clicked her tongue. "Bloody stubborn man."

"At least you know where I get it from." Amara grinned. "Sullivan's here too."

"So, the non-boyfriend came to the hospital to check on you," she teased.

Mum had been teasing Amara about him for weeks, claiming to notice she liked him as more than just a fuck buddy. She was constantly pointing out how her face lit up when he was mentioned or when she was headed out to see him. Much like her friends, her parents didn't understand how their relationship could stay purely physical when they saw the effect it had on her. But now...

"Oh God. I left him out there with Dad."

"You'd better go then."

Giving her mum another kiss, Amara left to find Dad and Sullivan in a conversation, rather than sitting awkwardly as she'd feared they would be. Dad spotted her first, said something to Sullivan then stood.

"Head home. I'll stay here while she's admitted."

Amara smiled. While he might not show outward affection, there was never any doubt that he was completely and utterly devoted to his wife.

"Mum said you should go home, too."

"The woman knows me better than that." He laughed. "I'll see you in the morning. Good to meet you, Sullivan."

"You too." Sullivan stood with a smile and wrapped an arm around Amara's waist in a sign of outward affection. Somehow, it made her feel branded and safe.

"Come on," he said once they were alone. "Let's get you home."

He draped his arm over her shoulder and held her close as they walked out of the emergency room towards her car.

"I'll follow you home."

She smiled up at him and tried to ignore the tingling in the small of her back and the warmth in her chest. "I'll be fine."

"Amara," he said in 'that' Dom tone. "This is not up for discussion."

She let out a small sigh. "Fine."

Sending texts to her brother and friends, she updated them before she left so that as soon as she got home, she could collapse into an exhausted heap.

* * * *

Sullivan followed Amara home, let himself inside, sent her to the shower, made sure she ate then began to massage her feet as she curled up on the couch. He was in full Dom mode, taking care of her as only he could. Finally, just because she needed to feel his arms around her, she collapsed into him. Resting her head on his chest, she inhaled his comforting scent of soap and man as the anxiety and stress-induced fatigue began to take over. It had been such a long time since someone else had truly cared for her that she'd forgotten how nice it felt. To have him fussing over her, bringing her water, running his hands up and down her back, pressing kisses to her head as he murmured to her.

He'd kissed her head, her cheeks, her forehead several times, but not once had he kissed her properly. And that just made her feel all kinds of alone again.

"You can leave whenever you want. I'll be fine," she told him even as she burrowed further into him.

"Do you want me to go?"

No. I want you to stay. She shook her head.

"Then I'll stay."

Shifting to sit up slightly, she looked at his perfect, handsome face and found nothing but sincerity as he watched her with those dark eyes she loved so much.

"You don't think that might be crossing a boundary?"

He gave her a heart-breaking smile that made his eyes dazzle in the dim lighting. "Amara, I've already crossed that boundary."

Running a gentle hand over her cheek, he continued to watch her. Pure joy filled her at his words. Even with all her reservations about beginning a relationship with him, that was exactly what she'd done tonight, whether she wanted to or not. She'd let him into her home and her heart. Goddamn, she wanted a real relationship with this man so badly. She just didn't want to screw it up.

Leaning forward, she pressed a soft kiss to his lips, smiling when he sighed into it and deepened it.

"I would love it if you stayed with me."

* * * *

Waking next to Sullivan the next morning was the best thing Amara had experienced in a long time. She came to lying on her side, his heavy arm draped over her waist, his hand palming her breast, his warm breath in her ear. She turned to face him, stretching out her aching, tense muscles and took a moment to watch him. Her fingertips itched to touch him. She reached up to trace his facial features, his dark brows, the straight line of his nose, the curve of his full lips, the sharp angle of his stubbled jaw.

"That feels nice," he mumbled, voice thick with sleep as his hand gripped at her waist.

"Morning."

His eyes fluttered open to look directly into hers. He smiled dreamily. "How are you feeling?"

"Better." She ran her thumb across his bottom lip, smiling when he kissed it. "Thank you for staying with me. I appreciate it."

"Any time." He gave her a crooked smile. "All you have to do is ask."

She wanted so badly to tell him she'd fallen for him. That she wanted him around all the time. But she didn't. She couldn't. She'd done it too soon with others and it had always ended up the same — with her heartbroken and alone, wishing she'd done things differently.

"I should get up."

He glanced down at his watch. "It's only seven. Hospital visiting hours don't begin until eight."

"And you know that how?"

"My mum was a patient there many times."

Right. She hadn't considered how being at the hospital with her worrying about her own mum might bring up painful memories for him.

"How about I take you out for breakfast?"

She bit the inside of her lip. As wonderful as that sounded, she felt the need to go to the hospital, to do her job as carer. Only she wasn't the only carer now. Her dad could take care of those things.

"Your dad is still at the hospital," he told her. "I got up before you woke, and his car isn't here."

She remained silent.

"He is capable of handling everything, Amara."

She knew that, but it was still hard for her to let go. He moved his warm hand to rest on her, squeezing gently.

"Remember what you promised me last week?"

"That I would do something for myself every day," she muttered.

"Breakfast with me can be the one selfish thing you do for yourself."

She smiled. She couldn't help it. What was it about this man that she was unable to resist?

"Okay. Do you want to go home first and change?"

"I have a change of clothes in my gym bag in my car."

"Of course you do."

He moved his hand beneath her singlet, bringing it to rest on her breast. He raised his brows and smiled when he found her nipples already hardened peaks. Having him half naked in her bed had left her aroused all night long. She'd woken to realise she was fucking wet. Pinching her nipples between his fingers, he grinned when it elicited a gasp from her each time. Then, right when her breasts were straining against her top, he removed his hand and rolled onto his back. The bastard grinned again when she groaned in frustration.

"You can't get me all excited and leave me hanging like that."

He raised one brow and looked down at her. "I believe I just did."

Narrowing her eyes at him, Amara moved to straddle his waist, resting her pussy against his underwear-clad cock, happy to find him rock-hard. She leant down and kissed him, softly and sweetly, hoping he would deepen it. He didn't, instead resting his hands on her waist, holding her still while she tried to writhe on him.

"I believe you were warned about trying to top from the bottom." His tone was deep and stern.

"That's not what I'm doing," she insisted as she ground herself against him, enjoying the shudder it spread through her body when his cock came into contact with her clit. "I'm just really horny and it's your fault. Isn't it your job to take care of me?"

"You're walking a fine line, Amara," he warned in that tone that made her insides melt.

"Please?" She gave him her best pout and wriggled on him once again. His dilated pupils didn't go unnoticed.

"That's it," he growled. "Get in the shower. You're getting spanked and fucked."

She giggled at the promise of shower sex and happily jumped off him, all but skipping out of her bedroom. He muttered "Brat" under his breath before he followed her.

* * * *

After a very long, very sexy shower, the two of them headed to breakfast. Sullivan took her to a little café near the hospital that he frequented with his gym friends. He ordered one of the biggest breakfasts she'd ever seen, while Amara settled for something far smaller. When he added a side of spinach and eggs to her order, she scowled at him.

"You'll be at the hospital all day. You need a good meal to start with. Besides, you undereat as it is. I don't want you losing any weight. I love your lush body just as it is."

He was right, dammit. She had been cutting down the amounts she ate since she'd started seeing him but had hoped it would go unnoticed. Looking down at her stomach, she noticed how it pouched out and rounded when she sat. Her thunder thighs hung over the edge of the chair. Her flabby arms were on display because, thanks to the summer heat, she wore a singlet top. It didn't go unnoticed that he made little comments about her body, but they were always positive ones. He was always telling her how beautiful she was, commenting on how much he loved her body, even when she saw nothing but flaws.

"I mean it, Amara. You have a wonderful, incredibly sexy body. I'm always at least semi-hard around you. My body loves yours."

She frowned.

"Did you just frown at me?"

She scowled at him this time. "I told you, I don't do D/s outside of the bedroom."

"Neither do I usually. But that doesn't mean I'm not keeping a tally of your bad behaviour for future use." He eyed her food. "But if you eat everything on your plate, I won't spank you later for that frown."

"Bastard," she said under her breath.

He let out a laugh and gathered her hand in his. Oh, how she loved that laugh. "There's never a dull moment with you, sweetheart."

The waitress dropped off their replacement drinks and Amara took a sip of her latte, watching Sullivan as he ate. All his casual movements held a subtle strength and dominance to them. Yet there was also a gentleness to his touch, an easy-going way about him. The man was a contradiction at times. Was it any surprise that she'd fallen so hard and so fast for him?

"So, you've met my dad."

"Yeah." He chuckled. "I wasn't thinking of that when I left for the hospital."

He'd made it clear last night the only thing on his mind was getting to her to comfort her. That comment had made her cry all over again.

"Did he say anything? Bad, I mean. He didn't try to scare you away?"

Not that she could ever imagine her dad doing that. He was always polite, even to a fault. When her first boyfriend had treated her like a doormat, he had kept a polite smile on his face and treated him with respect he didn't deserve, all because he was raised that way. He'd never be outwardly rude without a lot of prodding. And he was just instinctively friendly, a lot like Sullivan.

"On the contrary. He said he appreciated me being there for you, that you need someone to look out for you."

"That's funny. He's always wanted me to settle down. Just last week he was telling me he didn't understand how I could have a strictly physical relationship with you." She looked up at him. "I guess that's all out the window now, huh?"

"I can't say I'm sorry about that." His cheeks creased in a sexy way as he grinned at her.

"How long has it been since you were in a relationship?"

"About two years."

"It's been three for me."

"Is there any particular reason for that?"

She shrugged. "I'm just bad at relationships. I've told you that. After it didn't work out with the last guy, I just kind of gave up on finding someone and stuck to sex only." Daring to look at him, she asked the question he had always evaded. "Why have you been single for so long? You never did tell me."

He pursed his lips and clamped up for a moment. Like always. "I had a very bitter breakup."

She waited. She'd known that much but he never elaborated on it.

"My ex tried to take everything from me." His eyes darkened as he spoke, his frown growing. "She claimed she had a right to my money, my house, my business because we'd lived together for years. I ended up having to get a lawyer to protect myself. After that, I vowed never to get seriously involved with a woman again."

Amara dropped her fork and looked at the hurt and frustration on his face. He had been well and truly burned. And that definitely explained why he didn't see any of the submissives outside of the club.

"I haven't brought anyone into my home since her. That's why I prefer to play at the club. I like to keep subs at arm's length."

"Why didn't you do that with me? Why did you invite me into your home?"

He gave her a slow smile. "Because you're different, sweetheart. I either invited you into my home or didn't get to know you. And I couldn't imagine not knowing you."

A blush heated her cheeks. Wasn't that just something every woman wanted to hear?

"I really like you, Sullivan," she said, her voice slightly more timid than she'd expected.

"I really like you too, Amara."

"I'm glad I took a chance to get to know you." She truly was. She couldn't imagine her life without Sullivan in it.

After they finished their breakfast, Amara read a couple of texts she had received from her dad. The first just gave her a quick update, but the second told her to bring Sullivan to the hospital when she visited. Amara read the last one twice just to make sure she'd read it correctly. Mum wanted to meet him.

"What's that look for?" he queried, looking worried.

"My mum wants to meet you," she said tentatively. "Apparently she's mad that Dad got to meet you last night and she didn't."

"Well then." He pushed back his empty plate and grabbed his wallet and phone from the table. "We'd better not keep her waiting."

"Seriously?"

"Why not? I'd love to meet your mum."

And suddenly, she had a partner.

* * * *

Amara walked through the hospital, taking in the indecently strong scent of antiseptic as nerves ran rampant through her body. Sensing her trepidation, Sullivan stopped her outside of her mum's room and gave her a soft, sweet kiss that took her breath away, made her forget all her worries. He was very good at that.

"Better?" he asked with a grin.

She nodded. "I just... If she says something inappropriate, please don't take it to heart. She doesn't think before she speaks."

"It'll be fine. I was thrown in the deep end meeting your dad last night. Meeting your mum will be a piece of cake." He flashed her another grin before letting her lead him into the room.

Mum was sitting on the edge of the bed, her hair over her face, shoulders shaking. Amara's heart dropped as she prepared for the worst. But when Mum threw her head back, Amara saw she was laughing uncontrollably, not crying. Dad looked at her from his seat and shrugged.

"She got the giggles."

"Oh God," Amara said on a laugh. Once her mum got the giggles, there was no stopping her. She'd always been that way. "What triggered it?"

"I have no idea."

"I can't stop." Mum sucked in a breath. "Oh, what an introduction," she said when her eyes came to rest on Sullivan.

"At least I can see where Amara gets her gorgeous giggle from," Sullivan said with a smile. "It's a pleasure to meet you, Mrs Jones."

"Oh please." She waved a dismissive hand at him, still trying to stifle her laughter. "Call me Mari."

And just like that, Sullivan settled into an easy conversation with both of her parents. The entire time they chatted, he kept a hand on her in some way, whether it was holding hers, resting it on her waist or running his fingers through her hair as he spoke about her. She felt oddly treasured.

By the time her dad left the hospital, Amara realised it was nearly eleven and Sullivan had been there with them for over two hours. He hadn't made a single move to leave or hinted that he'd had to go. Yeah, he was definitely different from anyone else she'd ever dated.

"I'd better get going," he said eventually. "I've got a meeting at one and should check on the gym beforehand."

There was a hint of reluctance in his voice that Amara loved hearing.

"It was so lovely to meet you, Sullivan. Thank you for humouring a crazy old lady," Mum said from her position on the bed. "Thank you for being there for Amara. She deserves to be happy and you seem to make her happy."

Ugh, there she went, saying something completely inappropriate just because she thought it.

Rather than getting awkward, Sullivan looked at Amara with a shit-eating grin. "I'm glad to hear it because she makes me very happy too."

They said their goodbyes and Amara walked Sullivan to his car, keeping her hand in his for the entire time, not ever wanting to let him go.

"Thanks for doing that. Mum really appreciated you staying."

"Your parents are great." He wrapped his arms around her waist and pulled her against his warm, firm body. "I'll gladly spend time with them again."

He always knew just the right thing to say. Reaching up, Amara pulled his face down to meet hers and kissed him. He deepened the kiss, running his hands up and down her back as he turned to pin her between his body and the car. Arousal built quickly, tingling between her thighs as she became wet. He pushed his pelvis against hers, his erection pressing right up against her clit as he swallowed her gasp. He continued to devour her mouth, his fingers digging into her hips to the point of delicious pain that left Amara wanting so much more when he pulled away.

"Well, fuck," she muttered against his lips. "How the hell am I supposed to go back in there now?"

"Think of it as a parting gift." He kissed her once more. "A reminder of things to come tonight."

Body throbbing, she watched as he drove away, flashing her one last smile. The bastard had purposely left her aroused, knowing she would be suffering for the rest of the day. The only sense of satisfaction she got was knowing that he was in the exact same position.

* * * *

Later that afternoon, Sullivan picked up Amara from the hospital, forcing a smile as he kissed her in greeting. While he was definitely incredibly happy to see her, his depression had begun to take over this afternoon. After checking in on the gym, still on a high after seeing Amara, he called Grayson to update him on their relationship. He'd felt better than he had in a very long time. Then he had a psychologist appointment and everything went to hell.

The appointment had been a hard one. He'd begun by happily describing his relationship with Amara and how it had changed, that he'd met her parents and how important that was to him. Then came the inevitable issues with his own family. As much as he might have dealt with the loss, dredging up the past in therapy was always difficult and left him feeling exhausted. His psychologist had a way of digging deep inside of his soul and forcing him to face his hopes and fears. Today, she'd done exactly that, and it had ruined his mood, leaving him feeling like hell.

As he'd hoped, his fake smile and squared shoulders worked, and Amara seemed none the wiser. He'd had enough experience with depression to know how to fake a good mood. Now he just had to fool Amara for the rest of the night because she was stressed out enough and didn't need to deal with his depression and issues on top of her own.

They entered the dining area and she dropped her bag on the table and stopped in front of him, head cocked to one side.

"Tough day?" she asked in a knowing tone.

For a minute, he didn't answer. He went about setting their dinner on the table. She stopped him by placing a soft hand on his chest, then wrapped her arms around his waist and pulled him into her body. Melting at her touch, he buried his face in her hair as she ran her hands up and down his back in a soothing manner. His little sub certainly knew how to get to him. When he let out a slow breath, his chest loosened as he just enjoyed being held by her.

Amara pulled back, those light-brown eyes searching his, filled with worry.

Lie. Tell her you're fine.

"Sullivan," she pushed. "Tell me what's wrong."

"I'm fine, really."

She set her jaw and frowned up at him. Fuck, she was adorable.

"Sullivan."

With a low sigh, he tightened his arms around her shoulders. "I had a psychologist appointment today. It ended up being a tough one."

"Can I do anything?" She hesitated for a moment. "Should... Should I leave?"

"No," he answered a little too quickly. "Stay. I just..." He ran a hand over his weary face. "I'm not going to be up for much tonight."

Bastard. When he'd left her this morning, he'd promised her a good time. He'd wanted to fuck her into oblivion. But that wasn't going to happen. Depression completely decimated his sex drive.

Amara offered him that beautiful smile that lit up his entire world. "It's safe to say I'm no longer here just for the sex. I care about you. I want to make you feel better."

He broke away from her and moved to sit at the table, tapping his lap as he so often did with her. Having her sitting on his lap made everything better. He fucking loved it. Whether she realised it or not, she was often submissive outside of the bedroom. She obeyed him without question when they were alone together and tonight, he needed that. Needed to be in control, to be touching her, pleasing her. She assumed the position without hesitation and rested her arm over his shoulder, her other hand on his chest as she leant down to kiss his cheek oh so softly.

"Tell me what I can do."

"You can get me a plate of food. Then you'll let me feed you."

She opened her mouth to protest but, wisely, closed it when she saw his expression.

"Then we'll spend the night on the couch, where you'll be naked and on my lap for the entire night."

A delicious shudder spread throughout her body. Yes, she was definitely more submissive than she realised.

They made small talk while they ate, him feeding her from his fork. She didn't give one single protest. She accepted his titbits and snuggled into him while she ate. As she curled her arms around his shoulders, she told him of how her mum wouldn't stop talking about him all afternoon. Apparently, she called him a keeper. Happiness filled him upon hearing that.

Meeting her parents was a huge deal for both of them but he'd enjoyed every minute of it. Although it was quite obvious that Mari was disabled and her thought processes didn't work like they used to, he'd caught a few glimpses of the mother she must have been to Amara. Her love for her daughter was evident in the way she looked at her, how she'd called her peanut. While it had happened ahead of schedule, he was glad he'd gotten to meet Amara's parents because now she made more sense to him. It was evident she'd inherited her caring nature from her mother, and her emotional distance from her father. Drew was a nice guy, but he was not as forthcoming with praise and love as Mari was. He was more reserved than Sullivan had expected yet remained a very friendly and polite person. Sullivan could see himself getting to appreciate Drew for the man he was.

Amara kept pushing Sullivan to talk about the gym, his friends, anything that would distract him from the depression that hung over him like a heavy shadow. The sneaky little woman knew exactly what she was doing. And it was working. By the time they'd finished eating, he felt lighter.

She insisted on cleaning up for him while he settled on the couch. When she made a move to join him, he shook his head and gave her a stern look.

"What?"

"Undress," he told her. "I want you naked in my arms tonight."

There was nothing better than having his naked sub in his arms while he relaxed and tried to forget the day. A naked Amara was definitely his favourite thing in the world. He watched, his mouth watering as she stripped off her clothing slowly, leaving her panties for last. Noting the bruises from his bites earlier in the week, he asked her to turn for him and saw the bruising that remained on her ass and upper thighs from his hands and flogger. She marked and bruised so easily and healed quite slowly, he'd noticed. When he'd offered to take it easier on her, she'd actually scowled at him and told him *"Don't you fucking dare"* in a harsh tone. No, she enjoyed seeing the marks like a good little masochist.

"Come here, sweetheart." He held his arms out for her, all but grinning when she settled in his lap. "There's nothing like a nice armful of Amara."

Nuzzling her neck, he squeezed his arms around her and let out a long sigh. Content. That was how he felt. Completely and utterly fucking content.

After putting on a comedy they'd both seen before, they sat in a comfortable silence. He broke it when he realised that he'd never asked about her brother.

"How long is your brother staying for?"

"A week." She beamed. "It'll be the longest he's stayed with us since Mum got sick. I can't wait to see him."

"Do the two of you get along?"

She smiled. "We argue a lot, but yeah, we get along. We fight about stupid shit but get over it quickly. I got lucky to get him as a brother." She stuck a finger up at him. "But don't tell him I said that or he'll never let me live it down."

Sullivan offered a smile, realising he shouldn't have brought it up. All it did was remind him that he missed his own brother. He couldn't help but wonder what his and Brady's relationship would be like now. If they would still get along as well as they used to.

A soft hand came to rest on his cheek as she turned his head to force him to look at her. "Hey, what did I say?"

He shook his head. "Nothing. I'm fine."

"Sullivan."

"Really."

Letting out a sigh, she shuffled off his lap and curled up into herself. He immediately felt the loss.

"You're always pushing me to be honest with you. Why can't you do the same with me?"

He remained silent.

"If you're going to turn into one of the Doms who expects his sub to tell him everything but won't share his own feelings, then this relationship is going to be very short lived," she told him with no uncertainty. "I expect you to be as honest with me as I am with you. This goes both ways. I deserve that much."

She was right, of course. He knew that. He hated when his Dominant friends shut down on their own submissives. That must have hurt them to bare their souls but not receive the same in return.

Sullivan thought back to what his psychologist had said to him earlier. *"Open up to her. You're worried you're moving too fast, lean into it instead. You deserve to have her support."*

"I was thinking of Brady. Wondering what our relationship would be like now."

"And? Do you think you'd still be close?"

He smiled. "I like to think we'd be closer than Grayson and I am today. We did everything together. That wouldn't have changed. I really did idolise him. He was a great big brother, always looking out for me. He once beat up my bully for me when I was little."

"You had a bully?" she asked in disbelief.

"I was a very scrawny kid. I was shorter than most and some of the older kids thought I'd be an easy target."

He grinned at the memory of Brady threatening the older boy who had been beating up Sullivan for weeks. He told Sullivan that if anybody was going to beat up him, it would be him, not some random older kid. The very next day, he punched the other boy square in the nose for daring to touch his little brother. The bullies had laid off after that and Sullivan didn't have any more problems. Brady was a great big brother, only picking on him in the way an older brother would. But Sullivan never doubted he had his brother's love and support growing up. It was evident in his actions more than his words.

After the accident, Grayson had stepped into that role. He really was a surrogate brother for him. He'd taken him under his wing, continuing to look after him for his late best friend. And he never once abandoned him when life got hard. Even when he was in the hospital for two weeks, Grayson visited him every day he was allowed to.

"Brady and Grayson were allowed to pick on me all they liked, but the second someone else did, they stepped in."

"Because their bullying was done out of love." He nodded. "Jackson was the same. He picked on me a lot growing up, but the second someone else tried, he'd step up and scare the shit out of them. It was funny when we were teens because he turned into a big guy. He was always tall but once he started working out, nobody dared mess with either of us."

"Sounds a lot like Grayson. Even once he graduated high school, he would pick me up after school and check in with me, make sure nobody was hassling me. He's more like a brother to me than a friend."

"You're lucky to have that." She ran her fingers over his chest, her featherlight touch tickling. "I can see how close the two of you are."

"I'd like you to get to know him better."

"I've only technically met him once. That time at the club. I just feel like I know him because you talk about him so much."

"How about we visit the club next weekend and you can spend some time with him in his element. Get to know the Dom as well as the man."

Amara narrowed her eyes at him, a wicked smile spread across that cute face. "You just want an excuse to play at the club."

"Two birds, one stone." He shrugged.

"Okay, I'm in."

Sullivan thought back to something else his psychologist had said to him today about the bigger issue that he'd been trying to avoid all week. This upcoming Saturday was the anniversary of the accident and it was always a hard day for him, even twenty years on. He would visit his mum, just in case she remembered and needed some support, even though she never did. He thought it was far too soon, but the psych had suggested he ask Amara to join him and give him that support he desperately needed on what always turned out to be a difficult day for him.

"What was that thought?" she asked as she ran her fingers between his brows, down around his lips.

"I'm going to visit my mum next weekend." He hesitated, feeling like a fool. It was too soon. "I was wondering…"

No, it was definitely too soon to throw her into that messy part of his life.

Those beautiful eyes bore through his as she stared at him, waiting for him to continue.

"Would you come with me? My psychologist suggested having you there might help… I just…"

Amara was clearly taken aback by his request. Her eyes widened and her cheeks flushed. *Shit*. He'd overstepped. It was one thing for him to meet her family, but for her to meet his very ill, unhinged mother…

"I'd love to come with you."

He let out a breath he hadn't realised he was holding on to. "Thank you. Now get back onto my lap so I can kiss you properly."

She moved and he caught her lips immediately, cupping her face in his hands as he deepened the kiss, pouring his heart and soul into it. She responded in kind, touching her hands to his, holding him in place in that way that touched his heart. Touching him like he was precious, she continued to kiss him, eventually resting her forehead on his when he pulled away.

"Don't be afraid to tell or ask me anything, Sullivan," she told him with that determined little expression she got when she was refusing to give in. "It's healthy to discuss these things, especially with your partner. Besides, you always hear about my troubles and issues. I like hearing about yours. I enjoy helping you."

He shifted, pushing her back on his lap a bit to regard her with raised brows. "Did you just call yourself my partner?"

She wrinkled her nose in the cutest fucking way. "You noticed that, huh?"

"I did." He pressed a kiss to the tip of her perfect little nose. "And I love it."

"I guess that's what we are now. I want you to tell me everything about you. I expect it now."

He searched her gaze. Did she really mean it? Yes. She did. Because Amara chose her words very carefully before she spoke. She didn't say things she didn't mean.

"I'm so happy I took a chance on you that night at Haven."

"So am I, my sweet."

Chapter Fifteen

Amara's mum came home on Sunday morning. After spending the day hypervigilant because Mum had to use a walker short-term due to her affected balance, Amara was exhausted by the time she headed to the airport to pick up her brother from the airport. His fight was slightly delayed, so she parked and waited inside for him, eager to see him again. It had been four months since she'd laid eyes on her big brother.

At six foot five, broad-shouldered and well-muscled, he stood out amongst the other travellers. A broad grin spread across his handsome face when he spotted her and wove through the crowd. Wrapping her up in a big hug without a word, he held her tight. Amara and her brother didn't hug often, so she relished it when it did happen.

"Hey, sis." He ruffled her hair. "You look tired."

"Gee, thanks," she retorted sarcastically. "You always know how to make me feel good about myself."

The years he'd spent teasing her when they were young teens made her feel like he didn't like her at all. As she grew older, she realised that was his way of showing affection because he didn't do it in the traditional way. He had inherited it from their father, while Amara took after their emotional mother.

He slung an arm over her shoulder as they headed out the airport. He seemed different. Almost lighter than when she'd last seen him.

"I meant that as a concern. Have you been getting enough sleep?"

"I'm just tired today. Mum's using a walker for the next couple of weeks because the seizure affected her balance, so I've been on extra alert."

"How is she today?"

"Having a good day. She's just a little excited about you visiting."

"I've missed her." He smiled down at her. "I've missed all of you."

Amara put his suitcase in the boot of her car. "We missed you, too. It'll be good to have you around for the entire week."

"Carmen sends her love."

Jackson's wife was nice and very sweet, but Amara didn't have the relationship with her she'd always expected to have with a sister-in-law. Rather than gaining a sister like she'd hoped, they kept more of a cordial friendship purely because they didn't know each other that well. But Carmen made Jackson happy and that was all that mattered to Amara. Even if it did mean she'd stolen her brother away from their home and taken him to Sydney. Amara always hoped they would one day move back to Perth, but she had long since given up on that dream.

When they arrived at the house, Sullivan's car was already in the driveway.

"The boyfriend's already here, 'ey? Aren't you worried the parentals will scare him off?"

She scoffed. "He's already met them both. They like him. I'm more worried you'll try to scare him off."

Her brother laughed, the same big, booming hearty laugh he'd always had.

"It's a big brother's job to scare him a little. I'll be on my best behaviour. If you think he's good enough for you, I'm sure I'll approve."

* * * *

The five of them settled for dinner, carrying on a pleasant conversation without any lulls. Jackson updated them on his life in Sydney, telling them tales of his consultant job that Amara would never fully understand. Then her family began to grill Sullivan, asking for all the sordid details of his past. The man took it all in his stride.

Sullivan slipped into her family dynamic so easily — he took all their jokes and teasing, gave sarcastic comments back and seemed genuinely at ease. She watched him for signs of discomfort or depression, knowing that her family could sometimes be a little too invasive, but he appeared to be enjoying himself.

After dessert, he helped Amara clean up, doing the dishes despite her insistence she could do it herself. She rewarded him with a kiss so hot it left his cheeks pink when he pulled away, his pupils dilated with arousal, cock hard as it pressed against her abdomen. She loved when he got like that, knowing it was all for her.

He bent his head and nuzzled her neck, pressing his lips to the sensitive skin. "I don't suppose you'd want to come back to my place for a sleepover?"

"I could, couldn't I?"

Jackson would be around just in case Mum got up during the night, even though she hadn't done that all week.

"I'll make sure Jackson is okay to listen out tonight."

Sullivan headed home, saying goodbye to her dad and brother with a handshake before planting a kiss to her mum's cheek. She appreciated that more than she'd thought she would.

Jackson waited for her in her living room, leaving their parents to have some downtime.

"Do you mind listening out for Mum tonight while I stay at Sullivan's?"

"Sure. If she keeps me up, I can always nap tomorrow while you and Dad take over."

After packing a change of clothes and some toys Sullivan had asked her to bring, she left her bag by the front door, noting the slight rattle of her toys.

"So, what do you think of Sullivan?" she asked Jackson as she sat beside him.

He shrugged in that irritating non-committal way he always had. "He seems like a good guy. Does he make you happy?"

"He does," she said, feeling giddy. "He makes me really happy."

"That's what matters," Jackson told her. "You've always been a good judge of character. Besides, the man clearly adores you."

"You think?"

"You don't see the way he looks at you while you're not paying attention." He smirked. "The guy is completely smitten."

A blush heated her cheeks as she bit down on a smile.

"And judging by that look, you're smitten, too."

"I am. He treats me so well." She sighed. "Incredible is the only way to describe him. He's such an amazing man."

"And you're compatible in the bedroom if the rattling in your bag is anything to go by," Jackson teased.

"You should see all of his toys. His collection rivals that of any other Dom I've ever known."

"A Dom, is he?"

"Of course."

"Well, that's an extra point in his favour."

"Oh my God, definitely—"

"And you should leave before you decide to share the gory details of your sex life that I *definitely* don't want to hear."

Laughing, she stood and said goodnight to her brother before leaving to spend a very fun night with Sullivan.

* * * *

Amara got out of bed on Wednesday, more exhausted than she had been in weeks. Mum's higher dose of anti-seizure medication had made her more irritable, to the point where the doctor had also added antidepressants. On top of her bad moods, she wasn't using the walker and had already fallen a couple of times because of it. Amara had remained on edge all week because of it and felt herself beginning to burn out.

She made her way to the living room, finding Mum without the walker, just as she began to stumble backwards. Rushing to her, Amara lunged forward and caught her before she fell. A sharp stab of pain tore through Amara's right shoulder and chest as she barely maintained her hold on her mum. Biting down on a cry, pushing through the massive wave of nausea and agony that took over, she steadied her mum and moved them both into a standing position. Jackson heard the commotion and brought the walker out, taking over for Amara.

"Mum, you have to use this," he scolded.

"I don't need it." She sneered, clearly in a foul mood.

"It's only short-term…"

Amara tuned out her brother's words as she clutched her arm to her chest and tried her best not to throw up from the intense pain she felt. Her entire arm tingled and burned, her chest stabbing and wrenching as she tried to straighten herself. *Fuck.* She'd really hurt herself.

"Fine!" Amara heard Mum snap before the room began to spin around her.

"Are you okay?" Jackson caught her as her knees gave out from beneath her, propping her up in his strong arms.

She waved him off and staggered to the nearby couch. Sitting on the edge, she sucked in deep breaths that only added to the pain in her chest. Tears pricked her eyes as her stomach lurched. She'd injured herself a lot in her life, a side effect of being active as well as accident prone, but hadn't done something this bad in a very long time. It felt like the very muscle had torn from the bone. The pulsing heat that spread through her chest was similar to what she'd felt when she'd torn a pectoral muscle as a teen. Only this was much, much worse.

Cradling her arm to her torso, she leant forward to try to ease the pressure as she felt Jackson's large hand on her lower back, gently rubbing up and down.

"What did you do?" he asked from his perch next to her.

"I think I tore something when I caught her." Her voice was thick with pain. "I just need a minute."

"Once Tony gets here, I'll take you to the doctor."

"I'll be fine." But she wouldn't. The pain was beginning to spread, taking over her entire brain until she couldn't think straight. "Can you get me the strong painkillers from the bathroom cabinet? If I move, I'm going to throw up."

He disappeared and returned with the packet of pills and a glass of water. "It's not like you to feel sick from pain. You are a masochist, after all."

Her laugh sent a shockwave of pain throughout her entire right chest and arm. "Ow, my God. Don't make me laugh."

"Ring and make an appointment to see your doctor. I'll drive you."

"I'll be fine, I can drive with one arm."

"Amara." Jackson and his damn Dom tone.

Fucking Doms.

She scowled at her brother and took her phone he held out for her, dialling the number for her doctor. "Happy?"

With a grin, he replied, "Very," and left her.

* * * *

Amara took a long lunch break and went to see her doctor after she was unable to get an earlier appointment. She got a script for some very strong painkillers and a referral to get a scan done. The doctor assumed she'd torn her pectoral muscle and, judging by the dark bruising that was already spreading across her chest, that sounded about right. She was given orders to do nothing but rest and not use her arm for a few days. Yeah, like that was going to happen.

After a long day at work, combined with the excruciating pain she felt, Amara felt like shit on the drive home. She fought back tears, barely holding on. All she wanted to do was soak in the bathtub and see Sullivan. But she arrived home to hear her mum yelling.

Great.

She found Mum standing unsteadily in front of the couch, Dad holding her arm, Jackson holding the walker in front of her.

Jackson looked at Amara with tired eyes. He'd had a long day apparently. "She wants to go outside but refuses to use the walker."

"I don't fucking need it," Mum yelled.

She glared at Amara when she entered the room.

"Come on, Mum, I've had a rough day. Use the walker and come sit outside with me."

"I'm not using that stupid thing. I don't need it."

"We don't want you to fall like you did this morning."

She looked to Amara, her gaze conflicted as she tried to conjure a memory that was no longer there. "I didn't fall this morning."

"You did," she said using her soft voice. "That's where I got this from." She pulled her top down slightly to reveal a dark purple bruise that was spreading across her chest.

"Please use it so neither of you gets hurt again," Jackson told her.

Mum's eyes didn't soften, the glare remaining evident.

"How about you sit on it and I wheel you through the house?" Amara suggested.

"No." Mum stuck her chin out stubbornly and sat down. "I just won't go outside."

Dad sat beside her, clearly giving up, and Jackson followed suit.

"Come on, Mum…"

"I'm not using it. I don't fucking need it."

"Fine." Amara sighed, too tired and weak to fight. "Can I get you anything before I get changed?"

"Just leave me alone," she yelled.

Amara flinched at her tone but left the room. After changing very slowly to avoid causing herself further pain, she rubbed some ointment into her chest to help with the bruising and entered the living room where Jackson gestured for her to join him outside.

Settling on the lounge, Amara tried to ignore the constant throb in her chest that was now radiating down her arm. The painkillers only just took the edge off.

"Has she been like that all day?"

"Pretty much. She spent most of the day yelling at me and Tony."

It was a very bad day indeed if she'd been yelling at Tony. She was always on her best behaviour for him.

"She even called me a mistake earlier."

Amara saw the pain in her brother's eyes. "Goddammit." She rested a hand on his shoulder. "I'd hoped she'd be happier with you here."

"I know you usually have Wednesday nights off, but I think you should stay tonight. Dad hasn't handled her well this afternoon. It's too much for us to deal with."

Too much for them to deal with? Amara let out a huff. Two grown-arse men couldn't handle it but expected her to do it alone.

"I've had a really shitty day, Jackson. Can you guys not handle her for a couple more hours?"

"I can try, but I'm not built for this kind of thing."

"And you think I am?" she snapped.

"You're better at dealing with her than both of us are together. You know that."

"That doesn't mean it's easy for me," she told him, anger burning the blood in her veins. "For fuck's sake, I dealt with this twenty-four-seven for eighteen months, *by myself*. Good days and bad. It's no picnic. I think I deserve a break a few times a week."

He remained silent and avoided her eyes. Because he knew she was right. She did deserve her time off.

"I gave up my entire life to look after her. You have no idea what that was like. You giving up a couple of days won't kill you."

"I know it was hard, but someone had to be there to care for her."

"And it just had to be me, didn't it?" she snarled, old hostility mixed with her foul mood. "God forbid you put your perfect life on hold to help this family out."

"That's not fair," he scolded her.

No, it wasn't. But it also wasn't fair that Amara had been the solo carer for *their* mother while he got to live his life. For so long, she had held resentment towards her father and brother for not helping her. It was bound to come out at some point. Of course it was going to be tonight when tensions were high and they'd all had a day.

"Don't even start with me on what's fair," Amara growled. "I moved out of my home. I quit my job. I gave up my independence completely. I am starting from scratch now because I did the selfless thing and took care of the woman who took care of us. You have no idea what that felt like. You get to leave. You get to go back to your own life. I don't. This is my life now."

Jackson looked down at his hands, jaw clenched, eyes fierce. He had no comeback.

"I am going out tonight, for a couple of hours. You and Dad can handle it together."

"Just ask if she wants you to stay. If she does, please stay and help. Give Dad a break."

Regardless of the anger she felt, she agreed. Why? Because it was the right thing to do. And Amara always did the right thing.

After giving Mum her dinner and tea, Amara asked if she wanted her to stay at home tonight.

"I don't fucking care what you do," was her response.

Amara blinked back tears and looked at her brother. "There you have it. She doesn't want me here. I'm going out."

"Go, Amara. We have this handled," Dad chimed in.

Shooting one last glare at her brother, who really didn't deserve it, she thanked her dad and left.

* * * *

Amara drove to Sullivan's, absolutely furious at her brother. How dare he tell her it wasn't fair for him and Dad to look after Mum? *How fucking dare he*? He had no idea what Amara had given up. How much she struggled. How she spent every single night crying herself to sleep because she was so completely lost.

Amara knew that at the core of her anger—what really got her down—was that he had never once thanked her for looking after their mum. If he had just said thank you, she might not feel so much resentment towards him. Hell, it had worked with Dad. He'd thanked her, said he appreciated how much she'd given up and done for them, and most of her resentment had faded away.

That was all she wanted—to feel appreciated.

Still, as much as she loved her brother—and she did, more than she could express—he infuriated her.

"Fuck!" she yelled as she parked her car, fist slamming into the steering wheel. The move sent a jarring pain through her injured chest and arm, causing her to immediately regret the childish outburst.

She stomped up to the front door, feeling relief when Sullivan opened it for her. The relief soon disappeared when he looked down at her and noticed her cradled arm. His smile disappeared.

"What the hell happened to you?"

"Mum fell this morning. I caught her and tore my pec. I'll be fine."

He let her inside, waiting just inside the entry, his arms crossed over his chest, eyes colder than she'd ever seen. Shit, he was mad.

"And why am I only hearing about it now? Why didn't you tell me earlier?"

"There was nothing you could do. I knew I'd see you tonight."

"Let me see."

Pulling down the neck of her top, she winced as she saw the dark bruising that marred her chest and spread across her breast. She really had done a number on herself. His eyes became even colder as he inspected her, running a hand along her heated skin. Her bottom lip trembled as she avoided his harsh gaze, knowing she'd disappointed him by not telling him she'd hurt herself. First, she'd angered her family, now Sullivan. What else could she fuck up today?

"Oh, hell." He pulled her into his arms and held her, resting his chin on the top of her head.

She dropped her handbag to the floor and wrapped her good arm around him. This was what she needed, to be held by him. To have him make everything better in her world. Her anger began to melt away into fatigue and sadness. Because she'd had one hell of a day and didn't want to talk about it at all, she just wanted to feel no emotions.

"You should have told me. I would have come to you tonight."

"I really needed to get out of the house."

Hot tears blurred her vision as he pulled away from her and held her chin firmly in his hand.

"What happened?"

She shook her head and blinked away the tears. "I don't want to talk about it."

Without a word, he led her to the back patio, sitting her on the long outdoor lounge where they'd spent many evenings together enjoying the silence. Sullivan sat beside her, his knuckles gently running down her cheek as she closed her eyes and focussed on nothing but his touch.

"Did you get a scan of your chest done?"

A small nod. "The doctor called tonight, it's definitely a tear. Told me to rest for the next few days. But, really, it looks worse than it is."

"I'll be the judge of that."

He reached across to pull her top off, careful when moving the thin strap over her injured arm. His eyes lit up when he noticed she was braless, her nipples peaking under his gaze.

"I couldn't get my bra on this morning. And I didn't really want to have Jackson do it up for me. That's a little too weird," she explained. "As a result, my boobs and back are aching."

"I'm sure I can do something to ease the ache, sweetheart," he teased.

He shifted a chair to sit opposite her and, with the hands of a well-practised physiotherapist, he moved along her chest, poking and prodding gently. She made a small sound of pain when he reached one particular point, tears filling her eyes as a wave of nausea washed over her. He'd barely touched her but it felt like he'd just stabbed her with a knife. He grunted and sat back in his seat, a frown spreading across his handsome features.

"You're lucky it's not worse." He leant back and gathered his hands in his lap.

When she began to feel lonely because he wasn't touching her, Amara realised just how out her emotions were. She wasn't reacting rationally, and hadn't been all day.

"Now, why didn't you let me know what you'd done earlier?"

"I had it handled. There wasn't anything you could do."

"Okay." He furrowed his brow. "And how would you react if I did the same? Injured myself and didn't tell you about it?"

"Sullivan, I—"

"We're in a relationship, Amara. This goes both ways. If something happens to you, I expect you to tell me right away. I know you're used to being independent, dealing with things alone, but you don't have to do that anymore." He leant forward and ran a gentle hand along her thigh. "You have me to rely on now."

When she looked up into his dark eyes, her heart dropped. He was right. She should have told him. If he'd kept something like that from her, she would have been hurt and felt like he didn't trust her. But she hadn't wanted to bother him at work. She knew how busy he was.

"What else happened?"

"I had an argument with Jackson. But I really don't want to talk about it."

He kept watching her with those careful eyes, disappointment slowly filling them. Her vision blurred with more damn tears when she realised just how disappointed he appeared to be.

"Please don't make me talk about it right now."

"Sweetheart." He reached out and scooped her into his lap with very little effort and held her as she kept the tears at bay. "How about we get you into the spa and you can relax a bit, hmmm? We can ice your injury later."

She gave a small nod and stood from his lap. Moving her hands out of the way, he pulled off her leggings and underwear and carried her across the wooden deck to the large in-ground spa at the very edge of the patio.

He let her go and helped her into the hot bubbling water. Amara experienced instant relief as her muscles went languid and loose. The pain in her chest decreased significantly as her arm floated in the water, as did her breasts, taking the extra pressure off her back and neck. All the stress of the day began to melt away as she closed her eyes and rested her head back, giving herself over to the feeling of complete relaxation.

Once she threatened to turn into a prune, Sullivan helped her out of the tub and made her drink an entire bottle of water to rehydrate. Wrapped up in a warm, fluffy towel, she snuggled into herself, oddly content. When he knelt on the ground before her and spread her legs, she frowned down at him.

"What are you doing?"

Running his hands up her thighs, he teased the crease where they met her hips, just shy of her cunt. He pressed his lips along her inner thighs, sending shivers of pleasure through her.

"What does it look like?" he murmured into her sensitive flesh.

"It looks like you're being presumptuous again."

A slap on her inner thigh woke her up. "This is my body, sub. I will do with it what I wish, when I wish."

She went to refute him, but how the hell could she when she all but melted into his touch? He moved his mouth further up to that spot that begged for his tongue. Hands under her butt, he moved her until her ass was hanging off the edge of the couch and his mouth came down on her, instantly wiping all thought from her mind.

Lifting Amara's feet to rest on the edge of the lounge, Sullivan opened her up for him, keeping his eyes on her to make sure she wasn't in any discomfort or pain. The large bruise that marred her pale chest pained him to see. He inserted two fingers inside her cunt, watching with pride as she closed her eyes and parted her lips on a small sigh. She was so relaxed now that she would slip into subspace with very little coaxing. Then he would get her to talk about what was bothering her. He would force her to feel and let out the tears she'd so bravely been holding in.

What bothered him wasn't that she was injured or upset. It was the fact that she didn't share with him easily. She shared when it suited her, or when he forced it out of her. That wasn't how this relationship was going to work. She expected him to share his thoughts and feelings readily with her but wasn't willing to do the same. Something had to give. Amara had to know that he would always be there for her, to listen, to comfort, to hold her. All he wanted to do was help, but he couldn't do that if she continued to hide.

She made a little face, wincing slightly. Removing his fingers from her, he bent to press a kiss to her soft stomach.

"Is your chest okay?"

She gave a hasty nod.

"Amara."

She opened her glazed eyes. "Really, it's fine. I inhaled too deeply, that's all."

"If it happens again, tell me. Or I will stop completely, and I will punish you."

At his threat, she nodded quickly, eyes wide. He hadn't punished her yet. He hadn't needed to. But if she continued to lie to him, he would spank her. He had a feeling his hand would be spanking her sweet little ass before the night was over.

Inserting a finger into her cunt once again, he pumped in and out, watching her carefully. He added a second and saw nothing but pleasure on her face. *Good girl*. Her breathing increased, her breasts swelling and nipples peaking as she looked down at him with hooded eyes. He dipped his head and licked over her clit, down one side, up the other, before flicking ever so lightly over the top of the hardening nub. She sucked in a deep breath and winced but didn't say anything.

Goddammit.

Removing his hands and mouth from her, he sat on the chair, giving her his Dom look that made little submissives squirm. It did the same thing to her.

"I'm fine," she said. "Really, it only hurt for a second."

"Over my knees. Now."

"But…" She winced as she sat up. "I'm sorry…"

"Don't make me ask again, Amara. You won't like the outcome."

He'd allow her to push him farther than most Doms would, but when it came to her hurting herself, he had very little tolerance for that. He wouldn't stand by and let anyone hurt his woman, not even her.

She moved, positioning herself over his knee without further argument, even moving her round ass right up in the air. Now wasn't the best time to discipline her, not when she was injured, but she needed to learn to share with him. To trust him.

"Now my chest hurts," she told him with a small whine.

"Then keep still and I'll make this quick," he told her.

Running a hand over her ass cheeks to warm the skin a little, he gave her a few small smacks before resting his other arm over her lower back, to hold her in place. He brought his hand down on her arse, a loud slap filling the silent air around them.

"Count for me."

"One," she said instantly.

"You need to be honest with me, sweetheart." He spanked her again, careful to remain gentle. Waiting for her to say "two," he continued. "You will not get away with hiding things from me. Especially pain."

"I'm sorry…"

Smacking her hard enough that his hand tingled, he waited for her count, then ran his hand between her thighs, finding her sopping wet. Apparently, she enjoyed the spanking.

"You certainly will be sorry." He squeezed her cheeks before spanking her again, a little harder this time.

Her "four" came out on a sob. *One more ought to do it.* Running his fingers between her thighs again, he found her clit had hardened, practically begging for his touch. She squirmed as he ran his finger over it. Removing his hand, he brought it down on her one more time.

"Five," she cried.

He could hear the tears in her voice. Careful to be gentle with her, he helped her up and onto his lap. With a heavy heart, he held her, one arm around her like a steel trap, the other cradling her head while she cried into his shoulder.

"I didn't enjoy that, Amara." He really didn't. He had always hated spankings for punishment, but sometimes they were a necessary evil.

"I'm s-sorry," she sobbed into his chest.

"Let it out, sweetheart," he soothed. "I'm here."

* * * *

Once Amara's sobbing had stopped and her breathing slowed, Sullivan wiped her cheeks with the towel and kissed the red, tear-stained skin. He hated to see her cry but she'd needed a proper release. When she arrived tonight, she'd been so wound up he thought she might burst. Yet she still wouldn't share with him. He had thought he'd earned her trust, but clearly not enough. That was something he would need to work on.

"Now, tell me why I spanked you."

Bottom lip sticking out, she looked at him, vulnerability evident in her eyes. "Because I wasn't honest."

"About?"

"Hurting."

"And?"

She frowned at him, her fingers brushing across his chest gently in the way she always did when they were in this position. "I don't know…"

"Amara," he warned.

"I didn't want to talk. But sometimes I don't want—"

"I am your Dom. My job is to give you what you *need*, not what you want." He used his Dom tone, his face stern as he looked at her. "What you need right now is to feel, to talk about what is bothering you."

She continued to frown and pout at him. *Fuck, she's the cutest thing.*

"Now, let's try this again. What is bothering you?"

"I don't—" Cutting herself off, she held her hands in her lap and studied them. "I had a fight with Jackson. Mum had a bad day and he and Dad didn't handle it well. He told me to stay tonight, said it wasn't fair that Dad had to deal with it all afternoon."

Her heavy exhale came out a sob as fresh tears sprung to her eyes.

"I did it alone. For so long," she whispered. "Nobody cared. Nobody ever cared when I struggled."

She was angry, but she was also hurting. She was such a soft soul beneath her tough exterior. Lacking emotional support at home must have been very difficult for her to deal with. Sullivan tucked her head back into his shoulder, his heart aching for the woman he loved so much it hurt.

Love? Fuck. Where had that thought come from?

But he did love her. This little sub who tried so hard to pretend she could handle everything herself, who was far more sensitive than she let on. And she had been through so much, doing a lot of it alone. She needed someone on her side to look out for her.

"I have to start again... He doesn't." Her sobs ramped up a notch as tears spilled over her cheeks, wetting his shirt. "I left my home. I left my job. He did nothing."

"It's okay. I've got you, sweetheart. Tell me."

She pulled back and wiped at her cheeks, even as tears continued to fall. "I left my job, my house, lost most of my friends. All to help my family. To do the right thing. And nobody ever said thank you, not once. He's never said thank you." She hiccupped a sob as she buried her face in her hands. "He just... He triggered me... I had a really bad day today."

"I know," he mumbled into her hair. "What you did was incredibly selfless and brave. I don't know anyone else who would have given up their life like you did."

That was the absolute truth.

Once she'd regained her composure, she wiped her face and looked at him with red rimmed eyes. "I'm sorry…"

"If you apologise for crying and telling me how you feel, I'm going to spank you again. Except this time, you *really* won't enjoy it."

She pursed her lips. "It's hard for me."

"I know. But you'll learn."

He kissed her and ran his fingers along her hair, smoothing it out.

"You are to share everything with me from now on. No arguments. No apologies. Do you understand?"

"Yes, Sir."

Chapter Sixteen

Amara had called Sullivan 'Sir'. *Holy shit*. He had no idea what a big deal that was for her. She'd never once called a Dom 'Sir'. She felt it was too personal, that it gave them too much power over her. Now, she realised she'd never truly given everything over to a Dominant. But with Sullivan, she had given over every part of herself to him and trusted him with her body and mind. It made her feel absolutely complete.

After some very gentle lovemaking where he remained cautious of her injury, Amara left reluctantly, wanting nothing more than to stay curled up in his arms in his bed. But she had responsibilities at home.

Sir. She smiled to herself as she entered her parents' home. One simple word shouldn't have filled her with so much delight and warmth, but it did.

When she noticed the light on in her mum's living room, the good feeling came crashing down. Her brother was sprawled out on the couch where he'd clearly been waiting for her.

"She refused to go to bed without you."

And Amara's good mood was ruined. Mum really had become too reliant on her. How was Amara ever going to be able to move out on her own?

When Amara entered the room, her mum opened her eyes and scowled at her.

"Where have you been?"

"I went to Sullivan's."

"You left me."

Great, a guilt trip. "You told me to."

She frowned. "I don't remember that."

"Come on, let's get you to bed."

Amara helped Mum to her room without argument and got her changed before tucking her into bed. Jackson said goodnight and followed Amara to her bedroom, closing the door behind them, his face unreadable.

"About earlier…"

"Forget about it." She was too tired to start another argument with him. They'd both said things they shouldn't have and they knew it.

"I'm sorry for what I said. I didn't realise how hard it was. But I had a talk with Dad tonight and… I'm sorry."

"Thank you."

* * * *

Amara didn't sleep well that night, or the next. Her mind refused to quit thinking about the fight she'd had with Jackson. They hadn't discussed it since, not really. She hadn't had a chance to express that he'd triggered her. Not that that was out of the ordinary. Her dad and brother dealt with emotional outbursts by sweeping them under the rug. It was easier for them to pretend altercations didn't happen. As frustrating as it was, Amara had learned a long time ago not to push.

Saturday morning, she woke feeling a little more refreshed, which was good. She needed energy today. Today, she was meeting Sullivan's mother. He had warned her it might be draining and probably very awkward for her. She hadn't had to deal with dementia since her grandfather had died years earlier, but she knew how bad it could get.

"What are you doing today?" Mum asked, appearing very happy today.

"I'm going to meet Sullivan's mum."

Jackson perked up from his position in the kitchen. "Meeting the mother? Things really are getting serious."

"She's in a care home with severe dementia," she told her brother. "I'm going to support Sullivan. She probably won't even acknowledge my presence."

"Damn. The poor guy."

While her brother might not deal with Amara's emotions, he wasn't completely emotionless. He'd always shown empathy for others, just not Amara.

"He doesn't have any other family, does he?"

She shook her head.

"That explains why he's so happy to spend time with ours," he said quietly. "I can't imagine not having both parents."

Sullivan had spent the last two evenings at Amara's house with her family, getting to know them all better. It had been comforting to see him settle so easily into her family dynamic. Her parents adored him and Jackson got along well with him. The two of them had spent half an hour outside last night chatting. Sullivan wouldn't tell her what they spoke about, insisting it was man stuff, but she got the feeling Jackson was reading him the riot act.

For all his faults, her brother was very protective of her. He loved her—she knew that. Which made his attitude towards her difficulties all the more frustrating to deal with.

"Is he still coming tomorrow for dinner?"

"Yep. For some reason, he likes you."

Jackson flipped her the bird and gestured for her to join him in her living room, where he propped himself on the arm of the lounge.

"Listen, I'm sorry about the other night. I was out of line."

Yeah, he had been.

"I never really comprehended how hard it was. Looking after Mum for one day with Tony's help completely wiped me out. I have no idea how you did it alone."

"Now my cries for help make sense, don't they?"

Too bad they'd fallen on deaf ears.

"Yeah." He looked down and bit his lip. "I've been thinking and have discussed things with Carmen. I'm going to move back."

"Seriously?" Amara couldn't hide her surprise.

Jackson had been living in Sydney for seven years. His entire life was there. Even their mum almost dying hadn't convinced him to move back to Perth.

"Why now? You've never shown any interest before. I thought you would stay in Sydney forever."

"Things aren't working out with Carmen. They haven't been for a while now." He looked pained. "And with Mum being the way she is, I just feel I should be here helping you and Dad out."

"Wow." She didn't know what else to say. Her brother's marriage hadn't been perfect — what relationship was? But she'd had no clue they'd been having troubles.

"Why didn't you tell me about this earlier? You used to tell me everything."

"It's not exactly something I wanted to discuss over the phone. Besides, I was in a bit of denial. But this week has proved I need to be here, before it's too late. I've already missed so much. It's my turn to help and give you a break."

Amara's heart ached for her brother. She reached out and gave him a quick, tight hug.

"I'm sorry things didn't work out for you. But the selfish part of me is very happy you'll be coming home. You have no idea how much I've missed having you close by."

Before he'd left, the two of them had been so close. They'd been friends as well as siblings. That connection had been missing for years as they'd grown further apart.

"I do," he told her. "I've missed hanging out with you. I've missed having my little sister there for me no matter what. You really are the protector of our family and you don't even realise it."

There it was — validation of the role she'd taken over.

"So, what happened with Carmen? Do I need to fly over there and beat the crap out of her?"

That brought a smile to his face. She might be the younger sibling, but she'd always been fiercely protective of her big brother.

"We both changed and found we're no longer compatible. We want different things out of life. There's no bad blood. We've just been running through the motions for the last year or so and it's not good for either of us."

"That sucks."

"It's for the best." He shrugged. "To be honest, she's decided she wants no more D/s and wants to be strictly vanilla. You know as well as I do that's not an easy thing to give up."

She did know. She'd had vanilla relationships with really nice people that had crashed and burned all because she missed that D/s dynamic and couldn't live without it.

"I'll sort things out over the next month or so and move back here as soon as I can. I've discussed it with Mum and Dad and I'll stay here until I get on my feet."

"That's going to make for a very crowded house again."

"I don't plan on staying here for long."

"Neither did I," she said solemnly.

"Amara." He took in a deep breath and looked her dead in the eye. "I know I haven't said it before, but thank you. For stepping up and taking over when I wouldn't. I was selfish and had my head in the sand. It's my turn to step up now."

Those words. He had no idea how much they meant to her. With tears in her eyes, she hugged him again, laughing at his light groan when he begrudgingly hugged her back, holding her tight.

"You have no idea how long I've wanted to hear that from you."

"Go get ready," he said when she pulled away. "It sounds like you'll be having a stressful day today."

* * * *

Nerves filled Amara as she made her way through the car park of the care facility, plastered to Sullivan's side. The home looked like a nice place—with manicured gardens and peaceful surroundings, it appeared calm and serene from the outside. But she knew things could be very different on the inside. Squeezing his hand in hers, she felt a mixture of emotions radiating off him. A mixture of nervousness, hesitation and grief were written all over his face. He usually hid his emotions so well, but today they were all out there for everyone to see.

"Are you ready for this?" he asked in that unsure tone he'd had all day.

"Definitely," she told him, giving his fingers another squeeze.

She was ready to do nothing but support him just in case things went wrong. He'd warned her about his mother's mood swings, that she could well be very hostile today.

Sullivan signed them both in before he led her down a corridor to the locked wing of the facility. It opened to a large living area filled with couches, chairs and tables, some of them set up with games and puzzles. There was a large television on one wall, a couple of cupboards next to it filled with games, books and old DVDs. A couple of residents had visitors. One elderly man was surrounded by young children, and one elderly woman being visited by her partner, who stroked her hair lovingly. They appeared happy. But for each happy face there was a vacant one, staring into space, taking in nothing of the outside world.

Amara recognised Sullivan's mum before he pointed her out. Sitting in the corner alone at a table, she stared out of the large window. She appeared frailer than Amara had anticipated. All the photographs she'd seen of her in Sullivan's home were of a vibrant, curvy woman. The woman she approached, who was only in her early sixties, appeared as though she were in her late seventies. And she was absolutely tiny.

"Sullivan," a short female nurse greeted him with a smile. "I'm afraid she's not having a good day today."

"Is she aggressive?" he asked in a clipped tone that Amara had never heard before.

"No. The new medications appear to be working. We haven't had any incidents this week."

Amara listened to the two of them discuss her daily habits. From the sounds of it, she spent most of her days staring out the window or locked in her room. She refused to deal with the other residents. That absolutely broke Amara's heart. *What a lonely existence.*

As they made their way towards her, Sullivan slipped his hand from her hold and motioned for her to sit at the table opposite him. He bent and kissed his mum on the cheek before sitting.

"Hey, Mum." His tone was gentle, almost childlike.

His mum turned her head ever so slightly and looked at him with a blank expression. But there was so much emotion in Sullivan's eyes. Love. Pain. Sadness. Pure agony.

"Go away," the other woman said.

"I came to visit you. I even brought a friend to meet you."

She didn't turn, didn't acknowledge Amara at all. While she'd expected that, it still stung a little.

Smiling across the table to him, Amara watched as he tried to gain some form of response from his mum as he continued to talk to her. All of a sudden, she seemed to snap out of her trance and recognise him.

"My baby boy," she said in a sweet tone as she reached for his face.

Amara would never be able to describe the pure joy and heartache she saw in his eyes.

"Hey, Mum," he said quietly as his mother cradled his face.

"You've grown." She traced his beard stubble. "How?"

"I'm older than you remember."

Her demeanour changed and Amara caught a glimpse of the mother she must have once been.

"Where's your brother? I need to get him ready for basketball practice."

She stood. Sullivan was at her side in an instant. "Brady's not here, Mum."

"I need to get him ready. He can't be late."

"It's just me," he said softly. "It's just me."

Resting a gentle hand on her shoulder, he managed to get his mum to sit. She returned to her catatonic state, staring into the garden. She remained that way for the remainder of their visit until Sullivan made a move to leave.

"That's right." She sneered. "Leave like you always do."

"Mum, I'm here. I'll stay if you want me to."

She glared at him, nothing but hate in her eyes. "I don't want you. I want Brady. He should be here. Not you."

Somehow Sullivan managed to keep his resolve. "Brady's gone and so is Dad. I'm the only one you have left."

She sat silent for a moment, her angry gaze never leaving his. "I hate you." Her words were so sinister. So vile.

It took all Amara's strength not to interject. But, holy shit, she wanted to. Wanted to tell the woman to be grateful for the son she had left. Tell her how amazing he was. Loyal to her, loving her, regardless of the horrible things she'd said and done to him.

"Well, that's too bad. I'm all you've got," he snapped.

"Brady should be here."

The woman's hands and arms began to twitch as she became agitated. A young male nurse saw and approached the table.

"Violet, it's time for afternoon tea. Would you like me to get you something to eat?"

"They're all gone," she muttered, looking at the empty table. "My boys are all gone."

"That's not true," the nurse said. "Sullivan's right here."

"That's not my boy. My boy is gone. All my boys are gone."

She began to thrash beneath the nurse's touch, slapping his hands away as she fought to stand. The chair flew out from behind her, clattering loudly on the floor. Sullivan stood to steady her as she staggered, but she smacked his hands away.

"Don't touch me," she snapped. "I hate you. I hate you all!"

Amara watched in absolute disbelief, standing to get out of the way, as the previously sedate woman began to scream at the top of her lungs. She flipped the table and pushed Sullivan, slapping his face, hitting his chest, while everybody around them stared at the commotion. The nurse managed to usher her out of the common area and into her room. Amara followed Sullivan, staying a few steps behind him. Hands fisted at his side, eyes tight, lips pursed, he was barely hanging on. He tensed his shoulders when Amara reached up to touch him. She let her hand drop and hugged her arms around herself, feeling completely useless. What good was she if she couldn't even comfort him?

"Don't come back," his mum screamed at him. "I hate you. Do you hear me? I hate you!"

Too small to do any real damage, Sullivan's mum continued to lash out at the nurse while the short female nurse approached to help. All Amara could do was stand in the hallway and listen as the woman who had once been a loving, caring mother continued to yell at her son. He stepped out of her view and she eventually calmed.

The female nurse stayed in the room with her as she calmed down while the male nurse stepped out to speak with Sullivan.

"She hasn't been like that since last week."

"When I last visited," Sullivan stated, his voice cold and void of emotion.

"I'm sorry." The young man rested a gentle hand on his shoulder. "I know it's not easy."

Sullivan turned to leave, Amara following a step behind him, unsure of whether or not she should try to touch him again, to comfort him. Judging by his reaction when she tried in the hallway, she assumed she shouldn't. That he wouldn't welcome it. The expression on his face made her both afraid of him and worried about him.

The rage and hurt that filled Sullivan was palpable. He wanted to smash something, to fight someone, to lash out at the nearest person. But the nearest person was Amara and he would never *ever* lash out at her. Remaining silent on the drive home, he kept a white-knuckle grip on the steering wheel while he focussed on holding it together.

A few times, Amara made a move to reach for him, but backed off, clearly unsure of whether or not he would welcome her touch. He would have. God, he wanted her to hold him so badly. But he knew he would completely fall apart when she did. That was why he didn't welcome it in the care home. He had to wait until he got home. Then he could feel everything.

It had been an unpleasant visit but not a surprising one. Mum hadn't lashed out at him like that for weeks. "*I hate you.*" The words played in his mind over and over. How many times had she said that to him while drunk? They hurt every single time he heard them, but today of all days, they cut right through to his soul. His own mother hated him. He was well and truly alone.

Only that wasn't true. He had Amara now. They hadn't known each other long, but the bond he shared with her was stronger than anything he'd ever shared with another woman. But it still wasn't the same as having his own blood around.

Fuck, he missed them so much. Tears burned the backs of his eyes, his throat closing up as he fought to keep it together with each breath.

Stalking inside the house, he remained aware that Amara had slowly followed him, not daring to make a sound. Had he scared her? Because that was what it felt like. Bringing her to the home was a mistake. He should never have done it. There was a reason he'd never taken another woman to meet his mother, not even Katerina, and he lived with her for years. He'd hoped Mum would stay nonresponsive, that he could talk to her like he usually did, introduce her to Amara and have it all go well. Instead, it had gone about as badly as it could have.

He got himself a drink of water to quench the fire burning inside of him. It did little to help. He was on edge, tense, hurting, ready to completely fall apart. *Fuck.* He couldn't fall apart in front of Amara. He slammed his glass down on the counter so hard that it smashed into pieces.

Fuck.

Amara was on him in a second. With her arms wrapped around his waist from behind, she pinned herself to him. For a split second he thought of fighting her. No woman had ever seen him like this. He'd never let his guard down enough to lose control in front of anyone. But this was Amara. She was the strongest person he knew. She was everything to him. He turned in her arms, wrapped his around her waist and held on for dear life. She was his lifeline. His anchor. His love.

"It's okay." She ran a soothing hand over his hair, tangling her fingers in it. "Let it out."

Her words were a trigger. He let go, a sob escaping his throat as he held her. He let it all out. All the pain. The hurt. The frustration. The fucking grief that still hung over him like a dark cloud. The absolute loss he felt every year on this day. For the first time in a very long time, he allowed himself to cry.

Amara held him until he was completely emotionally drained. She ran her hands up and down his back, across his shoulders, through his hair, over and over, repeating the same comforting pattern while she pressed her lips against his temple, his forehead, cheeks and finally placed one small kiss at the tip of his nose.

The weight of the world lifted from his shoulders. *How did she do that? How does she make everything better? Because I love her. Bloody hell, I really do love her, so fucking much.*

She ushered him to the couch where he hauled her on top of him, needing the control of having her in his lap, right where she belonged. He wanted to feel her body wrapped around his. Placing her arms around his shoulders, Amara kissed his neck, filling him with warmth as she hugged him fiercely.

"I'm sorry today was so hard," she said quietly, almost nervously.

Filled with trepidation, he sucked in a deep breath and squeezed her. He…had to tell her the truth, had to explain why today had hit him so hard.

"Today's the twentieth anniversary of the accident." His voice was raw.

Shock and sadness filled her eyes as she sat back and looked at him, but he noted that the one thing she didn't portray was pity.

"Why didn't you say anything? If I'd known…"

"I wondered if she would remember," he admitted, sounding like a pathetic, needy teenage boy. The boy his mum had abandoned and turned him into each time he saw her.

"Thank you for coming today."

She kissed him and ran her fingers through his hair in that soothing manner of hers. "Of course. I'm here for you. Always."

Sullivan moved his hand to rest on Amara's inner thigh, need tearing through him like wildfire. The need to be in control. The need to forget the awful day. The need to forget, period. He gave her leg a squeeze, noting her deep inhale as she stiffened. His mouth was on hers a moment later, tongue plundering before she could even react. The kiss was raw and demanding and filled with emotion as he poured himself into it. Fuck, he needed her so badly right now.

Hand cupping her mound through her jeans, he applied just enough pressure to warn her what was about to happen. She sucked in another breath and tried to squirm back in his lap, but his arm stayed locked around her back. Forcing her mouth away from his, she looked at him with uncertainty in her eyes. She didn't understand his need to be in control right now. It was the same as her need to give it up.

"Sullivan," she breathed, a heady sound.

"Yes or no, Amara."

His eyes searched hers. *Please don't say no. I need this.* He needed her beneath him, her legs wrapped around him as he drove into her. Her arms wrapped around his shoulders while she rode out the orgasm he gave her. He needed his world to make sense again and, right now, the only thing that made sense to him was Amara.

"Yes," she whispered against his lips, a shudder running through her body. "It's always yes."

He was on her, taking over as she gave herself to him completely. With deft fingers, he undid her jeans and ordered her to lift her hips, in full Dom mode. Amara obeyed and lifted her legs, shoving her pants down. A beautiful whimper escaped her lips as his hand rested on her mound, applying pressure to her clit, which throbbed beneath the cotton of her panties. With one hand splayed on her back, he supported her while applying more pressure, groaning into her mouth as she caught his face between her hands in that incredibly sweet way he loved. Nothing ever felt so right as when she held him.

"Sullivan," she gasped when he moved his fingers beneath her panties.

He looked down at her fiercely. With wide, frightened eyes, she appeared fully submissive, in a way he'd rarely seen her without her being in subspace.

"Do not speak again, unless it's your safe word," he told her.

Her "yes, Sir," was barely a whisper as she spoke. Words he'd only ever heard from her once before, but fuck, he needed to hear them right now. To know that she trusted him enough to call him 'Sir' hit him square in the heart.

"Say that again," he growled.

Her small hands touched his cheeks, cradling his jaw. "Sir."

She knew exactly what she was doing to him.

"Bedroom. Now."

Scurrying off his lap, she rushed to the bedroom as he followed her closely, stalking her. His cock hardened further as he watched her sweet round ass jiggle with each step she took. Stopping in front of the bed, she kept her back to him. He grabbed her ass roughly, squeezing the globes in his hands hard enough to send a shiver of need down her spine. She leant into him, resting her back against his chest. His sweet little sub.

Fuck, he needed her.

"Strip for me."

She obeyed without hesitation, pulling her shirt over her head to reveal her breasts encased in a barely there lacy black bra. *Fuck, her tits are amazing*. He took a step back to watch her remove her undergarments, taking in the curves of her luscious body. He was so far gone he barely noticed the massive bruise that still marred her chest. He'd have to remember to be careful with her arm.

Her pupils dilated as she finished stripping, her cheeks flushing as she bit down on her bottom lip and looked up at him. The little vixen knew that look drove him wild. Using his size, he crowded her, pushing her back onto the bed before he captured her mouth. He glided his fingers between her legs, finding her pussy nice and wet. He loved how she was always ready for him.

"Can you clasp your hands up above your head?"

She did so without a wince, not showing any sign of pain from her injury. Even with a high threshold, her ability to get over the injury was impressive.

"Keep them there. Tell me the second it begins to hurt."

"It's fine. I promise," she reassured him, then pursed her lips and gave him a look of worry because she'd spoken.

He inserted two fingers inside her cunt, smiling when she gasped at the intrusion.

"I'm going to fuck you, Amara," he told her. "It's going to be hard. I'm going to use your body until I'm completely spent. And you have zero say in what happens."

Her cunt clenched around his fingers as she became even wetter. She wanted it. Wanted him. She swallowed and nodded, a delicious amount of anxiety in her eyes. Removing his fingers, he put them in his mouth and sucked them clean, enjoying her sweet honey taste.

Though she tried to hide it, he heard her whisper of "fuck" under her breath.

"Do not move."

In one movement, he thrust inside of her, filling her. Then he fucked her.

* * * *

Amara lay on the bed, trembling and quivering with aftershocks from an orgasm so intense she'd actually screamed so hard that she'd tasted blood. Her chest ached from her hands being pinned above her head for so long. Her legs hurt from being restrained in so many different positions. At one point, her ankles were up by her ears, so he could bury himself so deeply inside of her that she could still feel him. She'd never been so thoroughly used. And he had used her. He'd taken what he wanted, not giving a shit how hard he pushed her.

Sullivan went about moving her relaxed, sated body so she was curled into him. His chest was still heaving. He'd come hard, twice, and that did wonders for her self-esteem. She shuffled up further so her head rested on his pillow, her eyes level with his. He appeared spent and satisfied. But the haunted expression took over again. As soon as he was out of control, he was back to struggling with his emotions. And she would try her hardest to help him with it.

She ran her fingers over his stubbled cheek, enjoying the way his cheek creased beneath her touch. "What can I do?"

Continuing to touch him, she watched as the firmness of his brow slowly released. His lush lips were still pursed. Propping herself on one elbow, she ran her thumb over his lips, surprised and aroused when he pulled it into his mouth and sucked. The sensation sent jolts of arousal straight to her clit. God, the man brought a response out of her even when she was exhausted and couldn't handle any more.

"There must be something I can do," she mused as she continued to run her fingers over his face, down his throat to rest on his chest.

He considered her for a moment, tightening his arm around her. "Stay with me tonight."

She'd already said she was. "Sullivan—"

"Please. Just stay. That's all I need."

The look in his eyes almost broke her. He appeared so hurt.

"You know it's okay not to be okay," she told him, pressing her lips to his cheek as her fingers ran patterns around his chest.

"I just need you. Nothing more. Nothing less."

* * * *

They spent the evening in bed, snuggled under the covers and watching television. After dinner, Amara leant up for him and returned to her previous position, where she held him in her arms, his head resting comfortably on her breast. She caressed him, held him, loved him. He let her take care of him for once and she enjoyed every second of it.

Sullivan's phone sounded with a text message, startling Amara out of her comfortable daze. She caught the text over his shoulder and noted it was Grayson.

"Is he checking on you?"

"He would usually come with me today. I told him you were instead."

"Have you ever taken a girl to meet your mum before?"

He shook his head, his hair grazing her bare breasts in the most delicious way.

"Not even the ex you lived with?"

While he still might not have shared all that much about that relationship, Amara knew they'd lived together for a few years. She had to assume that woman had met his mother.

"The only person I've ever taken is Grayson. That's only because he knew her before."

The gravity of his words hit her. He'd never taken a partner to meet his mum. Yet he'd taken her. He had trusted her enough to help him afterwards. He'd allowed her to care for him all evening.

"I'm happy you have a friend like him to rely on." Tears burned her eyes and she willed them away. Now was not the time for her to get emotional. "Thank you for letting me be there for you today."

"Well, I—" He cut himself off. "You're special to me."

Heart caught in her throat, she waited as he moved to sit up and face her. Bringing one hand to touch her face tenderly, he dipped his head and kissed her, pouring his emotions into the kiss. It was so soft, sweet, gentle and filled with adoration that it made her ache.

"You're special to me, too." She rested her forehead on his in an intimate gesture. "I'm falling for you so hard and so fast…"

"It's scaring you."

Her cheeks flushed as he pinned her with his gaze. "Yeah. It is."

Never had she expected to find someone like Sullivan. Since her first relationship, she'd been careful to keep barriers around her heart, careful not to let anyone in. Somehow, Sullivan had smashed through them all, buried himself deep inside of her heart and was not letting go. He completed her in a way that had her missing him when they were apart. Amara thought she'd been in love before, but she had been so very wrong about that.

He kissed her, a brush of his lips against hers.

"I feel exactly the same way."

His phone made a sound again. He shifted to read. "Grayson is having a barbecue next weekend and invited you. Well, he said you're coming whether you like it or not."

Amara's breath caught in her throat. First, he'd taken her to meet his mother, and now she was going to meet his friends. That little scared part of her wanted to say no—the part that didn't want to acknowledge her true feelings for him. But it was small and easy to ignore.

"He sounds bossy."

"He is that. He's also the most dominant person I've ever met."

"Are all of your friends in the lifestyle?"

"Most, but not all." He regarded her with a small smile. "Are you nervous about meeting them all at once?"

"Just a little."

"Tell you what. Since we never made it to the club last night or last week…"

"And whose fault is that?" When she'd arrived ready to go to Haven last night, he'd taken one look at her and ordered her to strip.

"It's yours. You're dressing so damn seductively."

She hit his chest lightly and laughed.

"How about we actually visit the club this Friday and you can meet Grayson properly before I throw you in the deep end?"

She smiled, relief flooding through her. "That sounds like a good plan."

Chapter Seventeen

Amara squeezed Sullivan's hand as he led her through the main room of Haven. The sounds of slapping flesh, moans and cries made her shudder with anticipation. She'd only been here a few minutes and was already so wet she could feel it on her inner thighs. Attending the club with Sullivan was very different than being there alone. She was in a constant state of awareness and arousal.

Before, she'd been nervous, anxious at the thought of being hunted by Dominants she didn't know. Now, Amara was hot at the knowledge that Sullivan could do whatever he wanted to her, wherever, in a public place. But the thought of playing in public naked and on display still gave her so much anxiety it left her mouth dry.

He removed his hand from hers, running it down her back to her arse. His possessive grip had her looking up at him with wide eyes. She knew that touch well. Stopping dead in his tracks, Sullivan moved his other hand to grope her breast through the thin material of her top before he kissed her. The kiss was one of pure ownership, as though he had every right to do it. And he did. He'd just claimed her in front of everyone.

She'd agreed that, for tonight, she would be one-hundred-percent submissive with him. Once he was done with his dungeon monitor duties, she would leave herself entirely available to him, only speaking with permission, kneeling at his feet, not interacting with anyone else. But first, she would meet his best friend and was allowed to be herself with him.

His small hum of satisfaction was music to her ears and gave her a tingle in the small of her back. She gave him that silly grin she always did when she felt his possession and pressed herself against him.

"Remember, if Grayson gets called away, you either follow him or go straight to the subbie area until he retrieves you."

He kissed her again and ran a finger between her collar and her throat. While at the club, she would wear his collar to show that she was his and his alone. And it filled her with such joy she couldn't wipe the stupid smile from her face. He moved his hand further down and pulled the plunging neckline of her top to expose her breast. She instinctively covered herself up with her hand and stared at him in disbelief.

"Don't forget, little sub, this is *my* body. Do not cover it up."

She pursed her lips and frowned at him. "Permission to speak freely, Sir?"

He smiled. Calling him 'Sir' pleased him.

"Granted."

"I am aware we made an agreement. However, I am not going to meet your best friend with my tits hanging out." She stuck her chin out. "Sir."

A smile creased his cheek. "Nice save."

He covered her breast up. "Fair enough, sweetheart. But after I'm done with my duty, you will be naked and mine for the taking, regardless of whether my friends are around."

A shudder ran through her body at his threat and promise. Only he could get her excited about being naked in front of others.

Sullivan led her to the far back corner of the main room, to a slightly elevated roped-off area where Grayson sat in a chair alone. A king looking over his domain. Amara suddenly got very nervous. For all intents and purposes, this man was Sullivan's brother. His family. She needed to make a good impression on him.

The man exuded dominance. Sitting back lazily, his arm resting on the back of the dark leather lounge, he regarded them before a grin split his incredibly handsome face and he stood.

Amara had forgotten how tall he was. Grayson towered over her. He had to be six foot five, the same height as Jackson, but he carried himself very differently. He was broad, well-muscled and had a presence about him, an aura of importance.

"Grayson, you remember Amara."

Grayson held her hand in his, squeezing gently. "It's a pleasure to see you again, Amara."

"Likewise," she said and offered him a friendly smile.

God, the man brought out her submissive side. She barely fought the need to avoid his gaze and kneel at his feet.

He gestured for them to sit on the lounge next to his. She hesitated and glanced at Sullivan who sat and patted his lap. Of course he wanted her in his lap. Sitting in his lap, with the two of them, she couldn't help but wonder if the two men had ever tag-teamed a woman. They would definitely make a sub feel desired. Right now, Grayson was looking her up and down with the expression of an appreciative Dom. Everything about his movements spoke of confidence and a careful power, while Sullivan had a more laid-back grace and dominance. But both were very strong men.

The two men discussed club business for a few minutes before Sullivan had to leave to do his dungeon monitor duties. He ordered Amara to sit at Grayson's side and not move. Sitting next to the tall and broad man had her more than a little intimidated but somewhat at ease. How did a man so domineering also come across as friendly? She could sense that there was a softness to him that not many people got to see.

"I'm glad you came tonight. I've been wanting to speak with you alone."

"Oh? About what?"

"About Sullivan." He chuckled when he saw her wary expression. "Don't worry, I'm not going to warn you away from him or anything like that."

"Good. Because then we would definitely have a fight on our hands."

The lines around his eyes crinkled as he laughed openly. "I see why he enjoys you so much, little subbie."

The term of endearment from him made her smile.

"Before he started seeing you, my dear friend was withdrawing from us. Other than playing at the club, he wasn't socialising much. He was completely buried in work and showed no interest in dating at all."

Amara wasn't surprised. He'd told her as much when they began dating.

"Since he's started seeing you, however, he's turned back into his former self. I haven't seen him so happy in years, if ever. He reminds me of that happy little kid he used to be. He's enjoying life again and speaking of the future seriously, something he hasn't done since he was with his ex."

"She really did a number on him, didn't she?"

"The woman had us all fooled." Grayson pursed his lips and looked over the club. "But she completely betrayed his trust."

Anger rose in Amara at the thought of someone playing Sullivan for a fool, of taking advantage of his generous nature. He was the single most selfless man she'd ever met. If she ever saw the woman, she would bitch-slap her silly.

Grayson wrapped his fingers around her tightly fisted hands and smiled down at her.

"I see you're as protective of him as I am."

"I hate the thought of someone taking advantage of him," she all but growled.

"Amara." His voice held a hint of tenderness as he looked down at her. "Thank you for giving me my best friend back."

Amara smiled up at Grayson, grateful Sullivan had a friend like him to have his back.

"I can see why Sullivan loves you so much."

"Likewise," he said with a wink.

Sullivan looked to where his best friend sat with his love. With her legs crossed towards him, Amara looked at Grayson and laughed openly at something he said. He'd thought they would get along well but couldn't deny he'd been slightly anxious when he'd brought them together. They were quite similar in a lot of ways. Amara was as dominant and protective as Grayson was. Both were fiercely loyal and loved deeply. As did he.

He approached the two of them when his duties were finally done and enjoyed the way Amara's eyes lit up when she saw him.

"Would you like me to get you a drink?" she asked when he sat on the other lounge.

"Please, sweetheart. Just water would be great. Get yourself one, too. You're going to need it."

With an eager smile, she bounced to her feet and left.

"She's definitely something else," Grayson said. "I see why you love her."

"Is it that obvious?"

"I don't think anybody who doesn't know you well would be able to tell. Your reputation will hold up."

"My reputation is the last thing on my mind."

Sullivan thought about his player reputation amongst the lifestyle. He wasn't like that, not really. He'd hated it but it had been necessary to protect himself. Deep down, he was built to be monogamous. He had thought he'd never get that chance to trust again, then Amara came along and knocked down all the barriers he'd put up.

His little sub approached with two bottled waters and eyed the floor, obviously wondering if now was the time to kneel at his feet. He tapped his lap and brought her down to sit over his thighs instead. That seemed to please her. She undid the cap of one bottle and handed it to him, pressing a light kiss to his cheek as she did. The woman was so sweet, how could he not melt around her?

"Are you playing tonight?" Grayson asked.

"I've reserved an area in the dungeon for us. In fact, we'd better get going."

"Have fun, you two."

His friend gave him a knowing smile as Amara hopped off Sullivan's lap and waited for him to lead her away. She'd begun to think as they approached the roped-off scene area. Her shoulders had tensed, lips had pursed and her eyes were darting around the room as she looked at all the strangers.

"Stop thinking so hard," he growled in her ear.

She looked up at him and forced a smile. "I'm not."

"Now you're lying to me." He frowned down at her. "That's five swats."

She gaped, eyes wide as she looked at him with the cutest damned expression of shock and outrage. "You can't do that!"

"Want to make it ten?" He loved smacking that big round ass of hers.

She snapped her mouth shut and frowned. *Smart girl.* "No, Sir."

"Good girl." He gave her the endearment she loved. Sure enough, her cheeks flushed as she smiled and leant more of her weight into him.

Stepping into the area, he removed the reserved sign and placed his toy bag on the small table near the chains that hung from the ceiling beams. Gesturing for Amara to kneel in front of the station, he went about removing his tools for the night from his bag, setting them out for easy access. He turned to face her, looked up at the chains and played out the scene he'd been planning all week.

Thick adjustable chains hung from two bolt holes in the reinforced beams. After asking Amara to stand, Sullivan removed her flimsy top and watched as she fought the instinct to cover herself. It had been a long time since she'd been naked in public, and he could see her inner turmoil. The mere fact that she'd been willing to attempt a public scene meant the world to him, filling him with pride and joy as he realised that he'd earned her total trust.

He still couldn't understand why she lacked body confidence. Her body was purely mouth-watering, all softness and curves that he wanted to bury himself in. She had a body most Doms would dream of playing with. Why couldn't she see that? Before the night was through, she would.

Placing the cuffs he'd specifically bought for her on her wrists, he held out her arms before her. She noted the engraving of his initials and tears filled her eyes.

"From now on, when we're here or in a scene at home, you wear these. To show everybody that you're mine."

"Thank you, Sir." She ran her fingers over the lined cuffs, her smile growing as she looked up at him. "I love them."

He pressed a small kiss to her lips and moved her into position. Attaching the cuffs to the chains, he tightened them so her arms were positioned in a wide V, her back towards the main room.

"To begin with, you will face away from the audience. Then, when I wish, you will be on display." He ran his knuckles over her cheek as her anxiety-filled eyes glistened. "And you will do it because I want you to."

When her eyes showed true fear, he frowned. A healthy dose of anxiety was good for a scene, but true fear was not.

"Do you trust me, Amara?"

"Of course I do," she replied as though he'd just asked the most ridiculous question possible. "I'm just... I'm scared."

It took courage for her to admit that. He rewarded her with a long, deep kiss and caught her chin in his fingers when she tried to turn away from him.

"Sweetheart, would you like the blindfold?"

She gave him a small nod.

Offering a smile before he disappeared, he grabbed the blindfold he'd known he'd need and placed it over her eyes.

"You are a beautiful woman, Amara," he whispered as he tied it at the back of her head. "I love everything about your body and so should you."

"I'm trying." She pouted as she held her head up bravely.

"I know you are." She had been trying very hard recently, but it would take time for her to see her body the way he did. "I'm proud of you for taking this step tonight for me. If at any point you feel uncomfortable, you say yellow, and we'll slow down."

Another small nod.

"Now, no more speaking, little sub." He rubbed his cheek on hers and pressed a kiss to her lips, pleased when she tried to seek more as he pulled away.

Sullivan stood behind Amara, the flogger slowly hitting her skin in gentle strokes, warming up her skin.

She tried to get into the submissive headspace she'd been in but it had gone away when he took her top from her. Though the blindfold helped her not feel quite so self-conscious, it didn't remove the anxiety altogether. Her heart thudded against her chest, breath finally slowing down as his warm body pressed against her back.

"Nobody's opinion should matter to you but mine," he whispered into her ear. "Focus only on me, on my touch. *I* love your body. It's pure perfection."

One big hand came around her front to hold her breast. He ran his thumb over her nipple, smiling into her neck when it peaked beneath his touch.

"Your body responds to me nicely. Focus on that. I want only you and your perfect body."

He pressed a kiss to her neck and moved back to flog her once more. His touch did wonders. This was just like playing at home. And really, nobody was going to be paying attention to her, were they? They'd be too wrapped up in their own play to bother watching them. The only one looking at her was Sullivan. And he loved her body, always made her feel beautiful.

The flogger stopped again and his hand suddenly touched her mound, one thick finger invading her without warning. She sucked in a gasp as his solid body pressed against her back. He was shirtless now, his skin hot against her bare back. When he stuck to her, she realised she was covered in a thin sheen of sweat.

"You are utterly perfect, my sweet Amara," he whispered in her ear as he continued to play with her cunt.

One finger spread her wetness to her clit, which throbbed as he ran his finger along one side, then the other, never quite touching where she wanted him to.

He stepped away and began to flog her again. The strands were longer, thicker and heavier this time. When he took a break, he alternated between playing with her pussy and her breasts, teasing her into a frenzy. All other thoughts had been completely wiped from her mind and her sole focus was on Sullivan and what he was doing to her. One hand played with her breasts while the other played with her pussy. Two fingers thrust inside of her, bringing her up onto her toes as he finger-fucked her hard and fast. She cried out, needing just a little more…

"Come for me, sweetheart." The growled words in her ear pushed her over the edge.

She came on his fingers, crying out as her entire body tingled with awareness, her muscles relaxing. Loneliness swept over her, and even though she could feel his presence in front of her, no doubt assessing her, she wanted nothing more than a kiss. His kisses were everything to her. Tilting her head up, she whispered, "Please," sighing into his mouth when he obliged and kissed her softly and sweetly. It soon became hungry and oh, so dominant that it left her breathless, floating on a cloud.

His hands moved along her waist, down her back to the zipper of her skirt. Undoing it, he slid the material down her legs, the cool air wafting over her bare ass and pussy. Suddenly she felt very, very naked. Closing her legs in embarrassment, she felt his firm hands open them wide to her previous position. Only now she was open and bare for everyone to see.

Oh God. I can't do this.

She began to slowly relax again as he took his time to graze his hands up and down her legs. He caressed her skin, his lips following the trail up and down her legs, to her inner thighs towards the juncture of her thighs. Wanting his mouth on her so badly she ached, she whined in disappointment when his mouth left her skin. Cuffing her ankles, he placed a spreader bar between her feet, adding to the delicious helplessness that filled her.

The flogging began again, this time lightly on her front, across her breasts, down her stomach, her thighs, down, then back up again. Soon enough, she began to drift away, floating to that happy place where nothing else mattered but sensation. There was no fear, no worry, nothing but the feeling of her Dom pleasing her.

Sullivan watched as Amara's head dropped to rest on her upper arm as she lost herself in the sensations he was giving. He had turned her to face the crowd they'd attracted but she hadn't noticed. She was on full display now and couldn't have made him prouder. He continued playing with her, hitting her a little harder with his heavy flogger, working her body to its peak, losing himself in Domspace as he moved.

Adding another element to her pleasure, he picked up a medium-sized vibrator and inserted it into her pussy. She was so fucking wet it slipped in easily, staying in as she clenched around it. Switching on the vibration, he smiled at her breathy moan, his chest tightening at the sound.

Fuck, she really was the most gorgeous thing he'd ever seen, skin all pink and flushed, lips parted on a silent cry, head still resting on her arm. Her lips moved in a silent plea. She needed more. Happy to oblige, he got on his knees in front of her and bent his head, flicking his tongue over her clit. He worked the distended nub before placing his lips around it, sucking hard.

She came with a cry, her hips bucking into his face. Her entire body trembled when he wiggled the vibrator inside of her, tilting it so it touched her G-spot. She came again in an instant. A loud sob escaped her throat as her head dropped forward and a few tears slipped from beneath the blindfold.

Perfection.

Grasping her hair, he tilted her head back and kissed her thoroughly. He slipped off the blindfold and noted her glazed eyes barely registered his presence. A slow smile spread across her swollen lips as she looked up at him.

"I did it," she whispered.

"You did it," he agreed, heart swelling with pride. "I'm so fucking proud of you, my love."

He quickly went about removing the vibrator and packed away his things before he uncuffed her. Her knees buckled when he removed the spreader bar. She'd definitely had enough. He caught her and gestured for Grayson to help. His friend had watched the entire scene with a smile on his face. He knew what a big deal this was to Amara and to Sullivan.

Wrapping a subbie blanket around her, Sullivan scooped her into his arms and made his way to the quiet recovery corner, where Grayson met him with his bag. Huddled in his lap, Amara let out a small whimper as he moved to hold her properly. Like a content kitten, she curled up and rested her head on his shoulder, letting out small noises and hums of satisfaction.

"That was beautiful," a Domme whispered as she walked by and dropped a bar of plain milk chocolate on the table beside him.

Others made their way past, giving him their congratulations on the way, telling him what a beautiful scene it was. And it had been. She'd given herself over to him completely, given him all of her trust despite her reservations. He'd never been so complete before.

"I love you, Amara," he whispered into her hair as he pressed a kiss to the top of her head.

She murmured something unintelligible back and curled her fingers into his chest. He felt wetness on his skin and peered down to find her weeping silently. It had been emotional for both of them, but it had taken a lot out of her. He knew it would. His cute little sub soon fell asleep in his arms, going completely limp while remaining curled into him.

Grayson joined him and they conversed quietly while she slept. When she eventually began to stir, the club atmosphere was beginning to die down. While there was no official closing time to Haven, it was obvious very few people remained. He placed a bottle of water in her hands and forced her to drink. Amara downed the entire thing in no time and took the chocolate he fed her piece by piece, licking his fingers with each piece she took.

Fuck, she was something else.

"We need to get going, sweetheart," he told her once she was able to sit up unaided. "Let's get you dressed."

Realising she was completely naked, she looked at him with wide eyes and covered herself up further with the blanket.

He leant forward to nuzzle her neck. "Relax. You did it. You're done."

"I did it." She grinned up at him proudly, her face absolutely beaming. "I really did it."

Chapter Eighteen

Amara still felt a glow of pride the next day. She'd played in front of an audience, completely naked, and had let go, placing her trust in Sullivan one hundred percent. Still so proud of herself, she couldn't stop smiling each time she looked at him. He'd been so proud of her last night, it had filled her with the ultimate pleasure, that of pleasing her Dom.

People had approached them after, telling him how beautiful the scene was, how beautiful she was. Some even commented on her body, one woman calling her delicious, telling Sullivan what a lucky man he was. But no, she was the lucky one. Because of him, she'd overcome her fears of playing in front of others. She had feared it for nothing. Nobody had made a negative comment about her body. Nobody seemed to notice her flabby areas or her new stretch marks. Nobody had been as cruel as she had been to herself.

Now she couldn't wait to visit the club again to do a public scene. A weight had been lifted off her shoulders and she was excited by the thought of public play, just as she'd once been.

She had one more hurdle to overcome with Sullivan—meeting his friends today. The fact she'd spent time with Grayson last night made her feel a little more at ease as she entered his home. Grayson seemed like a great guy. He very openly cared for Sullivan and treated him like a brother. He'd grilled Amara about her past relationships, asking why they'd ended, if she'd ever cheated. He asked about her background, her family, her friends, filling in all the blanks. At the end of the night, it appeared he approved of her. He'd given her a kiss on the cheek, called her 'pet' and told her he couldn't wait to see her in a more relaxed environment. Amara liked the man.

Fidgeting with the clasp on her handbag, Amara smiled when Grayson spotted the two of them and made his way over. He greeted Amara with a kiss on the cheek, gave Sullivan a quick hug and led them to his backyard. Like Sullivan, he lived in a semi-rural area on acreage. Unlike Sullivan's house, Grayson's was completed and what a property it was.

Beautifully wild gardens lined the patio area, surrounding his gigantic pool and the stone paths that led to several different-sized sheds, one of which had the door open to reveal a huge dungeon.

"Want to go check it out?" Grayson asked her.

She looked to Sullivan for approval. "Go ahead. I'll get you a drink."

"Come on, pet. You're going to love this."

The massive shed was set up much like personal dungeons she'd seen, with equipment scattered everywhere, except this one also contained private sitting areas, a small, fully stocked bar and an entire wall set up with toys.

"This is my own personal dungeon, but I also have parties here."

"That explains all the lounges and chairs."

"I'm thinking of having one in a couple of weeks. I hope you and Van will attend."

"I'm sorry, Van?" she asked with a snicker.

"It's a childhood nickname."

"Oh wow. I'll definitely never call him that." She laughed again.

"It's better than squirt, which is what Brady and I used to call him."

"You're an arsehole," Sullivan called out from behind them before handing Amara a Pepsi Max. "You can't be telling her things like that."

"Sorry, squirt," Grayson said, then ruffled his hair playfully.

Amara stood back and watched the two of them interact with a big grin. She loved seeing them together.

"So, Amara, can you try to convince your Dom here to build himself a dungeon like this on his property? He's got more than enough room for one."

She all but beamed as she looked at Sullivan. She'd always wanted a personal dungeon to play in. And Sullivan could build a proverbial playground in his yard.

"Oh please, it would be so much fun to have our own wonderland to play in."

"I don't even have a garden yet. Let me work on that before you try to bombard me with dungeon ideas."

"Oh, about that." She poked his chest. "Belle said she'd come over and take a look. She'd love to tackle a property like yours and she'll do mates rates."

Sullivan grinned down at her. "Then bring her over and let's see what she suggests. I'll be helping her out with the hard work, though."

"My friend, Belle, runs a landscaping and maintenance service," she told Grayson. "I showed her a couple of photos of his yard and she was both mortified and excited to get her hands on it."

"Is this Ayden's Belle?"

Amara nodded. "The very same."

"I was surprised when she said she wasn't coming here today."

"She doesn't do things like that with her fuck buddies. Says it's too close to getting into a real relationship."

"That's a shame. She seems like an amazing woman from what I've seen."

"She really is. But she has her reasons for it."

And Amara would definitely not be going into those reasons with two nosy Doms who would take it upon themselves to fix her.

"Come on, let's introduce you to everyone," Sullivan said as he wrapped his arm around her.

* * * *

After being introduced to about a dozen different people, Amara worked hard to try to remember their names. Most of them were involved in the lifestyle, with a few of Grayson's vanilla work friends scattered amongst the crowd. The divide became evident as the afternoon wore on.

Amara settled into a very easy conversation with Ellie, who turned out to be absolutely delightful. And also a submissive who had watched their scene at Haven last night.

"So, Sullivan says you recently started working as a property manager again," the perky blonde said. "You do the routine inspections, right?"

Amara smirked, knowing exactly where she was going. Everybody always wanted to know what she'd walked in on during a routine inspection. More often than not the house was empty, but every now and then, she walked in on some people in compromising positions.

"What's the most embarrassing or interesting thing you've walked in on?"

"I've walked in on quite a few people fast asleep. Woken a few while wandering around the house. It's super awkward. But I think the most embarrassing thing was when I walked in on a couple having an afternoon delight."

"You're kidding." Grayson laughed.

"I'm not sure who was more embarrassed, me or them. They had totally forgotten I was showing up that day. I could hear them moving around inside the house and must have knocked five times before I let myself in. And then I found them, right there on the kitchen bench going to town on each other."

Those around her laughed, including Sullivan, even though he'd already heard the story. Only he got to hear about how she was so turned on from witnessing it that she had to sit in the car for several minutes to calm herself down.

"I felt like such a voyeur."

"There's nothing wrong with being a voyeur," Grayson commented. "Especially in the right setting."

Sullivan rolled his eyes and said to Amara, "I told you he was a pervert."

She giggled in response.

"Hey, I know what I like and I'm not going to apologise for it."

Amara's phone rang in her bag. She reached in to find Bridget calling her. *Shit. This can't be good.* Bridget never called her.

Excusing herself, Amara made her way inside where it was a little quieter.

"Hey, Bridget, what's up?"

"I know you're out and I'm sorry to interrupt, I just didn't want to text you with this," she said, her voice calm and collected. "Your mum had an awkward fall while we were on a little hike. She's fine now but she dislocated her elbow. We've got her at the hospital, they've set it and have given her painkillers, we're just waiting for discharge. Your dad asked that I call and let you know what happened."

Amara's mood dropped instantly. Why the fuck did these things happen when she was out having fun? Why did they happen, period?

"Is she okay? She's not in pain?"

"She's fine. You can speak to her, hang on." Amara heard Bridget change the phone to speaker mode. "She's just a bit loopy."

She heard Mum giggling away in the background as she did when she was high on painkillers.

"I can hear her."

"Drew and Dave will be here any minute. We've got it handled. Don't worry about a thing."

"Thanks, Bridget," Amara said with a sigh. "Tell her I'll see her tonight."

"No, you won't," Mum called out. "You're staying out. I want those grandchildren, dammit."

"Mum." Amara couldn't help but laugh at the inappropriate comment. Painkillers always turned her up a notch.

"If she needs extra help, I'll give your dad a hand. We were planning on staying well into the night anyway. You have fun, sweetie."

After a few moments, Amara agreed. They could handle it, right? Right. They were competent adults. Dad had been caring for Mum long enough now that he had it under control. And, if Amara was ever going to get back to living on her own, she had to hand over control.

"Thanks, Bridget."

As much as it put a dampener on her mood, she would rather have been called instead of getting home tomorrow to find out what had happened. Sullivan's warm hands closed over her shoulders and she all but melted into him. Blinking back tears, she turned to face him and allowed him to hold her. She hadn't been close to crying before, only when he'd approached. And why the hell was that?

Suck it up, woman. And that's what she did.

Sullivan watched Amara on the phone, her shoulders slumped as a defeated appearance came over her. Something had happened to Mari, that much was evident. Amara only got that weighted appearance when something happened to her mum. The amount of stress on her was too much for him to watch. She took on everything as though she had to handle it alone. But she wasn't alone. She had plenty of help now — she just had to recognise it.

When he rested his hands on her shoulders, she turned in his arms and rested against him. Blinking back tears, she insisted she was okay as she told him what had happened to Mari. The poor thing appeared so stressed he wanted to take her home right away and spend the rest of the evening pampering her. Instead, she put on that beautiful smile and insisted they stay, that she was having fun.

She'd fit right in with his friends, laughing, teasing, even having a little deep and meaningful conversation with Ellie at one point. He hadn't expected the two of them to hit it off so well, but was happy they had. Ellie was wise beyond her years, as was Amara. They'd both experienced challenges that not many others would understand. It seemed they had bonded over caring for their ill parents.

When the night was over, Sullivan drove home, his hand wrapped around Amara's. The second they left Grayson's driveway, Amara's energy dropped. Her shoulders slumped as she rested her arm against the window and stared out the windscreen. When she caught him looking at her, she offered him a genuine smile.

Brave little sub.

"How are you doing?"

"I'm okay," she answered, sounding more fatigued than she looked. "I'm just tired."

"You want to talk about it?"

"Can we just drive? I need a minute."

He agreed. The last thing he wanted to do was push her and ruin the great day they'd had. She gave his fingers a light squeeze but didn't let go as she slipped further down the seat.

Defeated. She looked defeated.

It was a far cry from the completion and happiness on her face last night and this morning. She'd had such a great day today, smiling almost constantly. He loved seeing that sparkle in her light eyes as she connected with his friends.

When they arrived home, she headed straight for the couch while he got her a water. Sitting down, he pulled her feet into his lap and began to rub them. It wasn't something she let him do often enough because, in her words, *"Feet are gross."* But he loved touching every single part of her, including her long and slender feet. Her toes curled as he rubbed his thumbs into her arch and a small shudder spread through her.

"Have you heard from your dad?"

Her phone had gone off as they drove in the driveway.

"He says she's fine," she said before yawning. "She's not feeling any pain yet. He's got it handled."

"Can I do anything for you?"

At his words, her face crumbled, tears springing to her eyes. She buried her face in her hands and snatched her feet from his grip to curl up into herself. To shut down as she often tried to when her emotions became too much for her to handle.

Oh no, you don't.

He scooped her onto his lap and held her, pushing her head to rest on his shoulder. Right where she belonged when she was upset.

"It's okay, sweetheart," he soothed. "I've got you."

He wanted to take away all her pain, all her worry, to make everything better. To make her feel safe. He'd been worried about Mari, too. His first reaction had been to leave his friend's house and drive to the hospital to see her. Not that there was anything they could do for her. But it was in his nature to care, just as it was Amara's. Now, he was just worried about Amara. She might try to put on a tough front, cover her emotions with sarcasm and jokes, but she was far more fragile than she realised. He hated seeing her upset. It broke something deep inside of him.

"I'm so tired," she muttered once she'd calmed a little. "Why don't I get one week without something happening to her? It seems like every time I try to live my life, something pulls me right back."

He didn't answer. That wasn't what she needed right now. She needed him to just listen.

"I feel so guilty for not being there all the time." Moving to sit up, she wiped her tear-stained cheeks. "I'm sorry. I never used to cry. Why do I always cry around you?"

"Because you know you're safe with me." He ran a hand over her cheek, pushing her hair behind her ear. "It's healthy to cry when you're overflowing with emotion." He pressed a soft kiss to her cheek. "But if you apologise for it again, I'm adding more swats to your tally. I still owe you five from last night."

"Don't joke about that." She looked down and fiddled with the buttons of his shirt.

"Who said I'm joking?" He was dead serious.

She looked at him and bit the inside of her bottom lip, lost in her thoughts again. "I feel so torn. I had so much fun today, being out with you, spending time with your friends without a care in the world. But part of me feels the need to be with Mum." A heavy sigh. "I'm having trouble letting go."

"I know, sweetheart." He really did understand where she was coming from. He'd gone through the same thing when he'd put his mum in the care facility

She gave him a weak smile, but it reached her eyes. "You do know, don't you? You're the only person who knows how it feels."

"I am." He touched her cheek gently, smiling when she leant into his touch.

"How did you do it? How did you let go?"

He watched her carefully, moving his hand up and down her legs as she remained curled up in his lap.

"It was hard. Carer's guilt is real. But at some point, you need to realise she's not going to get any better and you can't continue to live your life for her. You need to live for yourself. How many times has your mum told you to do just that?" He offered her a smile, moving his hand to run over her hair again. "I bet she told you to stay with me tonight, didn't she?"

"She did."

"Because she wants grandchildren soon." He laughed when she rolled her eyes. "Don't worry, we'll work on that later."

Unable to resist, he kissed her.

"You have two choices. You can either continue as you are, focussing on the guilt until you burn yourself into the ground and lose yourself completely. Or you can make a conscious effort to live. Let go a little more each day. Eventually it will become second nature just like caring did. It's all an adjustment."

He pressed his lips to her cheek, nuzzling her. "You still have a mum. One who loves and supports you. Focus on that rather than the guilt you feel each time you leave her."

He wiped a stray tear from her cheek and kissed her cheekbone. "Carer's guilt is normal. You'll probably always feel it. I know I still do. The key is not to dwell on it."

She didn't realise how much she had. He would have killed for some help while caring for his mum. To have a partner to talk things over with the way she now did with him. Amara remained silent for a few minutes before smiling at him as she brought her hands to rest on either side of his face.

"I'm so happy I found you."

"Me too," he all but whispered and rested his forehead against hers.

Every single day, he thanked the universe for bringing Amara into his life. He couldn't imagine himself without her. She was everything to him.

After her embarrassing outburst, Amara stayed curled up in Sullivan's lap, where she felt safe. Right up until her legs began to protest and cramp. Moving off his lap, she grinned when he pulled her feet back into his lap and rubbed them. She usually hated having her feet touched but had to admit it was different with him. When he massaged them, it was absolutely divine. It was just like a spanking. She'd never truly enjoyed being spanked before, but when he did it, it woke something deep inside of her. Everything he did felt right. Everything with him was different than it had been with anyone else.

She lay back against the arm of the couch and watched him, studying his perfect profile. Amara felt guilt for complaining to him about her difficulties. While he understood her troubles and reservations as a carer, he had lost so much more than she ever had. He shouldn't have been comforting her. Yet he'd held her, cuddled her, while she cried out her frustrations.

I love him so much.

She froze, eyes wide as she stared at him. *Holy shit.* Where had that thought come from? He stilled his movements and looked down at her.

"Well, what was that thought?"

She composed herself and offered him a smile. "Just a stray thought."

A very stray, completely inappropriate, absolutely terrifying thought. She couldn't love him. Not yet. Yet there it was.

"Are you staying tonight?"

"If that's okay with you."

He flashed her that sexy grin that made her insides shudder and melt. He was so beautiful it should have been a crime.

"If I had my way, you'd spend the night far more often."

She smiled. He was nothing if not honest. Sitting up, she moved her feet from his lap and asked for a kiss, then received a beautiful, soft and sweet one that made her toes curl.

"In fact, how about tomorrow we clear out some drawers and space in the wardrobe so you can leave some of your things here? Then you don't have to bring an overnight bag every time you visit."

Looking at him in surprise, she was shocked to realise she wasn't scared. Not like she should have been. She'd moved too fast with previous partners and felt trepidation at it, but this time she felt completely at ease, like it was the next natural step in their relationship.

"It would be nice to not have to carry a bag with me all the time," she reasoned, with herself more than him.

"Great. That's our plan for tomorrow then. We can go shopping and buy you some clothing specifically to keep here. We can even get you some new fetwear to show off at the club."

"I can't afford — "

He covered her mouth with his fingers. "My house, my rules."

She hated when he played that card. But she didn't let him pay for things often. They alternated buying food, and he understood when she said she didn't want him buying her gifts, even though he still did. But the fact was he got enjoyment out of spending his money on her — he'd often told her that.

"I'm getting a drink. Do you want anything?" she asked to cut off her thoughts before she went down the rabbit hole.

"A Pepsi Max please. And grab the chips from the bench."

She did as he asked and curled up at his side once more. It was so easy, being with him. She never felt the need to be anything other than her authentic self. Even when she let out a loud burp from drinking the soda, he laughed and hugged her closer. He fed her chips from his hand, kissed her every so often and when he moved to lie down, he entwined their fingers together and stayed that way.

He was always touching her in some way. It made her feel treasured. She'd never felt this way with anyone else. She could spend her entire life with him and feel complete.

Crap. She really did love him.

Chapter Nineteen

Over the next few weeks, Amara settled into a routine with Sullivan, spending Friday and Saturday nights at his house. She visited him on Wednesday evenings, he stayed Monday and Tuesday evenings at her house then they usually didn't see each other on Thursdays. There were exceptions, of course, but they had ended up spending almost all of their spare time with each other. So far, it was working. They hadn't gotten sick of each other. And her parents loved having him around.

He'd often help out with her mum, even tucking her in a couple of times at Mum's request. The revelation that she loved him had petrified her at the time. Part of her was telling her to pull away from him, not to lose herself in yet another relationship, but she didn't. She couldn't. She ignored that little voice, no matter how hard it had been at first.

God, she did love him, so fucking much. On Friday night, they'd visited Haven again, where he'd introduced her to everyone as either his partner or his submissive. That meant a lot to her, to be publicly claimed. She'd even felt a little smug when she'd gotten disgruntled looks from the other submissives.

Everything was going great for Amara.

So on Wednesday, when she woke with the entire world spinning around her, she wasn't particularly surprised that the universe had decided to throw her a curve ball. Each time she moved, a massive sharp pain stabbed through her head. Thousands of tiny men were jumping around her skull with jackhammers.

Fuck. She hadn't had a migraine in so long, she'd forgotten how bad they could be. She barely managed to get herself out of bed before her stomach lurched. But she had to get to work, had to get Mum ready for the day. First, she took some painkillers, managing to keep them down as she lay back on her bed. When she woke again, it was to her screeching alarm. That only made the pain worse.

Making her way to the living room, she found her mum sitting on the couch, eating her hot oats without a fucking spoon.

"Mum. Stop!"

Mum looked at her, shocked that she'd yelled, her hand still in the food. Amara ran a glass of cold water, pushing past the pain in her head, wiped off her mum's hand and placed her fingers in the water. Her stomach lurched again, her vision blurring as she sat down.

After a few minutes, she pulled Mum's hand out of the water. "Let me see."

She swore under her breath when she noted the bright red fingertips. Luckily, they hadn't blistered. Not yet at least.

"Why weren't you using a spoon?"

"I—" Mum frowned, clearly confused. "I thought I was."

"Does it hurt?"

She shook her head. Further proof that her brain wasn't processing properly. "What are you freaking out about?"

"You've burned your fingers. Hold them in the water until I get back."

She staggered to the bathroom, trying to ignore the golden aura that spread across her vision. Despite Amara having taken painkillers, the migraine continued to get worse. Grabbing the burn spray from her well-stocked first-aid kit in the bathroom, she stopped over the basin to wretch, crying out at the agony that shot through her abdomen.

Making her way to the living room, she sprayed Mum's fingers with the burn spray and regarded her for a minute. How could she ever leave her parents alone when things like this kept happening? It wasn't fair for Dad to deal with it by himself.

"That's life," Sullivan had told her. *"Accidents are going to happen whether you're there or not."*

She knew that, knew he was right. But knowing and accepting were two different things. God damn, she was too tired to deal with this today. The migraine raged on in her head as her vision blurred from the intense pain.

"You look like shit," Mum commented, ever tactful.

"Gee, thanks. I have a migraine."

Amara bit the bullet and called Larissa to let her know she wouldn't be making it into work today. There was no way she could get behind the wheel of a car feeling the way she did. She barely made it to the front door to let Tony in before she stumbled over her own feet.

"Go to bed, peanut," Mum told her as she let her hand graze over her forehead. "I'll look after you."

Too tired to refute her, Amara made her way back to her bedroom and promptly collapsed on the bed. She was out of it before her head hit the pillow.

When she came to, she was hallucinating. She imagined Sullivan's scent wrapping around her. His hand on her cheek, lips on her forehead. Smiling, she ran her fingers along his before giving a hum of gratitude as she swallowed the water he offered her.

"There," he whispered as he kissed her cheek. "Go back to sleep."

She did.

Sitting on the edge of Amara's bed, Sullivan watched her drift back off to sleep, a small smile on her face, a pang in his chest. He'd managed to get her to swallow the oxycodone and found himself glad that he hadn't thrown them out after his knee surgery years ago.

When Mari had texted him to let him know Amara was sick, he wasn't sure what to expect. He wasn't even sure how Mari had gotten his number. Turned out the woman was sneakier than she let on. She'd taken Amara's phone, used her resting face to unlock it and stolen his number. But he was glad she had. Amara looked like hell. Tony had said Amara complained of an aura and blurred vision as well as excruciating pain before she passed out.

Sullivan made his way back to Mari, then sat on the lounge opposite her. She looked a sight. One arm was still bandaged from when she dislocated her elbow and the fingers of the other were in bandages. Luckily, he had the afternoon off and was happy to help out.

It was just after four when he thought about dinner.

"What would you like for dinner? I'll get it started before Drew gets home," he said while Mari busied herself with the puzzle she was doing with Tony.

"You don't have to do that. I should be making you dinner."

He smiled. Even with crippled arms, she was ever the mother. His mum had been much the same before the accident. Nothing could keep her from looking after her kids.

"How about I do all the hard work, since you're injured, and you can supervise." He stood. "I'll make whatever you want."

Helping Mari to her feet, he noted she was much steadier on her feet than she had been in the weeks following her seizure. She hovered in the kitchen and rested her injured hand on the bench, instructing him on how to make Amara's favourite lasagne, which she had planned on making tomorrow night.

Drew arrived home at around five, surprised to find Sullivan there. He thanked him for his help. Sullivan really did like the man. He saw where Amara got her strength and stability from, but all her emotional strength came from her mum. Drew was a hard man, keeping his emotions buried, so very different from Sullivan's own father.

"You may as well stay for dinner, considering you made it," the other man said with a smile.

"I'd appreciate that." He wiped his hands on the tea towel after checking the lasagne. "Do you mind if I check on Amara?"

"Of course." The man waved him off and went to tend to his wife.

Sullivan watched him dote on her, feeling a pang of envy in his chest. They were so similar to his own parents. Growing up, he'd rarely seen his parents outwardly affectionate — they didn't kiss or hold hands, they didn't touch each other much at all, but the way they looked at each other, spoke to each other, cared for each other. They held a love so deep he had thought he'd never experience anything like it. Until he met Amara.

Sitting on the edge of her bed, he found her lying on her back with her hands over her eyes.

"Hey." He ran a hand down her arm gently.

She turned her head, eyes wide with surprise when she registered his presence. "What are you doing here?"

"Your mum texted me and told me you weren't feeling well. I came to relieve Tony. Even made you some dinner."

A tear slipped out of her glazed eye as she reached for his hand. "I love you," she said.

His heart leapt in his chest, swelling at the words. *She loves me.* It could just be the influence of the strong painkillers he'd fed her. Although everything in him wanted to say it back, he didn't. Instead, he wiped her tear and smiled down at her.

"How are you feeling?"

"The pain's almost gone," she slurred. "I feel fuzzy. I can't... My thoughts feel weird."

"That would be the oxy I gave you."

"You drugged me," she teased with a dopey grin. "You don't have to drug me to take advantage of me."

Her words were very slurred and tired. She was definitely under the influence. Smiling, he bent to kiss her. Her lips barely moved beneath his but she gave him that beautiful little hum of contentment that he loved so very much.

"Can you sit up? I'll bring you some dinner when it's ready."

She struggled into a half-seated position and complained the world spun around her. Running his fingers through her hair, he stayed still for a few moments, just enjoying looking at her.

"Has Tony gone?"

"Yes, and your dad is home. Everything's under control."

Tears glistened her red eyes. "She hurt herself this morning because I fell back to sleep."

"I know. It couldn't be helped."

She went to speak but he could see the wave of fatigue wash over her. Despite the strides she'd taken in recent weeks, her first instinct was to think of her mum. It was a hard habit for her to break.

In an effort to distract her, he leant across the bed and kissed her again. It worked a treat. Her hands raised to tangle in his hair. By the time he pulled away, she'd relaxed into the pillows, a lazy smile plastered on her face.

The oven timer went off and he jumped to attention. "Wait here, I'll get you some food."

* * * *

Sullivan spent the night with Amara, giving her another oxycodone so she would sleep through the night when her migraine came back. Mari got up once.

He'd heard instantly, as he'd been sleeping very lightly just in case she wandered. Her wandering reminded him of his own mum. It was hard to ignore the flashbacks that went through his mind. He'd heard her padding through the house and found her at the back door, fighting to unlock it, definitely sleepwalking.

"I'm going to weed the garden," she told him with such sincerity he couldn't help but smile.

"How about you wait until the morning and I'll help you."

She'd begun to argue then stopped mid-sentence. "I'm hungry."

"Let's get you a little snack then."

He ushered her to the kitchen where she had a drink of water, mumbled something about letting the cat out then wandered back to bed. That was something his mum had never done. She'd always fought him when he tried to get her back to bed. More often than not, she would hit him, too. She really had become incredibly abusive in those last few years.

Mari was nothing like his mum. Not really. She was sweet and obliging. She asked him to tuck her in and give her a goodnight kiss.

"You're a good boy, Sullivan," Mari said, tapping her hand gently on his cheek. "I see why Amara loves you."

There was that word again. He wanted to hear it so badly from a sober Amara. He'd thought about saying it to her before they went to sleep. Before the oxy started to affect her. But she'd said it while under the influence. That was good enough for him for now.

* * * *

Grayson was waiting for him the next morning when he arrived at his office. Letting him in, he began to work on his friend's knee immediately.

"Don't you look like the cat who got the cream?" his friend teased.

"I have no idea what you're talking about," Sullivan replied.

"You've got that shit-eating grin that says you got lucky last night and this morning."

Sullivan let out a laugh. "On the contrary. I spent the night looking after Amara who had a migraine, then I helped out with her mum."

"Well, damn, I guess I'm not as observant as I thought."

"You're losing your touch."

Grayson had always been an observant bastard. It was what made him such a good Dom. He seemed to know what was going on with Sullivan before he did.

"I bet looking after her mum brought back some memories, huh?" Grayson winced as Sullivan applied pressure to the outer thigh muscle. "How'd you do?"

"It was fine. Mari is far more compliant than Mum ever was. Didn't argue with me once, even called me a good boy."

Grayson laughed. "She sounds like a good woman."

"She really is."

Sullivan watched as Grayson's brows drew together. "Spit it out, I can hear your brain working overtime."

"You've only been with Amara a couple of months. Are you sure you're not moving too fast? I mean, spending time with her is one thing but you've been spending an awful lot of time with her family as well."

"I love her, man."

A grin spread across the other man's face. "I'm amazed you're admitting that."

"I want to tell her, but I don't want to scare her off. I almost let it slip this morning."

"Maybe you should tell her. It's obvious she loves you too. The way she was looking at you on Friday, I'm amazed she didn't let it slip then."

"Subspace is a wonderful thing, isn't it? When she's lost in it, she tells me exactly what's on her mind." He smiled at the memory of her curled up in his lap, telling him how incredible he was and how she'd never been with someone who came close to him. "She told me she loved me last night, but she was high on oxy. I'm sure that doesn't count."

"Maybe you need to get her blissed out and tell her how you feel, see how she responds. You know whatever answer you get will be an honest one."

"I did that a few weeks ago, after our first public scene." He grinned at his friend's shock. "She was too blissed out. I don't think she even heard me."

He moved to sit in his office chair. "She had a bad experience with an ex, said it too soon, moved too fast and completely lost everything. That's why I'm not pushing it. But fuck... It's so different with her."

"I don't think I've ever seen you so happy. Even with Katerina, you were never this content."

"I know."

"She definitely is something else, my friend."

"That she is."

Chapter Twenty

Amara woke panicking on Friday, sick to her stomach. A memory had just surfaced. In her drugged state on Wednesday night, she'd told Sullivan she loved him. *Oh God.* What had she done? It was too soon to say it. Way too soon. They'd only been together a couple of months. And yes, she definitely loved him. Sullivan completed her in ways she had never thought possible. She missed him when he wasn't around, longed to see him after a day at work. They spent every spare moment together. It felt right to say it to him at the time but still…

She'd already learned the harsh lesson of what saying "I love you" too soon could do. Her first ever boyfriend had said it after three weeks together and she had felt pressured to say it soon after. Then their relationship had moved much too fast. They had moved in together, had spent all of their time together. She'd wasted all her money and effort on making their house a home only to be kicked out and left with nothing. She wouldn't make that mistake again. Even if her relationship with Sullivan was completely different.

Then she realised she'd already begun turning Sullivan's house into her home. She'd moved clothing and toiletries in. Brought him artwork for his bare walls. She'd helped him pick out furniture for his empty formal lounge, something in both of their tastes, so they could use it. She was helping him with the landscaping on the property. *Goddamn.* She was already too involved in a house that wasn't hers. Why did she do that?

Still, it was all different with Sullivan. He'd genuinely wanted her opinion, valued it. He knew how much she loved gardening and had encouraged her to help him and Belle with the landscaping, not taking advantage of her but doing it because he knew it made her happy. And it had. Last weekend they'd spent both days buying and planting native plants around the patio. They'd had so much fun getting dirty together.

As happy as it made Amara, they were moving awfully fast. No, she was moving fast. He hadn't done anything but make her feel wanted, comfortable and loved. He'd told her how much he loved her touches in his house, how it made it feel more like a home than it had since he'd moved in. And that gave her all the warm and fuzzies.

She shook her shoulders out and moved to her small wardrobe to pick out clothing to wear tonight. Sullivan was taking her to Haven where she planned on meeting up with Larissa, Agin and Belle, as well as Grayson and Ayden. Belle and Ayden had recently stopped seeing each other, their relationship having run its course, so

Amara prepared herself for a little awkwardness between the two of them.

Dressed in a new tight black dress that Sullivan had recently bought for her, she smoothed it out and noted how nice it looked without any underwear on beneath it. Luckily it held up her breasts enough that she wouldn't feel constant pain when she went braless. Sullivan had gone full Dom and ordered her not to wear any underwear to the club. He wanted to have easy access to her body whenever they were there. And wasn't that something that made Amara feel damn hot?

She chatted with her parents while waiting for Sullivan to arrive. Of course, her mum quizzed her on what they were doing, where they were going, how late she was going to be out. Amusing her, Amara was thankful that her dad hadn't been around while Mum questioned her. Discussing her dating life in front of her dad had always been a tad more awkward.

Sullivan picked her up, waiting until they got to the car before he all but mauled her. Gripping at her arse, he kissed her thoroughly and pressed his body against hers, his very obvious erection pushing against her belly.

"Sullivan," she breathed. "We're in the middle of my driveway."

"I can't help it." He pulled away, his breath hot on her lips. "You look so fucking *hot*."

The hunger in his eyes was evident. Damn, the man always made her feel attractive, but when she got dressed up, she actually felt like the most beautiful woman in the world.

She pulled down the hem of the dress to where it should be, frowning when Sullivan dragged it back up.

"Tonight, your body is going to be on display." He nuzzled her neck. "I want it on show for everybody to see."

His words sent a shiver down her spine. She loved when he went full Dom on her.

On the drive to the club, she continued to fiddle with her dress, uncomfortable with just how far it had crept up when she sat down. Her pale thunder thighs were going to be on full show all night. While it was just her and Sullivan, that was fine, but in a room full of strangers? She was still getting used to that.

"You're unusually quiet tonight, sweetheart."

"Yeah, I feel a little off," she said quietly. "I think I've got a migraine hangover."

"If you'd prefer, we can spend the night at home," he said as he pulled into the car park of the club.

"No, I'm looking forward to tonight. Just my head's a little fuzzy. Don't blame me if I don't give it my all."

A sexy smile spread across his lips. "Oh, you'll give it your all tonight, whether you like it or not, sweetheart."

He offered her a kiss filled with promise and led her inside the club. After getting them drinks, Sullivan led her to Grayson's private sitting area where Larissa and Agin were already waiting. Agin chatted away to Grayson while his wife knelt at his feet, her head resting on his thigh. She appeared as content as ever. Larissa got off on high protocol, said it completed her, while it made Amara feel a little uneasy. While she would happily kneel at Sullivan's feet and fully expected to while in the club, waiting for permission to speak or move left her feeling a little on edge.

They greeted their friends and Sullivan sat on a large armchair, gesturing for Amara to take her position on the floor. She knelt between his knees, placing her drink on the coffee table in front of her face and slowly but surely relaxed into the position. He ran a gentle hand over her hair, closing his thighs around her shoulders, effectively trapping her. Feeling safe, secure and wanted, she smiled and leant into his touch, zoning out while the men spoke.

A little while later, when Amara had rested her head on his inner thigh, Sullivan leant forward to kiss her neck gently to get her attention.

"Why don't you get us another drink each, my sweet? Water for you. You're going to need to stay hydrated for what I have planned."

"Yes, Sir."

Shuddering as he ran his fingers along her bare shoulder, she stood and joined Larissa as they left the area. Larissa turned to face her as they left, a big grin on her face.

"Did you seriously just call him 'Sir'?"

Amara blushed. "Yeah. It slipped out a few weeks ago and just feels right."

"Wow. I've never heard you call a Dominant 'Sir' or 'Ma'am', ever."

"I never have. It hasn't felt right. I don't do it all the time with Sullivan, so when I do, it earns me brownie points. Often I get a nice little reward for it."

"I'm glad. I know what a big deal it is for you to hand over that power to him."

It really was. Amara looked around the club while they waited for their drinks. "Have you seen Belle yet?"

"She's doing a scene with Eddie." Larissa pointed to a scene area where their friend was strapped to a cross, nipples clamped, wrists and ankles restrained while Eddie went to town on her with his fingers and mouth.

Amara knew first-hand how good the man was. Her friend was in for a treat. He had a talent.

"I thought Eddie had a sub already."

"They share."

Amara saw the little brunette she'd seen him with weeks earlier kneeling just inside the scene area. Watching them intently, she had nothing but arousal in her eyes.

"Looks like we won't be seeing much of Belle tonight."

Their friend cried out as her orgasm approached. Eddie pulled his hands from her to kneel and go down on her.

"What do you guys have planned for tonight?" Amara asked.

"We've reserved a bondage table. He plans on spanking me publicly because I mouthed off to him earlier when he was too slow getting ready."

Amara laughed. "You know better than to mouth off to a sadist, you idiot."

"I may have done it so he would punish me tonight." Larissa's cheeks reddened as she picked up her drinks. "It's been a while since I had a good spanking. I get off on it being done in front of an audience. Are you doing anything public? Now that you're getting more comfortable with it."

"Sullivan has something planned but won't tell me what. He wants it to be a surprise so now I'm an even mix of terrified, anxious and excited."

"That's the best combination."

"I'm still nervous about public play, even though I've done it before."

"I'm sure it'll take a while to get used to it again. But you are the only one focussing on the negatives you see with your body. I bet you see flaws in how you look right now."

She was right. Her stomach had rounded out too much as she relaxed, sagging at the bottom near her mound. Her thighs were too jiggly when she walked, her arms too big. Amara felt like everybody was staring at her, judging her, even though in reality she knew nobody was. Nobody cared what she looked like. Only she had a problem with it.

"Look at her." Larissa gestured to a submissive, bigger than Amara, who was bent over the back of a lounge in a scene area.

Completely naked, she was totally on display, being fucked from behind. Her breasts flopped over the back of the couch, stretch marks evident, and her large, dimpled thighs were spread, jiggling deliciously each time her Dom ploughed into her. It was a beautiful scene to watch. They were both completely lost in it.

"She's bigger than you and look at the crowd she's gathered. Nobody is looking at the flaws in your body, only how it reacts when it's tormented and teased into a frenzy. And when there's a connection like there is between you and Sullivan, it's a beautiful thing to witness."

Amara thought back to the comments on their public scene weeks ago. Everybody had been positive about it, complimenting Sullivan on having such a responsive sub, one that clearly cared for him. Some people had even called her beautiful.

"You know I've never judged someone on their size. But it's different with me. I'm just not confident with the body I have now."

"Well, get confident in it, because it's one banging bod. Especially in that dress."

"Amen to that," a young man called out as he walked by them, giving Amara a wink.

She couldn't help but laugh as she looked back at her friend. Well, that certainly boosted her confidence.

"We'd better get back to our men," Larissa said when she spotted them watching.

"Yeah, I don't want to get punished tonight."

"Oh, I can't wait for my punishment." The little masochist grinned.

* * * *

Sullivan sat across from Grayson and Ayden and their two submissives for the night. Grayson's pretty little redhead sat curled up in his lap after doing a rather intense scene. Ayden's blonde knelt at his feet, appearing eager to do another scene with him. She looked up at him with big brown eyes before he finally gave in and agreed to take her upstairs. Then there was Sullivan's own sub. Sitting in his lap, breasts out and exposed while he amused himself with them, her thighs slightly parted at his request.

She'd done well being on display tonight. He hadn't wanted to push her too far, yet he knew she needed it. Over the last few weeks, he'd been working on her self-confidence, showing her how beautiful her body was. And it was. He loved every curve, every bump, every nook and cranny. He'd given her homework, asking her to write down one positive thing about her body each day, then they would discuss it. Her positive comments had come to her far easier than they had weeks ago.

A couple of weeks ago, he'd forced her to do ten laps of the club's main room topless, focussing on the positive looks and comments she received. Then he'd taken her upstairs as a reward. Last week, he'd done a scene with her in the main room where her pussy had been on display for everyone to see but he'd kept her breasts covered up. Tonight, he planned on getting her completely naked in an open scene area. He'd specifically reserved a bondage table so she would be wide open and on display for everyone to see. He just had to work her up a little so she would be in the right headspace for it.

Tweaking her nipples, he pinched them until they were taut peaks, then moved his hand beneath her dress, up her inner thighs. *Christ.* He found her so fucking wet she drenched his fingers when he touched her folds. Her mind may have had reservations about public play, but her body sure didn't.

"We're going to do a very public scene tonight, my sweet Amara," he said into her ear. "But first you need a little warm-up."

He gestured to where Ayden had his sub chained to the ceiling, standing in the centre of the scene room, quivering as he inserted a vibrator into her vagina. The woman let out a cry and Amara's cunt clenched around his fingers as he slipped them inside of her. The other woman threw her head back as Ayden sucked a nipple into his mouth and tweaked the other, on the edge of coming. Amara clenched again, licking her lips. She definitely got off on voyeurism—that much had been evident from their previous visits.

He moved his fingers out to glide up and around her clit, which pulsed beneath his touch. Dipping his head, Sullivan sucked one nipple into his mouth, enjoying the moan that came from her throat. He leant back on the armrest of the chair and feasted on her other breast, thrusting his fingers inside of her, his thumb playing with her clit.

Her hands became entangled in his hair. Fuck, he loved when she did that. She tugged slightly in time with his tongue flicking over her nipple. Closing his teeth over the hard peak, he smiled when she gasped and pulled even harder on his hair. Her hips wiggled beneath him, her pussy clenching around his intrusion as he pushed her higher. Pulling away from her breasts, he watched her. Breasts swollen and pink, cheeks red, lips parted, eyes hooded as she kept them on him…she was very close to the edge. He curled his fingers inside of her, finding that special spot, and applied pressure.

"Fuck," she cried out, her back arching as her thighs clamped around his wrist.

"That's my girl," he murmured before pressing a kiss to her breast. "Come for me, sweetheart."

She came, crying out loudly, her hips bucking, back arching further as she lost control. She came with her entire body. Her arms and legs twitched, her stomach dipped and shuddered, her shoulders shook. She completely let go and gave her body to him in earnest with each orgasm. Damned if it didn't make him feel proud of himself.

* * * *

Amara lay flat on the bondage table, her legs and arms strapped down. Feeling confident, she closed her eyes and sucked in a deep breath. She was naked and splayed open. But when Sullivan moved to strap her forehead to the table, extreme anxiety filled her. Being immobile, completely unable to move, was something that left her completely vulnerable, more than being strapped to the table with her pussy out for everyone to view.

"How we doing, my little sub?"

His voice calmed her. He ran his hands up and down her arms as he entered her field of vision.

"I'm okay," she said in a quiet voice. "Just a little nervous. I haven't had my head strapped down before."

"I know." He gave a small smile as he stroked her cheek.

"I…"

The way he looked down at her with nothing but sweetness and adoration in his eyes cut off her words.

"Do you trust me?"

"Absolutely and completely," she answered.

His cheeks creased as he smiled down at her. He ran a gentle hand over her hair. "Tonight is about pleasure only. I won't be hurting you, okay?"

She tried to nod. "Okay."

"Are you ready?"

"Yes, Sir."

He bent to kiss her, taking her mouth in a long, languid kiss that had arousal pooling in her core. In instinct, she tried to move, but her legs and hips remained in place. Heat filled her, pouring over her skin as he played with her breasts, licking and sucking his way around them while he ran his hands along her skin, awakening it. He continued to move down, pressing kisses to her exposed skin, her stomach, hips, the sensitive skin where her hips met her thighs.

Something cool and firm met her entrance — a vibrator, she assumed. After a few small pumps in and out, he pushed it completely inside of her. It was thin but the end curved over. A G-spot stimulator. *Shit.*

He'd bought it a few weeks ago but hadn't used it yet. And now he was going to use it on her, in the club. Force her to completely lose her shit in front of an audience. The tricky bastard.

The vibe came to life inside her at the exact moment he closed his lips around her clit. *Fuck.* She cried out, her chest heaving as an orgasm quickly approached. All too soon, the vibrations stopped. It moved, angled a little more, then turned on again.

"Aaaahhhhh."

Her orgasm ripped through her, a tidal wave crashing over her body, crushing her beneath its weight. Her entire body trembled from its pinned position, muscles quivering. She completely lost track of time after that.

Nipple clamps were applied, very lightly, a different vibe inserted inside her and a butterfly attached to rest right on top of her clit. She found herself awash with the different sensations but noted that Sullivan kept a reassuring hand on her at all times. His fingers massaged her muscles, teased her nipples, rubbed her clit. Taunted her until she'd come so many times she didn't know what was happening.

Sullivan's handsome face appeared in her blurred vision, smiling down at her. He spoke words she couldn't hear, no matter how hard she tried to focus. She wanted more. Wanted him buried deep inside of her. Instead, he began to remove the straps from her body.

"No," she whispered. "More. Please."

He smiled and said something to her. She tried to shake her head, tell him she wanted more but nothing came out. She began to drift into unconsciousness, the world around her blurring completely. Never before had she felt so out of control of her own body.

I love you.

* * * *

Amara came to, aware of Sullivan's arms wrapped around her, a blanket hugging her naked body. There were voices around her, but she couldn't make sense of any of them. Whatever Sullivan had done had completely overwhelmed her. She'd lost touch with reality. And she wanted more. The feeling slowly returned to her body. She wiggled her fingers and toes, shuffled slightly in his lap and eventually lifted her head to look at him.

"There she is."

Without a word, she leant forward to kiss him. A soft, gentle kiss that he reciprocated, tightening his arm around her back.

"How do you feel?"

"Like you fucked the life out of me without even fucking me." Her voice was quiet and husky. She'd definitely screamed during their scene.

God, she wished she could remember it all.

"Sir," a small voice sounded from in front of them. "My Master said you might want this." He handed Sullivan a bottle of water. "And said to say she is beautiful and congratulations."

The male sub walked back to his Master, an older man with silvering hair who gave Sullivan a small nod of acknowledgement. She looked at Sullivan in confusion as he unscrewed the bottle and wrapped her fingers around it.

"You've accrued quite a few fans, sweetheart. We gathered a bit of a crowd tonight."

"I was loud." She took a big gulp of water.

"Yes, you were." He laughed.

She buried her face in his chest. "How embarrassing."

"You mean beautiful. I've been getting non-stop compliments since I brought you over here."

"Really?"

He offered her a smile. "Really. Not that I need others to remind me of how lucky I am." A small kiss to her temple as he nuzzled her. "You pleased me immensely tonight, sweetheart."

Her heart swelled with pride. She loved knowing she'd pleased him.

Chapter Twenty-One

Sullivan woke up depressed the next morning. He'd had an amazing night with Amara, done the most fulfilling scene of his life. He should still be riding that high. Yet all he felt inside was emptiness. Depression was a real son of a bitch. It had no rhyme or reason and showed up whenever it felt like it.

With Amara spending the day with her friends, he'd planned on seeing Grayson. Instead, he cancelled and spent the day sprawled out on the couch staring mindlessly at the television. Fuck, he hated days where he was like this. Like nothing was good enough. Like he wasn't good enough. He needed Amara. But she needed to see her friends. It had been weeks since she'd had a girl's day. And he would see her tonight.

Seeing Amara always made him feel better. Nobody cheered him up like she did. Even Katerina had never managed to bring him out of a depressive state. Rather, she'd made him feel worse about himself. Whenever he cancelled date nights, she'd pouted. When they went for days without having sex, she'd given him the silent treatment. Now, years later, he realised just how unhealthy their relationship had been. He'd been fooled by her seemingly caring exterior and had ignored the manipulative behaviour that lurked beneath the surface. He thought he'd been in love with her, but he'd been an idiot. Amara was the real deal. He'd never been happier than when he was with her.

And she loved him. He knew that. She'd mumbled it last night while blissed out. That was the second time she'd let it slip. Did that mean he could tell her he loved her now without scaring her off? *Ugh.* Today was not the day to be thinking such things. His mind was muddled, his emotions off centre. He didn't do smart things when depressed.

Glancing at his watch, Sullivan noted that Amara would be back soon. He should shower and get ready to go out for dinner. But he couldn't bring himself to move. He had to hope she wouldn't be too disappointed with him for bailing on their night out.

His front door opened as Amara let herself in. She strolled through to the living area and straddled him where he lay on the couch. Flattening her body against his, she rested her head on his shoulder and held him. Inhaling her fruity, cherry scent, he found himself smiling, that hollow feeling in his chest filling. Because of her.

"I needed that," he said when she pulled away and sat up on his lap.

"Me too." She smiled down at him. "Do you still want to go out for dinner?"

He bit down on his lip and sat up, his chin resting on her breasts as he looked up at her. "Do you mind if I bail? I'm not having the best day."

"You're depressed again?" He nodded. "That's fine."

She ran her fingers through his hair in that soothing way he'd come to love so much. Looking into her eyes, he found nothing but sympathy and understanding. No, this woman didn't get upset when he cancelled plans because of a mental illness that wasn't his fault. She understood.

"Do you want to talk about it?"

"There's nothing wrong. I'm just really flat."

"Then how about I order some takeout and we spend the entire night watching comedies and horror to make you laugh?"

Yeah, he definitely loved this woman.

"I'm not feeling up for much more myself. I think I might be getting sick. I started feeling really lethargic a couple of hours ago."

"Aren't we a couple of bailers?"

"A perfect pair." She grinned at him.

He pulled her into his body, pressing his face into her cleavage where he placed several small kisses on the sensitive skin. She tugged on his hair and bent to kiss him. It was the softest, sweetest kiss he'd ever received. She deepened it ever so slightly, her tongue gliding along his before she nibbled on his bottom lip. Yet she didn't make any moves with her body, didn't try to grind against him, didn't press her chest to his. She was content to just kiss him.

* * * *

During the night, Sullivan woke feeling much better. The wave of depression had disappeared and he was feeling like himself again. Amara sprawled across his body, fast asleep. Moonlight streamed through the curtains illuminating her skin. Eyes closed, she rubbed her cheek against his bare chest, making a cute, sleepy sound, the vibrations rumbling against his chest.

With a little stretch, she stirred and shuffled off him, moving onto her back. Half asleep, she moved her hand to rest on his lower abdomen which had his cock hardening. He smiled and, unable to help himself, rolled over and moved down her body. Flicking his tongue over her nipple, he enjoyed the way it puckered and peaked. Always so responsive, his little sub, even when asleep. He gently palmed the other, running his thumb over the hardening peak.

Amara made a sleepy hum of pleasure but didn't open her eyes. Pulling her other nipple between his lips, he continued to play with her breasts until both nipples were hard, protruding from her round, swollen breasts. Running his hand over her stomach, along her waist, he smiled into her skin when her hips moved in response to him, beckoning for more.

Making that small whimper that he loved so much, she stirred and brought one hand down to tangle in his hair, still not fully awake. He kissed his way down her torso, nipping and suckling at her round stomach, her soft hips, then her mound. He ran a finger along her slit, through her folds, all but grinning when he found her wet for him. Was there anything better than a responsive submissive half asleep, ready and waiting for the taking?

Dipping a finger inside of her, he watched as her mouth opened on a gasp. She was definitely awake now. He rested his hand on her stomach, pinning her down, while he played with her, taking his time. He moved his finger out, to rub along either side of her clit, up one, down the other, teasing the hood of her clit, then brushing over the nub itself ever so slightly.

Amara whined when he touched her clit. "Nooooo."

He buried two fingers inside of her, her cunt clenching around the intrusion. Fuck, he loved when she did that. Shuffling down the bed, he parted her folds and licked directly over her hardening clit.

"Fuck!" she cried out, eyes open as she looked down at him while he worked.

Her clit hardened and grew beneath his tongue. A smug sense of pride filled him as she began to writhe, her hips moving in time with his pumping fingers. He focussed on bringing her to the edge. Right when she was teetering on the precipice, he removed his tongue and fingers, quickly replacing his fingers with his cock.

Her inner muscles clamped around him as he buried himself deep inside of her, keeping absolutely still. Pushing both of her thighs up and out so she was completely open to him, he watched her. Eyes darkened with arousal, cheeks flushed, lips parted ever so slightly, she was truly a beautiful sight.

"Hold your thighs open for me, sweetheart." He bent to kiss her. "Eyes on me. And don't move."

She complied, her pupils dilating further as she stared directly into his eyes, pure adoration and surrender in hers. Propping himself on his hands, he began to move, thrusting in and out in rhythmic movements, enjoying her small moans and whimpers as he used her body for his own pleasure.

He adjusted his hips, his cock brushing against her G-spot, enjoying the way she threw her head back but kept her eyes on him at all times. Moving a hand between them, he brushed a finger against her clit lightly and that was all it took. She came on a cry, slamming her eyes shut as she shook and trembled around him, bringing him down with her. Thrusting into her while her cunt milked him dry, he shuddered out his own orgasm, feeling spent. And absolutely complete.

"I love you, my sweet Amara," he said before he kissed her.

Amara opened her eyes, staring up at him in disbelief.

"Sullivan."

He kissed her again. "I don't expect you to say it back. I just needed you to know."

"No, I—" She paused, her tongue darting out to moisten her lips. "I came here tonight determined to tell you… But I lost my nerve."

She wrapped her arms around his shoulders, tightening her legs on his hips. "I love you, Sullivan. Absolutely and completely."

He felt his heart actually skip a beat. Damned if he didn't feel like the luckiest man in the world. He rewarded her with a kiss of pure love and adoration. Their tongues tangled in an intimate dance, their bodies remaining entwined as he gave himself over to her. Sullivan had never felt as complete as he did right in that moment.

* * * *

Amara woke wrapped in Sullivan's arms, feeling lighter than a cloud. He loved her. He really loved her. God, she felt amazing. Like everything in her life was finally coming together. All because of one man. A man who completed her in a way she never expected.

Sullivan woke first and brought her breakfast in bed. Fuck, he was the sweetest man alive. He joined her, stealing a piece of toast before giving her a quick kiss on the lips.

"I love you," she told him as he nuzzled her neck, tickling her sensitive skin.

"I love you too," he told her before sitting by her side.

"You know, I was absolutely terrified to tell you. I remember telling you while I was drugged up and was mortified."

"I wondered if you'd remember that."

"It took me a couple of days."

He finished off his food and leant back against the headboard. "You know you told me the other night at the club as well."

She looked at him, confused. "No, I—wait, when I was in subspace?"

He nodded as she removed the tray from over her lap.

"That doesn't count. Nothing said in subspace counts. I'm not fully aware of myself."

"On the contrary," he teased. "You're never more honest and open than when you're in subspace."

She pouted and frowned. He was right. That damn space was as effective as truth serum. It made submissives tell the honest, unabashed truth. It was how a lot of couples worked through their issues together. She'd half expected Sullivan to try to work through her body image issues that way, but he hadn't. No, he'd slowly worked with her, forcing her to say one positive thing about her body a day. Soon enough, she'd begun seeing herself in a new light, thinking positively without him prompting her. He'd succeeded. She saw herself differently. While she definitely wasn't cured, she didn't worry about others at the club judging her anymore. Not after all the compliments she'd received there.

Moving to face him, she curled her legs over his lap and rested on her elbow.

"So, if I said it the other night, why didn't you say it back?"

He gave a little smirk. "I said it to you after our first public scene together. Just to get the words out because I couldn't keep it in. You don't remember that?"

She frowned. "I don't remember the scene ending, let alone what happened afterwards. You cheater."

"I didn't want to say it too soon and scare you off." He ran a finger down her cheek, leaving a trail of heat in its wake. "I know you were worried we moved too fast, but how do you feel now?"

She bit the inside of her lip. How did she feel? Loved. In love. Amazing. Incredible. Fucking complete. "I'm no longer worried we moved too fast. It feels right."

"It really does."

Sullivan leant in to kiss her softly, tasting of coffee and toast and that underlying taste that was all him.

"Now we can work towards you moving in here."

That made her freeze.

"I don't mean right away. Or even full-time. But I built this house to make it a home." He cupped her cheek. "To fill it with love and laughter, to build a family. And I want to do that with you. There will never be anyone as good for me as you are, Amara. You're perfection."

Tears filled her words at his words, the honesty in his eyes.

"Now that we've gotten the 'I love yous' out of the way, we can move as slowly as you like. As long as you remain aware I'm not going anywhere. Ever."

"Neither am I. You're mine and mine alone."

She smiled and leant in to kiss him, completely aware that the man by her side would never leave her, no matter how chaotic her life got.

"I love you." Now that she'd said it, she couldn't stop.

Epilogue

Two months later

Amara watched as Jackson set down the last box of her belongings in Sullivan's living room and turned to look at Sullivan. Resting his butt against the kitchen bench, all long lean lines and muscle, he looked at her with a smile on his face.

"You're officially moved in," Jackson said. "And my job is done."

"Thanks for your help, bro. I appreciate it."

"Yeah, well, I guess I kind of owed you after you helped me out. I still want that free meal I was promised, though." He grinned at her. "I'll see you guys at the club tonight."

"You will."

With a quick wave to them both, he left to head back to his house. Technically it was Amara's house, but since her previous tenant had moved out, and Jackson was moving back to Perth, Amara had offered it to him for as long as he wanted. He'd said if he liked it, he would buy it off her, which Amara agreed to, especially since she wasn't going to be moving back there herself.

No. Now, she officially lived with Sullivan.

"I'm going to ask you one last time, before I start unpacking. Are you sure you want me living here?"

"Remember when I said if you asked me that one more time, I'd spank you?" He frowned as she wrapped her arms around his waist. "That's five."

"Oh, damn, I'd forgotten all about that," she teased.

"Brat."

"Seriously though, my things have been in storage for so long, I don't even know what's good or not anymore. We don't have to put any of it out. I could throw it away without a care."

"Amara. You're officially living here now. This is your home. I want it to be as much yours as it is mine. That includes having your belongings inside."

Over the last couple of months, they had been spending more time together, with Amara practically living at his house while she wasn't caring for her mum. With Jackson home, the two of them and Dad had sorted out a new schedule. Now, Amara stayed there on Monday and Tuesday, Jackson Wednesday and Thursday with Dad in charge Friday through Sunday. So far, it had worked out well and Amara was beginning to feel like she had some control of her life again.

She'd grown far more confident in her dad's and brother's ability to care for Mum. She was no longer as reliant on Amara as she had been. Having Jackson shift home helped with that a lot. And Dad was being far more vigilant that he had previously. Now, Amara was moving towards working an extra day each fortnight and they would hire another professional caregiver to pick up the slack.

Amara's life was finally on track and she was loving it. She felt lighter than she had in years. She was sleeping better and had even lost a little weight, which was an added bonus for her.

"You're really okay with me living here?"

"As I've said before, sweetheart, I would have had you living here months ago if it were up to me." He grinned down at her. "I'm very happy you finally decided it was time."

"Well, it was time. I miss you so much whenever we're apart. I feel like a clingy girlfriend with an obsession."

"The obsession goes both ways, so that's fine with me," he taunted and clasped his hands behind her back.

"I love you so much."

"Well, that's a relief, since we're now living together and you're mine forever."

With a little laugh, she stood on her toes and kissed him. Damned if it wasn't the sweetest, happiest kiss they'd ever shared.

Want to see more from this author? Here's a taster for you to enjoy!

Masters of Haven: Too Close
Liia Ann White

Coming July 2023

Excerpt

Belle was in a rut. For weeks—months—she'd had bad scene after bad scene. Everything was lacklustre, awash in a dusting of grey No emotions were involved, the bare minimum of sexual attraction was present with each scene. It simply wasn't enough for her to truly enjoy herself. And she couldn't seem to drag herself out of the pit she'd been sliding into. Right now, she was at the bottom, unable to see the light. It was grim.

Trying to concentrate on the Dom working on her, she focussed on the feeling of the light flogger working its way up and down her back. He was waking her skin, warming her up, but it wasn't having the desired effect on her mind, which wandered. She wasn't present. It wasn't fair to either of them.

All she'd wanted for tonight was to disappear into that submissive headspace she constantly craved. The one that helped her slip away from the real world and become enveloped in pure sensation. But the Dom she'd chosen tonight wasn't hard enough. He was a soft

Dom—despite him saying otherwise. He didn't command her submission, not like others had.

Belle had known she wasn't physically attracted to the man, despite him being objectively attractive, but he'd said he was a firm and strict Dom. Perhaps he was to other women—women who didn't have an independent and stubborn streak a mile long like she did. But for Belle, he wasn't hard enough. Now she couldn't understand why she'd agreed to play with him. She was probably self-sabotaging again. *My psychologist would be thrilled with that revelation.*

Closing her eyes, she let out a slow, controlled breath through pursed lips. *Just focus.* She tried to simply feel. *Whack. Whack. Whack.* The strands of leather hit her bare skin, tempting yet not capturing her attention. Shutting her mind off, Belle tried to lose herself, to concentrate on him but… just couldn't. There was not a single sign of arousal or submission in her.

God dammit.

Moving to stand before her, the Dom shoved a hand into her hair and closed it in a fist, tilting her head back until she looked at him. Even that did nothing for her. Not a damn thing. Most of the time, a simple tug on her hair was enough to make Belle want to melt. But with this man, it elicited nothing. He was too inexperienced.

Watching her, his eyes softened when he clearly caught the disappointment in her eyes.

"You're not into this at all, are you?" he asked, his own disappointment evident.

"I'm sorry," Belle mumbled.

Absolutely pathetic. Worthless sub.

After releasing her hair, he began to undo the restraints. Belle slipped on her top after he handed it to her and followed him out of the scene area.

"We'll try it again, another time," he said before leaving.

Belle knew better. There would be no other time. She was running out of single Doms to play with, especially that hard-asses that she was attracted to. Her choice to only play with a man once or twice before moving on was a choice made out of necessity, but it wasn't one she particularly enjoyed. Not anymore at least.

Deep down, Belle wanted a man to call her own… a Dom to claim her. Someone to care for her, someone she could care for. Someone she could love. She wanted what her friends had. But to find that, she would have to open herself up. That wasn't her strong suit. She simply didn't know how to do it anymore. Belle was a closed book to men.

And now she was failing as a submissive. She visited Haven, her favourite BDSM club, each week because it gave her a safe space to explore her kinks. Each member was vetted and had a mutual goal — exploration and pleasure. It was the only place she could find experienced Doms. They were very difficult to find in the vanilla world.

Unfortunately, Haven's community was small and close knit. Most of the members knew of the incident she'd had with Bryce. They had cut him out of the community as a whole and blacklisted him. They'd had her back. But a lot of them still looked at Belle as that broken woman who'd had a panic attack the first time that she tried to scene afterwards. Even new members seemed to know of her and what had happened. It was humiliating. The BDSM community in Perth was too small sometimes.

Soon, word would get out that she could no longer perform as a submissive and her reputation would be ruined. Perhaps it was time for a break, to take a step back from the lifestyle and focus on other aspects of her life for a while.

A familiar deep voice called her name. She turned to find her friend and ex-Dom approaching. Ayden strode toward her in all his charming, handsome, powerful glory. The aura of dominance about him meant he never went unnoticed. The eyes of each available submissive nearby went to him. The man was considered a commodity in the club. And Belle definitely understood why.

Sighing, she forced a smile when she looked up at him, his large body towering over her. If only things had worked out between them, she wouldn't be in her current predicament. They'd seen each other for a couple of months last year, but their spark had flamed out quickly. Since their mutual separation, Ayden had become one of her closest friends. It had happened slowly, but he had crawled beneath her skin and now she couldn't get rid of him. Not that she'd want to. Even if he did tease and irritate her from time to time.

"What happened to your scene?" he asked.

Belle shook her head, the pit in her gut becoming even deeper. "It wasn't happening. I'm going to say bye to the others and head home."

Ayden gave her a look—that irritating Dom look that said they would discuss her issues later, whether she liked it or not. He tugged at the silver-trimmed dungeon monitor vest he wore and looked around the room.

"I'm almost done with my DM shift. Go sit with the others and I'll be there in a few minutes."

She knew better than to argue with him when he was in Dom mode. Within the club's walls, she had to show him the same respect she would any other dominant. Outside, she didn't listen to him. She taunted and teased him as she did her other friends. As a Master of Haven, Ayden had the right to hand her off to other dominants for punishment or reprimand. He had the further right to order her around because Belle was considered under his protection. He had never once taken advantage of the power she'd given him, though. It was probably the only reason she listened to him.

Heading for the bar with her head held high, Belle ordered herself a Dr Pepper and looked around the main club room while waiting. Amara soon approached, looking quite the sight. Amusement bubbled inside Belle. Dark brown hair messed, lips swollen, cheeks pink, eyes all glassy—Amara appeared to have been thoroughly used. Belle couldn't help the pang of envy that struck her right in the chest.

Amara had met her Dom and fiancé, Sullivan, last year. The man completed her in ways Belle couldn't fathom. Since then, Amara had returned to her old self. Positive, fun-loving and, above all else, happy. That was all Belle wanted out of life—happiness. She couldn't remember what it felt like to be truly happy anymore. Her life was a mess.

With both of her friends now partnered up, Belle was becoming sick of feeling like the third wheel when she visited one of their houses. She'd always been the odd one out, though. She should have been used to it. With her family, with the few friends she had growing up and now she was again. And it sucked.

Mentally shaking her head, Belle pushed away the negative thoughts and smiled at her friend and confidant. "Don't you look like you just got thoroughly fucked?"

"Sullivan used a damn spanking bench. I thought it was going to be a quick scene, but he ended up taking me right there, in front of everyone."

Belle laughed genuinely. "And you loved every second of it."

"I really did." The other woman grinned.

She smiled at her friend, happy to see how far the other woman had come in recent months. Amara had had a rough go of it over the previous couple of years. Then she had met Sullivan and gained her confidence back. Last year she would never have partaken in a public scene — now she couldn't get enough of them.

"Are you doing anything else tonight?"

Everybody knew that Sullivan was insatiable when it came to Amara. The man was practically in a constant state of arousal around his fiancée.

"He threatened to take me upstairs once he's had a break." She shuddered. "I just want to go home. I'm wrecked. The bastard already beat on me at home, earlier today."

"Oh, please, you love it."

Amara was a submissive and masochist. Having Sullivan "beat" her was one of her favourite things. While Belle used to enjoy a moderate amount of pain in her kink play, she could never endure what Amara enjoyed.

The other woman got that dreamy look in her eyes, the one caused by love. "I really do."

That damn pang of envy returned. Belle took a sip of her Dr Pepper and allowed the fizz to calm her churning stomach.

"I thought you were playing," Amara said with the slightest hint of worry in her tone.

"I couldn't get into it," she replied, trying to ignore that familiar wave of shame and disappointment that threatened to take over and ruin her mood entirely. "I don't know what's wrong with me."

"Oh sweetie." Amara rested a gentle hand on Belle's arm. "There's nothing wrong with you. You're tired and depressed. Don't even try to deny it."

"You know you living with Sullivan has become a real pain in my ass, don't you? I used to be able to hide my depression and anxiety from you."

Sullivan lived with clinical depression. Belle had post-traumatic stress disorder which often resulted in bouts of depression and anxiety, even panic attacks. Two years after the incident, she was still trying to get used to the mood swings and panic attacks, still trying to recognise her triggers.

Previously, she'd been able to hide her symptoms from her friends, plaster that fake smile on her face and pretend everything was okay while she was dying on the inside. But now that Amara lived with Sullivan, she recognised the signs far easier and pointed out whenever Belle was depressed or anxious. And, right now, Amara was right. Belle was depressed.

"Well, you can't hide anything from me now, so you just have to deal with it." Amara, the brat, stuck her tongue out and grabbed her drinks off the bar top. "Come on, let's join the others."

* * * *

Sitting on a black leather lounge by herself, Belle looked to the two happy couples who were her closest friends and smiled despite her sadness. Amara was perched on Sullivan's lap, as usual, while Larissa knelt on the floor between her husband Agin's legs, her head resting on his thigh in a sign of comfort. Belle became hyper aware of her loneliness as the feeling of longing grew inside of her. That was what she wanted. To have the look of contentment that all of her friends had.

All her life, Belle had simply wanted to belong. Her parents had made sure she knew she never belonged at home. She'd fumbled through life, seeking validation in all the wrong places, until she'd met Larissa and Amara. They were the first true friends she'd ever had. They had taken her in, treated her like family from the beginning of their tentative friendship. Now they were her sisters. She couldn't imagine life without them. But that key piece was still missing—a partner to call her own.

But that was probably something she would never have. After all, what man would choose a thirty-year-old with a lifetime of trust issues and trauma? No sane one.

The couch dipped beside her as Ayden sat and slung one arm over the back of the lounge. Smiling at him despite the darkness weighing on her soul, Belle looked at his objectively handsome face. It truly was a shame there was no sexual chemistry between the two of them anymore. He was the first man since Bryce that she'd began to trust.

"So, sweetness." He used her pet name on purpose. "Are you really going to give up and go home?"

She fought the urge to roll her eyes as she looked away from him. While Ayden had men and women begging—sometimes literally—to play with him, Belle didn't have that luxury. The men willing to play with her now were few and far between. She was pretty enough and experienced, but her height turned a lot of men off. At five feet ten inches, she was far taller than most women, even a lot of men. Most Doms preferred their women short, round and soft, not tall and toned like Belle. Thanks to genetics and her physical job, she would never be soft and round like she'd always wanted to be. She'd longed for a small, feminine figure.

"I'm going to finish my drink in peace then head home," she told him in no uncertain terms.

As she was looking around at the scenes nearby, one in particular caught Belle's attention. A big Dom, tall, muscular and intimidating—exactly her type—had a submissive strapped to a bondage table. With a plug in her butt and a vibrator in her pussy, the woman writhed against restraints as the big man ravaged her breasts with his hands and mouth.

He pulled away and stood over the women. Belle noticed it was Master Ambrose, the latest Dom to be voted in as Master by Haven's members. Though he was a close friend of Ayden's, she hadn't met him yet. She'd avoided him purely based on his size. Big men scared her now. Though she'd always been physically attracted to big, strong men, they now intimidated her and made her panic. All because of Bryce. The only reason she wasn't scared by her large male friends was because there was no sexual interest for them. It made Belle feel safer.

Master Ambrose had quite the reputation of being strict and firm yet fair. He was very popular amongst the female submissives. All the women she'd spoken to who had played with him had said that he was sweet yet stern, strong and caring. He also doled out punishments to misbehaving submissives. He was exactly the kind of Dom Belle would have once drooled over and sought out.

But that wasn't the sort of man she looked for any longer. She preferred shorter men, ones who wouldn't be able to overpower her as easily as a big man would.

The man moved like a predator—large and graceful—down the woman's body until his mouth came down on her most intimate area. Belle felt herself becoming aroused for the first time in weeks as she watched, mesmerised by the scene. The woman cried out in pleasure and pulled against the restraints, her hips bucking against his face while he pinned her down with strong, knowledgeable hands. He looked up and said something to the submissive that had her eyes bulging, her head shaking rapidly.

What Belle wouldn't give to be that woman. The man looked like he knew exactly how to work a woman into a frenzy.

Another man stepped into Belle's line of vision, speaking down to the submissive. He must have been the other woman's Dom. It wasn't uncommon for Doms to ask one of the Masters to step in a dish out a punishment or do a specific kink for their submissive if they weren't comfortable in doing it. It required an extra layer of trust in the relationship. Just one more thing for Belle to envy.

Removing the vibrator, Master Ambrose replaced it with his fingers, fucking her until she threw her head back on a cry, her entire body shaking as she came. *Jesus fuck*. Belle's thighs definitely clenched this time, but she couldn't tear her gaze from the scene. The woman lay on her back, completely sated, her chest heaving with strained breaths. But Master Ambrose wasn't done. He continued his movements and coaxed another orgasm from the woman. This one had her screaming loud enough that the sound travelled to Belle's ears and sent a shudder down her spine.

Belle's skin tingled, her clit throbbing as she watched the aftermath of the scene. The Dom and Master undid the restraints, both murmuring to the woman before Master Ambrose said something to the other Dom. He packed his things away, moving with unnerving confidence. Belle hadn't seen anything like it. He was beautiful and enticing—hot as fuck.

"I see Master Ambrose caught your attention," Ayden said, his smirk evident in his tone.

Belle startled, having completely forgotten he was beside her. Embarrassment washed over her as she realised that she'd been caught watching like a voyeur. Larissa smirked as well. Narrowing her eyes at her friend, she hoped that nobody had caught onto her arousal.

"He would love to scene with you if you want me to ask."

"No," Belle snapped. She would not do a scene with that man. He was too big, too dominant, too everything she was looking for. And far, far too intimidating.

"Did you seriously just roll your eyes at me?" Ayden narrowed his gaze as he looked down at her.

"I am perfectly capable of setting up my own scenes. I don't need you playing matchmaker all the time."

The second she saw Larissa's and Amara's jaws drop, she realised what she'd done. She'd just snapped at a Dom inside of Haven, completely unnecessarily. A Master no less. That was a serious no-no.

Shit.

"You know what you need? You need to be reminded of your place here."

Belle tensed with fear. *Crap. Shit.* Looking at him, she shook her head. "No. I really don't. Please. I'm sorry, sir. I'm just tired and… I forgot where we were."

She recognised the set of his jaw, that piercing look in his blue eyes, and sighed. She was doomed no matter how hard she grovelled. Tears of shame and disappointment burned her eyes.

"Fuck," she muttered.

"Fuck indeed, little sub." He stood and pulled her with him. "Come. You're getting a punishment."

Receiving sympathetic looks from her girlfriends and smirks from the Doms, she allowed Ayden — Master Ayden — to pull her away. Ayden was a bit of a sadist. He loved spanking unruly, badly behaved submissives. She'd been on the receiving end of it once and had hated every single second of it.

"I'm sorry I snapped at you, sir," she said while trying to blink away tears that blurred her vision.

Don't cry. Only babies cry. Are you a baby? She had learned from a very young age that crying got her nowhere. She saved her tears for moments when she was alone.

"You will be," was all he said.

Belle did her best to appear the good submissive. Once upon a time, she'd been a brat, but Bryce had trained that out of her, emotionally beating her down until she no longer found it fun to mouth off. The last time she had acted the brat, he'd restrained her, gagged her and set her on the couch, then left her for two hours while he watched a movie in the other room. It had left her feeling so unbelievably alone, she'd cried until she felt sick.

Now, Belle knew that was abuse. No good Dom would ever do that to a submissive, especially one with abandonment issues. But at the time she'd been blindsided by what she thought was love. So now she obeyed without question. Because that was what Doms wanted.

Ayden led her through the main room toward the scene area where Master Ambrose had been. When he stopped, her heart dropped into her gut. He'd led her straight to Master Ambrose.

Fuck.

Masters and Mistresses of Haven were all expected to undertake basic tasks when it came to submissives and dominants alike, but certain Masters had specific jobs. Agin was in charge of the beginner training program for Doms, Sullivan was in charge of new male dominants, Mistress Ashely the females, Ayden was in charge of helping new and unattached submissives and Master Harvey, the sadist, was the enforcer of all submissives. But now Master Ambrose had taken over some tasks as enforcer to the single females. And tonight, that included Belle.

Looking up to Master Ambrose, Belle found herself having to actually crane her neck to meet his eyes. He was taller than she'd realised, about six feet five inches, she guessed... and built. The man was deliciously broad—he had a chest she wanted to run her hands over, and muscled shoulders she wanted to hang off, have her legs draped over. Her mouth watered as she looked him up and down, noting the fit of his black button down, the way his dark jeans clung to powerful-looking thighs. He was attractive, but more than that, he had a build that would make her feel small and feminine.

"Master Ambrose," Ayden said. "I have a disrespectful little submissive for you to punish, if you're up for it."

He reached back to grab her arm just hard enough to remind her she had no say in what happened to her unless she used her safe word.

"This one mouthed off to me, completely forgetting her place in the hierarchy. She needs a reminder of where she stands."

Belle sucked in a breath and tried to ignore the sudden tightness in her chest. She deserved to be punished. She'd done the wrong thing in front of others. But all she wanted right now was to go home, curl up on her couch and cry herself to sleep.

Eyes shimmering in the dim lighting like two dark emeralds, Master Ambrose looked at her. Belle suddenly felt very, very small.

"It would be my pleasure, Master Ayden."

His voice was smooth, rich and deep, wrapping around Belle's exposed skin, enveloping her in a satisfying warmth. For a moment, she imagined what it would be like to have him whisper sweet nothings in her ear, to hear him murmur dirty words while he did unspeakable things to her… ordered her to come.

Arousal trickled down her inner thighs when he shot her a half smile. How could she be so aroused by the simple sound of his voice?

He continued to watch her, assessing her with that deep green gaze. He really was gorgeous to look at. His light brown hair fell over his forehead, cut just long enough for a woman to tangle her fingers in. His jaw was chiselled to perfection, his full pink lips appeared soft, but it was his eyes that transfixed her. Two pools of pure forest green that held so much strength it made her want to melt into a puddle at his feet. They were absolutely beautiful. While he wasn't classically handsome, he was drop-dead sexy.

Yes, he scared her. How on earth could she be attracted to yet fearful of a man at the same time? She really was broken.

"Give us a moment, sweetness." Ayden's voice broke through the silence before he and Master Ambrose stepped away.

Belle stood alone, hugging herself as tears of fear and disappointment in herself burned her eyes. It was just another reminder she was alone, in every sense of the word. God, when had she become so negative and needy? She was meant to be a strong, independent woman. She should be happy to be alone and not need a man. But she wasn't like that deep down.

Biting her lip to distract herself from the emotional turmoil, Belle forced the tears away. She would not cry. She didn't cry in front of others. She'd never cried during a scene. Not even during a spanking. She refused to cry in front of a stranger.

"Belle." Ayden tipped her chin up with a finger. "You understand why I'm doing this?"

Her bottom lip quivered as she nodded. "I'm sorry, sir."

"I know you are," he said. "But we have rules for a reason."

He pressed a gentle kiss to her forehead. "This will be good for you."

Yeah, right.

"Come on, little sub," Master Ambrose said after Ayden left. "Let's have a chat."

"But…" She didn't want to talk. She wanted to get her punishment done so she could leave.

Judging by the hard stare he gave her, there would be no arguing with Master Ambrose. Closing her mouth, Belle obeyed and tried to ignore the sinking feeling in her stomach. She followed him to one of the quieter sitting areas near the recovery corner, specifically designed for people to negotiate in.

Seated beside Master Ambrose, Belle couldn't hide her surprise when he pressed his thigh against hers and slung one arm over the back of the lounge, behind her. He gripped her chin with his free hand, firm but not rough, and forced her to look at him. Those gorgeous eyes held a hint of a smile despite his hard expression.

Arousal continued to flutter through her veins at his proximity. Her skin heated at the burning tears returned to her eyes. Belle fought the urge to crawl into his lap and cry. He was not the comforting sort of Dom, based on what she'd heard. Regardless, she suddenly couldn't wait to be spanked by this man. This Master.

About the Author

A born and bred Aussie, Liia hails from Perth, Western Australia. After spending her childhood years dreaming of far-off lands, she eventually discovered her love of romance and hasn't looked back since.

A self-proclaimed geek, she loves all things Disney and Star Wars. Being a bisexual, bipolar and ADHD battler, she is passionate about mental health and LGBTQIA+ rights, as well as advocating for animal rights.

When not writing, she can be found curled up with a good book, with her two dogs by her side.

Liia loves to hear from readers. You can find her contact information, website details and author profile page at https://www.totallybound.com

Home of Erotic Romance

Sign up for our newsletter and find out about all our romance book releases, eBook sales and promotions, sneak peeks and FREE romance books!

www.ingramcontent.com/pod-product-compliance
Lightning Source LLC
Chambersburg PA
CBHW030809260626
47169CB00001B/249